AF557802

HOW THE WORLD WAS BORN

Also by Lopamudra Maitra

The Collected Stories of Upendrakishore Ray Chowdhury

The Owl Delivered the Good News All Night Long: Folktales, Legends, and Modern Lore of India

India, Sri Lanka and the SAARC Region: History, Popular Culture and Heritage

Folk Festivals and Beliefs of Radh Bengal: Understanding Through Ethnoarchaeology

Stories of Colonial Architecture: Kolkata–Colombo

HOW THE WORLD WAS BORN

WONDROUS INDIAN MYTHS AND LEGENDS

retold by
LOPAMUDRA MAITRA

ALEPH

ALEPH BOOK COMPANY
An independent publishing firm
promoted by ***Rupa Publications India***

First published in India in 2024
by Aleph Book Company
7/16 Ansari Road, Daryaganj
New Delhi 110 002

ISBN: 978-93-93852-93-9

1 3 5 7 9 10 8 6 4 2

Printed in India

To those memorable conversations from yesterday
which sometimes began with
'Shey onekdin ageykaar kotha
(This is a story from long ago.)'

Contents

Eastern Region

Western Region

Central Region

Southern Region

Water Bodies: Bay, Ocean, Sea, and Others

Editor's Note

A charming story of the Wancho community of Arunachal Pradesh, of northeast India, narrates the origin of the earth, water bodies, and the sky.

In the beginning, there was no earth, but only sky. Rang, the God of the sky, threw a star into the sky, which, after many years, turned into the earth. There was no water at first, but it gradually oozed up from under the ground from a great lake of water. This underground lake is vital, and there is a large snake in it. The earth rests on the snake's head. Sometimes, when the snake moves, it causes earthquakes. This great lake has other importance, as well. All the rivers from all around, flow down across the world and collect in this great lake below. Then the water from this lake rises up into the sky and reaches Rang. He sends the water back to the earth as rain. Fog and mist also go up to Rang and form a thick layer across the sky, which sometimes forms into a pile of stones. These fall back on the earth as hail.

When the water oozed out of the underground lake, it flowed towards different directions and cut through the ground. Thus were formed hills in some places and plains in others. These waters were full of fish and Rang was very fond of them. Sometimes when he is hungry, he comes down to the earth by the rainbow to catch them. Thus, the rainbow is formed every now and then.[*]

Myths, by their very spirit, are woven into the fabric of nature, her ecosystem, and all her elements. As much as these

---

[*]Verrier Elwin, *Myths of the North-east Frontier of India*, New Delhi: Gyan Publishing, 2017, pp. 82–83.

stories amuse and appeal, they are also a reminder of how much they have been a part of our sociocultural ethos for centuries, interlaced intricately within our shared and natural surroundings. This imparts an almost mystical aura to the world of myths. An interesting story from the Khasi community of Meghalaya speaks about this deific and almost spiritual connection.

Long, long ago, a Khasi man one day, received a document from God. He saw the document and realized that it contained religious and philosophical teachings as well as guidelines for performing rites and rituals. He realized that the document was of utmost importance and he packed it up and set off for his home. Unfortunately, on the way to his village, he lost this very important document. Now, fearing the rage from his kinsmen, he informed everyone in his village when he returned, that all the teachings of God were recorded in his mind and that he would orally pass them onto others.

Thus began the tradition of the stories of mythologies—about Gods and Goddesses, life and existence, origin, destruction, recreations, migrations, and resettlements. This tradition continues till date.

And true indeed, having survived through generations orally, myths have found their natural echo through stories and storytelling. They quintessentially form an important aspect of all the communities around the globe. This book aims to showcase various myths and legends from across the extensive regions of India. Since it is not only impossible, but to a great extent, inhumane to compartmentalise these stories according to specific political units, this book represents 108 stories across a broader division of various geographical segments of India. However, at the very outset, it should also be mentioned that, just like languages, stories too, cannot be restricted to mere regions. Thus, there are many storylines which have common echo in the neighbouring regions. For the time being, to avoid complications, this book follows a simple geographical division of the length and breadth of the nation, including the northern, central, southern, western, eastern, and northeastern regions. Finally, there is a section about water bodies, comprising of the bay, ocean, and the sea; smaller ones like wells, ponds, and rainfall; bigger ones like single drop waterfalls, rivers, their many tributaries, and deltas. Each section thus represents various landforms and topographies, including the four major types of terrains—mountains, hills, plateaus, plains, and also the different water bodies lying therein. When I sat down to write this book, the first fact that came to my mind was how water bodies form 71 per cent of the surface of the earth. The oceans hold about 96.5 per cent of the earth's water. It is also present in the air in the form of vapour, as well as in the ground as soil moisture. Aquifers and human bodies contain almost 60 per cent of water, while other animals have between 70–76 per cent and plants can have up to 95 per cent of water. Water has helped to sustain life forms through ages, as we know it, and down the course of history. The earth is distinguished as the 'Blue Planet' due to the abundant presence of water on its surface and this sets it apart as a unique representation in our solar system. I was captivated by the myths and legends about water bodies, and it was my conscious choice to share an extensive segment about it in this publication with my readers. While writing about these myths and legends, it was a pleasant surprise to explore the uniqueness and diversity within each story, representing a different platform in time and space. Each of the stories in this publication has been further explained with an accompanying note. I believe this will help the readers to further understand the various communities, as well as the representational aspects of the respective stories,

Myths and legends are often also preserved through various elements of intangible cultural heritage (ICH). This book also explores many elements of ICH from across India, which has stayed alive through the retellings of many mythological stories and legends of different communities. The elements of ICH explored within the book are folk songs, art and performative art, dances, festivals and puppetry, among others.

The legends and myths gathered from folk art, include the story of Bhagat Dhanna Ji from the tipanu scrolls of Gujarat; stories from the kaavi wall paintings of Morjim in Goa, in the temple of Morjai, which is also linked to the folklore of the seven sisters and one brother of the region; the story of the Nabagunjara from Odisha, which is variously depicted on ganjifa playing cards, on various handicraft items and also blended into the architecture of the Jagannath temple in the Puri district of Odisha; the mythological story about the creation of the world by Bada Dev through the Gond paintings of Madhya Pradesh; the story about the elaborate and intricate tattoos of the Baiga community of Madhya Pradesh, Chhatisgarh, Jharkhand, and Uttar Pradesh; the various stories from the temple architecture and patachitra folk paintings of West Bengal, including the depiction of the story of machher biye (the wedding of the fish); the story of the creation of the world from the Santhal community; stories from the Chandi Mangal Kavya and Manasa Mangal Kavya, and last, but not the least, the story of the portrayal of Kanseri Mata—the deity of corn, through the Warli paintings of Daman and Diu, and Dadra and Nagar Haveli.

Many folk songs also retell stories from the myths and legends of different regions. The ones included in this book are the Abhangs of Sant Tukaram from Dehu in Maharashtra; a narrative from the songs of the Kota communities of the Nilgiris; the ballad of Nallathangal from the Tholpavakoothu performances of shadow puppetry in Kerala; a Jhoria Muria Gond song in reverence of Lingo, the founder of the Gotul; a famous lyrical epic of the Kondhs, sung by the Boguas; the song by Godabarish Mishra of Odisha, which retells a sad legend of Jaai of Chilika Lake; a legend from the songs of weaving of the Dimasa community in Assam and Nagaland, as they continue their work on their daophang (traditional loom), and a myth retold through the song 'Sangpangtu Kan' of the Ao Naga community of Nagaland, which retells how humans learned to comprehend the nature of animals.

Storytelling, as a mode of communication and also as an art form, has been an integral part of our societies since time immemorial. The formats of narration and the mediums used, may have changed, however, they are all intrinsically woven into the sociocultural ethos of various communities whom they represent. Thus, they form a very important aspect of ICH of India. It was indeed a pleasure to explore many aspects of the art form of storytelling for this book, including the story of Kanseri Mata. It forms part of a ritualistic narration from Maharashtra, that usually takes place at night, during the harvesting season, on a threshing floor, to the accompaniment of the two-stringed musical instrument—the ghangali; the story of Bonbibi and Dakkhin Rai from West Bengal, which are often portrayed through rural theatre and folk paintings; the legend of Bhasmasura as portrayed through the Gavri nachh (dance) or Rai nachh by the Bhils of Rajasthan; the story from the Tendong-faat ritual dance of Sikkim, which is performed to worship the Tendong Hill; various poems in Bengali down the course of history, which have narrated the story of Prince Vijay sailing from erstwhile Bengal region to Sri Lanka; the story of Usha and Aniruddha which have been variously depicted in popular culture and paintings.

Festivals have always been an interesting milieu of people, ideas, thoughts, and expressions, making them an integral part of ICH and conveying an array of significant and diverse expressions. Some interesting stories from the festivals of various communities of India, which are included in this publication, include the story of Jamshed and the Parsi festival of Jamshed-i-

Naoroz celebrated across the nation and in different parts of the world; the story of Chand Saudagar of Madhukar nouko pujo (boat puja) held across Assam Brahmaputra Valley and Barak Valley; the story related to the celebration of the Sanjan Day of the Parsis at the Sanjan Memorial Column in Gujarat; the agricultural story from the Mizo festival of Pawl Kut; the story from the Riju Dune autumnal dance of the Adi tribe of Arunachal Pradesh; the story associated with the Pushkaram river festival of India; the story of Goddess Anahita from the Avan nu Parab or Parab of Ava of the Parsis celebrated across the nation; the story of the origin of the Karam festival of the Baiga, Majhwar, Sahis, Savar, the Gond communities of Madhya Pradesh and few adjoining regions; the story from the Brata Katha of Kojagari Lakshmi puja of Ashwin (September–October); the story of the origin of the festival of Bhadu and its songs from the region of West Bengal; the legend of Tapoi, recited through the festival of Khudurukini Osha of Odisha; the legend surrounding the origin of offering Poovan bananas to Mother Mary by the Syro-Malabar Catholic Community during the Lady's Feast at Koratty in Kerala; the feast of Sao Joao of Goa held every year in June; the story of the origin of Phulaich, the flower festival of Himachal Pradesh; the story of the origin of the Charkula dance from the Braj region of Madhya Pradesh and Uttar Pradesh, which is held on the third day after Holi.

Finally, as much as they provide for light reading, myths and legends also remain an interesting source that often goads one to look into many existential questions. They often endure as one of the best ways to understand and deliberate upon our infinitesimal existence, along with our worldly yet miniscule affairs. Amidst a gargantuan universe with its enormous splendours, expressions and surprises, it has taken centuries to be voiced through thousands of sets of stories, which try to explain, in their own rudimentary methods, the ways of nature and of the world. Yet, many questions remain unanswered.

I hope that this publication may inspire thoughtful contemplation on the myriad complexities of these colossal set of questions.

Happy reading, thinking, and exploring.

Lopamudra
Kolkata
February 2024

Introduction

One of my earliest memories of listening to a mythological tale was when my father shared a story with me during a summer vacation. I must have been four or five and we were visiting our large ancestral home in the Maldah district of West Bengal. Those were the days of extended power fluctuations and power failures, followed by kerosene lamps, providing enough light to reach a few feet, rendering everything within that vicinity into various shades of yellowish grey and black. These would form very elongated silhouettes on the nearby wall, which sometimes seemed to be more prominent than the person sitting in front of the lamp. Every time a gust of wind blew, the little yellow and orange flame of the lamp would flicker, and the long shadows on the wall would do a quick dance. I remember one late evening, sitting on the wide terrace of our home with my elder cousin on a sataranchi (a type of hand woven rug) during one such episode of power failure with the ubiquitous oil lamp in front of us. Only this time, there were no shadows as the lamp opened up into the late evening sky, dotted with stars, peeping through the gathering of sparse, pre-monsoon clouds on the horizon. The light of the lamp danced gently in the mild breeze on the terrace as both of us sat silently—at least, I did. My cousin must have been around seven or eight at that time. She took charge of most of the conversation, leaving me captivated as I absorbed her words. Coming from a different city, all her words seemed rather enchanting to my petite mind, discovering a new thing in almost every sentence. As she sat, enlightening me during one of her many discussions, we were joined by my father, who had come to the terrace for some work and stayed back. As he sat down on the large satarанchi next to us, there was an almost immediate request for a story from my cousin. A very courteous man, especially considerate to children, my father immediately obliged. He reflected a little, and then looked up at the sky. He pondered for a moment, as if searching for something, and asked, if my cousin knew the story of the Dhruv tara or the Pole Star. My cousin did not. Neither did I. Thus, what ensued thereafter was around fifteen minutes of storytelling, transforming the dark blue and black of the late evening sky into a palette of characters, settings, and most importantly, imaginings. This was also the first time, I learnt that constellations represent not only patterns, but images and pictures, which are also connected to stories—and some very interesting ones as well, especially for a child of five. I was intrigued. Until now, I had only listened to the regular and incredibly well-known stories from Bengali folklore found in compiled books by famous authors dating back to more than a century ago—Upendrakishore Roy Chowdhury or Dakkhnaranjan Mitra Majumdar. It was the first time, when the sky took the form of a narrator, and to my fledgling mind, this revelation in itself was absolutely mesmerising. Much younger than my cousin, the mythological story that followed, unfolded in its own way in my little, yet vivid imagination. In between the session of the storytelling, I remember distinctly gazing up at the deep blue early night sky, speckled with dim and bright stars. That night, I discovered the Ursa Minor constellation, resembling a wheelbarrow, and became acquainted with the presence of the Pole Star. As the tail of the Ursa Minor constellation directed me to a new story, the Pole Star, at the very tip of that tail, seemed just a tad little brighter.

The story of little Dhruv actually frightened me. The very thought of the little boy, almost my age, leaving his home and parents and going all alone into the wilderness to pray, where he stayed for a long time, till Lord Vishnu came and blessed him, unsettled me. I was full of admiration for the courage and confidence of little Dhruva, for which he was rewarded by being placed in the sky—a laudable reward indeed. As the story of Dhruva tara goes:

> Long ago, there was a king named Uttanapada, who was the son of Manu. One day, a son was born to him from his first wife, Suniti. This was Dhruva. Soon after, another son, Uttama, was born to Uttanapada's second wife Suruchi, who was the younger queen. Suruchi was the centre of the king's affection. She knew very well that it was Dhruva who would become the king one day and not her son. So, she was always looking for ways to steal the king's attention, to shower on her son. One day, when Dhruva was five years old, he saw his younger brother sitting on their father's lap on the throne. Dhruva, too, wanted to sit on his father's lap and as he struggled to get on, he was rudely berated by his step-mother, Suruchi. Dhruva protested and wanted to know why he couldn't sit on his father's lap. In response, Suruchi angrily suggested that Dhruva should seek an answer about this from Lord Vishnu, asking him to grant him birth from her womb before he can sit on the king's lap. Dhruva was crestfallen at such an answer. He went to speak to his mother, who upon hearing everything, wanted to console the distraught child. But Dhruva was determined to seek the answer from Lord Vishnu about his rightful place in the universe. Seeing his determination, Suniti could not say much, but had to agree to allow her little son to leave for the forest for meditation. Soon, Dhruva left for the deep forest to meditate. In the meanwhile, sage Narada saw the little child all alone in the forest and wanted to make him return to his parents. However, Dhruva was steadfast in his determination. Upon seeing the firm

resolve at such a tender age, Narada decided to teach him all the rituals and mantras of meditation to seek blessings from Vishnu. One mantra that Narada taught him, which Dhruva used by repeating it continuously was: Om Namo Bhagavate Vasudevaya. Dhruva went without food or water for six months and the austerity of his meditation shook the heavens. Finally, Vishnu decided to reveal himself to Dhruva. However, so immersed was he in his deep meditative thought and image of Vishnu in his mind, that Dhruva did not even feel the presence in front of him. Finally, Vishnu had to make Dhruva's inner vision disappear and only then did he open his eyes. At first, Dhruva was extremely overwhelmed to see the vision in his mind, right in front of his eyes. He could barely utter a single word and stood silently. Then, Vishnu touched Dhruva's right cheek with his conch and this sparked off his speech, and he started narrating verses in praise of the Lord. He recited twelve beautiful verses, which together are called 'Dhruva-stuti'. Having spent a long time in meditation, Dhruva also had forgotten his initial reason for beginning the tapasya. Finally, he only asked for a life, in memory of the Lord. Being pleased with him, Vishnu granted him his wish and also said that he would attain Dhruva-pada or a state, where he would become a celestial body, which would not be even touched by the Maha Pralaya. Then, Dhruva returned home to his parents. He was warmly received by his mother and also his father, who had been informed about Dhruva's tapasya by Narada. He was full of remorse for the little child who had been praying amidst the wilderness and seeking an answer to the prejudiced behaviour which had occurred before his eyes. He had understood, how unjustly Dhruva was treated. Thus, Uttanapada was very happy to receive Dhruva back home. He attained the crown at

> the age of six and ruled for many decades in a fair and just manner. After his death, he and his mother, entered the region of Dhruva-loka, and they live there peacefully till date, as the Dhruva tara—the Pole Star.
>
> According to the 'Vishnu Purana', there is another version of the story. When Vishnu was pleased with Dhruva's meditation, he told him to ask for a wish, to which Dhruva sought the knowledge of stuti (hymn). He never desired worldly pleasures and only desired knowledge for eternal peace. Thus, the Saptarshi (Seven Rishis or sages) conferred upon Dhruva the most revered seat of a star—the Pole Star.

A few years later, I came across this same story, aided with vivid visuals as a colourful graphic novel from the Amar Chitra Katha publications. I still remember most of the images of the Dhruv tara from this graphic novel—my second round of initiation into the world of mythologies. From then till now, it has been an enriching journey, exploring not only myths and legends, but oral traditions, and the intangible cultural heritage of India and South Asia. As this process of learning unfolds, it consistently proves to be a fulfilling and gratifying educational journey. The story of the Dhruv nakshatra or tara (star) is part of the Vishnu Purana and Bhagavata Purana. The Mahabharata also mentions Dhruva as a devotee of Vishnu, as the son of Uttanapada and the grandson of Manu. The Dhruv tara is a special star in the sky, as it is believed to be located exactly over the North Pole and it points to the north. Thus, it is a natural compass and a GPS, which has helped travellers, navigators, and sailors across centuries. It is believed that the position of this star remains more or less permanent, and it always points towards the north. There is an interesting story to elucidate how the Pole Star changes after several millennia. As far back as the time of the ancient Greeks, it was believed that the Pole Star does not exactly point towards the North

Pole, but only a section of it towards the north. This is because the earth's axis moves slowly backwards and forwards over several centuries and thousands of years, and the star nearest to the North Pole thus changes over time. The Pole Star points towards a celestial section of the sky, towards the northern pole, and the star nearest to this section assumes the responsibility of being the Pole Star, till the position of the earth shifts once again, and it is the time for another star to resume the duty. At present, the Pole Star is the Polaris, which belongs to the Ursa Minor or the Little Bear constellation. It is in fact, the last star at the very end of the Bear's tail. Five thousand years ago, a star called the Thuban was the Pole Star and in about five thousand years from now, a star called Alderamin from the constellation Cepheus will be nearest to the North Pole. In about 28,000 years the Polaris will be the Pole Star once again—for a while. It is also interesting to note that the Polaris is, in fact, what astronomers call a 'supergiant'. These are the brightest and largest stars and are often many hundreds of times larger than the Sun in our Solar System. However, the Polaris does not look very bright when seen through the naked eye from the earth because it is very far away—431 light years away from the earth (over 6,400 million kilometres or 4,000 million miles). Nevertheless, the Pole Star remains an important landmark in the sky and has helped thousands down the course of history because it does point towards the northern part of the earth. So, it is not surprising that there are many stories in oral traditions in various cultures about the Pole Star, and many of them date back to very ancient times from many parts of the world. There is an interesting story from ancient Greek mythology, which also mentions how the Ursa Major and Ursa Minor got their other names of the Great Bear and the Little Bear. According to this ancient Greek story,

> Zeus, the king of Gods fell in love with a mortal woman name Callisto. However, Zeus's wife, Hera, grew extremely

jealous and she turned poor Callisto into a bear, but since Hera had kept her human memory alive, Callisto was a very sad bear, and she would roam throughout the woods with a forlorn face. One day, she suddenly met her son, Arcas. An accomplished hunter, Arcas did not recognize his mother, but since Callisto had her human memory, she could identify her son immediately. When he saw the bear, Arcas picked up his bow to shoot. Just then, Zeus intervened and turned Arcas also into a bear. Now, Arcas recognized his mother. Zeus wanted both to stay close to each other, and thus put them in the sky by holding them by their tails and throwing them up towards the sky, where we can see them now. These turned into the Great Bear, or the Ursa Major, and the Little Bear, or the Ursa Minor, constellations. And because Zeus held them by their tails, both the bears grew long tails. These constellations are also called the Big Dipper and the Little Dipper, and the Pole Star is the very last star at the end of the Little Bear's tail.

There are many other variants about the Pole Star from the old books of mythology from several parts of the world.

During the medieval period, Polaris was also known as Stella Maris or 'Star of the Sea' as it helped greatly during navigation.

In ancient Norse mythology, the Pole Star was considered as the jewel on the end of the spike which the Gods used to stick through the universe. They believe that the sky revolves around this.

In ancient Japan, the Pole Star was referred to as God Myoken, who is also known as Sonjo-O. He is mainly worshipped in the Shingon, Tendai, and Nichiren schools of Japanese Buddhism.

In ancient China, the mythical emperor of ancient

China—Zhuanxu is believed to be the God of the Polaris, along with God Taiyi.

Old Mongolian mythology believed that the Pole Star was a peg which held the world together.

Old Arabic mythology speaks of this as an evil star, which killed a great warrior of the sky and this warrior is said to lie in the coffin of the 'Funeral Bier' constellation—the name for the constellation of Ursa Major or Great Bear.

Stories amuse us. They can create worlds and emotions and perhaps even make the mundane seem interesting and take us on incredible journeys. This very essence of a quintessential connection with the listener, reader, or spectator is what underlines the popularity of stories across ages and across various cultures of the world. This world of stories, myths, and legends occupy a special place, as they help in portraying timeless and universal themes which are relevant to the art of storytelling and to human experiences. They also give a perspective of a bygone era, and an understanding about similarities or differences with the present. A closer look and a deeper study of these references of stories from long ago also helps us, to a great extent, to understand the psychology and the thought processes that went behind the framing of these stories in the first place. Thus, legends and myths appeal, engage, and connect to the listeners of all ages, across all cultures of the world, and has held a special place through generations.

Legends are commonly known as traditional narratives recounting specific individuals, events, or locations. They frequently delve into the realm of spirituality, the supernatural or extraordinary occurrences associated with a particular region or individual. They often connect to historical incidents or persons and though the storyline may have been created over a period of time, often, some part or parts of the main story is believed to be true or to have taken place in the past. On the other hand, the word 'mythology' as is common knowledge, comes from the Greek word mythos, meaning 'story of the people' and logos meaning 'word' or 'speech'. Thus, it exists as the oral narrative of the people, about sacred tales of a culture which deal with both the aspects of good and evil of the human condition. They look into the stories of origin of various aspects of existence and a celestial connection amidst all, which imparts an essence of spiritualism and often a connection with the divinity. This very spirit also makes mythologies ever so special across cultures of the world, as they have been part of civilisations through thousands of years. The earliest recorded indication of myths as evidenced from burial practices and tomb paintings from ancient Egypt, and dating to as far back as 4000 BCE.

Legends and myths have a commonality in the way they endure across generations and centuries, thanks to oral traditions, a fundamentally significant and captivating element of human existence. From across India, there are abundant examples of both, e.g. the numerous legends about many saints, kings, queens, or philanthropists of India or the mythological stories from *Jataka, Panchatantra, Hitopodesha* or the great Indian epics the Ramayana and Mahabharata. Having passed down through centuries and through generations, these stories have survived as oral traditions, till they were penned down or published. Today, thanks to the magic of modern printing, publication, marketing, the audio-visual media, and the world wide web, these stories have not only managed to survive but have also reached a diverse set of audiences, many of whom are also geographically far away from the region of origin of these stories. The methods of storytelling of myths and legends may have changed, but the essence continues to connect people.

Over a broad scale, and through a more academic understanding, there are various critical analyses of the different types of myths, primarily focusing on these three expansive categories:

> Etiological Myths: stories of origin explaining how a particular thing or element came to be.
>
> Historical Myths: these are mostly related to retellings of an event from the past but with greater impetus. Often legends and Historical myths correspond with each other.
>
> Psychological Myths: they represent a journey from the known to the unknown, as if in an attempt to balance the external world with the internal consciousness. This is akin to discovering a path, which is taken as a personal lesson for self.

However, for the time being, I will leave the analyses of the various types of mythologies for a more academic reading and move on to looking at various sections within this book, over a broader platform. All these forms and types of myths can help to enthral an audience equally as they have a way of explaining things, when the mind is either at rest or in trouble. Perhaps this can be attributed to the mystical allure embedded in mythologies. They enquire, ask questions, and provide answers, and leave us with a knowledge, which might be pleasing as well as overwhelming. Here, I would like to add an interesting observation. During the extensive research for this book, it appeared to me that the term 'legend' is more readily accepted in regular communication than the word 'mythology'. Though there remains a basic structural difference between mythologies and legends, yet it is interesting to note how in common parlance, both are interchangeably used and the word mythology is at many times only restricted to the many well-known tales from the Puranas or the epics—Ramayana and Mahabharata or *Jatakas, Panchatantra*, and others. While it is true that for centuries, these stories have moulded thought processes and formed very important repositories of information, yet, the commonly held notion often omits the hundreds of myths and legends as part of narratives from many communities. This includes languages and dialects and religious backgrounds, from across the nation, which remain outside the paradigms of this platform of renowned mythological tales. The colossal number of these lesser-known stories is equally interesting and captivating, for one seems more fascinating than the previous one. They are equally beguiling and insightful and provide a helpful and holistic picture of the many answers about questions of creation, origin, or existence.

In most mythologies, almost all natural heavenly bodies, such as the sun, moon, stars, comets, etc. are accorded a divine identity. This is due to the belief that they are part of the heavens, and, as such, considered to be the closest to the Supreme Being or the Gods. In many mythologies across India, the sun, moon, and stars have been the centre of many interesting mythological retellings. Like the story of 'Samudra Manthan', which not only speaks of the origin of the lunar and the solar eclipses, but also provides a narrative about the formation of the earth and the origin of the many natural spectacles and occurrences of the world. Thus, goes the story of the 'Samudra Manthan':

> Once sage Durvasa offered a garland to the king of the Gods—Indra. At that moment, Indra was sitting atop his elephant mount Airavat. In an act of great happiness, Indra accepted the garland and put it on the forehead of Airavat lovingly, however, the strong scent of the flowers of the garland irritated Airavat and he got upset. Immediately, he picked up the garland with his tusk and threw it on the ground. This greatly angered sage Durvasa. Though Indra pleaded with him, nothing could lessen Durvasa's anger. He cursed not only Indra but also all the Gods, stating that they had become too vain and thus deserved to lose all their wealth, power, and immortality. And truly, the Gods lost their wealth soon, and Lakshmi, the Goddess of fortune and prosperity, also left. She took shelter in the depths of Kshir Sagar or the Ocean of Milk. When Lakshmi left, she parted ways with her consort, Lord Vishnu. The luminous

Chandra or the moon, disappeared from the matted locks of Lord Shiva's head. In such an overwhelmed state and robbed of their strength, the Gods soon realized they are no match for the Asuras or demons as they started to lose all the battles against them. They ended up losing their kingdom altogether, and Indra, followed by all the Gods, left their heavenly abode. Indra's throne was occupied by the victorious Asura king Bali, who started to rule over the entire universe.

Seeking help, the Gods, led by Indra approached Prajapati Brahma, who informed them that this is a mighty challenge and the right person to help them in this hour of dire crisis is Lord Vishnu. Thus, all the Gods went to seek help from Vishnu, who listened to them patiently. He then prepared an elaborate plan for making the Gods regain their wealth, energy, and kingdom. The final solution was that they should partake the nectar, amrit, which is also the source of immortality, and the only way this could be achieved was through Samudra Manthan or the churning of the ocean of milk. Finally, Vishnu mentioned that the whole process is a challenging one and will need a lot of effort as well as the contribution of the Asuras. Now, this indeed seemed a difficult situation, but the Gods agreed. Soon, an invitation was sent to the Asuras, who readily agreed for Samudra Manthan, thinking of the benefits they may get.

Vishnu remained the main adviser of the event and as per his instructions, Mount Mandara was chosen as the churning rod which was to act as a stirrer. Lord Vasuki, who adorned Lord Shiva's neck was selected as a churning rope. Finally, the day arrived and the event began. Under Vishnu's instructions, the Gods were advised to take the tail end of Vasuki. The Asuras were more than happy to hold on to the head, thinking that it might be beneficial. This act of allocating the tail end to the Gods was the forethought of Vishnu, who could visualise an upcoming fatal incident as a result of the churning.

Finally, when everything was set, the Asuras and the Gods took their respective positions. Vasuki got ready, wrapped a few times around Mount Mandara and the churning began, but no sooner had it started, the mountain started to sink. It was too heavy to remain afloat on the ocean. There needed to be a stable platform which would hold up Mount Mandara. Vishnu once again helped the situation by taking the avatar of a kurma or tortoise and placing himself under Mount Mandara. To provide an additional aid, which would act as a stable platform, Brahma was advised by Vishnu to sit at the top of Mount Mandara. Thus, the mountain stopped wobbling and stood firm on the back of the kurma. Once again, the churning began.

Soon, various things started to come out of the ocean of milk. In total, fourteen jewels or ratna were obtained from the Samudra Manthan and these ratnas have been variously described in different scriptures.

Soon after, the beginning of the churning of the Ocean of Milk the rigorous pull from both ends created a tremendous stress on Vasuki's body and a dangerous poison started to emit from his mouth. This was halahal and it had the potential to completely destroy all living creatures across the three worlds—the heaven, earth, and the netherworld. The poison soon started to get mixed with air and as the Asuras were closest to the mouth, many started to fall sick or perish from inhaling the poison. The churning came to a stop, but nobody from the Gods or Asuras had the power to stop the halahal from spreading. Finally, Lord Shiva stepped in from Mount Kailash. He directed all the poison onto the closed palm of his hands and consumed it. Goddess Parvati, Shiva's consort, made the halahal stay only within the throat of Shiva, but the ferocity of the poison caused Shiva's neck to take on a deep blue colour. Ever since, Lord Shiva is also known as 'Neelkanth' or the one with the blue neck.

Soon, the churning continued and brought out Airavat, in another avatar or form, which was a white-coloured winged being with six trunks and six pairs of tusks. He dug his trunk deep into the ground, and could reach an otherwise inaccessible water table below the earth. Then, he would draw that water and spray it on the earth as monsoon showers. After appearing from the Cosmic Ocean, Airavat chose to once again serve his master—Lord Indra.

From the churning two more animals emerged—the seven-headed flying horse—Uchchaihshravas, who was taken as a mount by Indra, and Kamdhenu—the cow, who is considered as the mother of all cattle. She is depicted with the face of a woman, and the body of a cow, with a pair of wings, and the tail of a peacock. She was given to the Saptarishi, or the seven sages, to provide them with ample milk to prepare curd and ghee regularly for their sacred rituals.

The churning also made heavenly Apsaras appear. They were beautiful spirits of Devlok, and experts in the performing arts—music and dance. They chose the Gandharvas as their companions, who served as musicians in Indra's court.

The churning also produced the beautiful Parijat tree. The tree had small white flowers, with tiny orange stalks and a scent that travelled across the universe. This tree was taken by Indra and planted in the heavenly garden.

The churning also produced Vishnu's Sharanga bow, Panchajanya Conch, and Kaustubh Mani. Crafted by the heavenly craftsman Vishwakarma, the Sharanga bow was used by Vishnu's three avatars or forms—

Parshurama, Rama, and Krishna. Finally, the Sharanga bow was returned to the God of oceans—Lord Varuna. The Panchajanya Conch was utilised by Vishnu symbolically in various avatars to state his role as a preserver of the universe. The conch was also blown through time to signify the beginning of war and to save humankind. Finally, the Kaustubh Mani was a sacred gemstone, embedded in a necklace that adorned Vishnu's neck. The exotic stone looked as beautiful as a lotus and as radiant as the sun.

From the churning, also emerged Lord Chandra, or the moon, and Goddesses Lakshmi and Alakshmi. Chandra took refuge in Shiva's matted locks once again, and Lakshmi, being Vishnu's consort, was once again reunited with him. She appeared draped in a red and gold saree, sitting atop a beautiful lotus, and holding smaller lotuses in her hand. Her arrival brought back the prosperity of Devlok. The arrival of Lakshmi was followed by Alakshmi—her elder sister, who wore white, had unkempt hair and is the Goddess of misfortune, poverty, and misery. She is said to visit houses filled with ego, pride, selfishness, and envy.

Then, finally emerged Dhanvantari, the physician of the Gods, holding the pot of amrit, or the nectar of immortality. Dhanvantari was responsible for teaching mankind the ancient knowledge of medical science and ayurveda. As soon as the pot of Amrit emerged, the Asuras snatched it and wanted to consume all of it. The Gods realized the problem and once again sought Lord Vishnu's help. He appeared in the form of a beautiful lady, named Mohini and allured the Asuras to hand over the pot of elixir, so that it could be served by herself in an orderly manner. Fooled by the beauty of Mohini, the Asuras agreed and both the Gods and the Asuras lined up to partake the Amrita. Vishnu, disguised as Mohini, began serving the Gods first. The Asuras, still under the spell of Mohini's charm, did not suspect anything. However, one Asura named Saimhikeya, disguised himself as a God and joined the queue of the Gods. Mohini had served him Amrita and Saimhikeya had drunk it, but right at that moment, the two Gods—Chandra or the moon and Surya or the sun realized that he was indeed an Asura disguised as a God. They shouted out the truth to Mohini. Vishnu assumed his original form and immediately cut off Saimhikeya's head with his Sudarshan Chakra or the flying-disc weapon which he always held in his hand. The body of Saimhikeya was cut into two halves and as the Amrita had reached till the throat, the head of the Asura remained alive. These two parts of the body evolved into the Asuras Rahu and Ketu—Rahu being formed from the head and Ketu from the body. They remained angry at Chandra and Surya for revealing the truth. There is a popular myth about lunar and solar eclipses associated with this story. It is believed that since Rahu and Ketu remained angry at Chandra and Surya, they try to gobble them up. However, the attempts remain unsuccessful as the headless body can never ingest either the sun or the moon and very soon after being gobbled up, both reappear. Thus, both the sun and the moon reappear soon after an eclipse has taken place. This legend of the eclipses is mentioned in the Kampa Ramayana (also known as Kamba Ramayana) and the Bhagavata Ashtama Skandha.

Despite the hindrances, all the Gods were served the amrit elixir. They regained their kingdom, wealth, and prosperity by defeating the Asuras. Peace returned to Devlok once again.

Such stories of creation are also found in various other cultures of the world and also many other communities of India as well.

It is also often believed that these stories[*] and similar ones, which have identical patterns to 'Samudra Manthan' and speak about the creation of the world, have tried to provide within an embryonic outline, the explanation of the creation of the universe. This includes the formation of the earth and all life forms, the existence of water being the source of life on earth, the formation of the moon from the earth, or the emergence of larger forms of life from the simpler aquatic ones, among others. Though these are often criticized, a closer look at the stories, which took centuries to be formulated, reflect a belief about biodiversity, the environment, and above all, the very belief of water being the source of sustenance for life on earth. This is a recurring symbolism in many myths from across India. Here is an example from a Santhali story.

> This is a story from a time long, long ago, when the entire universe was a great mass of water. One day, Bonga (God) decided to create the world. So, he called up all the mukhiyas (headmen) of the water land and advised them to collect mud from the waterbed. Firstly, the crabs carried the mud and piled it up, but it got washed away. After that, the tortoise did it, but he too failed. Finally, the earthworms picked up mud and placed it on the back of the tortoise which was sitting there. Thus, land was created. Soon, many other things were created, including the highlands, lowlands, mountains, and seas. Though the earth looked stable, yet human life was missing. Thus, God created birds from the seed of 'Sirom Grass'—a gander and a goose. Two eggs were laid. Two human beings were born—one was called Pilchu Haram and the other Pilchu Burhi. The Santal were born out of them. They started

[*]'Samudra Manthan: The legend behind eclipses', *Amar Chitra Katha*, India: Amar Chitra Katha, 26 September 2020; 'The Ratnas of Samudra Manthan', *Amar Chitra Katha*, India: Amar Chitra Katha, 14 May 2021.

cultivating in the barren hilly land and thus started their life.*

This version of the creation myth, according to Durga Bhagwat, is perhaps the earliest version of the creation story of the Santhals. She also suggests that the close bond shared by the community with ducks, their high fertility, and people deriving sustenance from duck eggs probably led to the special mention of ducks in the story. The story also speaks about the hierarchic social set-up and the concept of a class divided society, which have been explained by a headman or a mukhiya. This version of the creation story also reflects an archaic faith in all living beings, especially the unknown, as deities or divinities. This is a remnant of the pantheistic outlook. Assigning creatures a social status, identical to that of the humans, sprung out of a hierarchical social structure, typical of the post primitive era. Such similar tales of the creation of the earth are also common among various other communities as well.

Often Creation myths also embody the concepts of the 'Great Flood' or the 'Great Deluge'. These are also parts of the mythological stories of many communities from across India and the world. These stories of the Great Flood, also multifariously explain the birth of life and of creation after destruction, which are variously measured across many religions to span over a period of time. This measurement of time is an ongoing process and is mentioned in many religious ideologies of the world, including India. All stories pertaining to the Great Flood also mention the earth, which renews herself as life starts afresh after the floods. These stories explain the peaceful harmony of recreation, immediately after an episode of cataclysmic destruction of all forms of life. These stories do not only portray hope, but also underline a continuous struggle between man and nature and the struggle for survival

---

*Durga Bhagwat, *Indian Anthropologist,* 36:1 & 2, 2006, pp. 23–44.

of either. Often, it has been critiqued that these stories took birth as a kernel from the memories of the last ice age, which ended around 10,000 years ago. On the other hand, there are also different sets of opinions which refute these claims. They discuss these tales of the flood as representations of natural calamities and tragedies across history, and part and parcel of human existence. One such story of the 'Great Flood' of the Oraon community is as follows:

> A very long time ago, when there was nothing, God created heaven and earth in seven days. He created a couple according to his likes and filled up the entire earth with such couples. However, soon, their nature changed. Many became wicked and crooked, and God did not like this. He soon decided that he would destroy everything with a great flood. This was sensed by one deity named 'Bhabi', who was the beloved of one God. Since she realized that all creation will end soon, she hid a couple first within her garments, and then finally, within a crabhole on earth. As quite rightly 'Bhabi' had sensed, soon enough, God sent a massive flood on earth. Everything was inundated and destroyed. When the waters receded, God could see destruction everywhere and there was no sign of life. God suddenly realized that there remained nobody to even worship him, or offer him sacrifices or prasad. Thus, he went in search of any signs of life on earth, along with his dog named, Lili Bhuli Khairikuti (female dog). 'Bhabi' also accompanied him and instructed the couple to come out of the crabhole within which they were hiding. When the couple saw the barking dog of God, they were frightened at first, but God called out to them: 'Natiiro (grandchildren), do not be afraid of my dog. She will bring you no harm. Come with me and I will give you a proper shelter.' Upon hearing the endearing word 'Natiiro', the couple went with God, who provided them a safe place

> to stay, clean clothes to wear, and good food to eat. He then prepared them for the night. At first, God had made a bamboo fence to separate the couple as they slept at night. After a few days, God lifted the fence, and thus, he instituted the very first matrimony. Some days later, the couple asked God to show them the way and means to live. He instructed them to clear the jungle and dam the rivers within, and they did so. God soon made the sun, moon, and stars, and made them rise and set at specific times. He also made the plough and taught the couple how to use them. Then the couple ploughed the upland and the low fields, but they did not have any seed to sow. Thus, they asked God for seeds to sow. He gave them pumpkin seeds and also sent rain, wind, and warmth for the seeds to survive. Thus, when the fruit was ripe, God instructed the couple to break open the fruit. From one pumpkin, a variety of paddy crops, pulses, oilseeds, and vegetable seeds came out. The couple was very happy. They took out the seeds and planted them at suitable places. Thus, crops spread gradually.

Creation myths, also impart a symbolic understanding of the respective world within particular natural surroundings, which helps to form a pattern of thinking. In doing so, these stories also often speak of migration, settlements, and resettlements. Illustratively a story from The Andaman and Nicobar Islands, recounts the floods and the creation thereafter. Interestingly enough, in these oral traditions from the Andamans, the memory of the forefathers and their frequent encounter with storms and tsunamis are etched in space. Severe thunderstorms and cyclonic weather are common occurrences in the Andamans due to their geographical position. The islanders have faced them through centuries. These stories now act as a repository of the memories from the past. One similar story[*], which highlights storms, destruction, and recreation, is a famous one from the Akakede and A-Pucikwar languages. Both are extinct languages at present, and are said to have ceased to officially exist between1930–1950. The Akakede belonged to the Great Andamanese North Kede language family and was seen in and around the central, north central, and middle Andaman Islands. The A-Pucikwar belonged to the Great Andamanese family and was formerly spoken by the Pucikwar people of the south coast of Middle Andaman, the northeast coast of South Andaman and the Baratang Island. According to this Akakede story:

> The world was created by God Puluga, who then made a man named Tomo, who was the first human. He looked exactly like the present people from the region, but was much taller and had a very bushy beard. Puluga showed him many fruit trees in the jungle, which only existed in Wota-emi—a place in the country of the A-Pucikwar tribe. The wife of Tomo was Cana Elewadi (Lady Crab). Tomo lived to a great old age and had many children. They grew so many in number that their home could no longer accomodate them. Finally, at Puluga's bidding, these numerous children were provided with the necessary things that one might need to settle down, including weapons, implements, and fire. Then Puluga scattered them all over the country in pairs. During the time of this exodus, Puluga also provided each party with a distinct dialect and also taught each member to live by certain rules and behaviour.

---

[*]Alfred Radcliffe Brown, *Puluga of Andaman,* UK: Cambridge University Press, 1933, pp. 196–97; Edward Horace Man, *The Andaman Islanders: On the Aboriginal Inhabitants of the Andaman Islands, Report of Researches into the Language of the South Andaman Island,* UK: White Lotus Press, 1885, pp. 202–03, 212–13.

This would make life easy for each member and would also reduce confrontations between settlements. Thus, it is believed that the various tribes dispersed all over the region of the Andaman and Nicobar Islands, and each also developed their own specific languages or dialects, which is followed till date.

Now, one day, Tomo and his wife disappeared from the community at Wota-emi. Thus, the duties of leading the community fell upon one of their grandchildren—Kolwot. He was a distinguished person and was deft in many things, including being the first to spear and catch turtles. Life in the community continued well during the lifetime of Kolwot; however, things started to go haywire after his death. People became disobedient and stopped following the commands, which were provided by the Supreme deity at the time of creation. Thus, Puluga stopped visiting them and grew very angry at the lawlessness. So, one day, Puluga's anger burst out in the form of a massive flood. This inundated the region and destroyed all living creatures—all except four, who were made to stay alive by Puluga to continue life after the deluge. These were two men, Lora-lola and Poi-lola and two women, Ka-lola and Rima-lola. These four people were saved as they were in a canoe when the catastrophe occurred, and somehow they managed to stay afloat in spite of the rough waters all around.

When the water subsided, they found themselves near Wota-emi. They set out to explore the area in hopes of finding signs of life, only to discover with disappointment that every living being on the island had perished, and there was no trace of a burning fire, crucial for their survival. Now, Puluga helped these four people to resettle in the same island and recreated the animals, birds and fishes, but he did not provide fire, until he was tricked

> into doing so by one of the survivors' recently drowned friends who reappeared in the form of a kingfisher. It so happened that since Puluga did not want to give fire to the ancestors, one night, the Lirtit or the kingfisher went slowly to the abode of Puluga to steal fire while he was sleeping. While the kingfisher was running away with the fire, Puluga woke up and threw a pearl shell at him, which cut off his wings and tail. The helpless kingfisher dived into the water and swam instead with the fire in his mouth to Bet-ra-kudu. He gave it to Tepe, who in turn gave the fire to Mite, or the bronze-winged dove, and it was from Mite that all the ancestors received fire.
>
> Soon, however, the population increased for a second time to such an extent that it became impossible to stay in a single place. Thus, another exodus occurred in pairs, with each group provided with essentials, including fire. They left for various directions, settled in different regions, adopted a new and separate dialect, and also a distinct name. It is believed that the current communities descended from these settlements.

This story and similar ones from the Andaman and the Nicobar have been popular for centuries and were also documented by E. H. Man (1885) in his account of the South Andaman and later by A. R. Radcliffe-Brown (1922). Many Andamanese mythologies centre round Puluga and Tomo. It is also believed that everything which is natural is attributed to or believed to be the creation of Puluga. It is important to note the mention of fire in the story. Fire, originally obtained from nature, was considered a sacrosanct part of existence, which faced threat from floods and storms and thus needed protection to survive. On the other hand, the mention of the floods is part of several local narratives of the region, and these reveal many aspects of geological and environmental changes and occurrences.

Creation myths can help to revive traditions and identities

as well. Through these preserved identities, one can also, often witness a particular ideology of a community. One such example is the Donyi-Poloism of Arunachal Pradesh (from the name Donyi-Polo, meaning 'Sun-Moon'—a name given by the people in the 1970s). According to one creation myth of Donyi-Polo

> All living things on earth were made from parts of the body of Sedi. His hair became plants; his tears became rain and water; his bones became rocks; and from his eyes were formed Donyi or Mother Sun and Polo or Father Moon. After creation, Sedi continues to keep a watch over all his creations. Interestingly enough, Donyi and Polo are the male and female energies of nature, which create harmony and balance of existence.

Religious rituals and theological thinking are not particular to any one single community or religion. They share their space with similar patterns of thought processes with other communities. Thus, many symbols and motifs within stories also follow a pattern. These have also been extensively studied throughout the last century, and thus, we come to an understanding of how stories of creation are closely connected to stories of life, destruction, and finally, representation of various marginalized thought processes, including those related to caste, creed, or gender. Within the many layers of understanding of the retelling of a myth, it is the subtext of these representations which form an interesting read, and to a great extent, I believe, calls for greater and deeper attention. They impart a very different perspective towards the regular storylines, or a clichéd format, or setting. This publication is a miniscule attempt to bring forth, some of these interesting storylines and representations which often lie in oblivion.

As one looks deeper into the many folds of representation, one is also surprised to witness the many stories of nature which manifest themselves amid humans, where the lifeforce of bipeds and that of nature is explained in an interesting interchangeable manner. Often, being left with a melancholic end, these myths and legends seem to highlight a possible psychological and emotional tussle of women and men with nature—one with whom they have to live, but often are helpless in front of its might and fervour. Following this, one is reminded of the famous legend of Aonglemla* from the Ao Naga community of Nagaland.

> The Aonglemla is a creature from the land of the lore of the Ao Naga, and is said to be a feminine spirit that manifests itself as a gigantic humanoid, covered in hairs from head to toe, while its feet are turned backwards. Though considered basically harmless her wails terrify people. Often, people claim to have seen her, and then it is considered a bad omen; even seeing her footprints is still considered a curse. Thus, while venturing into the jungles, people take special precautions to avoid meeting her or her footprints.

While social scientists and anthropologists have endeavoured to elucidate the presence of Aonglemla over the years, the conviction in a 'strange and hairy creature with a shrill cry' persists uniquely within the local community's beliefs. One such explanation about the Aonglemla mentions that the stories have come from the sighting of the Hoolock Gibbon (Genus Hoolock) an endangered primate species found in Eastern Bangladesh, Northeast India, Northwest Myanmar, and Southwest China. This assumption is based on the fact that both the gibbon and Aonglemla, are tiny, agile, and live in the deep forest, and share similar taste in food, including leaves, insects, and worms. The

---

*The Mizos, 'Aonglemlatsu- 5 Nasty Mythical Creatures from Northeast India', 11 October 2021; Talilula Longchar, *She Who Walks with Feet Facing Backwards and Laughs in the Wilderness- Ao Naga Narratives of Aonglemla*, New Delhi: Zubaan Books, 2019, p. 35.

Hoolock also calls out loudly, just like the Aonglemla. In this book, there are some captivating legends about supernatural beasts or famous creatures which are considered as half man and half beast. Once again, these stories need to be understood through the layers of representation that they speak of. These stories are significant and reflect an important thread of thought within various communities.

Since this book looks into myths and legends about nature and environment, an important part of the same are the tales about water bodies. An attempt has been made within this book, with the scope and limitation in mind, to include a variety of representations of water and waterbodies in India. Water in mythology holds a special place and there are many stories pertaining to the different forms of water, including rains, rivers, and waterfalls, among others. Rivers, particularly, have always been associated with spiritualism. The concept involves crossing over from the world of ignorance, delusion, and the bondage of materialistic hurdles to that of a state of enlightenment, awareness, and salvation. Thus, often the rivers are worshipped, just like in temples, with or without fire (aarti) and offerings are made. Often, such pujas are also commemorative of events and occasions from the past, about a period of prosperity. On the other hand, the worship of rains forms an integral part of the worship, especially in an agrarian economy like ours. Thus, the excess of rainfall, as well as the lack of it, are both often the central highlights of worship, especially during the mid-monsoon months of July through September, when there is often very heavy rainfall. On the other hand, such worship pertaining to rainfall is also seen during the hot summer months of May and June, when the southwestern monsoon rains are yet to set in. The entire landscape of the subcontinent waits patiently for the first drops of rain to quench the thirst of the parched land. Through a conscious attempt, this book accords a large section to mythological stories concerning water bodies, including the bay, ocean and the sea, as well as a variety of others, including rivers, waterfalls, delta, lakes, wells, and rainfall.

The tradition of storytelling is an important one among all communities. In the tumult of life, one may get lost among the plethora of methods to which we are exposed as part of storytelling, but nevertheless we are surrounded by stories from almost all directions. It is the same with the various elements of intangible cultural heritage (ICH) of India as many tales of myths and legends lie woven within the tapestry of folk songs, art, dances, festivals, and puppetry, among others. Some of these tales from ICH of India are part of the 108 stories in this book. They represent various big and small linguistic and religious communities and range across seven geographical sections of India—northern, central, western, eastern, northeastern, southern, and water bodies—consisting of the bays, oceans, seas, and others. However, as mentioned at the beginning of this introduction, I would also like to specify that these stories are peripatetic by nature, and they cannot be compartmentalized into sections and divisions of topography, linguistics, or politics. The segments in this book are merely for the benefit of representing specific historically significant episodes or periods, and represent particular communities which are still largely seen to reside in a particular region. Being peripatetic by nature, there can be various versions of a myth or legend. Thus, many of the stories mentioned within a specific region within this publication, may also be found in the neighbouring regions and across other communities as well. Long ago, anthropologist Levi-Strauss had stressed the significance of understanding all the versions of a myth, in order to comprehend the structure of a myth. All versions of a myth are relevant to the function of a myth as a whole, as they show a spiral growth of the myth, which is continuous, while the structure itself is not. All of these also highlight specific important aspects of communities or their beliefs within varied time frames, at which point, presumably, the different versions are supposed to have been created. Many versions of the myths and legends have also found a place in popular culture, including graphic novels and cinema. With many being international productions and publications. They reach a very wide and different set of audiences worldwide. In this book, some of the myths and legends, along with their different versions mentioned, have also been cited with a very brief note about communities, festivals, arts, crafts, or specific and important written or oral literature. These might aid the general query of readers and help to understand how all the stories within this publication touch upon various aspects of biodiversity, and in their own specific ways, draw attention to the significant courses of conservation and preservation.

Finally, this publication is a collection of very old and new tales, with many of the stories even lost from the pages of modern lores or publications. There are also stories from languages and dialects, which have ceased to exist nearly a century ago (according to official reports of the Census of India). These elements also help to portray a significant aspect of tales from a bygone era. Myths primarily serve as descriptive rather than explanatory guides, offering insights into traditional, pre-industrial societies from historical records. They employ unique methods to depict aspects that individuals cannot directly observe. However, this search is more complex. As much as it is closely connected to finding a position within a complex system of relationships, it also helps at the microlevels of the self, pertaining to social life and survival. This depends on the making of distinctions between hosts of decisions, upon which the very existence of the self depends. Myths and legends almost provide a map for questions and answers within which individuals dwell, almost like the story of the Dhruv tara or the Pole Star, providing a navigational mean through centuries and generations. Thus, the stories go on....

Northern Region

1

The Hare-shaped Mark on the Surface of the Moon

Long ago, when king Brahmadatta sat on the throne of Benaras, the Bodhisattva came to life as a hare in a forest. He had three very close friends—an otter, a monkey, and a jackal. The little forest where all of them lived was surrounded on one side by the foot of a mountain, on another side there was a river, and on the third side there was a border village. The hare was unanimously elected as the leader of the group because all the friends considered him the wisest of all, and also thought that he had a divine persona. The wise hare taught his friends the way of admonition and preached the Truth. He taught that alms are to be given, about the moral laws, and about the holy days which are to be observed. They accepted his preaching and went to their respective homes in different parts of the jungle. One day, the Bodhisattva, by looking at the sky, understood that the following day was to be a day of fasting. Thus, he summoned all his three friends and said, 'Tomorrow is a day of fasting. We should observe the holy day and give alms to the poor, and food from our own table to any beggar who comes by.' All the three friends listened, nodded their heads, and went back to their own dwellings.

The next day, on the day of fasting, a fisherman had caught seven red fish from the river Ganga. He stringed the seven fish, buried them in the sand, and went back to catch some more. At that time, the otter was out searching for food. He came upon the seven red fish, dug them out, and cried three times,

'Do these fish belong to anybody?' The words did not reach the fisherman, so nobody answered. The otter waited for sometime and when nobody came to claim the fish, he understood that he could take the fish with him without any hesitation. So, the otter brought the fish home. Then suddenly he remembered that it was the day of fast. Thus, the otter decided to keep the fish away and eat it only the next day. The otter felt happy that he could control his greed and considered himself to be very virtuous.

On the same day, the jackal had also gone out to hunt. He came upon a hut in a field, within which there was a large piece of roasted meat and a pot of curd. The jackal also cried out loudly three times. 'Do these belong to anybody?' However, he did not receive any reply. Relieved, the jackal took the meat and the pot of curd with him to his home, only to realize later that it was a day of fast. So, the jackal kept the meat aside for the next day.

In a similar manner, the monkey had also gone out to look for food. He came across some mangoes and on realizing that they belonged to no one, brought them home and kept them aside for the next day.

On the very same day, the hare, while sitting on kusa grass, on which he used to feed, thought of all the people who might be hungry and starving. He wondered, 'What will I offer if anybody came begging for food from me? Will I offer this kusa grass? I cannot offer him this, and I have no rice or oil. I will offer him my own flesh to eat.'

As soon as the Bodhisattva thought about this, the throne of Sakra grew hot and started shaking. This always happened when a great event was planned or done on earth. Sakra wanted to know why his throne became hot and looked down at the hare. He knew about the pious thoughts of the hare and wanted to test his sincerity.

Sakra assumed the form of a Brahmin priest and descended

on earth. He went to each of the animals and asked for food. First, he went to the otter and asked for food and the otter replied, 'I have brought seven red fish from the banks of the Ganga. O Brahmin, please eat these and stay within the woods.' Sakra, disguised as the Brahmin priest, replied, 'Keep it till tomorrow and I will see if I want to eat it.'

Next, Sakra went to the jackal and asked for some food and the jackal replied, 'I have a pot of curd and a piece of meat. This is my evening's meal. O Brahmin, please eat these and stay with us for a while in these woods.' The Brahmin once again replied, 'Let it wait till tomorrow and I will see if I want to eat it.' The same incident happened with the monkey as well, and the Brahmin replied that he will wait until the next day and moved on. Finally, Sakra reached the hare and asked for food. The hare realized that he had nothing to give and thus offered himself, and asked the Brahmin to set up a fire. Sakra, still in disguise, set up few live charcoals and informed the hare. The little hare got up from the kusa grass on which he was sitting. He shook himself a few times to free himself of any insect which might be alive in his fur, lest they too die in the fire. Then the hare sprang up in the air like a swan and jumped into the live charcoal, but the flames did not even touch the fur on its body. The flames of the fire had turned icy cold. The hare looked at the Brahmin and said, 'Brahmin, this fire has turned cold and it fails to heat up even the slightest hair of my body.' Then the Brahmin replied, 'O hare, I am no Brahmin. I am Sakra and I came to test your virtue.' To this the hare replied, 'O Sakra, if it was not a Brahmin but any other person, I would have still not made him return empty-handed.' Then Sakra replied, 'O wise hare, I know your virtue and it should be known throughout the land.' Saying this, he squeezed the nearby mountain, and with the juice thus extracted, drew the sign of the hare on the surface of the moon. After this, Sakra made the Bodhisattva return to his abode of kusa grass, and he lived harmoniously with his three friends in the forest—observing holy days, fasts, and fulfilling the moral law.

Thus, there is a hare mark on the moon.

2

How the Parijat Tree Came Down to Earth from the Heavens

Many many years ago, the Parijat tree, rose out of the milk ocean from Samudra Manthan (Churning of the Ocean), and Indra, the king of the Gods, planted it in the garden in his heavenly abode in Amravati.

The Parijat tree was indeed beautiful. It was not like any other tree. The bark of the tree was of gold, and it was embellished with young, copper-coloured sprouting leaves and fruit stalks, bearing numerous clusters of fragrant fruits. The little flowers were not only pretty, but adored by one and all.

Once, sage Narada brought one of these beautiful Parijat flowers from heaven to the kingdom of Dwarka and presented it to his friend Lord Krishna, the king of Dwarka at that time. Narada also wanted to see to which of his wives Krishna would give the flower. It so happened that Rukmini was passing by the main chamber where the king and his ministers were holding court. When Krishna saw her, he remembered the flower that Narada had gifted him and promptly presented it to her. Now, the flower was given to Rukmini without favouritism, however, Narada thought that it was an act of preference over Krishna's wife Satyabhama. He went straight to Satyabhama, who noticed that Narada looked sad. When asked, Narada replied, 'I brought the glorious Parijat flower from heaven and gifted it to Lord Krishna to give it to his wife. I thought that you were his favourite wife and the Lord would give the gift of the wonderful Parijat to you. However, I just noticed that the Lord gave the flower to Rukmini. I am saddened.' Saying so, Narada became quiet, while Satyabhama began to think, 'Am I wrong to doubt the Lord's affection? I always thought that he would never prefer one of us over the other. But, can I be wrong?' and Satyabhama's thoughts took the better of her. She started to feel a pang of jealousy towards Rukmini and said to Narada, 'O wise and noble one, I am so happy to see that you care for me so. But am I supposed to doubt the Lord's affection?'

Narada replied, 'No one should ever doubt it, for the Lord is always impartial to all on heaven and earth, but still, the flower was only given to one, while not to the other. I do not know what else to make out of it.'

Satyabhama was still thinking. Finally, she asked Narada, 'O wise one, do tell me what to do now?'

Narada thought for a moment and replied, 'Why don't you ask, not for a single flower, but the entire heavenly tree itself, and ask the Lord to plant it near your house?'

To Satyabhama, this sounded like a just advice and she went on to ask Krishna for the whole Parijat tree as he had already gifted the flower to Rukmini. The Lord understood the reason for Satyabhama's request and knew that she was advised by Narada. However, he was placed in a challenging situation and found no other way, but to agree to Satyabhama's demand.

Narada, on the other hand, knew that the Parijat tree was in the heavenly garden of Indra, the king of Gods. From Satyabhama's quarters Narada went straight to Indra's court. The king was busy at the time with his ministers. He asked Narada, 'O wise one, let me know what I can do for you?'

Narada replied, 'I just came to warn you that you should guard your Parijat tree carefully as there is a risk of it being stolen.'

'The whole tree will be stolen? By whom?' Indra could not believe what he was hearing and it all sounded too sudden.

'Yes, the whole tree. Guard it well, for within a day or two, it will be stolen,' and so saying, Narada left.

That same night, Krishna stole into Amravati, the heavenly abode of King Indra. As Krishna started to uproot the tree, the loud noises of digging brought out Indra to his garden. He was completely astonished to see Krishna digging and pulling out the entire Parijat tree from the garden. Indra could not believe his eyes. He remembered what Narada had told him that very morning, yet he was surprised for he never ever imagined that Krishna would be stealing the Parijat tree. Indra did try to question and stop Krishna, but finally let him have the tree. Krishna took the tree with him to Dwarka and put it outside Satyabhama's chamber.

It is believed that after the death of Lord Krishna, Dwarka got submerged in the ocean and the Parijat tree was taken back to heaven.

3

How Hariti Became a Protector of Children and Also a Part of Sculpture

Once, during the time of Buddha, there lived a Yakshini in Rajagriha by the name Abhirati, who was born so because of a wicked vow she took in her previous birth. She was married to Panchika, a Yaksha general of the Gandhara region.

Abhirati and Panchika had five hundred children, and to feed herself and her many children, she took to cannibalism. She used to steal and devour a child every day at Rajagriha. All the people of Rajagriha became extremely worried because of the alarming incidents every night. Everyone was fearful and finally decided to approach Buddha to seek advice. Abhirati came to be referred to as Hariti, i.e. one who steals. Buddha listened to the worrisome people of the city and decided to pay a visit to Hariti. He came to the city of Rajagriha and went from door to door seeking alms and food. Finally, he arrived at Hariti's house. At that time, Hariti was not at home and all her children were alone. Buddha knew that the youngest child, named Pingala, was Hariti's favourite. The Buddha hid Pingala in the begging bowl and returned to the monastery.

Hariti returned after sometime and became increasingly restless upon not finding Pingala. Overwhelmed with grief, Hariti started searching for him everywhere in an anxious quest to find him. Finally, she came to the Buddha and requested him to find the boy. In silence, Buddha listened to her sorrowful lamentations. Finally when she stopped, he replied, 'I have listened to you attentively. I can completely understand the grief of a mother. I will help you, but you have to promise me something.' The Buddha became silent, waiting for Hariti's reply.

Hariti was overjoyed at the very thought of meeting her dear son once again and immediately replied, 'Anything you say, My Lord.'

The Buddha replied, 'You have to promise me that you will give up cannibalism and also follow my precepts.' The Buddha was silent once again, waiting for Hariti's answer.

Hariti replied, 'Yes, my Lord. I will listen to your commands. Not only myself, but I will also make my children follow your path and your wise words. But if you permit, I have a question to ask you.'

'Please tell me what is on your mind,' said the Buddha.

'My Lord, I know I devour children and destroy lives, but I do it to sustain myself and my children. If I stop eating, how will my children and I survive?' Hariti sounded worried.

The Buddha replied calmly, 'Please do not worry about that. I will never ask anybody to give up food and to starve their children, but the way you were leading your life was proving to be extremely fatal to many innocent lives, and that is not the correct path of life. I have ordered all the monks at the monastery to serve you abundant food for your sustenance. This will continue throughout time. You will also be remembered at every monastery. People will always talk about you as a protector of children, rather than a malevolent force.' Hariti bowed down in salutation and the Buddha blessed her. Soon, she met her son Pingala and she was overjoyed, but she remembered her promise to the Buddha. She became a lay worshipper to the Sangha. Buddha called all the monks and ordered them to serve Hariti food every day to sustain her children and herself. The monks followed his orders faithfully and to this day, Hariti is seen as a reverent part of every monastery across India. In return for the services of the monks and the monasteries, Hariti and her children became the custodians of Buddhist monasteries in India, and her conversion to the faith introduced a new phase in her life. Thanks to the blessings of the Buddha, Hariti was ordained as an Upasika, and from a devourer of children, she became their protector and a deity. Very soon, a popular cult grew around Hariti.

Thus, Hariti's presence is seen within all monasteries across India. Her sculpture is found either in the porch or in a corner of the dining hall of all the Indian monasteries. Her sculpture depicts her carrying a baby in her arms and three or five children around her knees.

4

Legend of Surdas's Compositions about Lord Krishna

An important Bhakti poet of Brajbhumi, Surdas loved Lord Krishna dearly and composed songs in the praise of the Lord. His songs are usually considered to be the finest expressions of Brajbhasha, one of Hindi's two principal literary dialects. Surdas was visually impaired, and though it is often mentioned that he suffered this impairment in the latter part of his life, the Vallabhite tradition describes him to be so from birth. Surdas's life is said to have been difficult at home, with unhappy situations, because of his visual impairment. However, he had a deep love for music from his very childhood, and also loved to listen to the music of groups of singers who would often pass by his house. It is said that he left home when he was around six years of age with one of these groups of singers. Unfortunately, they soon abandoned him, but the child managed to survive and began composing poems and songs. At the age of eighteen, Surdas moved to Gaughat and lived there till he was thirty-one. At this point he met Vallabhacharya. By then, Surdas had accumulated many followers and was well-known for his padas (stanzas and paragraphs of songs), and he was appointed as the official devotional singer at the temple of Shrinathji by Vallabhacharya in Braj area. A popular legend speaks of how Surdas was destined to visit Brajbhumi. According to this story, he once dreamt of Lord Krishna calling him to Brajbhumi. After visiting the region, he met his guru Sri Vallabhacharya, who asked him to dedicate his life to Lord

Krishna. Surdas stayed in Brajbhumi for the rest of his life, and it is popularly belived that he composed 125,000 padas in praise of Lord Krishna. He died in Parasoli, in the presence of Vallabhacharya's son and successor, Vitthal Nath.

Another legend recounts how Surdas used to compose a pada at the Shrinathji temple every evening. The people who had gathered at the temple would look on in astonishment as the poet would sit each day and compose a new song in praise of The Lord, and describe the attire and the ornaments as well. The priests and the devotees used to wonder in amazement. Thus, one evening, they thought of testing Surdas and did not adorn the deity with any attire or ornaments. When Surdas arrived that evening, he surprised everyone by composing a song in honour of the natural tone of Lord Krishna (meghashyama, meaning dark clouds), sans the adornment. At that moment, everyone realized that even though Surdas was visually impaired, he was endowed with a divine vision that enabled him to see the splendour of his Lord. To this, Surdas spoke of the mercy of Lord Krishna—

> I worship the feet of the great Hari
> Whose grace enables the crippled to cross mountains
> and makes the blind see
> By His grace, the deaf hears, the dumb speaks once
> more,
> and the poor hold the royal chhatra (umbrella)
> above their heads.
> Sur says: The Lord, is merciful; I worship His feet
> again and again.*

Many stories speak of Surdas meeting emperor Akbar in his court, as the latter desired to meet the famous poet. This was

*Six Poems from Surdas Author(s): Surdas Source: Mahfil, 1963, Vol. 1, No. 2 (1963), pp. 24-26 Published by: Asian Studies Center, Michigan State University

made possible through the court poet of Akbar, Tansen. A legend also speaks about Akbar, like the rest of the common people, asking the poet about his precise description of Lord Krishna as he was visually impaired. To this, Surdas seems to have replied thus—

No more room
remains in my heart.
It is the son of Nanda
who lives there
always, all the time.
How is it, then, possible
to let someone else
even come in?
In the waking hours
in the dreams at night
His face
never goes away from my heart
not even for a moment.
People tell tales, O Uddho,
They try to tempt me.
But what can I do?
My heart so full of love
is like a clay pitcher
into which an ocean cannot be poured.
Surdas sings only of dark
And lotus-faced Krishna
of His soft and sweet smile.
It is for the vision of him
that my eyes thirst
eternally.*

---

*Usha Nilsson, *Surdas* (*Makers of Indian Literature*), Sahitya Akademi, New Delhi, 1969.

5

The Story of Aditi:
The Divine Mother of All

Aditi is the divine mother and is also considered to represent all that is positive. In the Vedas, she is Devamata (mother of the celestial Gods) and it is through her that all heavenly bodies were born.

According to the Shiva Purana and the Bhagavata Purana, Aditi was the daughter of King Daksha, who married off all his daughters including Aditi and sixteen others to sage Kashyapa.

Amongst the other wives of Kashyapa, was Aditi's sister by the name Diti and she was very dissimilar and different from Aditi. When they were living in the ashrama (hermitage) with Kashyapa, the latter was very pleased to see Aditi's services, and told her to ask for a boon. Aditi prayed for one ideal son and accordingly Lord Indra was born. He became the king of Gods. Later, Aditi also gave birth to other divinities, including Varuna, Parjanya, Mitra, Ansh, Pushan, Dhatri, Aryaman, Surya, Bhaga, and Vamana. Thus, they were referred to as Adityas. With Kashyapa, Aditi had thirty-tree sons, out of which twelve are called Adityas, eleven are called Rudras, and eight are called Vasus.

6

To Stand United Like Trees in a Forest

The Buddha shared this profound narrative while sitting near the river Rohini in the Siwalik Hills in Kapilavastu. Through the story, the Buddha's message was to speak about the unity among kinsfolk, and the need to support and protect each other during times of danger. As the story goes, a new king who sat on the throne of Varanasi, sent an important message to all kinds of plants, including trees, shrubs, bushes, climbers, creepers, and to all the tree fairies. He instructed all the tree fairies to choose the abode of a specific tree and to reside within it. They were also free to allow the tree to grow at any desired place that they wanted. In those days, the Bodhisattva had been reborn as a tree fairy in a sal (*Shorea robusta*) forest in the Himalayas. The wisest of all, he advised his kinsfolk and other tree fairies to choose their habitation wisely and to stay closer to the sal forest. He said this was important, keeping in mind any emergency situation in the future.

The wise tree fairies listened to the Bodhisattva and they all took up their abode around the sal forest, while the foolish ones went to hunt secluded spaces, which were outside the forest or within the dwellings of mankind. They also thought, 'The trees which dwell amidst the habitations of mankind receive the richest of offerings and worships. Why should we abandon all of these and go and live in the Himalayas in a sal forest?' Thus, these few unwise tree fairies went in search of haunts within the town and in open spaces.

Shortly thereafter, during the night, a powerful gale swept through the town. The storm was intense, wreaking havoc and causing the complete destruction of everything in its path. Numerous houses were damaged, countless animals found themselves without shelter, and everyone was plunged into significant hardship. The massive storm left a trail of devastation as it departed the town. Along with this were also the secluded trees. Many were uprooted, or their branches were snapped off, or their barks were broken midway. Many trees fell on houses, causing more devastation. People, animals, and plants suffered equally as a result of the storm. The lonely trees lay stranded, withered, bare, and broken between the town and the open spaces. Numerous trees lay shattered and irreparably damaged, succumbing to their final breaths. The aftermath presented a harrowing and devastating spectacle. That same night, when the storm hit the sal forest in the Himalayas, it could do little damage. Only some leaves were scattered and some flowers were blown away, but the ferocity of the wind could do no harm to the trees. None of the trees were uprooted or broken, as the cumulative power of the large trees within the sal forest cushioned the wrath of the storm, and also protected the smaller ones within the forest. When the storm subsided, the sal forest, including all the shrubs and bushes, stood as strong as ever.

In the town, the forlorn tree fairies, who had lost their dwellings, decided to go and speak to the Bodhisattva. They picked up their belongings and their children and headed towards the sal forest. Once they met the Bodhisattva, they narrated their sad stories and he said, 'You have suffered because you did not listen and think wisely, and went to stand in secluded spaces. If you had stayed in unity and within the forest, together we would have helped you. It is always important for kinsfolk to stand together in unity, like the trees in a forest. Then, no storm will be able to overthrow them, like a solitary tree.'

The wise tree fairies in the story were the Buddha's followers, and he himself was the wise fairy of the sal forest who guided others.

7

Amir Khusro's Unbound Devotion for His Pir

A great poet, musician, scholar, and historian, Amir Khusro was a great devotee of Hazrat Nizamuddin Auliya, a revered Sufi saint of the Chishti order. Many of Khusro's compositions, especially his masnavis, are full of praise for his Pir. There are many legends about the wonderful compositions, music, and the great devotion of Amir Khusro. According to one such story, once his father, Amir Saifuddin Mahmood took the infant, wrapped in a cloth to a Sufi of high spiritual standing. The saint took a look at the baby and said that the child will be inspired by God, and will be unique when he grows up. He also said that his name will be remembered till doomsday and will surpass Khaqani (royal). After four years, his father took him from Patiala to Delhi and made the best arrangements for his education and moral training.

Another legend speaks of Khusro's devotion for Hazrat Nizamuddin. According to this story, once a poor man travelled to meet Hazrat Nizamuddin to ask for financial assistance. He had travelled from a distant region to Delhi, as he had heard that Hazrat Nizamuddin never made anybody return empty-handed. Unfortunately, the saint had nothing else to offer the poor man other than his old shoes. The old man was disappointed, but nevertheless, thanked Hazrat Nizamuddin and left for his home.

On the way, he coincidentally met Amir Khusro, who was travelling from the other side. Suddenly, Khusro remarked that he could smell his Pir's fragrance. After discovering the source of the scent, Khusro understood that the old man had gone to meet Hazrat Nizamuddin and was carrying his shoes. The old man narrated his story in detail and said that he was indeed looking for financial assistance. Khusro immediately asked for the shoes from the old man and promised to pay him handsomely. Overjoyed at his totally unexpected good fortune, the poor man thanked Khusro and went away rejoicing with the money. Khusro soon met his Pir and placed the pair of shoes at his feet. He then explained how he had exchanged it for all the wealth he had.

8

The Legend of Shambhala

There is a myth about the kingdom of Shambhala found in Kalachakra Tantra of Vajrayana Buddhism. Sakyamuni Buddha is believed to have taught the Kalachakra on request of King Suchandra of Shambhala.

According to the myth about the origin of Shambhala, long, long ago, when King Manjusrikirti, ruled over a kingdom of more than three lakh followers, there were many who worshipped the sun and the rest were followers of the Kalachakra. Once, the king had ordered the sun worshippers to follow Kalachakra and they left the kingdom in protest. After they left, the king realized that these were the wisest of the wise and the most honest and truthful people in his kingdom and he needed them for the prosperity of his kingdom. So, King Manjusrikirti requested all those people who had left to return, but only a few of them came back and resettled in the kingdom of Manjusrikirti. Those who did not return, are said to have formed the kingdom of Shambhala. Manjusrikirti is said to have abdicated his throne to his son Pundarika and soon after that, he passed away.

The myth of Shambhala also mentions how it is a place of complete honesty and truthfulness. It is also said to be a place which will usher a Golden Age in the near future at a very crucial time, when there is a need to fight Dark Forces. This Golden Age will defeat the Dark Forces. This is mentioned in another story in the Kalachakra, which narrates that sometime in the future, when Shambhala would be ruled by the future Buddha Maitreya, the Dark Forces, united under their evil king, would conquer all and everything around us. After conquering and destroying everything on earth, when life would have almost come to a standstill, the mists surrounding Shambhala will gradually drift apart and the mountainous kingdom will reveal itself. Seeing the pristine kingdom of Shambhala, the evil king will also try to attack it with his huge army and dreadful weapons. It is at that time that the king of Shambhala—Maitreya, will emerge with a huge and righteous army and vanquish the Dark Forces. This final battle is prophesied for the year 2424 or 2425, which also marks 3,304 years after the death of Buddha. Thus, after the fall of the Dark Forces, there will be a Golden Age.

9

The Dreams of Queen Trishala

Lord Mahavira was born in a Kshatriya family of the Ikshvaku dynasty. His father was King Siddhartha, who was the ruler of Nata, Ainwar, Gyat, or Jnatri clan in Kshatriya Kundagrama, a suburb of Vaishali of modern-day Bihar. Mahavir's mother was a Lichhavi princess, Trishala, who was the daughter of King Chetaka of Vaishali, according to Jain text Uttarapurana (though the Jain text Uttarapurana identifies Trishala as the daughter of King Chetaka, alternative historical accounts describe her as his sister). Trishala was also known as Priyakarini. Both Trishala and her husband were followers of Parsvanath, the twenty-third Tirthankara.

According to the Svetambara text, Kalpasutra, Trishala gave birth to Mahavir after a pregnancy of nine months and seven and a half days. The text also describes how Mahavir was originally formed as the foetus of a Brahmin woman, Devananda. However, when Saudharma Indra, the king of angels, realized that the Lord was being born into a non-royal background, he sent an angel named Harinaigamesin, to transfer the foetus of Devananda into the womb of Queen Trishala and that of Trishala, who was also pregnant at that time, into the womb of Devananda. During the short time when Devananda was pregnant with the Lord, it is said that she too had the fourteen unusual dreams. Though Digambaras do not recognize the story of the transfer of the foetuses, they both speak about the many dreams mother Trishala had during her pregnancy. The Digambaras speak of Trishala having sixteen dreams, while the Svetambaras speak of her having fourteen dreams.

According to this story of the dreams of Queen Trishala, one night, when she was pregnant, she had fourteen consecutive dreams. She woke up and reflected about them. Then she also woke her husband up, King Siddhartha, and narrated what she saw in the dreams. Astounded by the words of his queen, the king understood that these dreams had some underlying significance. Thus, the next day, he summoned the great scholars to his court to seek their advice and also to speak to them about the dreams. The queen saw many things related to nature in her dreams and each one had a deep symbolism.

The first dream queen Trishala had was of a big and impetous elephant with four tusks. The elephant had all the desirable auspicious marks of excellence.

The second dream was of a noble bull, which had a majestic hump, fine body hair, and superbly sharp, pointed horns.

The third dream was of a magnificent lion with a long tail and beautiful claws, well-rounded head, sharp teeth, and glowing eyes. The queen saw this lion descending towards her and entering her mouth.

In her fourth dream, the queen saw Goddess Lakshmi—the deity of wealth, prosperity, and power. She sat on a lotus with a garland of pearls, emeralds, and gold, and a pair of dazzling earrings.

The fifth dream was of a beautiful and fragrant garland descending from the sky. Each of the flowers blossomed at different seasons and their fragrance spread throughout the world.

In her sixth dream, the queen witnessed a full moon. The light of the moon was so bright that it even awoke the lilies in the pond.

The queen saw the bright sun in her seventh dream. It shone in all its dazzling glory like a wild forest fire, vanquishing all evil and destroying darkness.

In her eighth dream the queen saw a very large flag with the picture of a lion on it. It was tied to a golden pole and fluttered gently in the breeze, attracting all and everyone around it.

In her ninth dream, the queen saw a magnificent and beautiful golden vase filled with clear water. The vase was also decorated with a garland.

In her tenth dream the queen saw a lake full of fragrant lotuses. All of them blossomed at the touch of the rays of the sun.

The queen saw a vast ocean in her eleventh dream and its water rose to great heights in all directions as a gentle wind created waves on the ocean.

In her twelfth dream the queen witnessed a heavenly plane that echoed with pleasant music and a wonderful aroma of the incense.

The queen saw a big heap of jewels, made of gems and precious stones in her thirteenth dream.

In her fourteenth dream, the queen saw a smokeless fire burning intensely.

The queen saw a pair of fish in her fifteenth dream.

And in her sixteenth dream, the queen saw a high and lofty throne.

When the wise scholars in the court of King Siddhartha heard about the dreams, they understood that the child to be born would be a virtuous child, a blessing from the heavens being sent down to earth for ending the misery of man, and to help one and all attain spiritual liberation. They interpreted each dream for the King. These interpretations made them understand the metaphor within the dreams.

It was explained that the dream of the elephant meant that the child would be of an exceptionally high character. The four tusks of the elephant meant that the child would guide the spiritual chariot with its four components—monks, nuns, laymen, and laywomen.

The dream of the bull meant that the child would help cultivate the region.

The dream of the lion conveyed that the child would be as strong and powerful as that of a lion, and he would fearlessly rule the world one day.

The dream about Lakshmi was explained as a boon from the Goddess for the child, who would one day benefit all, and enjoy prosperity and splendour all his life and thereafter.

The dream of the garland meant that just like its fragrance, the teaching of the son would one day spread throughout the world.

The dream of the full moon meant that the child would end the sufferings of all through the path of spirituality. He would bring peace to mankind.

The dream of the sun meant that just like the sun, the child would one day dispel the darkness of mankind through the path of spiritual awakening.

The dream of the flag meant that the child would be a leader one day and carry the banner of religion. He would reinstate religious order throughout the world.

The dream of the golden vase meant that the son would be virtuous and full of compassion for all living beings

The dream about the lake of lotuses meant that the child would be beyond worldly and material attachments, and that he would also help others to get detangled from the cycles of birth, death, and misery.

The dream about the ocean with great waves signified a person with very high knowledge and a great personality. He would escape the rigmaroles of the ocean of life—signified by birth, misery, and death—and thus, the child's soul would attain Moksha (liberation).

The dream about the heavenly plane indicated that every angel of heaven would respect and honour the child's spiritual teachings.

The dream about the heap of jewels meant that the child would possess infinite wisdom and virtues, and would also attain the supreme spirit.

The dream about the fire meant that the child would reform religious beliefs and do away with blind faith and orthodox rituals. He would also burn and destroy his karma, and attain salvation.

The dream about a pair of fish meant that the child would be very handsome.

Finally, the dream about the high and lofty throne meant that the child would have a very high spiritual status.

Thus, it was summarized that the child who was to be born would be full of virtues, strong, and courageous. He would grow up to be the spiritual leader for many, reach throughout the world and guide people onto the path of righteousness. He would forgo all worldly desires, abandon the life of riches, and attain salvation.

Lord Mahavira was born on the thirteenth day of the bright half of the month of Chaitra, 543 years before the Vikram Era calendar (this is believed to be 599 BCE according to Svetambaras, while Digambaras believe that Mahavira was born in 615 BCE).

10

Some Tales from the Janamsakhis

Water, according to the holy book the Sri Guru Granth Sahib, is considered to be the most important aspect for the origin of life, as God is supposed to have created the world by combining air, water, and fire. In the Janamsakhis, there are many legends concerning spiritualism and water. According to one such legend from the Janamsakhis, it was through water that Guru Nanak Dev Ji had the ultimate spiritual encounter with God. As the narrative mentions, one day, accompanied by Mardana, Nanak went to have a bath in a river. After a dip however, he could not be found anywhere. It was as if he had disappeared. The friend became frantic and started to search for him but could not locate him anywhere. Deeply saddened, he then returned to Sultanpur, along with the clothes which Nanak had left on the banks. However, three days later, he reappeared from the water and spoke about his encounter with God. This transformative experience had a profound impact on him, leading him to express a belief in the unity of all religions. Consequently, he decided to embrace the path of God. Guru Nanak Dev Ji also spoke about his mystical encounter with God in one of his hymns, where he mentions that he was taken to the court of God and given a cup of divine nectar, or amrit, to drink. Therefore, God bestowed his blessings upon Nanak and selected him to serve as a guide and preacher, spreading the message of the Divine. Another story from the Janamsakhis, which has also variously been depicted in painting, concerns the mystical and spiritual powers of water. According to this story, once Guru Nanak Dev Ji wanted to travel across the ocean to an island. He was to be accompanied by Mardana and Bala. Faced with the daunting prospect of crossing a vast expanse of water, Mardana sought guidance from Nanak, questioning the feasibility of such a journey. To this, Nanak replied that they would be travelling on the back of a giant fish. Though surprised, Mardana and Bala both realized that it was indeed a miracle. Finally, after travelling for three days and three nights on the back of a giant fish, when all of them reached the shore, Mardana finally saw the face of the giant fish, which had opened its mouth large and wide. Mardana was filled with dread at the sight, worried that the fish would soon consume them. However, Bala reassured him to trust in God. Much to their amazement, the giant fish emptied its stomach, revealing an abundance of food for Nanak and his companions. Finally, Nanak asked the fish to reveal its true identity. At this, the fish replied that he was cursed to be born as a fish in the present life as he was a lazy person in his previous life. The fish added that it had once served Nanak but frequently avoided work. On one occasion, Nanak had compared his reluctance to work to the troublesome situation of a fish out of water. Thus, the person was reborn as a fish in the present life, and he was waiting all along to serve Nanak once again to attain salvation. Thus, Nanak blessed the fish and freed his soul, and they continued on their journey.

11

The Stories of Saint Lal Ded

Saint Lal Ded, is famous for her 'vakhs' (sayings and verses). There are many legends about her and her miracles. According to one of these legends, Lal Ded would go to the river to fetch water every day at her in-laws' house. Once, as she was bringing water home, which she had balanced on her head, she faced a delay. Upset by her tardiness, the husband vented his frustration by striking the clay pitcher with a hefty stick. It shattered into several pieces, and scattered all over; nevertheless, miraculously, the water within the pitcher remained as it was atop her head, appearing as if frozen in air. Lal Ded used the water to fill all the containers in her home, and there was still some excess water. This she threw out of her kitchen window, which is said to have become a pond. This pond came to be called the Lalla Trag. However, it is said to have dried up by the beginning of the twentieth century. This miracle established Lal Ded as a person with divine abilities. As the word spread around, many people from the neighbouring villages started to visit her to seek her blessings.

With a rope of loose-spun thread am I towing
my boat upon the sea.
Would that God heard my prayer
and brought me safe across!
Like water in cups of unbaked clay
I run to waste.

Would God I were to reach my home![*]

Lal Ded spent her life as an ascetic, wandering from place to place, meditating and singing praises of the Lord.

I, Lalla, entered
the gate of the mind's garden and saw
Shiva united with Shakti.
I was immersed in the lake of undying bliss. Here, in this lifetime,
I've been unchained from the wheel
of birth and death.
What can the world do to me?[†]

She became famous for her vakhs, and people would be often seen seeking her blessings at various occasions.

Now I saw a stream flowing;
Now neither bank nor bridge was seen.
Now I saw a bush in bloom;
Now neither rose nor thorn was seen.[‡]

There is another famous legend about how Lal Ded, as she was popularly referred to, disappeared one day. According to this story, after leading the life of a saint, it is believed that when she was about fifty, she was singing her verses one day. A small crowd had gathered around her to listen to her vakhs,

---

[*]Lal Ded 1st verse- From- Kaul, Jayalal 2018 Lal Ded. Sahitya Akademi: New Delhi. Parimoo, B.N. 2013 The Ascent of Self. Motilal Banarsidass: New Delhi. pp-206

[†]Lal Ded 2nd verse- Schelling, Andrew 2018 (February 6) Five poems by Lal Ded, the Kashmiri mystic who merged erotic and spiritual longing in her poetry. In Scroll.in. https://scroll.in/article/867201/five-poems-by-lal-ded-the-kashmiri-mystic-who-merged-erotic-and-spiritual-longing-in-her-poetry.

[‡]Lal Ded- 3rd vakh- Kaul, Jayalal 2018 Lal Ded. Sahitya Akademi: New Delhi. Kotru, Nil Kanth 1989 Lal Ded Her life and sayings. Utpal publications: Srinagar.

which was already very famous. The listeners stood in rapt attention. Little did they know what lay in store for them, for soon, and to their great astonishment, Lal Ded disappeared forever. When she finished singing, she descended and sat down inside a large earthen pot. Then she pulled up another huge pot over herself, which completely covered her. After a while, when she did not emerge from within the two large pots, the people started to wonder, and they went forward to open the pots. But to their surprise, they could not find anyone inside the pots. They were empty. Lal Ded had vanished and merged with the divinity.

For ever we come, for ever we go;
For ever, day and night, we are on the move.
Whence we come, thither we go,
For ever in the round of birth and death,
From nothingness to nothingness.
But sure, a mystery here abides,
A Something is there for us to know.
(It cannot all be meaningless).*

*Lal Ded- 4th vakh- from- Kaul, Jayalal 2018 Lal Ded. Sahitya Akademi: New Delhi. Parimoo, B.N. 2013 The Ascent of Self. Motilal Banarsidass: New Delhi. Kotru, Nil Kanth 1989 Lal Ded Her life and sayings. Utpal publications: Srinagar.

12

Phulaich: Flower Festival of Himachal Pradesh

The Phulaich festival of Himachal Pradesh is the only flower festival of its kind. It is held on the sixteenth day of the Indian agricultural month of Bhadrapada (September–October), and is a stunning festival with myriad flowers in various shapes, sizes, and colours, mesmerizing any onlooker.

Legend has it that the festival originated long ago when ten men ventured uphill to gather vibrant flowers that were known to bloom on the slopes of the mountain. Mesmerized by the beauty of the flowers and their heavenly fragrance, the ten men stayed there the whole day, and even the day after. Finally, they came down with a divine bouquet of flowers for all to see, emanating a fragrance that spread far and wide across the valley. This charmed the people of the village, as they had never experienced anything like this in their lives. However, the scent of the flowers was so strong that soon people started to feel excited. Everyone sensed that the fragrance of the flowers possessed a magical quality that brought joy to the mind, body, and soul. Thus, they felt that they should celebrate this new arrival. The eighteenth of the same month was celebrated with much fun and fervour, along with music, under the deodar trees. They took it as a blessing from the Gods and thanked all the deities for a prosperous year, along with the hope for a bountiful year ahead. This celebration went on for a week and it continues till date. Even today, by the twenty-third of the month, all the deities are brought back to their original temples, and offerings are made, marking the end of the festival. Along with the deities, this festival is also celebrated to remember those who have departed. In their remembrance, offerings of wine, rice, and other items of food are presented. Food is also served to the needy. The festival is viewed as a period for sharing, caring, and respectfully recalling both the deities and the ancestors.

13

The Story of the Charkula Dance

The Charkula is a famous folk dance, especially in the Braj region of Uttar Pradesh and Madhya Pradesh. There are many legends which speak of the origin of the dance. According to one such legend, it is believed that at the news of the birth of Radha, her grandmother ran out of the house in excitement, carrying charkula or oil lamps on her head. This day, it is believed, was the third day after Holi. Ever since, the dance is performed by womenfolk with oil lamps on their heads on various auspicious occasions, and especially on the third day after Holi.

There is another legend which speaks of Lord Krishna lifting up the mighty Govardhan Mountain to save the people from heavy rainfall. According to this story, the people of Vrindavan were preparing for their regular annual puja and sacrifices to appease Lord Indra for better rainfall. Lord Krishna, who was growing up in Vrindavan as the son of the village head, Nand Maharaj, was still a little boy at that time. He observed the villagers gathering for the puja, so he stepped in and addressed them. He urged them to focus on their karma as farmers and pastoralists, emphasising the importance of performing their duties rather than engaging in prayers or offering sacrifices for natural phenomena. Krishna specifically highlighted the role of the mighty Govardhan Mountain in aiding this process, such as accumulating clouds to facilitate rainfall. Thus explained, the people of Vrindavan realized that indeed it was not necessary to perform the puja and instead went over to worship the Govardhan Mountain. When Lord Indra, the king of the

Gods and also the Lord of Thunder, heard that the people of Vrindavan had stopped the puja, he grew angry at the audacity of a small village boy, instructing the villagers to act otherwise. In his arrogance, Indra had forgotten that the little boy was none other than the avatar (form) of Lord Vishnu. In his fury, Indra summoned the samvartaka clouds of devastation, which were used to destroy the whole cosmic manifestation at the end of a kalpa (a duration of time, covering a complete cosmic cycle from the origin of a world system to its destruction). He instructed the clouds to proceed to Vrindavan and drown the entire region. As instructed, the clouds started lashing out rains over Vrindavan, accompanied by thunder, lightning, and howling winds, causing great misery to the people. The entire region started to get inundated. People and animals, started to look for shelters from the rainfall and the deluge, but there were none to be found. Finally, they decided to approach their head, Nand Maharaj. Little Krishna also stood by his father, listening to the apathy of the villagers, and finally instructed them to follow him. He led them to the area of the Govardhan Mountain. Then he prayed to the mountain and asked for his cooperation. Finally, little Krishna lifted up the Govardhan Mountain on his little finger and instructed all the villagers and their animals to take shelter under the mountain. Krishna stood, holding the mighty Govardhan Mountain like a large umbrella, protecting them from the lashing rain. The villagers were astonished, but realized that it was the only place which would save them and their animals. Thus, everyone took shelter under the Govardhan Mountain and were saved from the rain. On the other hand, Indra realized who Krishna was and immediately recalled the clouds. The rains stopped and the people of Vrindavan returned to their houses, along with their animals. Finally, Indra appeared in front of Krishna and bowed in reverence. Krishna blessed him and asked him to seek a boon. In response, Indra asked Krishna to provide guidance to his son, Arjuna, ensuring that he walks the righteous path in the future. Krishna blessed him and granted him his boon.

Thus, it is believed that milkmaids of Mathura re-enacted the story by performing this dance with a large array of oil lamps on their heads, resembling the Govardhan Mountain, on the third day after Holi. Ever since, the dance is celebrated by womenfolk with a large decoration of oil lamps on their heads.

14

Hariyali Devi of Uttarakhand

There are many stories about the origin of the Hariyali Devi of Uttarakhand. According to one such legend, she was born as Mahamaya to Yashoda and was swapped with baby Lord Krishna, when he was born to Princess Devaki in a prison cell.

King Kangsa, who was the brother of Devaki, was the ruler of Vrishni kingdom with his capital at Mathura. A very ruthless ruler, Kangsa had imprisoned his father, Ugrasena, to usurp the throne. He had also imprisoned his sister, Devaki, and brother-in-law, Vasudev, as there was a daiva-vaani (divine utterance or a voice from heaven) that Kangsa will meet his end at the hands of Devaki's children. Thus, a fearful Kangsa imprisoned his sister and brother-in-law and everytime a child was born, the prison guards went and informed their king. Immediately, Kangsa used to come down to the cell and kill the child mercilessly. This continued for seven times and on the eighth time, when Kangsa came down to kill the newborn, he snatched the child by the legs, and just when he hurled it to the floor, it is said that the child split up into many pieces and then disappeared in thin air. Immediately, Goddess Mahamaya appeared and announced, 'The one who will slay you, is growing up in Gokul.' Popular stories mention that the many parts of the deity in the form of the newborn girl, got scattered across the world. It is believed that the hand of the Goddess fell on the spot where the Hariyali Devi shrine stands today.

Northeastern Region

15

The Origin of the Daophang among the Dimasa

The daophang is the traditional loom of the Dimasa community of Assam. Many folktales and songs describe its origin to have been at the very beginning of time, when the whole of creation was taking place, and gods had just been created. During that period, there was only water everywhere. There was complete silence and there was no air or sound. Into this state appeared the male and female gods—Bangla Raja, who is also the father of Dimasa gods and the king of earthquake, and his wife, Arikhidima, who was the mother of all the Dimasa gods and had wings like a fairy. Soon, they had seven sons, who had divine and magical powers. They grew up to be handsome men and their mother thought that they would now make good use of their magical powers. Arikhidima wanted her sons to use their divine powers to make the world a much better place for all. However, the sons never desired to do anything like that, and they were simply contented with their way of life. This made Arikhidima sad, and soon, one day, when she realized that she was pregnant once again, she left her home to find a better place to lay her eggs.

Searching far and wide, Arikhidima found a nice and quiet place in a banyan tree, which was situated between the confluence of two rivers—Dilaobra and Sanibra. This was indeed the ideal place that Arikhidima was searching for. It was a place like no other, as the tall branches of the banyan tree were so strong that no storm could break them. The tall and wide branches of the tree could help thousands of birds to nestle, and the shade provided by the tree was so vast that it could hold thousands of animals. Arikhidima immediately liked the place, laid her eggs there, and promptly flew away.

Seven days later, when all the seven eggs hatched, mankind was gifted with their gods—both evil and good. From the first egg came out Lord Sibrai, from the second came Doo Raja, from the third came Wah Raja, from the fourth came Gonyung Raja, from the fifth came Brayung Raja and finally from the sixth came Hamyadao. From the seventh egg came many evil spirits who started to spread diseases, evil, and negative thoughts and practices in the world. They entered the homes and minds of all the people, and there they remain till the present.

The first of the six children became one of the principal deities of the Dimasas. When they grew up, they wanted to meet their mother, so they decided to go out looking for her. They searched far and wide, but could not locate her anywhere. Then finally, while returning home one day, all the six brothers found their mother weaving under the magical and divine banyan tree in which she had once laid her seven eggs. She sat under the tree, weaving on a daophang. In the end, the six gods found their mother, and people learned the use of the traditional loom—the daophang, a divine gift from the gods.

16

The Legend of Keibu Keioiba from Manipur

Meitei mythology of Manipur speaks of the mythical creature Keibu Keioiba. There are various stories about how Keibu Keioiba came to exist. According to one such story, he was a clever, shrewd, and vain priest by the name, Kabui Salan Maiba, who had supernatural powers. He used these powers to transform into a tiger. However, his excessive pride proved to be his downfall, as one day he failed to return entirely to his human form. As a consequence, he remained trapped in a state of half-man and half-tiger. There is another version of the myth that describes Keibu Keioiba as originally being a very gifted physician. He was well-known and revered all across the region for his remarkable medical skills and knowledge, and he was always looking forward to strengthening his knowledge further. His increasing thirst for knowledge also began to fuel his vanity. He found pride in the extensive knowledge he had gained, enabling him to effortlessly master magical powers. And thus, with the help of a newly acquired skill, he wanted to transform himself into a tiger. He also taught his wife how to make him revert to his human self. However, as soon as he turned himself into a half tiger-like creature, he developed the instincts of a tiger and started to roar and frighten people. In fear, even his wife ran away. Now, there was nobody to help him transform into his original form. Thus, it is believed that he remained a tiger-like creature, which is often described as being half-man and half-tiger. This creature was Keibu Keioiba. Thus, Keibu began to be feared by one and all. He began terrorising people, initially preying on smaller animals in the village, and then progressing to targeting humans.

One night, Keibu Keioiba arrived to prey upon an old lady who was staying alone in a hut. To save herself, the old lady immediately thought of a wicked plan—she told Keibu Keioiba that she was old and wrinkled, and that he would never get the desired taste while eating her. So, she implored him instead to eat a beautiful young girl named Thabaton, who was her neighbour. After the deceptive lady enticed Keibu Keioiba, the cruel plan began to unfold. She informed him that Thabaton, who lived with her seven elder brothers, was currently home alone as all of them were away at work. She also taught Keibu Keioiba some tricks which he could use to make Thabaton open the entrance door. Thus, soon, that very same day, Keibu Keioiba left for Thabaton's house and, as he had learned from the wicked old lady, tricked Thabaton into opening her door.

When Thabaton opened her door, Keibu Keioiba abducted her and ran away to his hut in the deep jungles. When the seven brothers returned home, they could not find their sister. They made enquiries about their missing sister and were informed by the old lady that Keibu Keioiba had taken her away. The brothers were furious. They sharpened their weapons and went in search of Thabaton. They searched far and wide, but could not find her. A couple of years passed by thus.

In the meanwhile, Keibu Keioiba had not killed Thabaton, but had married her and by now, they had a son. They lived in a hut in the woods, where Keibu Keioiba kept strict vigilance over Thabaton, so that she would never be able to escape. One day, the seven brothers spotted their sister in the forest. They kept waiting for Keibu Keioiba to leave the house. Soon enough, towards evening, Keibu Keioiba was ready to go out for hunting his prey. And when the sister was alone, all the seven brothers entered the house. The sister was delighted to see her brothers and narrated her sad story. The brothers stayed back throughout the night and thought of a plan to rescue their sister. Accordingly, next morning, when Keibu Keioiba returned home, Thabaton gave Keibu Keioiba an utong (bamboo pipe) and asked him to go to the nearby stream to fetch some water. Thus, Keibu Keioiba left home. Immediately, the seven brothers killed the son and ran away with their sister, after setting the house on fire.

In the meanwhile, Keibu Keioiba sat next to the stream, trying to fill up the utong with water but what he did not realize was that the utong was hollow on both sides. As he filled it with water, it flowed out through the opposite side. Now, a crow was sitting atop a tree watching Keibu Keioiba. He knew that Keibu Keioiba had a wife, who was also his prisoner, and that they also had a child. Thus, seeing Keibu Keioiba struggling with the utong, he cried out sharply, 'Keibu Keioiba Naning Namang Hotrong Ho, Natu Leima Kangkok,' bringing to his attention that he was doing something foolish and that his prisoner-wife had escaped. At first, Keibu Keioiba did not pay much heed to the crow's calls. But when he finally did, he realized that probably he was being fooled. He ran towards his house. To his great dismay, his house lay burned down, his son dead, and there was no sign of his wife. He was furious and decided to take revenge on Thabaton. He ran towards the house where Thabaton lived. The seven brothers knew that Keibu Keioiba would soon come seeking revenge and they were ready with their weapons. They fought Keibu Keioiba and finally killed him. After the death of Keibu Keioiba, Thabaton, her seven brothers, and all the villagers lived in peace. Till date all the people remember the story of Keibu Keioiba and how he had terrorized people all over the region.

17

How the Mizo Festival of Pawl Kut Originated

Various myths recount the origin of the story of the Mizo agricultural festival—Pawl Kut. All these stories speak about the beginning of the festival from a time when the Mizos used to live in Burma. According to one such story, the festival began with catching rats (Zu pawl), which were found in a heap of straw. Another story mentions the initiation of the festival when the Mizos used to live in Kabaw Valley, in Burma's western Sagaing division. They specify the period to be between 1450–1700 CE. Once the famine subsided, they are said to have celebrated with a feast, marking the beginning of the festival of Pawl Kut. According to this story, when the Mizos were living in western Burma, in the Chin Hills, there was a devastating famine that persisted for a span of three years. This widespread scarcity affected not only humans but also took a toll on plants and animals, plunging the entire community into a state of suffering. The rivers dried up and the fields lay barren and cracked up. The parched lands lay desolate with a vacant look that could only speak about a time of gloom. However, luck smiled upon the inhabitants of the valley in the fourth year as there was sufficient rainfall, and agriculture returned to its previous state. After three years of sorrow during the harvesting period, people rejoiced when a variety of crops were successfully grown and harvested. They believed that after three years, their supreme God, Chung Pathian, had blessed them with sufficient food and they wanted to thank him. Thus, the Pawl Kut festival began.

18

The Lushai Stories of the Creation of the World

It is believed that a long, long time ago, there was no land, and the whole world was only one vast stretch of sea. Here, lived a gigantic worm. One day, the creator had an important conversation with this worm. He went to the worm, and dropped a small piece of clay and said, 'I mean to make land from this piece of clay and also make man and woman, animals, and plants. I want this piece of land to prosper as their habitation region.' The worm laughed. He said, almost in a mocking manner, 'You really think that you can make such a large habitable piece of area from such a small piece of clay? This is absurd. Just see how small this piece of clay is. I can easily swallow it,' and saying so, the worm swallowed the small piece of clay. As the worm was swallowing the clay, God smiled and the vain worm did not know a surprise was in store for him as soon as he swallowed the clay. It immediately came out of his body and kept increasing in size. The lump of clay grew larger and larger and soon, it had become even larger than the worm. The worm stood aside looking in wonder as the clay proceeded to increase in size. Soon, it was the biggest lump of clay that one could ever imagine, and thus was formed the earth. When this was completed with the magic of the gods, women and men came out of this clay. Gradually the Gods also added plants and animals to the land and the waters.

It is also believed that when the world was created and there were people, plants, and animals on it, it was finally encircled by a huge serpent. It was so huge that even after encircling, its head and tail almost touched each other. To this day, the snake remains so. For most of the year, the snake lies down quietly and sleeps; however, at times when it wakes up, it sees the end of the tail in front of him and always mistakes it for another serpent. It gets angry and tries to attack it. This causes commotion, and then there is an earthquake, which is harmful for the earth and all its creatures.

19

The Origin of Some Ethnic Communities of Manipur

According to the myths of the Anal tribe, two brothers came out of a cave on the Haubi peak. The elder became the ancestor of the Anals, while the younger went to the valley of Manipur and became the king of the valley.

There is yet another story which states that the Manipuris, Anals, and Thadous are the descendants of three men, whose father was the son of Pakhangba, the mythical snake-man ancestor of the Manipuri royal family.

The stories of the origin of the Chiru tribe describe their long travel to their present place in Manipur. They claim to have originated from the land where kongrap (land snail) originated. The word 'Chiru' means the seeds of a plant, and they are believed to have travelled from the far away land of Mongolia (between Russia and China). Their legends also detail their movements through Mizoram and Tripura, and finally to Manipur in around the twelfth century CE.

The Lamkang speaks of an interesting story. They say that long ago, on the Kang Mang hill there was a cave. One day, from that cave emerged a man and a woman. However, the moment they stepped out, they were eaten by a tiger, who was watching them. God Benglam, who had two horns, saw this and was furious at the horrible sight. In anger, he drove away the tiger and kept waiting for the next man and woman to come out of the cave. When the next couple came out, Benglam tricked the tiger with his bow and arrow and made safe passage for his people to escape. This incident is often repeated in their oral traditions. They have a famous proverb that says 'Benglampa jalthurthu' (meaning Benglam's style of pulling out an arrow). There is also a folk song which narrates this story of their origin. The Lamkang oral tradition also recounts their original travels from the cave into the regions of Khurpii village, from where they further went onto Kokpii, Pheidul, Damdul, and Arhong villages.

The Purum tribe has a similar story, which also connects them closely to the Lamkang myth. According to the Purum story, they are descendents of Tonring and Tonshu, who came out from the clay of the earth. However, they also were about to be killed by a tiger, but narrowly escaped. Thus, the word 'Pu rum' means 'hide from the tiger' (as suggested many decades ago by anthropologist Late Tarakchandra Das and British writer Late John Shakespear) which thus connects to the Lamkang story.

The Koireng people, originally known as Kolren, recount that their forebears emerged from Khurpui (the great hole) along with a basket and a spear. They lived at Talching and had a son named Nairung and a daughter named Shaithatpal. There are many who believe that they are the direct descendants of these children, and there are many legends about them.

20

How Tezpur Got Its Name

Long, long ago, when Krishna was still the king of Dwarka, the region, presently known as Tezpur, was ruled by king Banasura. He was the son of King Bali and grandson of King Prahlad. He was also a great devotee of Lord Shiva. He once performed a severe penance for which Shiva blessed him with a thousand arms. However, this made Banasura extremely vain and egotistical. Upon witnessing this, Shiva cautioned Banasura that his conceit would crumble in the near future, leading to the destruction of his arrogance and ultimately resulting in his downfall. However, Banasura did not pay much heed and continued to be a severe and despotic ruler.

Banasura lived in a large palace, along with his family. He had a very beautiful daughter—Usha. Banasura was overly protective of his daughter and aimed to exercise great discernment in choosing the right partner for her. Thus, Banasura kept her isolated in the palace, and away from everyone, and only a select few were allowed to the inner chambers of the princess. Among these trusted people was Usha's dear friend Chitralekha, who was the daughter of Banasura's minister.

Chitralekha was no ordinary friend; she had magical powers. One night, Usha dreamt about a handsome young man and fell in love with the man from her dream. However, she knew that it was almost an impossible feat to see him, as it was just a dream. When Princess Usha spoke about her dream to Chitralekha, she wanted to help her friend and drew a portrait based on Usha's descriptions. She identified the man on the canvas as Aniruddha, the grandson of Krishna and

Rukmini, the king and queen of Dwarka. Aniruddha was the son of Krishna's son Pradyumna and his wife Rukmavati. He stayed in his palace in Dwarka and was endowed with many of the virtues of his grandfather, Krishna.

Meanwhile, in order to help her friend Usha, Chitralekha used her magical powers to travel to Aniruddha's palace, abduct him at night while he was sleeping, and take him back to Usha's chamber in the palace of Banasura. When Aniruddha woke up, he saw the beautiful Usha in front of him. Both fell in love with each other and got married through the Gandharva form of marriage.

When news reached Banasura of the intruder in the inner chambers, he was furious and immediately tied up Aniruddha with snakes. Aniruddha tried to fight at first, but was eventually defeated at the hands of Banasura's large army. He remained in captivity for a month, until one day, sage Narada delivered the news to Dwarka. An angry Krishna immediately left for Banasura's palace and reached in no time. On the other hand, when Banasura heard about Krishna's arrival, he prepared for a fight and challenged him in a battle. Balaram, the elder brother of Krishna, also joined the battle and fought against Banasura's commander. Seeing the beginning of the fierce confrontation, Shiva arrived on the battlefield on his Nandi vahana (carrier) to help his ardent devotee against Krishna, who was the avatar (form) of Lord Vishnu. Thus, what ensued was a mammoth fight between Shiva and Vishnu. It was a prolonged battle between mighty equals, causing widespread destruction. There was death and bloodshed all over the place. Finally, when Balaram defeated Banasura's commander, King Banasura was the only one left alive in the army. Krishna took his Sudarshan Chakra and started to chop off the thousand arms of Banasura. At this point, Shiva approached Krishna and requested him not to kill Banasura. Krishna respected Shiva's request and also remembered that he had promised Banasura's father, Bali, that he would not kill any member of his family. He also remembered that Banasura was the grandson of Prahlad, who was an ardent devotee of Vishnu. Thus, Krishna chose to spare Banasura's life, allowing him to go free, and Banasura eventually realized his error. Banasura's arrogance was vanquished as he lost his thousand arms, and Shiva's prophecy came true. Finally, Banasura retired to the Himalayas, after arranging for the marriage of Usha and Aniruddha, and bidding them farewell as they left for Dwarka along with Krishna.

After the destructive wreckage caused by the fierce battle, it is said that the city of Tezpur got its name, where 'Tez' (from tejas) means energy or inner spiritual energy in Sanskrit, and 'Pura' means city. Tezpur is located in Sonitpur district of Assam, where the word 'Sonit' means blood.

21

The Story of Riju Dune

The Riju Dune dance is performed by the Gallong segment of the Adi tribe of Arunachal Pradesh. There is a myth associated with this performance. According to this story, the summer God, Gute Cambre departs from the world of humans and returns to his heavenly abode by the end of September. Along with him, the summer season also departs. This helps to prepare nature for the arrival of the winter God, Podi-Barji's visit to earth. As the summer season departs, it also takes away with it many of the vices of the season, including blood sucking insects and snakes. This brings relief to all the humans.

Once Podi-Barji visits the world of humans towards the end of October, he stays till the advent of spring. It is to welcome the fresh season of autumn that the Riju Dune dance is performed.

22

The Legend of the Origin of the Great Hornbill

The Great Hornbill is regarded with great respect in Nagaland. There are many legends associated with how it came to be.

According to one legend, the Great Hornbill was formed from a very sad, orphaned little boy, who was raised by his relatives, who used to constantly ill-treat him. As the little boy grew into a young man, he was sent to the fields to work. His stepmother used to give him rice mixed with rat dung to eat, and a porcupine spine to separate and eat the rice from the mess.

In the fields, all the young people used to sit together and eat, however, the young man never liked to sit with the rest of them, lest anybody saw what he brought for his lunch. Thus, he would sit quietly in a secluded spot each day and have his lunch. Among the youngsters, there were two young girls who used to like the man, and they wanted to speak with him. However, they felt it was strange that he would shy away from everybody. Thus, one day, when the young man had chosen his secluded spot for lunch, kept his lunchbox and gone to wash his hands, the two young girls came to speak to him. Upon realizing he had gone to wash his hands, the two young girls seized the opportunity to uncover the contents of his lunch box, a mystery he meticulously concealed from everyone. They were overwhelmed with horror to see the rice mixed with rat dung. They did not know what to do, and instantly decided that they would replace this with a little of their own food. Thus, after sharing their food, the two girls went away. When the young man returned, he was pleasantly surprised to see the good food in his box. He knew that someone had inspected his lunch box and changed its contents. He disliked being the object of pity, and immediately went over to the place where all the other youngsters were sitting and having their lunch. When questioned, no one claimed responsibility for removing and replacing the contents of the lunch box. Dazed and overcome with sadness and grief at his own pitiable condition, the young man did not touch any of the good food in his box.

This continued for several days. Every time the young man went to wash his hands, the two girls would replace the vile contents of his lunch box, and each day the young man went without his lunch. He understood who was putting the food in his box one day, and decided to put a stop to the whole thing. Yet he felt sorry for the girls' love, which he knew would go unrequited. He felt sadder for his forlorn life and how it gave him nothing but sadness and pity. He decided to put an end to it all. So, he approached one of the two girls he favoured the most and inquired about her preference between him and her clothes. When the girl confessed her love for him, he told her, 'Then get me your skirt and a black top.' She did as she was told. The young man put these on and asked for the cap of her water bottle. He put this near his mouth like a beak and started to climb a tall tree nearby. Upon reaching the top branches of the tree, he asked the girl how he looked. This time, the young girl started to feel uneasy and began to plead with the young man to come down from the tree. However, he did not; instead, he climbed even higher and went and sat on one of the highest branches of the tree. As the man settled down on the branches of the tree, to the utter disbelief of the girl, he gradually turned into a Great Hornbill and started to chirp harshly. The girl was stunned and began to cry. She kept pleading to the boy to come down and to return to their village, but being a hornbill, he had no intention of returning to his mortal life. He wanted to fly away now. He raised his magnificent wings and flew away saying, 'I will return once a year. When you hear the flapping of the wings of hornbills, do come out to see. I will be the last one of the flock in the sky. If you come out to see me, I will drop one of my finest feathers down for you. You may keep that,' and the hornbill flew away. The young girl returned to her village weeping. Shortly after that, she got married, but kept thinking about the Great Hornbill. Soon, one day, when she heard the flapping of wings from the sky, she rushed out to have a look and to her surprise, indeed, there was a flock of hornbills flying just above her hut and the last one of the flock suddenly dropped a glorious feather towards her. The girl received this token of love and took it inside her home. At the same time, the cruel, adoptive mother of the young man was also watching the Great Hornbill drop a beautiful feather for the girl. Greedily, she asked, 'Oh! Give me something as well!' but all that landed right on her face were the droppings of a bird, which blinded her.

The girl kept the feather in a special place and it brought them luck. She and her husband always had a great harvest and soon became very rich. They led a very comfortable life forever—thanks to the good fortune brought by the Great Hornbill.

The hornbill is still considered very auspicious to the Nagas.

According to another version, the Great Hornbill was born out of a sad lover—Kivigho, who was in love with a girl—Kahauli. Despite their love for each other, a hindrance to their marriage existed due to Kahauli's affluent background and Kivigho's impoverished status. Eventually, Kahauli got married to a wealthy man from another village. Kivigho was devastated, but decided to go to Kahauli's new village by carrying flaming and burning coal in his hands, to prove his love for Kahauli. When Kivigho finally reached the village, it was already night-time and he hid behind some bushes. Suddenly, he saw Kahauli coming out of her house. Kivigho called out to her immediately. Kahauli recognized the voice. They met and decided to return to their own village. Thus, they started off. On the way, Kahauli felt hungry. Kivigho climbed a fruit tree swiftly to pluck some fruits, but unfortunately as he climbed up, all the lower branches broke off. The tree only had the remaining branches at the very top where Kivigho sat. Thus, Kivigho was unable to climb down, and he sat on the high branches on the top of the tree. As time passed by, slowly and gradually something magical happened. He turned into a colourful bird—the Great Hornbill. He shouted out to Kahauli, saying that whenever people speak about an exotic bird, she would know that Kivigho has come.

A very sad and heartbroken Kahauli returned to her husband's home in her new village. Soon, one day, she heard people talking about an exotic bird flying high in the sky. She came running out too and saw the most beautiful, colourful, and exotic bird that the entire village had ever seen. It was flying just above the village. This was the Great Hornbill. Suddenly, a feather fell on Kahauli, and she kept it with her during her entire lifetime as the symbol of her love. To this day, every tribe in Nagaland keeps a hornbill feather in their traditional headgear made of bear's fur. This is a traditional symbol of never-ending love and affection.

23

The Legend of U Thlen

In very ancient times, there used to live a bloodthirsty evil creature named U Thlen, also popularly referred to as Thlen. He was an evil creature with supernatural powers, who lived in the depths of the wilderness in Sohra, better known as Cherrapunji. Thlen had supernatural magical powers and he could take any shape and size. Among all the shapes, the one that he liked to take was that of a gargantuan python. It is believed that it would lie with its massive mouth open at the entrance of the cave near Pomdoloi Falls, which later came to be referred to as Dainthlen. This was a place in the western suburbs of Sohra. The tail of the monstrous serpent lay long and wide and tapering and reached till Lingkhrong, which was several kilometres away from the main area of Sohra. Thlen had a history of being born as a demigod. His grandfather was the great U Mawlong Syiem, the chief God around the area of Mawsmai, and his mother was Ka Kma Kharai, who had become completely disobedient and unmanageable. She would not listen to her father and this pained and angered U Mawlong Syiem always. Finally, one day, Ka Kma Kharai gave birth to a son out of wedlock. As the child started to grow up, his antics revealed that it was the son of the netherworlds, and was endowed with evil, supernatural powers. This angered U Mawlong Syiem further, and one day, in a fit of anger, he banished Ka Kma Kharai and the child from his home. Moving from place to place with her child, Ka Kma Kharai kept wishing to run free and away, leaving the child behind. Finally, when she reached the northern regions of Sohra, she thought that it was the ideal place to leave the child behind and go on her way. She particularly chose a place at the foothills of the Pomdoloi falls as she knew that the child would soon start feeding on human flesh. She knew that the cave was on the route to Rangjyrteh, a large town to the west of Sohra, which also had the biggest market area in Ri Hynniewtrep. Thus, many people would pass by the cave to reach the market and this Ka Kma Kharai thought, would provide human flesh for her son to feast upon. Soon, Ka Kma Kharai left the child and went away forever, never to be seen again.

By and by as the child grew up, it started to feast on human flesh, especially an individual from a group of odd number of people passing by. One person from a group of three, five, or seven, would be devoured in such a manner and no trace of the straggler would be left. The person to be devoured first thus, was a marketeer from Sylhet, who was passing by alone. When suddenly he went missing, a search party was organized, which combed the entire area of Pomdoloi Falls, from Sylhet to Ri Hynniewtrep. The people in the search party could not find anybody, not even the body of the missing person. Soon, they realized that more and more people had started to vanish from the search party, leaving no trace whatsoever. This frightened the people, and they decided to approach their God, who advised them to approach the U Syiem Syrmoh by the name of Suitnoh. He was the patron God of villages and also the chief of all guardian spirits, and it was also his duty to look after and restore health and virtue in the world.

Thus, when the villagers approached Suitnoh and told him their story of misery, he grew angry and decided to teach Thlen a lesson. He came down to earth and made a stop at the house of the Lyngdoh, or the chief priest. He appeared in human form in front of the Lyngdoh and ordered him to make him a smithy some distance away from the cave of Thlen. He also ordered the Lyngdoh to make a huge iron ball and a pair of very large and strong tongs. Once the items were finished, Suitnoh approached the cave where Thlen lived. Knowing each other, as both were from the world of spirits, he greeted Thlen in a manner of a long-lost friend. He told him that he was on his way to the bazaar and asked him if he would like to get him something to eat. To this request, Thlen asked him to bring him some Sohra pork, about which he had heard much. He also added that a change of flavour would appeal to him as he had a desire to consume something other than human flesh. Suitnoh heard him, smiled to himself and set off for the place where he had set up the smithy. There he ordered the massive iron ball to be heated to the maximum. When the ball was burning as brightly as the sun, Suitnoh took it within his large tongs and went in front of Thlen's cave. He then told the snake to open his mouth wide for the pork, which Suitnoh claimed to have brought from the market. Not suspecting anything, Thlen opened his giant mouth in anticipation of a large and luscious piece of Sohra pork. Immediately Suitnoh threw the iron ball into the large cavity, holding it steadfastly with the large tongs. The ball rolled right into the body of Thlen and started to burn him up. He started to writhe in pain, twist and turn, and struggle. Soon he was dead from the hot burning iron ball. At this point Suitnoh called all the villagers and instructed each of them to finish off the entire body of the large reptile. He told them to cut the flesh of the reptile into small pieces and distribute it among the people to be cooked and eaten the very same day. He also instructed that the remaining bones and skin were to be burned the very same day as well. Lastly, he once again added that everyone should be careful that no piece of flesh or any part of the body, including the skin or the bones, should remain, for it would bring calamity. Thus, all the people gathered, lit up the fire, and fixed up large cauldrons. The flesh of Thlen was cut into small pieces and eaten by one and all, young and old. Finally, after the feast, when all the young men, women, and children had departed, the elderly stayed back to thank the Gods for their kind blessings. They also carved out on the rocks a figure of Thlen and all the articles used in the feast. This, they did, for all the future generations to see and remember—the story of the demonic creature. It is believed that these markings are still visible in the place. Finally, before leaving the place, they also renamed the Pomdoloi Falls as Kshaid Dainthlen or Dainthlen Falls—the place where Thlen was killed and carved up. Finally, all the elders also left the area of the feast and returned to their respective homes.

Among these elders, there was an aged lady, who had kept a piece of Thlen's meat for her son. She wanted to give it to her son when he would return home, but forgot about it completely. Finally, after many days, the old lady suddenly heard a voice emanating from the bamboo basket where the meat was kept. She peered into it and saw a small snake, speaking to her. It said, 'Keep me old woman and take good care of me. I will give you all the riches, gold, and silver you can ever imagine. Feed me and I will reward you well.' Thlen had resurrected from the leftover piece of flesh which the old woman had brought home, against the instructions of Suitnoh.

The old woman was horrified. Now she realized why Suitnoh had categorically warned against retaining any fragment of the demon's flesh.As she sat thinking in stupefied silence, Thlen added, 'Think again wisely. If you speak to the villagers about me, they will not spare you as you have not followed the orders of Suitnoh, but if you listen to me, you will be handsomely rewarded.' The old woman pondered about this for a long time. She realized that if she told the villagers, she would incur their wrath; on the other hand, she can lead a life of luxury if she gave refuge to the snake. Thus, with greed in her heart, the old woman agreed to keep Thlen, who soon changed her fortune. She became rich within a very short time.

One day, as Thlen grew increasingly impatient, he addressed

the elderly woman, 'I have kept my promise, but you are yet to keep yours. I want to feast on the Khasi people. Bring me one person every day or else I will start feasting on your family members.' And true enough, soon, the old woman noticed that one of her grandsons had gone missing. He was never to be found again. She realized that Thlen had started to take his revenge. Hence, she finally took a drastic decision, which changed her and her family's life forever—she decided to search for men, who would kill for money. She paid them to kill other people, and bring a person to her house every day for Thlen. This routine persisted for months and it propagated the practice of hiring paid killers for Thlen. It is said that the old woman and her family kept Thlen and the paid killers for many more years—incurring the family a notorious reputation. Even today, many people speak about and believe in the existence of Thlen.

24

How Eclipses Began

According to a legend of the Bugun tribe of Arunachal Pradesh, the sun is the Rani (queen) of the day and the moon is the Raja (king) of the night. However, the great serpent, named Ettong, who resides in the sky, is jealous of both and wants to kill them once and for all. He wants to become the Supreme Lord of the Sky in their place. Therefore, as an act of vengeance, the serpent occasionally ascends to the sky and seizes the sun or the moon. This is believed to cause an eclipse, resulting in either a solar or a lunar eclipse. It is also believed that every time Ettong gobbles up the sun or the moon, all the people on earth start shouting, 'Let it go, let it go!' and the cumulative noise from all the people frightens the serpent, who immediately releases the sun or the moon from the clutches of his venomous fangs. Thus, the sun or the moon reappears within a very short time after an eclipse.

25

Why Houses Are Built on Stilts in Mizoram

This is a story from long ago. A heavenly creature had suddenly swallowed the moon, and the whole earth was plunged into darkness. Light is an essential element for the survival of life on earth, without which, everything would perish. Thus, when darkness descended all around, it became a catastrophic situation on earth. Seeing this, the Goddess, Khuazingnu was worried about the future of mankind. In order to safeguard everyone, she selected a pair from every human clan and representatives from all animal species, placing them within an expansive pit. Subsequently she sealed the pit's entrance with a colossal rock. This gigantic rock was called the Chhinlung.

The pit remained sealed for several generations and then one day, the Goddess decided to open the mouth of the pit. She briefly moved Chhinlung and immediately hordes of humans—all men, women, and children, poured out of the pit. The Goddess waited for a while, till she confirmed that there were enough people on earth. Then she closed the Chhinlung once again. Among the people who emerged from the large pit, one was very powerful and he was made the king. His name was Thlanrawkpa. To celebrate his appointment as the king he organized a feast. This feast came to be known later as the Thlanrawkpa Khuangchawi. The grand preparation of the feast began and soon, it was the day of the feast. However, there remained one problem, which everyone had forgotten about, for Thlanrawkpa had forgotten to invite his father-in-law, Sabereka. On hearing that the feast had commenced without him, Sabereka grew furious and in a fit of anger, caused severe thunderstorms and rainfall which washed away all the earth of the village. Only the mighty Chhinlung rock remained. The rainwater completely inundated and destroyed everything. Not only did it teach Thlanrawkpa a lesson, but also made people realize the might and strength of water. It is because of this rainfall that the Mizos started to build their houses on stilts, so that the houses are saved, if such a calamity occurs again. Ever since, all traditional Mizo houses are built on stilts.

26

How Humans Learnt to Understand the Nature of Animals

This is a myth which is recited through the song 'Sangpangtu Kan' of Nagaland by the Ao Naga community.

According to this story, the ancestors of the Ao Nagas believed that man was living in suppressed fear of powerful and large predatory animals like the lion. Since they did not understand the nature of any of the animals, they also did not know how to be safe from them and live peacefully. This created a constant fear among the people. To find a solution to this problem, the villagers approached an old lady, who had spiritual powers and could also predict the future. After listening to the woes of the villagers, the old lady informed that the God of water is not happy with the villagers. To please him, the village well needs to be consecrated. On hearing this, all the villagers gathered together and purified the village well. It is said that ever since, humans understood the nature of animals and learnt to live peacefully along with them.

27

The Sad Legend of Nohkalikai Falls

The Nohkalikai Falls in Meghalaya is also known as 'The Leap of Ka Likai' in the local language. Associated with this name is a tragic legend, which reverberates across the region even today.

According to this legend, long ago, in a village Rangjyrteh, upstream from Nohkalikai Falls, there used to live a woman by the name Likai. In Khasi, she was referred to as Ka Likai, as the former is a prefix for feminine gender in Khasi. She became a widow, when her only child, a daughter, was still very small. Her late husband used to work as a porter and after his death, she took up the job and started working as a porter as she had no other options. One day, she decided to remarry to provide a stable life for her daughter, and married a man from her village. However, this marriage did not work as Ka Likai had planned. Her new husband soon became abusive towards both her and her daughter. He started to feel jealous of the attention that Ka Likai used to shower on her toddler and thus, the husband would often abuse or bully the child when the mother was not around. Finally, to teach Ka Likai a lesson, the husband left his work and started staying at home. This was his way of not providing any monetary assistance to Ka Likai, and instead, he started to coerce money out of Ka Likai's earnings. Ka Likai had no other choice but to surrender to her fate and a life of abuse. Fighting with her husband was useless as he would mercilessly beat up both of them.

One day, Ka Likai had to travel far away for work. In the meantime, the cruel husband killed Ka Likai's daughter.

By evening, when Ka Likai returned, she was surprised to see the husband in a better mood. When she enquired about the whereabouts of her daughter, the husband replied that she was most probably playing somewhere. Ka Likai did not suspect any gruesome act behind such an answer and thus, she prepared her dinner and finished eating. After dinner, Ka Likai was in the habit of chewing betel quids. As it was her regular habit, after dinner, she reached for the bamboo basket where she kept her betel leaves. When she opened the basket, to her horror, she found her little, darling daughter, lying dead inside the basket. Ka Likai was horrified. She jumped up and fell on the floor in disbelief. She could neither scream, shout, nor cry, for she was so overwhelmed; she could not even force any tears. Confronted by Ka Likai's ferocious shrieks, the husband confessed to the crime as she lunged at him. The answer was no consolation for Ka Likai. She stood stupefied. Her whole world came crumbling down. She finally got up as if in a daze and started running towards the door. She kept running until she reached the end of a precipice, from where she threw herself into the depths of the abyss. It is believed that her fall caused a waterfall, which became famous as the Nohkalikai Falls. It is also believed that the howling of the wind across the Nohkalikai Falls is the anguished cries of Ka Likai, echoing across the valley.

28

The Legends of Unakoti

The word Unakoti translates to less than a crore. One myth explains how the carvings on the stone came to be. According to this story, once, during one of his trips to Kashi, Lord Shiva was accompanied by 9,999,999 Gods and Goddesses. They stopped to rest overnight at the place where the site is located at present. Shiva instructed everyone that they should wake up very early the next morning, and continue before dawn to reach Kashi on time. However, unfortunately, none of the other Gods except Shiva woke up on time. Enraged at his companions, Shiva unleashed his fury on all the other deities and went on his way to Kashi. This fury turned them all into stone. Thus, as there were 9,999,999 deities, the place was named 'Unakoti'—one less than a crore.

Another myth also speaks of the origin of the name. According to this version of the story, there was a very skilful artisan by the name Kallu Kumbhar. He was accompanying Lord Shiva and Goddess Parvati and 9,999,999 other deities on their journey to Mount Kailash. When the travellers reached the present site, Parvati suggested that Kallu build one crore (10,000,000) stone sculptures of Shiva and his accompanying deities. This task was difficult as the group was to stopover at the site for only one night, and Kallu only had a night to finish the work. Kallu was a skilled sculptor and he set to work immediately. Kallu had only one more sculpture to complete, but as dawn broke, he could continue no more. Thus, the place got its name, 'Unakoti' or one less than a crore.

Eastern Region

29

The Nabagunjara from Sarala Das's Mahabharata

This is the story of the Nabagunjara from the version of the Mahabharata by the famous fifteenth century Odia poet, Sarala Das. The creature is Das's innovative creation, where Krishna assumes a chimeral avatar (form) by the name of Nabagunjara, who consists of parts from nine different types of animals.

According to the story by Sarala Das, once Arjuna was doing penance on a hill. At that moment, Krishna-Vishnu emerged in front of him as Nabagunjara; the word 'naba' means nine. This was a unique animal, and Arjuna had not seen anything like that before in his life. It stood on three feet and each one represented a different animal. Thus, there was a foot of an elephant, a second foot of a tiger, and finally a third foot of a deer or a horse. The fourth limb was a raised human hand, which carried a blossomed lotus. The animal had the head of a rooster, the neck of a peacock, the hump of a bull on its back, and the waist of a lion. Finally, the animal also had a long tail which resembled that of a serpent.

As the very unique Nabagunjara, representing nine animals, stood tall in front of the mighty Arjuna, he was petrified. Upon composing himself, he was overwhelmed, and in an act of sudden astonishment, lifted his bow to shoot an arrow at the strange animal. At that very moment Arjuna calmed himself and realized that the animal in front of him was no ordinary one and had to be a manifestation of the Divine.

He understood that it was an avatar of Vishnu. Arjuna then dropped his weapon, sat down on his knees, and bowed in reverence to Nabagunjara.

30

A Munda Song of Birth and Death

My mother, the sun rose
A son was born.
My mother, the moon rose
A daughter was born.
A son was born
The cowshed was depleted;
A daughter was born
The cowshed filled up.

31

How the Kojagari Lakshmi Puja Came to Be Popular

The king of a particular kingdom had vowed to buy the leftovers from any merchant if he had not managed to sell his lot by the end of the day. A merchant from the neighbouring kingdom was in the city and wanted to sell a statue of a lady—made of iron. However, being unable to do so, he approached the king at dusk and told him this was Alakshmi (a misfortune) and hence he was not able to sell it. But under a vow, the king still bought the statue and gradually, over the next three days witnessed three forms of the Goddess Lakshmi departing from his kingdom. While leaving, all the Goddesses informed the king that the reason they were departing was because the king had willingly placed Alakshmi in the house.

This left the king in an extreme state of penury. Having lost most of his wealth, the king was forced to shun all luxury, including consuming ghee (clarified butter) regularly with his rice at mealtimes. At the sight of the king's rice plate—devoid of ghee—even the passing ants started mocking the fate of the poor king. Rebuked and pestered by his queen, the irritated king also banished his queen to the forest where she performed the puja of Lakshmi by offering chinrey (flattened rice), coconut, palm fruits, and other seasonal fruits and distributing them among many people. The misfortune of the king gradually faded away. He welcomed the queen once again to the palace and they lived happily amidst the restored prosperity. Thus, people started worshipping the deity all the year-round.

32

The Origin of the Karens of the Andamans

Once upon a time, Htaw Meh Pa, who was the founder of the Karen, lived with his family in an unnamed and unknown land in the north. The regular rhythm of life was disturbed by a great wild boar, which came ravaging the fields across the region. Thus, one day, Htaw Meh Pa went out and killed the boar and made a comb from the tusks of the animal. However, since Htaw Meh Pa made it, it was no ordinary comb and had magical powers. It had the power of blessing anybody who uses it, with eternal youth. Hence, everytime Htaw Meh Pa combed his hair, he shed a few white hairs and thus he started to return to his youth. In this manner, Htaw Meh Pa remained immortal forever and bore hundreds of children, who became the ancestors of the Karens. However, soon, the land started to become overpopulated. Thus, in an attempt to search for new land, they headed to the south and reached the Andaman Islands. Htaw Meh Pa too travelled with them. Soon, they came to a river called Hti She Meh Ywa (river of the running sand). Many attempted to cook shellfish, though they did not know how to, while Htaw Meh Pa advised all to follow him, and he began to clear forests and wild plantain growths and set the clearance ablaze. Htaw Meh Pa advised all to follow the blazing path. However, the people were delayed as the original inhabitants of the land came along and started to teach them how to cook shellfish. They cooked and ate the shellfish and consequently, they learned how to cook. After sometime, when the people remembered and realized Htaw Meh Pa's words, they started to search for the marks of the burned and singed path. But it was too late by then. The plantain stocks, which Htaw Meh Pa had chopped off, had grown very tall by then. There was no trace of the road made by Htaw Meh Pa. Nobody found that path anymore. Thus, the Karens settled down in this vicinity and Htaw Meh Pa could not be found. He went missing in the woods and many Karens still believe that Htaw Meh Pa is still around there, somewhere.

33

Limbu Myth about Ritual Offering of Newly Harvested Food Grains

According to Yapon Pokma mundhum, when Mujikna Kheyongna came down to the visible world to visit her numerous offspring, she was shocked by what she saw. She had descended from the heaven above, which is considered as the invisible world, and saw that all mortals in the visible world were starving for survival from the grip of hunger and famine, and yet they did not know how to grow food grains. Mujikna Kheyongna was greatly saddened on seeing this sorry plight of her grandchildren in the visible world, and she wanted to think about a solution so as to save them from this condition of complete destruction. She returned to the heaven or the invisible world and went to consult Tagera Niwaphuma to seek advice and blessings for a complete solution. After a long discussion, when Mujikna Kheyongna once again descended upon earth, she was carrying a handful of grains. She called all her grandchildren and advised each and every one of them to sow the food grains in the fields. She told them that with the end of each season, the seeds will ripen and produce a bumper crop. The grandchildren listened carefully and they planted all the seeds accordingly. They were amazed to see the massive agricultural produce. They started consuming it and this saved everyone from starvation and hunger. Thus, it is a ritual to offer newly harvested food grains to every household deity—Yuma Mang, and this is carried out in the Limbu community in each and every harvesting season.

34

Creation Myths of Birds, Beasts, and Fishes of the Andaman

Various stories from across the Andaman Islands speak about the creation of animals of the forest and the sea. It is interesting to note the similarities and uniqueness in all these stories. Here are some of the popular myths about the origin and nature of the various extinct, and almost extinct dialects of the North Andaman.

An Akachari myth recounts that Maia Dik or Sir Prawn had discovered fire by striking a piece of parano wood. However, one day, he was angry, and in a fit of rage he started to throw fire at men. Struck by the fire, they all turned into birds and fishes. As the birds flew into the jungles, the fishes swam into the sea. Thus, Maia Dik, the large prawn, helped to create all the animals of the sea and the forest.

An Akajeru myth from the same North Andaman comes very close to this version. Once, when all mankind was asleep, Maia Kolo or Sir Sea-eagle came and threw fire among men. Everyone woke up in terrible fright and ran hither and thither. In an attempt to save themselves from the fire, many started to take refuge in water or between trees. Thus, some ran into the sea, and some into the jungles. Those who ran into the sea became fishes and turtles, and those who took shelter within the dense trees of the jungles turned into birds.

An Akakol myth of the same region says that in the beginning, everything was just a vast expanse of forests and water. There were no birds in the jungle or fishes in the sea, but there were the cicadae, who were the children of Biliku—the Goddess of rain, thunder, lightning, floods, and also of the northeastern monsoons. Everyone knew that Biliku loved her children, the cicadae, and loved to hear them sing. She got angry if anyone made noise while her children sang. Thus, men needed to keep quiet whenever the cicadae would sing and everyone obeyed the strict rule of Biliku. However, one day, men forgot about this rule while the cicadae were singing. Men were busy playing games, laughing, and making merry across the forests and the shores of the sea. The noise of the men was so loud that it started to disturb the singing of the cicadae, and Biliku was furious on witnessing the disrespect shown to her children. In a fit of anger, Biliku sent a powerful cyclone. The wrath of the cyclone turned all the people into birds, fishes, turtles, and jungle beasts and they were distributed across the forests and the sea.

35

How Bonbibi Has Been Protecting the Sundarbans

This is a story from long ago. There used to live a Brahmin sage by the name Dakkhin Rai or king of the south. He took the form of a tiger one day and decided to feed on humans. He had magical powers which helped to change his shape at his will. Over time, his greed increased, and he wanted to keep all the resources of the forest only to himself, and not share it with any human. As the intensity of Dokkhin Rai's slaughters increased, he started to call these 'kar' or tax, suggesting that he was making the humans pay as the jungle was rightfully considered as 'his' jungle. His arrogance and greed knew no bounds and he claimed that he was the master of the whole Sundarbans mangrove area, and all the beings inhabiting it, including the 370 million spirits, demons, and tigers. As his threats increased, he became a rakkhosh or a demon, who preyed only on humans. Now, tigers and spirits, which became emboldened by Dokkhin Rai, also started to terrorise people. The petrified humans were too scared to trust the tigers at all times. The situation in the Sundarbans—the athero bhatir desh (or the land of the eighteen tides)—was becoming pensive with each passing day, and the humans lived in fear, day and night.

On seeing the plight of the humans, Allah took pity on the humans and decided to put a stop to the misery of man. He chose Bonbibi, a young girl living in the forest for the task. Bonbibi's father, Ibrahim, following his second wife's wishes, had abandoned his first wife, Gulalbibi in a forest, while she was pregnant. Gulalbibi had given birth to twins—a girl and a boy, but she feared that she would not be able to raise both, and thus decided to abandon the girl child and only keep her son, Shah Jongoli. The newborn baby girl lay abandoned in the forest, when a passing deer took pity on her and adopted her as her own. She became her foster mother. Thus, Bonbibi grew up surrounded by nature. Several years later, one day, when she had grown up, she heard Allah instructing her to free the athero bhatir desh from the torture of the vicious man, who had taken the form of a tiger—Dokkhin Rai. At the same time, Ibrahim was visiting the forest, trying to find his first wife and children, who had all been abandoned there. However, as her mother and brother prepared to leave, Bonbibi called out to her brother, Shah Jongoli, to accompany her on an urgent task. They set off to go to Mecca and Medina.

Together, the siblings set out on their pilgrimage. They left for Medina and received the blessings of Fatima. From there, they went to Mecca and brought back some holy earth. Finally, they returned to the Sundarbans, called out Allah's name and mixed the holy earth with the soil of the Sundarbans. Dokkhin Rai was visibly upset on hearing their loud noises and decided to drive them away. At this time, Dokkhin Rai's mother, Narayani, intervened and advised her son that since Bonbibi was a woman, it is only right that a woman should fight with her. Thus, she decided to take on Bonbibi. However, Bonbibi was no match for Narayani and she was soon losing the battle. When she saw that she was losing, Narayani started to call Bonbibi as her soi (friend). Now, Bonbibi, gratified with this appellation, accepted Narayani's friendship and they stopped the battle.

This story of Bonbibi is mostly followed by Dukhey's tale. Dukhey, literally meaning someone who is sad, was a young boy who used to live with his widowed mother, grazing other people's animals. One day, Dhona, who was his village uncle, lured him into joining his team to work in the forest as a honey collector. Now, Dhona was also a wealthy man, and his name signified *Dhon,* or wealth. Though Dukhey's mother was at first reluctant to let him go to work in the forest, she agreed finally, however, with a promise that he should call out to Ma Bonbibi if he meets with any danger. The team left for the forest but was unable to locate any beehive. Dokkhin Rai appeared in front of Dhona, the uncle, and promised him seven boats full of honey and wax if he could give him Dukhey in return. Dhona deliberated for a few moments but the offer sounded too enticing to him. He left Dukhey on the banks of Kedokhali Island and sailed off. Poor Dukhey was left all alone on the island and Dokkhin Rai, finding an opportune moment got ready to pounce on him. Just as he was about to be devoured by Dokkhin Rai, he called out to Bonbibi, just as his mother had instructed him. Bonbibi came to his rescue and she sent her brother Shah Jongoli to beat up Dokkhin Rai. Now, Dokkhin Rai, in great fear, ran for his life to his trusted friend, the Gazi, who was a pir. The Gazi gave him wise advice that Dokkhin Rai should call out to Bonbibi as 'mother' and also ask for her forgiveness. The Gazi then took Dokkhin Rai to Bonbibi and pleaded on Dokkhin Rai's behalf. Bonbibi listened carefully and showing deference to the Gazi's words, accepted the apologies. She also accepted Dokkhin Rai as her son. Now, seeing that Bonbibi was finally appeased, Dokkhin Rai did put in a wise word. He stated that humans cannot be considered as the supreme being of all and given a free reign. For if that is allowed, then there will be no forest left at all. To be fair and ensure that Dokkhin Rai and his retinue of tigers and spirits stop being a threat to humans and vice-versa, Bonbibi made Dukhey, Dokkhin Rai, and Gazi promise each other that they should consider each other as brothers, and always act and behave amicably. She accomplished this by making Dokkhin Rai and Gazi part with some of their wood and gold respectively and making Dukhey promise that he and the rest of mankind should only enter the forest with a *pobitro mon* (a pure heart and mind), and also khali hatey (empty handed). She then sent off Dukhey back to the village, a rich man, taking care that he would not have to work in the forest again.

36

A Halbi Story of the Moon, Stars, and the Sun

Once, there was the Sun, who was the brother and the Moon, who was the sister. They had many children. One day, it so happened that they were hungry. Then, the Sun said to the Moon, 'O Noni,' and the Moon replied, 'What is it, older brother?' The Sun said, 'Let's eat our children.' A horrified Moon replied, 'Oh! How can we eat our children?' But the Sun kept insisting and thus, the Sun and the Moon gulped all their children. However, the Moon kept her own children in her cheeks and did not swallow them. Much later, a considerate Moon told the Sun, 'Please release all our children.' And she spat out all the children from her mouth as she had carefully kept them within her cheeks. However, the Sun could not spit out any of his children as he had already swallowed them. The Moon was horrified to see this. So, ever since, she has been hiding all her children within her cheeks throughout the day fearing that the Sun would eat them. The children that the moon spits out become stars. It is believed that if the children of the Sun were still around, there would be so much sunshine all around that it will burn everything in sight. The children of the Moon, the stars, do not harm anybody, as they can only be seen at night when they come out of the protective cheeks of the Moon. In the morning they hide within the mouth of the Moon.

37

The Legend of Tai Pak Kung or Tong Atchew

While Chinese travellers and chroniclers, like Hieun Tsang and Fa Hien, have made their way into India down the course of history, this is the story of one Chinese settler in Bengal, who became a revered legend with time. This is the story from the eighteenth century of a Chinese trader, Tong Atchew, as mentioned in the British colonial records.

Also referred varyingly as Yang Dazhao, Yang Daijang, and Yang Tai Chow, little is known about the early life of Atchew, except for the fact that he was probably a tea trader, who travelled for decades. Today, Atchew is revered as a sacrosanct figure, like a deity, and forms an important part of local beliefs.

The Budge Budge Ferry Ghat, near Kolkata, is a serene place. Thirty-three kilometres from Kolkata, it is a historical place and is famous as Swami Vivekananda landed here on 19 February 1897, after returning from his famous Chicago trip. However, what is least known is that very close to the Ferry Ghat stands a small town—Achipur, famous for a Chinese legend associated with Tong Atchew, or as he is famously referred to, simply 'Achi Saheb.' Among the local Chinese population from various parts of the region, including Kolkata, he is famously known even today as Tai Pak Kung, meaning 'biggest grandfather' or 'godfather'.

The story of the association of Tong Atchew with Bengal began a few centuries ago. A Chinese businessman by profession, Tong Atchew, arrived in the region, and settled down there around the late eighteenth century. In the British Gazeteer, he is also referred to as Yang Dazhao, Yang Daijang, and Yang

Tai Chow. However, there is very little evidence about his early life and his life before he arrived in India. Atchew was most probably a businessman who dealt in the trading of tea. According to British records, after his arrival in Bengal, in 1778 Atchew applied to the colonial government, requesting for a piece of land to set up a sugar mill. At that time, Warren Hastings was the Governor-General of colonial India (1772–1785). He was very keen to increase trading contacts with China, and make profits for the British East India Company. He was trying to open up new routes and connections with China. To fulfil this mission, he was eager to send envoys to the east. One of his envoys to the east was Samuel Turner. He was Hasting's cousin, and was also a diplomat and a traveller. He was sent to Tibet to bring tea saplings for the plantations, which were just spreading across the Assam region in colonial India. Thus, Hastings saw the request of Atchew as an immediate reason to be connected with, and granted him the land to build his factory.

Atchew was granted a land of 650 bighas with an annual rent of Rs 45. Gradually, the little town became popular because of Atchew's mill. To work in his mill, Atchew got indentured labourers from China, who also settled down in the region. Over a period of time, many more Chinese immigrants came over to the same area and settled down. From the mid-eighteenth century onwards, the community of Chinese grew. More settlements grew in and around the erstwhile region of Kolkata, including Bowbazar, and much later spread to Tangra. Both of these regions are at present, part of northern and southern Kolkata. The reason for the many migrants seeking a life outside their homeland was the unrest in southern China, which intensified by the eighteenth century. This made many Cantonese migrants from Sihui County search for settlements abroad. By mid-nineteenth century many other migrants travelled from Guangzhao (Canton) to Malaya and also British India. Later, many migrants from Siyi and Hakka also came to Kolkata. With the local Chinese community growing substantially, the popularity of the local beliefs and customs also found their unique platform of expression. The name of Tong Atchew was already famous, as were the stories of his local business providing work to many Chinese migrants across several years. The name Atchew gradually became a word of reverence and through time, acquired a sacrosanct space among the local Chinese population. The pronunciation of the name also changed and gradually Atchew was mispronounced as 'Achu', from which it became 'Achi'. It is from this word that the little town is referred to as 'Achipur'.

Atchew was probably manufacturing alcohol, along with sugar, which is evident from the final sale notice of the mill that was issued after his death in 1783. According to a letter from an East India Company attorney, attempting to extract money from the executor of Atchew's estate, a notice was issued for the reselling of the factory. This notice of sale is found in the Calcutta Gazette, dated 15 November 1804. This notice mentioned that the estate, along with 'all buildings, stills, sugar mills and other fixtures' were up for sale. The very mention of the stills indicate that probably Atchew was also brewing alcohol from the sugarcane. With the closure of the factory, all the labourers were disbanded and many started to move towards Kolkata. Thus, the local Chinese community kept growing in Kolkata till as recent as the 1950s.

Today, there remains no trace of Atchew's mill in Achipur and one can only see Atchew's tomb. Located in an area called Chinamantala, the tomb is within a compound which also has a Chinese temple and the temples of Bogong and Bopo, the God and Goddess of the earth, locally referred to as Khuda and Khudi. It is also locally believed that these deities originally belonged to Atchew. After him, they were placed within the temple, and ever since, the locals have been worshipping them as their own. Atchew's tomb is a horseshoe shaped structure, painted red, and the precinct is very close to the banks of the Hooghly River. It is also stated that the original tomb was washed away due to the changing courses of the river. However, the existing tomb and temple is still venerated in remembrance of the prosperous trading days, a historical past, and a beginning from centuries ago.

Though Atchew is often mentioned as the first Chinese to arrive in the Bengal region in common parlance, historians state otherwise and mention that when Atchew came to the region, there were already many Chinese migrant workers living in the erstwhile Bengal region. However, many Chinese residents in Kolkata still maintain the belief that Atchew was the first settler in the region, arriving from their homeland in China. According to this belief Yang Da Zhao, known as Atchew, holds the distinction of being the first to land on the shores of the Hooghly River. Many Chinese from Kolkata also recollect paying a visit to the place of the ancestor, who they refer to as 'Thongyeng Pakkung', or 'sugar plantation master'. The tomb was reconstructed in 2004 by the Yixing huiguan, which is the oldest Cantonese guild in Kolkata, dating to 1838.

Following tradition, Chinese from various parts of Kolkata often pay a visit to the sacred place, and visit the tomb of Tai Pak Kung. This pilgrimage is their way of paying homage to the departed soul and also seeking blessings for a prosperous future. To the inhabitants of Achipur, Atchew remains a historical figure from the days of yore. On the banks of the river Hooghly, he is fondly referred to as Achi-saheb. The legend also connects to the general belief that Achi-saheb will look after the well-being of all the creations of nature.

Why the Sky Was Pushed Back from the Earth

This is a story from a time when the Santhals lived in Champa and the Kiskus were their kings. The Santhals were very simple and religious. They only used to worship Thakur Jiu, and the deity also took good care of mankind. In those days, the sky was very close to the earth, and Thakur Jiu would easily come down to earth and visit the various houses. He took care that food was easily available in all the houses, and man did not need to do any hardwork. So, rice grew unhusked, and without any covering, and cotton bushes bore clothes. Thus, man did not have to either husk the rice or make clothes out of cotton from the trees. Man also had the wonderful ability to remove their heads from their shoulders, comb, and take care of their hair. They used to take off their heads, oil it or take out lice, and after grooming, once again put it back on their shoulders. Life was made very simple by Thakur Jiu. This did not last long, as man started to take things for granted and pollute nature by throwing garbage and filth, or discarding food and leftovers everywhere. Thakur Jiu was very angry. Then, one day, Thakur Jiu also saw that even the people serving under the raja or the king were contaminating the place, which made him angrier. He saw that the servants of the king were wiping their hands on the very cotton clothes which Thakur Jiu was providing for them directly from the trees. They were cleaning the cowsheds and wiping their hands on their clothes. The clothes became soiled and no one was bothered about it. Thakur Jiu saw that all around, it was the same condition. Man had taken everything for granted, and had developed very unclean and dirty habits. He thought of teaching man a lesson. Thus, he took away all the privileges which he had bestowed on man. The heads of men were permanently fixed to their necks. No one could remove and groom their heads anymore. He made husks grow around rice so that man had to dehusk the rice to eat it and this was hardwork. Finally, Thakur Jiu stopped the cotton clothes from growing on trees, and only made sure that the trees produced raw cotton. Since then, man had to make clothes out of the cotton from the trees. However, man still did not learn his lesson. As Thakur Jiu saw, after eating, man was still throwing their dirty leaf plates here and there, and outside their doors. One day, a woman, after eating, had just discarded her dirty leaf plate outside her home. A gust of wind carried the plate to the sky, and to the home of Thakur Jiu. He was deeply disturbed when he realized that humanity seemed unwilling to learn from their mistakes. Convinced that their persistent unclean habits warranted no further regular visits from him, he felt angered by their lack of improvement. Thus, in anger, he pushed away the sky from the earth and resolved that if man kept their houses unclean, he would not visit those specific houses. Since then, the sky remains far away from the surface of the earth. It is believed that to have the blessings of Thakur Jiu, one needs to keep the house and the surroundings clean, and discard the garbage and filth in their proper places.

How the Twelve Months of the Lepcha Calendar Came into Being

In the very beginning, when the earth was yet to be formed, God Aitbu Deburoom created the first man and woman out of fresh fallen snow from Mount Kangchenjunga. God named the man Fudongthing and the woman Nazong Nyu. The very generous God even gave them immortality, but then he thought that he would refer to them as brother and sister instead of man and woman. So, he put in a word of warning to both, that they should always refrain from physical relations and consider themselves to be brother and sister. However, this was not meant to be. As their bodies matured, both Fudongthing and Nazong Nyu started to feel attracted towards each other. Soon, a son was born to them. This was Laso Mung Pano. This first son was followed by six more children, and both parents remained ashamed of what they had done. They felt that they could not show their face to God again. So, one day they discarded all the six toddlers in a deep forest. This had a very bad effect on the children. They grew up alone in the forest and became demons. They were angry because they believed that their parents never wanted them and discarded them in the forest. These demon kids were led by Laso Mung Pano, the firstborn son of Fudongthing and Nazong Nyu. Now soon, their mother Nazong Nyu was pregnant again and this time she gave birth to twins—a girl and a boy. The girl was named Rilbu and the boy Singbu. News reached the demon children that their mother was very affectionate towards the newborn children. Though Nazong Nyu often felt extremely sad about all her abandoned seven children, she did not understand that the children had grown up to be dangerous demons, and now they were even jealous of her love for the newborn twins. This jealousy and hatred from all the seven demons created so much of negative energy that it finally killed Rilbu and Singbu. Though Fudongthing and Nzong Nyu had more children, yet all of them died soon from the evil energies of the demons. All the children of Fudongthing and Nazong Nyu were the Lepcha people. Because of the wrath of the demons and the death caused thereby, mankind became mortal.

Now, the demons, led by Laso Mung Pano, continued to torment the Lepchas and seeing the plight of the people, God decided to intervene and create a priest who could control the evil spirits. Thus, God created the very first priest out of the purest of snowflakes from Mount Pandim and gave him two names—Azaor Boongthing and Taamsangthing. God then granted him immense powers, knowledge, and strength. Soon, a great war started between Taamsangthing and Laso Mung Pano.

This battle continued for twelve long years and finally, Laso Mung Pano was killed. However, it was not a very easy battle. In the twelve long years, Laso Mung Pano changed his form twelve times, and he assumed the form of a mouse, an ox, a tiger, a rabbit, a python, a snake, a horse, a sheep, a monkey, a bird, a dog, and a pig. All these animals now designate the twelve months of a Lepcha calendar. Finally, after Taamsangthing won the battle, he also ensured that the demons or Laso Mung Pano did not cause anymore disturbance. So he created his representatives and bestowed them with his powers. They became the shamans of the Lepchas, known as Boongthing.

40

The Story of the Origin of Bhadu Songs

This is a story from Kashipur of Purulia district in Bengal. According to this legend, many centuries ago, in the month of Bhadrapada (August–September), a baby was found by the temple priest of Kashipur. He called the village headman and the king of Kashipur, Nilmoni Singha Deo. Both arrived and were pleasantly surprised to see the newborn. The baby looked divine. There was a spiritual aura surrounding her, and both immediately wanted to adopt the child. As the village headman could not rise above the commands of the king, Nilmani Singha Deo understood that the final decision rested with him. Thus, he decided that the child will be a part of the royal family, but will remain with the village headman in the village, and he will not take her away to the palace. The child was named Bhadrabati, as she was born in the month of Bhadrapada. A different version of the story however states that Bhadrabati is the own daughter, and not the adopted daughter of Nilmani Singha Deo of Purulia's Kashipur (of Raghunathganj subdivision) and his wife, who is variously referred to as both Anupkumari and Kalavati.

While there are multiple accounts surrounding the origins of Bhadrabati, they all depict her maturing into a happy and delightful child. Everyone loved and admired her as she had a very sweet nature and persona, and was empathetic, kind, and gentle with all. Slowly, as Bhadrabati grew into a young woman, people started to identify her sweet nature as having the blessings of Goddess Lakshmi—known as Bhadradebi in Purulia. However, the joy was not meant to last for long, as

Bhadrabati fell in love with a local boy from a caste which was considered to be inferior to her own. News reached the king who immediately gave orders to imprison the boy. Bhadrabati was shocked and in grief as the boy was put behind bars. With tears in her eyes she pleaded with everyone, sang songs, and prayed for the release of her lover. These songs came to be known as Bhadu songs.

The story took a different turn as soon as the king, Nilmani Singha Deo, was arrested by the British colonial police. He was accused of being part of the freedom fighters, and was contributing to the fight for freedom in the region under the colonial rule. Nilmani Singha Deo was put behind bars. In prison, the king realized that it was important for his daughter to be happy. He resented his decision of imprisoning the young boy, and he decided to change the situation as soon as he returned. On his return however, the king was shocked to hear that both the boy and Bhadrabati were dead. The boy had breathed his last in prison, and on hearing the news, Bhadrabati died of a broken heart. Coincidentally, Bhadrabati also died in the same month in which she was born—Bhadrapada. Thus, it is said that her grieving father started a month-long mourning with a final puja on the Sankranti (last day of the month) in which Bhadrabati was born and died. Thus, to this day, Bhadu festival is observed with a month-long celebration of brata songs by womenfolk, and a final puja held on Sankranti.

There are however few other versions of the story. According to one of them, Bhadrabati was the daughter of the king of Kashipur. It was arranged that she would be married to the prince of Burdwan. But on the day of the marriage, the prince is said to have lost his life in a struggle with bandits while travelling to reach Kashipur to get married. On hearing the grave news, Bhadrabati is said to have taken her own life.

According to another version, Princess Bhadrabati of Kashipur was a great devotee of Lord Krishna, and she had taken him to be her husband. She had thus, vowed that she will never get married to another mortal. However, the King arranged for her to get married to a prince of the neighbouring kingdom. In grief, Bhadrabati is said to have passed away while meditating in the temple. She chose this path to avoid being compelled into a marriage against her will.

41

The Story of Tapoi

Tapoi was a very sweet girl, born into the family of a prosperous merchant. She had seven elder brothers, and all of them, including her parents, brothers, and sisters-in-law, used to love her dearly and would shower her with all kinds of gifts, and anything else she wished for. One day, she desired to get the moon (a moon-shaped gold ornament). Inspite of some obstacles, the parents arranged the present for their daughter, but unfortunately, by the time the jewellery was completed, they were no more. The passing away of the parents was a shock for the family, and the days of financial constraints began. Soon, the seven brothers left for a long voyage to Southeast Asia, and left Tapoi in the care of their wives.

The initial days went by without any hassles, however, one day everything began to change with the arrival of a wicked Brahmin widow, who came visiting. She spoke to all the seven sisters-in-law about Tapoi being an extra mouth to feed in the time of dire stress. As a result Tapoi was asked to leave the house. Among all the sisters-in-law, the elder six were easily influenced by the words of the elderly woman; however, the youngest one shared a special bond with Tapoi, and she remained aloof. She understood that the elder six wives will soon create all kinds of hindrances for Tapoi. True enough, the life of Tapoi gradually started to change. There were no more days of smile and laughter. Tapoi started to face harassment of various kinds every day at the hands of the six sisters-in-law. The youngest one remained helpless under the circumstances, unable to extend any form of support towards Tapoi.

One day, not being able to take the harassment anymore, Tapoi left home in anguish. She only took some khuda (broken rice) to feed herself. While wandering through a forest, Tapoi saw some young girls worshipping Goddess Mangala, and she too joined them. She offered whatever khuda was remaining with her and prayed to Goddess Mangala to relieve her of her distress, and for the safe return of her brothers very soon. She also pledged to fast every Sunday. Goddess Mangala heard Tapoi's prayers and took pity on her. Soon, with the blessings of the deity, all seven of Tapoi's brothers returned. They found Tapoi in the forest and heard the story of her misfortune. They took her to their large ship and decked her with various expensive items which they had brought back from their trade and business abroad. Tapoi resembled a Goddess as she sat on the large vessel. By now, the news of the return of their husbands had reached the wives. All seven of them came running to the ship, and were dumbfounded to see Tapoi sitting brilliantly attired, dressed in expensive clothes and jewellery. Finally, Tapoi avenged her oppression by cutting off the noses of six sisters-in-law, except the youngest one, who remained Tapoi's good friend. Since then, Goddess Mangala has been worshipped by young women for the welfare of their brothers.

42

The Mahabharata and the Many Connections with Purnia

Purnia division is an administrative unit of the state of Bihar, with its administrative headquarter in Purnia town. This region extends from the Ganga River, northwards to the frontier of Nepal. An otherwise unassuming geographical unit, very less is spoken about the many legends about the origin of the region, which connects it to various episodes from the Mahabharata. According to some passages in the Mahabharata (Sabha Parva, Adhyay 30), the region was bound on the east by the river Karataya, on the west by the modern Mahananda, which separated it from Anga, on the south by the modern Padma, and on the north by the hills, which were inhabited by aboriginal hill tribes such as the Kiratas. Bhima, of the Pandava brothers, is said to have travelled to this region of Purnia in eastern India and conquered many regions and defeated many local rulers, including the Mahanja king of Kaushikikachha. It is a tract lying between Modagiri (modern Monghyr) and the land of the Pundras, which is identified with modern day South Purnia. Bhima is also said to have defeated Karna, the king of Anga and also conquered the hill tribes and killed the king of Modagiri (Monghyr) in various battles. He is said to have also subdued the powerful Pundra king, Vasudeva, who is described as the king of the Vangas, Pundras, and Kiratas.

Many legends across the region of Purnia highlight various episodes from the Mahabharata even today. The Mahabharata mentions a Kirata woman from the Morang or Tarai to have been the wife of Raja Birat. He gave shelter to Yudhisthira, his wife, mother, and brothers during their twelve years of exile. Some broken ruins and stone at Thakurganj in the north of the district is believed to be the palace of Birat Raja. A big pond, called Bhatdola, to the west of Thakurganj is said to have been used by Draupadi for cooking rice for the Pandavas when they were living at Birat's palace. Furthermore, there is another place called Kichakabadh, around three to four miles from Thakurganj, where the brother-in-law of Birat, Kichaka, is said to have resided. He was a lascivious man with evil intentions towards Draupadi. It is believed that Bhima slayed Kichaka here. An annual fair is held here for a day, to pay homage to the fountain where Kichaka was killed, in remembrance of the act of victory of truth over evil.

The region of Manihari of Purnia division, has a busy ghat (riverbank) for travellers. According to local belief, the origin of the name Manihari is also connected to the Mahabharata. It is said that Lord Krishna came to this place and lost a mani (jewel). Thus, it came to be known as 'maniharan', which changed to Manihari. An area around eight kilometres to the east of Manihari is believed to be the place where Raja Birat kept his cows. He constructed a bathan (a shed to house and maintain cattle), making it an important part of India's agrarian institution for community herding of the cattle of the village.

been the wife of Raja Birat. There is a shrine to Yudhisthira, his wife, mother and brothers during their twelve years of exile. Some broken ruins and stones at Thakurgaon, in the north of the district, is believed to be the palace of Birat Raja. A big pond called Bhim [illegible] near Thakurgaon is said to have been used by Bhima [illegible] for the Pandavas when they were living in Birat's palace. Furthermore, there is another place called Kichakdaha, around three or four miles from Thakurgaon, where the brother-in-law of Birat, Kichaka, is said to have resided. He was a lecherous man with evil intentions toward Draupadi. It is believed that Bhima slayed Kichaka here. An important [illegible] is held here for a day [illegible] month [illegible] where Kichaka was killed, in remembrance of the [illegible].

The [illegible] of Madhupur [illegible] division, has a busy ghat [illegible] for travellers. According to local [illegible], the origin of the name Madhuban is also connected to the Mahabharata. It is said that [illegible] Krishna came to this place and lost a [illegible]. This [illegible] came to be known as [illegible], which changed to Madhuban. An area around [illegible] kilometres to the [illegible] of [illegible] is believed to be the place where Raja Birat kept his cows. [illegible] dedicated to house and [illegible] an important part of [illegible] in [illegible] feeling of the [illegible] of the village.

Western Region

43

How Corn Was Created for the Humans

> O, Mother Corn, I bow to thee at dead of night. This man of blackhead seeks your protection. Where was the corn deity born and where was she brought up? She is the creation of God and moves in the eight worlds (khanda).

The Warli bows to the corn deity with reverence. This story of the corn deity also speaks of the narrator, listener, and the supreme place of God amidst all. According to Warli mythology, at the very beginning of the world, there were two primordial beings—the narrator called the Kahankar and the assimilator, called the Ahankar. As the Kahankar started to speak, the Ahankar started to listen. The two remained like this for many years and even died in the same position. Many years later, people found two heaps of bones in their respective places. They put these into a large vessel and floated all the bones into the water. Some bones floated on, while others sank. The ones which floated on were those of Kahankar, and his bones floated as he distributed knowledge; the bones which sank were of Ahankar and the bones sank as he had accumulated everything. Of the stories thus narrated, the story of Mother Corn or Kanseri Mata is an important part of the storytelling tradition.

Once, the Gods assembled to find out a means to construct earth. They got stones from the pathrat lok (stoneworkers) and built the earth. The Gods also made the mountains, which became the Rishis. They planted twelve herbs and made the earth very firm. A lamp was lighted for this dark world. This was the Sun, and the Moon was made as his companion. All big and small creatures were created thereafter, and it was destined that one creature would live on another—establishing the food chain as it is known to all of us today. A man of black head was finally created by the Gods. Brahmins were made to write books and educate people. The winds were asked to blow over the world. There was however, no food for these creatures. Naran Dev prepared a plot of land for sowing eighteen seeds. He meditated upon Mother Corn or Kanseri Mata and went deep into the darkness looking for her. He arrived finally at the city of Dhanol, which was full of corn, but Kanseri refused to leave the place and accompany him to the Assembly of Gods. In order to propitiate Kanseri, Naran Dev brought cow dung, burnt it, and applied the ash to his body. He also held some ash in his hand and resembled an ascetic. He persuaded Kanseri in his new disguise and took her to the Divine Assembly. The Gods requested Kanseri to be pleased with mankind and give them food as a means of livelihood. At last, Kanseri, the head of eighteen corns, gave permission to mankind to create corn. Thus, man started to harvest corn, and the Gods too were offered abundant corn as a *Prasad*. They soon got tired of the corn and said, 'We do not wish to have this black beauty (Nagli) in our kingdom. Find a husband for her and drive her out.' Kanseri Mata was furious at this insult and immediately left the abode of the Gods.

The Gods soon began to feel the corn deity's absence. They began to starve as their stock of food was exhausted. Cows stopped giving milk and the wells dried up. The Gods thought to themselves that they were much more prosperous when 'Black-beauty' (corn) was with them. Thus, they requested Naran Dev to request Kanseri to return, or else, the whole world would perish from starvation.

Naran Dev crossed the seven seas in search of Kanseri Mata and when the Goddess heard that Naran Dev was searching for her, she changed her form into that of a weeping child. When Naran saw the child in the cradle, he suspected it to be Kanseri. So, he pounced upon the cradle, took the baby, and wrapped it in a piece of cloth. Then, he tied the baby onto his back and started for his place. On the way, the child turned itself into a little frog and jumped into the sea. With the help of the sacred ash which Naran Dev still had with him, he changed his form into that of a fish and dived into the water. He saw that the frog was swallowed by a crocodile. He grabbed the crocodile and cut it open to rescue the frog. Kanseri realized that Naran Dev was more than a match for her. 'I am not willing to follow you to the Kingdom of Gods,' said Kanseri to Naran Dev finally, and added, 'But, I will give you five drops of my blood.' Naran Dev accepted the proposal. Thus, Kanseri cut one of her fingers and gave five drops of blood to Naran. He took it and sprinkled it over the world and that is the reason why there are five ears on the corn. Naran thought that the Gods would not take care of the corn, but if it is entrusted to the farmer, he would certainly regard it as his wealth. From that day, the farmer was associated with corn.

Bhagat Dhannaji

Saint Dhanna Bhagat was born in the village of Duan Kalan in Tonk district of Rajasthan in April 1415 to Bhai Panna. As the only son in the family, he never received any formal education. But from very early in his life, he is said to have been closely observing the teachings of various saints and scholars, which made him deeply spiritual, and also wise about the process of growing up. He used to worship the Shaligram Shila and Lord Vishnu. Bhagat Dhanna is said to have received the blessings of Lord Krishna, who is an avatar (form) of Vishnu. It is also believed that Krishna blessed him variously during the chores and challenges in his field. Krishna is believed to have even helped him in the harvesting work in his field. Slowly, Bhagat Dhanna came to be recognized as a Param Sant.

According to a popular story, Bhagat Dhanna was once ploughing his fields and suddenly, a large number of sadhus came to him, asking for food. Bhagat Dhanna did not have anything with him to feed so many people, but he knew that it was important to feed hungry people, and he remembered all the seeds he had stored for sowing in his field. Bhagat Dhanna distributed these seeds among the sadhus. Then he ploughed his field without the seeds. No food grain came forth from the field, but gourds. Soon, it was time for the Jagirdar to collect taxes. As he came for tax collection, Bhagat Dhanna offered him two gourds as he had no money without his regular crops. The Jagirdar felt insulted, and in a fit of anger, he broke the gourds by flinging them onto the ground. To everyone's astonishment, the gourds were full of pearls. Even Bhakti-saint Meerabai had referred to this story in her poem 'sun lijo biati mori, main sharan gahi prabhu teri.'

The story of Bhagat Dhanna's devotion towards Vishnu is still remembered and depicted through the Garoda painters of Dhola near Bhavnagar, Gujarat. These paintings often tell the story of how Vishnu blessed Bhagat Dhanna and his fields yielded crops of gems and pearls.

45

The Story of Jamshed and Jamshed-i-Naoroz

The poet Firdaus mentions in his *Shah Nameh Book of Kings* about Jamshed, son of Tehmooraz of the Peshdadian dynasty of Iran, the fourth king of the world, and the story of the creation of the world, including mankind. He was considered the greatest of all kings and an 'Illustrious protector of the flock, most glorious among men, most resembling the sun among mortals.'

Jamshed was also the High Priest of Hormozd, which is middle Persian for Ahura Mazda. He created many things which helped mankind and their lives on earth, including the creation of armour and weapons for defence, and also many other things for everyday use like various metal ores. He also taught mankind to make things for everyday needs like weaving, and dyeing clothes made from cotton, wool, linen, and silk. He taught man to build houses, gain knowledge of medicine, and also sail in ships to get connected with other regions. He is said to have also taught man to mine jewels and make luxury products like jewellery, wine, and perfumes. He created wonderful music and many other things which made life beautiful for mankind and animals on earth. He also created the sudreh, which in Avestan language means the special undergarment worn by Zoroastrians, and finally, Jamshed also taught man about kushti or the sacred girdle worn around the waist by Zoroastrians. Thus, from a simple life of skin clad followers, humanity rose to a great civilisation during Jamshed's time. Finally, he is said to have divided people into four groups—Katouzians or priests who performed the worship of Hormozd, Neysarians, or the warriors who protected the people by the might of their arms, Nasoudians or the farmers who grew the grains to feed people, and Hotokhoshians or the artisans who produced goods for making life easy for everyone. Jamshed became the most renowned monarch that the world had known and a radiant splendour burned about him by divine favour—the farr. He is also said to have a magical seven-ringed cup—the Jam-e Jam, which was filled with the elixir of immortality and allowed him to observe the universe.

It is also believed that Jamshed saved all mankind and rescued everyone from a very long winter, by initiating the New Year in spring. According to this popular legend, Jamshed was thinking of a way out as there were no formal clocks to determine time. The mighty king sought the help of important mathematicians and astronomers of his time to figure out a solution. They devised a calendar, which was known as Tacquin-e-Nowrooze-e-Sheheriyari. The king accordingly decided that Naoroz or the New Year would start on the Vernal Equinox, when night and day were of equal duration. This is also the beginning of spring and the celebration of new life after the harsh winter months. This celebration takes place every year on 20 or 21 March. Another legend speaks of the beginning of the Jamshed-i-Naoroz. According to this story, one day, Jamshed sat on a jewel studded throne and the divs or Zoroastrian supernatural entities, who served Jamshed, raised his throne up into the air and he flew through the sky. All of mankind rejoiced at the sight and praised him. There, in the sky, he shone brighter than the sun, and thus, a new day was born, and Jamshed saved the world from an apocalypse that came in the form of a very prolonged and dark winter. This special day was the first day of the month of Farvardin and this was celebrated as the 'new day' or Naoroz. Thus, in honour of Jamshed, all of mankind started to celebrate the first day of the month of Farvardin as Jamshed-i-Naoroz. Jamshed is said to have created the Persian or the Shahenshahi calendar, which is followed in India in a celebration held across July–August each year. Naoroz became the last and the greatest of the seven feasts of the Zoroastrians, which is in honour of the seventh creation: the fire, and devoted to its great guardian–Asa. Thus, Naoroz celebrates the coming together of the seven elements or the Amesha Spenta, who are the guardians of creation.

Jamshed ruled for over 300 years and it was a very prosperous time when sickness receded and longevity increased. However all the prosperity also made Jamshed vain, and his pride grew in time. He forgot that all the prosperity was because of the blessings of the Almighty. He started to think of himself as the Supreme Creator and began to demand suitable honours from mankind. With the growing pride, the farr departed from Jamshed. People began to murmur and rebel against him. Though Jamshed repented in his heart, he never regained his lost glory. There was more sadness to follow as Ahriman or the destructive evil spirit and the main adversary of Ahura Mazda in Zoroastrianism, stepped in to create chaos. Ahriman influenced the vassal ruler of Arabia, Zahhak, to declare war against Jamshed. Many of Jamshed's dissatisfied subjects also rebelled against him and he fled from his capital. Finally, after a fierce struggle and running across half the world, as Jamshed breathed his last, sad times once again descended upon earth—after seven hundred years.

The Abhangs of Saint Tukaram and How They Became Famous

Trees, creepers and the creatures of the forest
Are my kith and kin
And the birds that sweetly sing
This is bliss! How I love being alone!
Here I am beyond good and evil;
The sky is my canopy, the earth my throne.
My mind is free to dwell wherever it will.
A piece of cloth, one all-purpose bowl
Take care of all my bodily needs.
The win tells me the time.
I feast on the cuisine of Hari's lore,
A delighted connoisseur.
Says Tuka, I talk to myself
For argument's sake.

These words of Sant Tukaram reflect an important thread of his abhangs and kirtans, and show how all nature, flora, and fauna are related to man. Tukaram reminds us that all living beings are interdependent, and it combines environment, ecology, and energy together. There is a need to impart a balance in life, and that God resides and represents all.

...Bless me
O Lord
That these trees
These shrubs

These stones
Will relate to my blood....

Nature is not separate and is a part of our very core and existence, and the realisation of God reveals itself through an understanding that he is omnipresent. The poems of Sant Tukaram show the significance of every being. These compositions, however, had a tumultuous journey for survival. This is the story of the great Saint poet Tukaram, born in Dehu in Maharashtra, on the banks of the river Indrayani in 1608 in a non-Brahmin family. Tukaram's father had inherited the position of Mahajan or collector of revenue from traders, from his father, and in turn, Tukaram also inherited the same position. Soon after the death of his father, he was the Mahajan of Dehu village. His parents died very young and by the age of twenty-one, Tukaram was shouldering all the responsibilities of his wife and six children, as well as the household, and also the village. However, things took a bitter turn with the devastating famine of 1629. Tukaram lost his wife and some of his children. Though he was made to remarry soon, yet the distress and death had made him lose all interest in the life of a householder, in materialistic pursuits, and life's conundrums. A challenging time followed. He could not sustain his second marriage and children properly, and was facing a terrible situation of penury and bankruptcy. He was stripped off his position as the village Mahajan as well.

Facing one of the most challenging moments of his life, Tukaram sought solace in his unwavering devotion to Lord Vitthal or Vitthoba, the deity revered by his family. He started to find solace amid the misery of life through the kirtans of God. These are his famous abhangs, which are also believed to have had a divine blessing and a sacred beginning. It is said that Vitthal himself appeared in the dreams of Tukaram and instructed him to compose abhangs, and make them the best expressions of his life. It is also believed that soon after that,

Namdeo, a great poet-saint of the thirteenth century, also came to Tukaram in his dreams, requesting the same.

Tukaram used to sing his abhangs every day and this was attended by many sadhus and devotees from various upper and lower castes, and different communities. They all returned with an overwhelmed heart, full of revered love for Vitthal. However, this was not appreciated by many from the Brahmin community. They also did not like that Tukaram was reinterpreting religion, despite being a non-Brahmin, and that he was composing in Marathi rather than Sanskrit. It is also believed that Tukaram threw his manuscripts away into the river, and there is a sad story about it. According to this story, when Tukaram was composing and reciting his abhangs, and people used to gather all around him to listen in rapt attention, there was a person by the name Rameshwara Bhatt in Dehu. A learned Pundit himself, he was very well versed in the shastras, and was also preaching about Dharmashastras. He slowly started to realize that he was losing his followers to Tukaram. As his listeners reduced in number, he could distinctly perceive the number of listeners of Tukaram's abhangs were steadily growing each day. Rameshwara Bhatt was not happy about this. He confronted Tukaram and told him, that he was not well versed with the shastras, and so, he was not proficient to preach in Marathi. Bhatt also added that he himself was only repeating what the rishis, munis, and the great sages have been saying for centuries, but Tukaram was spoiling the sacrosanct knowledge from the shastras with his own interpretations. Tukaram listened to him carefully but did not get angry, as he believed that Rameshwara Bhatt was indeed a learned man, and he himself might have made a mistake somewhere. Tukaram prostrated before him, did pranam, and asked him if he had made a mistake by composing his abhangs. He was rebuked by saying that he was sinning in composing his own interpretations, and he should stop maligning the sacrosanct expressions of the shastras. Tukaram was also told that he was sinning by making others listen to his compositions. Eyes brimming with tears, an overwhelmed Tukaram said, with folded hands, that he was unaware about the sin he was committing, and asked him to suggest a way out, as he considered Rameshwara Bhatt a very learned person. Bhatt instructed him to stop his compositions, and also throw his existing manuscripts into the river.

Tukaram returned home, tied all his writings in a silk cloth and with tears in his eyes decided to throw all his compositions into the river. He then took the bundle of his compositions to the Indrayani River. Sitting under a tree on the banks of the river, Tukaram once again looked at his compositions. They were about the beauty of Vitthal, Namamahima, Gurumahima, Ekadashimahima, Prahalada, Dhruva, and other bhakthas. He realized that Vitthal remained in each and every line of his abhangs, and it filled him with pain to part with them. He knew he could not sing anymore, as he had made a promise to Bhatt, and so he threw the silk bundle into the waters of the Indrayani. Tukaram sat on the banks of Indrayani, under a tree, weeping and only uttering—Panduranga, Panduranga—another name for Vitthal, knowing well that his life's most precious possessions were gone forever and he could never sing again or even write about Vitthal. His wife and children came looking for him, but were equally sad to see him in such a sorry state. In despair, Tukaram began a fast until death, which continued for thirteen days.

> Today it is thirteen days since I began to fast not even drinking water
> And yet O my Almighty Parent, You have not emerged
> O Lord of the Senses what is wrong with You?
> Why do You cover Yourself with stone?
> I will sacrifice my life at Your altar now
> Pandurang, I'll kill myself:
> O Vitthabai, my Mother, I had hoped so much!

Now my being is all I can destroy, Pandurang.
Says Tuka, I am about to leave now,
I shall give up my life unto You.

Soon, a miracle occurred which made him finally come out of his state of despair. It so happened that thirteen days after the incident, the priest of the local Vitthal temple in Dehu was opening the main door of the temple one early morning. Suddenly, he spotted a bundle on the head of the sculpture of Vitthal. He rushed to remove it and realized that it was a thick silk bundle that was completely wet. He opened it—this was the same bundle which Tukaram had thrown into the Indrayani River, and it contained all his compositions. All the compositions were intact, though the cloth was wet. The priest understood that the abhangs survived through a miracle and with the blessings of Vitthal. He took the bundle and set off in search of Tukaram. He was not to be found in his home. Thus, the priest searched the whole village and finally spotted him sitting under the tree on the banks of the river, still weeping from his misfortune and the loss of his compositions. When the priest showed him the manuscripts, Tukaram thought that he had picked them up from the river. The priest described how he had found the bundle of manuscripts. Tukaram listened with amazement and realized that it was Vitthal, who had saved the manuscripts. He also realized that there was nothing wrong in his compositions, that the deity was indeed pleased with his abhangs, and rescued them from the river.

No blade was about to fall on my head
Nor was I going to be stabbed in the back;
Yet I howled so much, O Hari! As though it was the very end.
You divided Yourself equally on either side;
You were with me and deep inside the river, too.
In neither place did You allow

The tiniest trace of damage to be done.
For much smaller crimes,
Real parents would kill their own children.
What you have forgiven was
An offence only you could bear with.
Says Tuka, O Merciful One!
There is none more generous than you.
What more can I say?
I have become speechless.

The news soon reached the ears of Rameshwara Bhatt and he came running to meet Tukaram. He realized what a great mistake he had made in trying to discourage a true devotee of Vitthal. He did pranam in front of Tukaram and asked for his forgiveness. Bhatt said that he was a true mahatma and sought Tukaram's blessings. Tukaram, being his true self, was not angry at all, but said that being a learned man of the shastras, Bhatt should not seek forgiveness from him, but just recognize the blessings of Lord Vitthal. Tukaram mentioned that it was indeed divine intervention which rescued his abhangs, and that Vitthal was pleased with his songs.

I have committed this beastly blunder once;
To force you to stand in the river
And protect my notebooks.
I did not pause to think
What right I had to ask your help,
Why the Almighty One should bear my burden....

Tukaram's abhangs were already famous and the news of this incident further spread across the region, and everyone got to know about his compositions, which came to be referred to as Vaishnava Veda. Many of Tukaram's detractors turned into his followers, and in the following years of his life, he attained the stature of a saint.

Tuka has descended into Tuka;
Heaven, earth, hell watch in wonder.
My only performance of penance
Is my singing of His praises.
Tuka sits in heaven's vehicle
As all the saints bear witness.
God starves after pure devotion
So much, He lifts Tuka to heaven!

In the forty-eighth year of his life, in 1649, Tukaram disappeared. Many of his followers believed that Vitthal himself carried him away, while many others hold the belief that he could have fallen victim to a conspiracy instigated by those who opposed his work and preaching, though this assertion remains shrouded in uncertainty.

I burnt the seed myself
And pop it went
Now I have gone beyond
Life and death
What space can enclose my form?
My body itself is God
Sugar does not become Sugarcane again.
We will never grow
In another womb.
Says Tuka,
This is absolute awakening;
There is Pandurang
In everything.

Tukaram is also said to have continued the tradition of making an annual pilgrimage to the Vitthal temple at Pandharpur in the month of 'Ashad' (July–August), which was further continued and modified under his youngest son Narayan Maharaj in 1685, who started carrying the 'paduka' or wooden sandals of the saint to the Vitthal temple in Pandharpur, along with the 'paduka' of Sant Dnyaneshwar. He was joined in his pilgrimage, called the 'wari' by many devotees, called 'warkaris', and this tradition of the annual pilgrimage of the warkaris continues till date, as thousands travel to Pandharpur. The term 'warkari' in Marathi means 'one who performs the Wari' or 'one who venerates Vitthoba'.

There is a whole tree within a seed
And a seed at the end of each tree
That is how it is between you and me
One contains the Other.
There is a ripple on water
That is itself water.
Says Tuka, the image
Merges with the mirror.

47

The Story of Gugga Pir

Once, a child was born to a king and a queen after twelve long years of wanting to have a family heir. They were King Jewar Singh and Queen Bachhal of Rajasthan. The Guru Gorakhnath had rolled the eldest son of the snake–Anantnag into an incense and the Queen Bachhal got pregnant by smelling it. This child was named Goga. As the child was born with the blessings of Guru Gorakhnath, he was revered across the country, wherever the cult of Gorakhnath is popular.

When Goga became an adult, he decided to leave for Bengal to get married to Princess Siliar. The marriage took place and a contended Goga settled down in Bengal and stayed back for twelve years, while his sister looked after the kingdom, awaiting the return of her brother. One day, there was a crisis situation at home, which made Goga return immediately, along with his wife. There was a conspiracy planned by his cousins Arjan and Sarjan against Goga, along with King Anangpal Tomar of Delhi. As Goga was on his way to his kingdom, the conspirators attacked him and his envoy. In the struggle that ensued, Goga killed his two cousins and, on this account, he drew upon himself the anger of his mother. Queen Bachhal, was furious and she cursed Goga, who entered the earth at the very spot where his cousins lay. Princess Siliar came to know that her husband was still alive, but underground and sitting on his cousin's graves. She smeared her room with cow dung, lit a lamp, and called for him. Hearing his wife, Goga came to her and stayed with her till the cow dung on the floor dried up. This continued regularly, till one day Queen Bachhal heard about this. She asked Siliar to mix oil in cow dung so that the floor doesn't dry at all. However, Goga discovered this and was insulted by the deception. Thereafter, he refused to visit every night. It is believed that, since then, he only visits once, for a period of only nine days each year between Rakhi Purnima and Gugganavami. This is the story of Gugga Pir, who is considered as an incarnation of Anantnag.

Why the City of Punvaranogad Lay Desolate

Once upon a time, more than a thousand years ago, around AD 878, there lived a cruel person by the name of Punvar. He was the son of Ghaa or Ghav, the chief of Kera in Kutch. Punvar was also a nephew of Lakho Phulani. As cruel as he was, Punvar was also very vain and quarrelsome. Upon a stiff argument with his family, Punvar resolved to create a city and call it after his own name. Thus, a city was built, and when it was completed, Punvar ordered to have both the hands of the architects cut off so that they would be unable to build another city for anybody else.

One day, soon after, seven devotees—who were renowned for their virtues and pious devotion—arrived in Punvaranogad from Rum-Sham, which are the older names of the regions of Anatolia and Syria. These seven devotees settled in a high hill near Punvaranogad. Gradually, the news of their devotion spread all around, and one day it reached the ears of the queen, the wife of Punvar. The queen was childless, and she wished to seek the blessings of the holy men to have an heir in the family. She wanted to visit the holy men and be a part of their regular puja. However, it was difficult for a queen to travel so far in broad daylight, so the queen had an underground passage dug from her chamber in her palace to the high hill where the seven devotees were staying. Once the queen started to pay a visit to the holymen, she continued it the next day and the next and so on. Like this, the queen became a regular participant at the puja of the devotees, and became a worshipper of their deity, Yaksh or Jakh, who was considered their God from

Western Asia. After praying to the deity for six months, the queen asked for the blessing of a child, to which the devotees replied that the sin committed by her husband by cutting off the hands of the architect needs to be first atoned, and only then would the deity bless the queen. The devotees also said that they can help her in performing a puja in her home to seek atonement for the sin of her husband, Punvar. The queen listened gravely and agreed to perform the puja at her home.

The seven devotees reached the queen's quarters by travelling through the underground passage to perform the puja. As the rituals were underway, news reached the ears of Punvar about the entry and activities of strange men within the inner chambers of the women's quarters. He immediately reached the place where the rituals were being performed, seized the devotees, and took them out to be punished. He made them set out on their bare feet to tread corn in a threshing floor which was bristling with spikes. The devotees were made to suffer thus, while passers-by watched the frightful plight of the holy men in horror. One kind-hearted passer-by, a barber, took pity on the devotees and offered to take the place of one of the devotees, who immediately went to pray to Yaksh. The deity heard the prayers and was furious. There was a tremendous earthquake that shook the high hill and Yaksh sent his brothers and a sister to the rescue. They appeared in the form of cavalry with seventy-one brothers and one sister—Sayari. The horsemen drove to Punvar's palace and called on him to release the holy men. Punvar refused. The enraged deities sitting on their horses then started to shoot arrows at Punvar. However, nothing happened as he was protected by a gifted magical amulet which was tied to his hand, and none of the arrows could injure him. The deities realized that they will need to remove the amulet to defeat Punvar. Sayari, the sister among the cavalry, took the form of a mosquito and bit Punvar on the arm, where the amulet was tied. It was a severe and sharp bite and Punvar twitched and jerked his hand in pain. The movement made the amulet drop off from his hand. The battle continued between the cavalry and Punvar. Suddenly, a very large stone dislodged from the roof and fell on Punvar's head. Punvar died instantly.The battle ended, and Yaksh cursed the town. Since then, Punvaranogad, has lain desolate, but shows signs of once being a large and peopled city. The ruins are located about two miles to the northwest of the present-day village of Majal, in the Kutch district in Gujarat.

It is said that the cavalry also blessed many childless women, including the queen, Punvar's wife, and set off for Delhi. Thus, throughout the twentieth century, till today, villagers in Kutch continue to make statues of the seventy-two horses, offer sweet rice to the cavalry, and ask them for boons.

49

How the Town of Jejuri Became Khandobachi Jejuri

A long time ago, the seven rishis (sages) used to live among the beautiful surroundings in the Manichura Mountain and carry on with their daily rituals and meditations peacefully. All the flora and the fauna of the mountain were happy with the rishis as the latter never disturbed the peaceful life of the forests in the mountain, and the animals in turn, never used to bother or harm the rishis. However, this peace was not long-lived as the rishis began to be harassed by two demon brothers, Malla and his younger brother Mani. Both of these brothers had gained a boon of invincibility from Brahma, and with the incredible power, came their greed to rule over heaven and earth.

Now, both brothers used to regularly frequent various parts of the Manichura Mountain in search of food. During their many hunting expeditions, the animals and plants of the forest were left terrified as the demons demolished and ransacked anything that came within their way, and randomly destroyed large parts of the mountain. These two demon brothers, one day, found the hermitage, and they thought that the area was a hindrance in their path. So, they started to destroy the hermitage and harass the rishis. This torture became a regular phenomenon and Malla and Mani started to return every single day to destroy some parts of the hermitage. The rishis on the other hand, laboured each day to set things right and carry on their lives with much difficulty. Though they did try to prevent the onslaught of the demon brothers, they were no match to their mighty strength. Finally, they decided to seek help from the Gods. Thus, the rishis went to meet Indra, the king of gods, but he expressed his incapacity to go into combat with the demon brothers. Then the rishis went to Vishnu to ask for help, and he too expressed his inability to fight the brothers as they were made exceptionally strong by the boon of Brahma. Finally, the rishis thought of approaching Shiva. At the abode of Shiva, the rishis explained their pitiful condition and their long struggle with the demon brothers, and said, 'Lord! We pray that you please help us and rescue us from our misery. The harassment of the demon brothers knows no bounds and it is increasing with each passing day. If this continues, we will have nowhere to go and the demon brothers will rule over the entire mountain.'

Shiva was angry and said, 'This cannot be. I will help you and fight the demon brothers.' And thus saying, Shiva assumed the avatar (form) of Martanda Bhairava, as the Mahatmya calls Khandoba. He rode atop the bull, Nandi, and led an army of Gods. Covered in turmeric he shone like gold and the sun. Thus, he came to be known as Haridra. He had three eyes and a crescent moon on his forehead. The army of Gods, led by the mighty Khandoba went into battle against the demon brothers, Malla and Mani.

A fierce battle ensued between the army of the Gods and the army of the demons. Finally, the demon army was defeated and Khandoba killed Malla and Mani. As Mani lay dying, he offered his white horse to Khandoba as a gesture of repentance and asked for a boon. 'Lord, grant me the boon that all of humankind be blessed by you. I seek your blessing to be present in every shrine of yours.' Shiva granted him his wish and Mani was transformed into a demigod. Ever since, Mani is part of every Khandoba shrine. His white horse is seen as a mount for Khandoba, and thus at the most important locale of Khandoba worship in Jejuri, in Maharashtra, the deity can be seen sitting atop the white horse of Mani.

As the story goes, the battle continued even after Mani was slayed. Malla approached Khandoba. After a fierce battle, Malla was also killed, and as he lay dying, Khandoba asked if he sought a boon or repentance. However, unlike Mani, Malla did not ask for a positive blessing, but sought the destruction of the world and human flesh. This angered Khandoba, who decapitated him. The head fell at the temple stairs, where it was trampled upon by the devotees entering the temple.

As the battle came to an end, the rishis requested Khandoba to remain on the mountain and in their midst. He did so in the form of a Swayambhu double lingam (a lingam which is self evolved and not shaped or crafted by human hands). Soon, thereafter, and gradually with time, a city grew on the spot and was named Prem-puri, or the town of love. According to the Malhari Mahatmya, Khandoba first appeared on Champasashti, which was a Sunday at Prempur. This is identified as Pember, Mailarpur or Khanapur near Bidar in Karnataka. Oral traditions also narrate that Khandoba came originally from Prempuri and then went to Naldurg, Pali, and finally to Jejuri. Thus, this final place in Jejuri came to be referred to as Khandobachi Jejuri, Khanderayachi Jejuri, or Khandoba's Jejuri.

Khandoba is also said to have two wives from two different communities—Mhalsabai, who is supposed to be from the Lingayat merchant or Vani community. Behind the image of Khandoba, she is seen riding and attended by a dog. She had a regular and ritualistic marriage with Khandoba. The second wife of Khandoba is Banai, who is even referred to as Banu or Banubai. She is said to belong to the Dangar community and had a love marriage. Often, Mhalsabai is associated with Parvati, and Banubai with Ganga. Khandoba stands in between the two wives and is seen riding a yellow horse. His flag is yellow and the demons he killed were also yellow.

It is also believed that the brother-in-law of Khandoba, Hegadi Pradhan, who was also his minister and the brother of Mhalsabai, as well as the faithful dog, who helped Khandoba to kill the demons, and also the horse given by the demon, Mani, were all avatars (forms) of Vishnu, Nandi, and the demons Madhu-Kaitabha respectively.

There is also another variation of the myth, which mentions that Khandoba killed a single demon named Manimalla, who offered his white horse to the deity. There is also a mention that both wives of Khandoba tried to help in the fierce battle with the demon Mani, as every drop of the blood was creating a new demon. It was then that the dog of Khandoba swallowed all the blood to help the deity win the battle. Sometimes, Mhalsa and very rarely Banai, are also described to be seated atop the horse and behind Khandoba, fighting with a sword or a spear.

The legend also describes Khandoba as a just king. He rules from his fortress and holds court, where he distributes gold and often goes on hunting expeditions.

50

The Legend of How the Siddi Rulers of Janjira Took Over the Fort

The fort of Janjira is an important example of architecture in Maharashtra, which began from a small wooden construction. Having an excellent command over the Arabian Sea, it served as an observation post and a naval base for the rulers in the past. In preparation for any surprise attack, this fort was equipped with big guns and long-range cannons under the Siddi rulers. Detailed descriptions of this are found in the old colonial Gazetteer (1883) which mentions that the bastions and the walls had ten guns, three of which were local-made and seven were from Europe.

This Murud-Janjira fort, which grew under the Siddi rulers of Ethiopian descent, who were locally referred to as Habshi, has an interesting legend that narrates how they overtook the fort from the hands of the local Koli chief. This legend is popularly believed to have taken place around the last quarter of the fifteenth century. A Siddi Admiral, Piram Khan was instructed by the Admednagar Sultanate to capture the fort. However, the local chief, Ram Patil, and his men proved to be a difficult match and Piram Khan had to deduce a plan of deceit. He and his men disguised as merchants, trading in silk and wine, travelled from Surat. They declared that they had arrived for trading purposes, and carried three hundred boxes with them. Ram Patil was requested to guard these boxes. That night, the disguised Piram Khan threw a party with wine for all the hosts. Well past midnight, the hosts were heavily intoxicated and fell into a deep sleep. Piram Khan took the opportunity and opened the boxes which contained his men. Thus, they overtook the fort easily. The Siddi rulers of the Janjira fort thereby continued to rule for a couple of centuries.

Subsequent cordial relations of the Siddi rulers with the Ottomans and the Mughals, allowed them to fortify the island and establish control over the region. The Janjira navy was unrivalled and survived many attacks by the Mahrattas. With the British on their side, the Siddis continued on through the eighteenth century, till the British themselves took over the administration.

51

The Waddar Community and Their Traditional Work

This is a story, which is almost forgotten. It has featured among the very old colonial publications.

Many years ago, on a very hot summer day, a thirsty Lord Shiva and Parvati, were travelling through a parched landscape. They became very thirsty and started looking around desperately for a drink of water. Lord Shiva created a Waddar man and woman out of the drops of sweat from his body to dig a well, to quench his and his wife Parvati's thirst. The man and woman were provided with a crowbar, a pickaxe, and a basket for the task of digging the well. They soon finished digging the well and the deities quenched their thirst from the fresh water of the well. On being gratified, Lord Shiva asked the couple for a boon, but the excessive demands of the man and the woman made the Lord angry. Instead of a boon, the Lord cursed them, decreeing that the couple and all their future generations would endure a life of hard labour, digging wells and tanks, and remain in a perpetual state of poverty.

There is also another story which speaks of the association of the Waddars with the Sahasra Linga Talav near Pattan, Gujarat, dating to the twelfth century. According to this story, associated with Jasma Devi, the Waddars are said to have descended from the Surya Dynasty. It is believed that Jasma was the wife of a simple pond digger, a man by the name, Rooda, who belonged to the Waddar tribe. Jasma was a very beautiful lady, and everyone praised her beauty while also acknowledging her loyalty towards her husband. However, once, when King Siddhraj Jaisingh heard about her beauty, he wanted to see her. Thus, one day, when he did see Jasma Devi, he was completely mesmerized by her beauty and he expressed his wish to marry Jasma Devi and make her the queen of Gujarat. Jasma's loyalty towards her husband and self-respect made her spurn the offer, but she knew that it also meant that it will be a tough time ahead for her husband as well as for all the people of her community. She knew that since she had offended Siddhraj Jaisingh's ego he would try to seek revenge. Thus, to save the honour of her community and that of her husband, Jasma Devi committed sati or self-immolation. It is believed that her curse made the tank waterless, and the king was left without an heir to the throne.

A third legend also associates the tank-digging activity of the Waddars to Bhagirath, who brought down the river Ganga from heaven to earth to propitiate and release the soul of his 60,000 ancestors. King Bhagirath used his architectural skills to excavate through the peak of the mountain, shaped like Lord Shiva's coiled hair. He then constructed the canal with the help of the Waddar community from his kingdom.

Karni Mata: The Protector of Cows and Krishna Saara Mriga

Karni Mata was born in 1387 as Riddhi Bai to Meha ji Charan and Deval Bai of Suwap village in Jodhpur district. After growing up, she was married to Depa ji Charan of Sathika village. However, Riddhi Bai had no desire for material pleasures even after her marriage. At her in-laws's residence, her general attitude to shun all family responsibilities was thought to be a momentary phase at first. Even her husband thought so, but she soon arranged for her husband to marry her younger sister Gulab, so that he might have a proper married life and she could remain a celibate all her life. Riddhi Bai's husband agreed to her decision and supported her till his death in 1454.

Riddhi Bai, now revered as Karni Mata, lived in her husband's village for two years and she finally left, along with her followers and a herd of cattle, to lead a nomadic life.

One day, while Karni Mata and her followers were camping in the village of Jangloo, a servant of Rao Kanha refused the group and their cattle access to water. Karni Mata declared her follower, Rao Ridmal, as the new ruler of the village instead, and set off on her way, along with her followers and cattle. Finally, she stopped wandering at the village Deshnok, near Bikaner. This is where her most popular temple is located.

A popular story states how Karni Mata helped her devotee Jagadu Shah in the sea. One day, while Karni Mata was milking her cow, she heard Jagadu Shah, a devotee calling her name. Jagadu, a trader, was caught in a fierce storm at sea and was praying to her. Karni Mata rescued him, and Jagadu reached the Porbandar port safely. He immediately went to Karni Mata and sought her blessings. As he expressed his desire to construct a temple for her, Karni Mata advised him to build a temple at Porbandar. This is the Harsiddhi temple.

Karni Mata is also said to have solved the enmity between the Rathore and the Bhati families, and laid the foundation stone of the fort of Bikaner at the request of Rao Bika.

Karni Mata was very close to her sister, Gulab Bai's son, Lakhan. According to a popular story, once, Karni Mata heard that Lakhan had drowned and died in the Kapil Sarovar in the nearby village of Kolayat. Lakhan had gone visiting to the village with his friends. When Gulab Bai saw Lakhan's body, she broke down. As the news reached Karni Mata, she too reached the place and was shocked to see her sister sobbing near Lakhan's lifeless body, lying on the floor. She took Lakhan's body inside a room and shut the door. After sometime, when she opened the door and walked out, Karni Mata was followed by Lakhan. It is believed that Mata fought with Dharmaraj or the Lord of Death, to bring Lakhan back to life, and Dharmaraj also promised her that from that time, her descendants will become kabas or rats after death and all kabas in turn will become human after death. Thus, the temple at Deshnok also became famous as the temple of kabas. Finally, one day while travelling with Lakhan, Mataji disappeared forever. Karni Mata, along with her followers and Lakhan were returning after paying a visit to the Maharaja of Jaisalmer. They were travelling back to Deshnok. Near Gadiyala and Girajsar of the Kolayat tehsil of Bikaner in Rajasthan, the processions stopped as Karni Mata wanted to drink water. It is believed that from there, she disappeared and could not be traced anywhere. Karni Mata continued to be worshipped by all and also became a protector of all animals, especially an important deity for the protection of cows and Krishna Saara Mriga or Blackbuck.

53

The Story of Tana and Riri

The story of Tana and Riri occupies a special place as they are associated with the annual music festival held in Vadnagar in Gujarat.

As the famous story of Tana and Riri goes, in the past, there were two sisters, who were gifted with the ability to sing raag Malhar in its most perfect form. They were born around the middle of the sixteenth century in the northern Gujarat town of Vadnagar, near Visnagar. They belonged to the Nagar community and their mother's name was Sarmishtha, while their grandfather was the famous Narsinh Mehta, the great saint, who was also a very important singer of bhajan and Bhakti. The girls were equally gifted like their grandfather. When the girls were growing up, it was the time of Emperor Akbar in the court of Delhi, and his court was adorned by the Nava Ratna or nine gems. The nine gems were nine distinguished and acclaimed people from various walks of life, including arts and culture. The famous singer Tansen was among these nine gems in Akbar's court. It was popularly believed that Tansen's music, especially Raag Deepak always lit up diyas or oil lamps. Now, it was also believed that it is next to impossible to sing the raag in its perfect repertoire, and if one did manage to sing it to perfection, apart from the diyas lighting up on their own, the singer would also experience a burning sensation all over his body from the feisty nature of the raag. This could only be calmed by the cooling showers brought down by singing the Raag Megh Malhar to absolute perfection. Thus, one day, when Tansen did sing Raag Deepak on Akbar's insistence, all the diyas lit up all around. Everyone was mesmerized by the magic, including the emperor. However, after Tansen finished singing, his body started to burn with the fierceness of Raag Deepak. It was a challenging predicament for Tansen, and he started to roam all across the kingdom, seeking a cure and a possible singer, who could sing Raag Megh Malhar to perfection. Ministers and soldiers were sent out of Akbar's palace, to even distant places, to aid the singer in his search. One day, the commander-in-chief of the army, Amjad Khan, reached Vadnagar, along with Tansen as he had heard about the two sisters from Vadnagar and their magical ability to sing Raag Megh Malhar to perfection. The Chief of the Army knew that he would soon find a solution to the problem and true, the girls, with the approval of their community and their mother, did help out an ailing Tansen by singing Raag Megh Malhar. Rains came down in torrents and calmed Tansen's burning sensation. When Akbar heard about the story from the Army Chief, he desired to meet the singers. Thus, the Army Chief returned to ask the two sisters to accompany him to Akbar's court. This was a difficult situation for Tana and Riri as they did not want to make the emperor angry, but also were not willing to perform their music for entertainment as they would only sing for their village deity. The sisters left their home and took their own lives by drowning themselves in the talab, or pond. Many days later, when Akbar received the news of the sad death of the two sisters, Tana and Riri, he apologized to the community and the parents of the girls, and also requested Tansen to create a new genre of musical piece in honour of Tana and Riri.

There is another slightly different version of the story. According to this version, while Tansen was searching for a cure across India, he reached Vadnagar. Tansen knew that the people of Gujarat were famous for their music, and he hoped that he could find an antidote there. At night, Tansen sat down to rest under a tree on the bank of the river Sarmishtha. Early next morning, Tansen was surprised to witness an interesting feat. With the break of dawn, women from the village gradually crowded around the river bank to fill up their pitchers. Among the many women, were two sisters, who looked very different from the others, and they were doing something strange which drew Tansen's attention. One of the sisters was filling up her pitcher and emptying it again. The other stood patiently, in anticipation as if something was about to happen. The sister, who was holding the pitcher, said aloud, 'I will not fill up the pitcher till I hear the tunes of the Raag Megh Malhar from the flowing waters in the pitcher.' Thus, she kept on emptying her pitcher for sometime and finally, she was satisfied when the water in the pitcher started to emit the perfect repertoire of Raag Megh Malhar. These were the two sisters, Tana and Riri. Tansen understood immediately that only these two sisters could save him. Just as the girls started on their path to return to their village, Tansen approached them and with folded hands pleaded, 'I am a poor Brahmin and at the emperor's insistence, I sang Raag Deepak and now my entire body is burning under the feisty spell of the raag. I just saw that you are the masters of Raag Malhar. Can you please sing it to me so that my body can calm down and I can return peacefully? Otherwise, I will perish soon as I cannot take this burning sensation much longer.'

The two sisters were shocked at the strange request from a complete stranger, and they informed Tansen that they would seek the approval of the village elders first. The parents of the girls and all the village elders were equally amazed at the request, but in order to help an ailing person, allowed the girls to perform and save the poor Brahmin's agony. Tana and Riri, however, had understood that it was the famous singer Tansen in disguise, as only he could have sung Raag Deepak to such perfection. Anyhow, they started to sing and soon grey and black clouds filled up the sky, and it started to rain torrentially. Tansen got completely drenched and it cooled down his burning sensation, and he was ready to return to the palace of the emperor. Tana and Riri mentioned that they understood who Tansen really was, and though he was taken aback at first, he thanked with folded arms and bid goodbye to the village, and Tana and Riri.

In Delhi, Akbar was greatly surprised to hear the story from Tansen about Tana and Riri and their magical singing abilities. He immediately desired to meet them. Now, as Tansen was narrating the story to Akbar, two princes overheard the story. They were amazed and could not believe their ears. They immediately wanted to visit the village and get the two women singers to the palace. Thus, the two princes reached the village and hid themselves on the bank of river Sarmishtha. Early next day, as the women of the village arrived to fill up their pitchers from the river, Tana and Riri arrived as well. Even from a distance the two princes could differentiate the two sisters from the rest of the crowd. They noticed their unique way of filling up the pitcher, and they approached the girls to speak to them. At that moment, all the women were surprised to see two strange men, and they started to shout. In the commotion that ensued, the villagers came out to rescue the women, and in the tussle the two princes and their horses were killed. The two princes and their horses, were buried on the banks of the river.

Soon, an impatient emperor understood that two princes were missing for a few days from his palace. He sent men to search for them. Shortly, his spies informed him that the two princes had gone to Vadnagar, and were killed by the people. An angry emperor gave orders to teach the people of Vadnagar a lesson. Thus, the army of the emperor marched and reached Vadnagar. They massacred and killed many and imprisoned the two sisters, Tana and Riri. The two sisters were put into a palanquin, and it set off for Delhi. However, the two sisters never wanted to leave Vadnagar, as they had vowed to only sing for their deity and never for entertainment. The sisters saw no other choice but to end their lives. Thus, just as the palanquin had reached the Mahakaleshwar temple at the border of Vadnagar, they took their own lives by swallowing the diamond from their rings. The two sisters were cremated there. Later two structures, resembling temples, were built in the area in memory of the two sisters, and their sacrifice.

The region still remembers the two sisters and the temple in their name. The annual Tana Riri music festival is a monument to the piety and power of music.

The Story of the Seven Sisters and One Brother of Goa

Long ago, seven sisters, along with their younger brother, travelled on an elephant across the Western Ghats, via Chorla ghat to Borda in Bicholim taluka (administrative district) in Goa, which was previously known as Bhatagram. It is said that the elephant that they travelled on, can be seen at Vydanar, near Mayem village, very close to the temple of Maya-Kelbai or Kelambika. It is carved in laterite stone on top of a hillock. The names of the sisters were, Kelbai, Mahamaya, Lairai, Mirabai, who later came to be also known as Milagres, Morjai, Sheetalai and Ajidipa, and the brother was Khetoba. At Bicholim, the presiding deity was already there and she was Shantadurga. So, the seven sisters and one brother were advised to go to the nearby Mayem village, where they set up their home.

One day, Kelbai, the eldest sister, sent the brother, Khetoba to arrange the fire for cooking food, but as he did not return even after a long time, Kelbai sent Lairai to look for him. A worried Lairai went out looking for the brother. She did finally find him, but was furious to see that he was playing with his friends instead of doing the work assigned to him. Livid, she kicked the back of Khetoba and he, unfortunately, while trying to escape, twisted his back. From that time onward the icons of Khetoba portray him like that. As the brother became angry at being hit, he refused to return and went to Vainguinim village. Till today, he stays there.

When Kelbai heard what happened, she scolded Lairai and felt responsible for the brother's departure, and decided to go to Mulgaon to do penance. She vowed to walk with fire on her head with five hundred followers called Dhonds. This tradition continues till date. Lairai, on the other hand also immediately left home, feeling sorry for her anger and sudden outburst. She went and settled in Shirgao in Goa, but did vow to return every year to walk barefoot on fire as a penance with seven hundred Dhonds. To this day, this is done by the devotees of Lairai at the zatra festival in May, at her temple.

Lairai's favourite sister was Mirabai and she became Milagres Saibin, after the Portuguese came to the area. On the feast of Our Lady of Miracles Church at Mapusa, Milagres Saibin is worshipped inside the church and oil is poured on the idol. The popular belief still speaks of a close bond between the two sisters, Lairai and Milagres or Mirabai. Lairai is said to gift a causo of oil to Milagres during the feast, Milagres in turn gifts a basket of mogra flowers—Arabian Jasmine (*Jasminum sambac*) to Lairai during Shirgao zatra. This story is reflected in Milagres's devotees offering Lairai her favourite flower—mogra—at the annual Dhondachi zatra festival. Lairai has no icon and is only represented by a pot full of water with a bud of mogra, and both are symbolisms of life and the womb.

Morjai settled in Morjim and her temple has the famous kaavi wall paintings. On the other hand, Mahamaya was afraid to settle in Mayem because of the presence of an evil spirit there. Kelbai came from Mulgao to ensure her sister's safety and till today, every year, Kelbai's dhoti-clad devotees wear garlands of her favourite flower—aboli (*Crossandra infundibuliformis*) and undertake the Peth zatra—carrying a wicker basket or peth with masks of four idols, and run eight kilometres to Mayem temple.

Thus, all the seven sisters and the brother settled at various places according to popular mythology, and they continue to be worshipped at these places. These are: Lairai in Shirgaon, Kelbai in Mulgaon, Mahamaya in Mayem, Mirabai or Milagres in Mapusa, Morjai in Morjim. No temples can be seen of Ajidipa, who is said to have settled in the Anjidipa Island near Karwar, and Shitalai is believed to have gone to paataal or the netherworld.

55

The Story of Waghoba

This is a Warli story centred on Waghoba, or the tiger, who is revered and worshipped.

According to the story, many years ago, there was once a wagh or a tiger, who was terrorizing the village of Kartod in Maharashtra. It kept entering the houses of people, causing mayhem and killing many. The houses, at that time, were made of thick leaves, and it was not very difficult for the wild cats to easily enter and prey. This continued for a long time and finally, being fed up with living in fear, people abandoned the village and moved into other areas and settlements.

Then one night, in one of the new settlements, a wagh approached once again, hearing the wailings of a crying baby. However, the mother of the baby arrived just on time and started to frantically beat the wagh with a thick stick. In her frenzy, she ended up killing the tiger. This incident scared the mother and all the villagers as they feared that this unfortunate incident will bring a curse on the entire village. Thus, everyone decided to approach the shaman for help. After listening, the shaman agreed that a grave mistake had been committed, and the sin needed to be atoned. He advised to build a temple in the honour of wagh, the presiding spirit of Waghoba. This was meant to pacify him and his spirit. Soon, they began to offer animal sacrifices in its honour, and also started to observe the festival of Waghbaras on the first day of Diwali. In Kartod, the deity continues to be worshipped on special events of the community and on Waghbaras. Hence, this festival started to be observed across all the shrines. The worship of Waghoba helps to understand sociocultural constructs in aiding shared spaces, as well as, renders an understanding for a need for conservation, and focus on ecological dimensions.

56

Sao Joao Festival of Goa

The feast of Sao Joao in Goa celebrates the birthday of St John the Baptist. St John was the son of St Elizabeth, who was related to Mary, the mother of Jesus. The feast is celebrated on 24 June, three months after the Feast of Annunciation on 25 March. It is believed that on the day of Annunciation, the angel Gabriel informed Mary that she would soon bear a son, Jesus. At that time, Elizabeth was already pregnant for six months with a son. Mary visited Elizabeth, and when the latter heard Mary's greetings, it is believed that the little baby in Elizabeth's womb 'leapt' in joy in anticipation of hearing the voice of the mother of Jesus, and also as it understood that baby Jesus was soon to be born.

When John grew up, he used to wear only simple clothes made from camel's hair with a leather belt around his waist, and eat only things which are naturally available to him. When asked by Jewish priests and Pharisees, he never described himself as a religious leader or a prophet, but spoke about himself as the 'voice of one crying in the wilderness'. He is said to have foretold the coming of the Messiah, Jesus. And when Jesus was thirty years old, he baptised him on the banks of the river Jordan.

Central Region

57

How Bada Dev Created the World

According to Gond mythology, Bada Dev, the supreme deity, was sitting on a lotus leaf, when he suddenly thought of creating the world. He accumulated some dirt by rubbing his chest. From this dirt, he created a crow. Then Bada Dev gave the crow the responsibility to go look for mud as there was only water all around. Unfortunately, the crow was unable to find any sign of mud, and all he could see everywhere and all around was only water, but he knew that perhaps at the bottom of this, there lay mud. Suddenly, the crow met Kekda Mal, the crab, and the two of them were able to find an earthworm. Now, with the knowledge that earthworms consume mud, they comprehended that earthworms possess the ability to locate areas where mud is abundant. To make this mud available above water, the crow and Kekda Mal made the earthworm spew out his food. What came out of the earthworm was soil. Seeing the soil above water, Bada Dev called for Makdi Dev, who was the spider king. Bada Dev then advised him to weave a large and vast web across the water. Once the web was woven, Bada Dev scattered the soil which the earthworm had brought, over the large web. Thus, land was created. Then when the soil was stable, Bada Dev realized the need for living creatures. So, he made all living beings, including plants, humans, and animals, and then scattered them across the land. Thus, all the earth was formed.

58

How the Santals Learnt Music and Dancing from the Gods

This is a very old story and is part of many colonial publications.

According to the story, in the very beginning, the Santals worshipped no deities. They also did not know the use of musical instruments or anything about dancing. One day, two people from their community were wandering through the forest, and by evening they had gradually entered into the deeper sections of the forest. Here, they suddenly heard some noise. This was music emanating from a specific area, but the two men had never heard music and to them, it sounded like a strange noise. Curious, both men proceeded to see where the sound was coming from. Moving towards the direction of the sound, both men realized that they had approached a bunch of thick trees. They climbed on top of the trees and were overcome with fear by what they saw. They saw Moreko, Jaher-era, Maarang Buru, and Gosae-era—all the Gods moving around rhythmically. The Gods were dancing, but the men did not know this as they had never seen or even heard about anything called 'dance' in their lives, neither did they know about the Gods. Suddenly, one of the dancers stopped moving and said aloud, 'There are humans nearby and I can smell them.' To this, Jaher-era replied aloud, 'Whether they be men or beast, we will do them no harm. They should come over here'. Seeing this open invitation, the two men climbed down from the trees and approached the Gods, and all night long, they danced with them. For the first time, they learnt to dance. By morning, the Gods gave the two men two drums and told them, 'Go and inform your people all about us, respect us, and annually offer sacrifices to us. You must also instruct them to play music and dance to its rhythm. We also order you to teach the people of twelve villages every night.' Thus instructed, the two men left. They did as the Gods had instructed them. Thus the Santals learnt the use of musical instruments and also learnt dancing.

Koya Punem of the Gonds and the Legend of Pahandi Pari Kupar Lingo

Several thousand years ago, during the reign of Sambhu-Gaura, a son was born to a Gond kingdom's chief, Pulashiva. The son was called Rupolang Pahandi Pari Kupar Lingo. He became the leader of the Koyas, served for the welfare of the Gondi community, and established the code of conduct, the 'Gondi Punem', which teaches the lifestyle values that are followed by the Gonds to this day. There are many legends which speak of the birth of Kupar Lingo and this is one of them.

More than a thousand years ago, Kali Kankali was living in the forests of Central India, along with her thirty-three children. They were raised in Raitad Jungo's ashram.

One day, the deities Shambhu and Gaura saw the children playing and offered them food, but were enraged when they did some mischief. A furious Shambhu imprisoned them in the Kachargarh cave for twelve years. This cave had an opening, through which a mythical bird used to serve them food and within the cave, there was a pond, from which the children drank water.

Kali Kankali was distressed at the confinement of her children and she appealed to Shambhu. Though at first he was reluctant, finally, Raitad Jungo intervened and stated that Lingo will release the children. This is the story of the birth of Lingo.

Shambhu advised Jalka Dau and his wife Hirodai, both residents of Pari Pator Bijli Pura to give him their son Ru

Polang, to be brought up as a king to lead and guide them in the future. Though the boy was just a new born baby at that time, both Jalka Dau and Hirodai were very loyal to Shambhu-Gaura and thus gave away their son. Shambhu took the newborn baby and placed him under a tree in the garden of king Pulashiva. As a mark of protection, Shambhu had tied his own necklace around the neck of the baby—Bhujang.

Soon, in the same garden, the queen came out for a walk. She suddenly heard the cry of a newborn baby. On enquiring, her servants found the baby and brought the queen to where the baby was lying. The queen and her servants were amazed to see that the baby was crying under a huge tree, but he was encircled by a massive snake. The large hood of the snake shielded the child from the rays of the sun, as if it was protecting the child. The snake did not seem to be harming the baby, neither did the baby seem to be scared of the large reptile. To the queen and her servants, the sight was indeed a spectacle. In great fear, the queen became speechless and quickly closed her eyes. After sometime, when she opened her eyes, she could not locate the snake anywhere in the garden, and saw that the baby was sleeping peacefully under the tree, in the same place. All this seemed like a miracle to the queen and her servants. The queen picked up the baby and took him inside to show to king Pulashiva. On narrating the unusual incident in the garden, the king was surprised and took the child to be a boon of Phadapen. Soon, a naming ceremony was arranged and the baby boy was named Kupar.

When Kupar grew up, he freed Kali Kankali's children from the cave. Kupar approached Hirasuka Patalir—a traditional bard in the Gond community, who played a tune on his kingri. Hearing this music, for the very first time, the children desired to see the world outside, and they came out of the cave by pushing aside the heavy boulder that covered the mouth of the cave. This was like the birth of a newborn, though the heavy boulder crushed Patalir. This site then became the kotayur, or 'one born of the womb'. They were thirty-three in number and all of them got initiated into the Gondi way of life. Kupar initiated and educated them to Gondi Punem or Gondi way of life and divided them into Samaven branches or clans, and they were assigned certain social roles. A specific kinship structure was established. The Gondi pilgrims often narrate the Kachargarh as the utpatti sthal or the place of beginning. All thirty-three propagated Gondi Punem, travelling across 'koyamooree' land, disseminating and preaching the teachings of their mentor, Pari Kupar Lingo. The religion was established with the aim of fostering human development. The belief is that nature was created from zero and it gave all the power to man to move ahead in life. Kupar Lingo instituted 'koya-punem' into a natural, truth seeking, and intellectual religion.

60

Why the Vindhyan Range Is Lower Than the Himalayas

This is a story from long ago, when the Vindhya Mountain lived a happy life knowing that he was the tallest mountain. However, this happiness was short-lived as he soon got to know that the Himalayas from the north is even taller than him. The Vindhyas enquired about it from the sun God and he too replied that it is indeed true. Now, the Vindhyas wanted to compete with the Himalayas and thus wished to grow. Indeed, with such an eager wish, the Vindhyas started to grow by an inch.

As the Vindhyas kept growing taller and taller, it started to create various natural imbalances, and slowly, the tall height also started to obstruct the sun. This created a very difficult situation for southern and western India. The sun God himself was deeply troubled to see the problem, as he knew that all living beings would perish without his life-giving touches. Thus, he approached sage Agastya, who was considered as the greatest Guru.

Agastya understood the problem and assured that he would find a solution. A short-statured man, Agastya started his journey towards the Vindhya Mountains from his abode in the north. After travelling for long, Agastya finally reached the Vindhyas, and on seeing him, the Vindhyas bowed down in reverence.

Agastya explained that he was in a hurry to travel towards the southern direction and requested the Vindhyas to lower himself. He also mentioned that it was indeed very difficult for a short-statured man as himself to climb such a massive mountain, as the Vindhyas had grown to an enormous height.

The Vindhyas had great respect for sage Agastya, and understood the practical problems of a short-statured man crossing over a mountainous and forested path. He did not suspect anything else, and thus did pranam to Agastya, and lowered his height in reverence, so that the sage could travel across easily.

As Agastya crossed over, he also mentioned to the Vindhyas that he would be back soon and once again it will be a problem if the mountain maintains the enormous height, and so, advised that he should retain the low height till he returns.

Once again, the Vindhyas did not suspect anything, and bowed down and bid Agastya farewell as he continued on his journey towards southern India. The Vindhyas maintained its low height and kept waiting for the sage to return from southern India. Agastya, on the other hand, never returned and settled in the south. The Vindhya Mountains, true to its word, never grew further in height. It is believed that, till this day, the mountain range is still awaiting the return of the sage, and thus, has maintained a lower height in comparison to the Himalayas.

This myth has various versions with other characters woven in, which also extends the main storyline. According to one such version, it was sage Narada, who wanted to play a trick and thus teased Vindhya about the Himalayas being taller. In another version, the Vindhya himself enquired about the tallest peak from a crow, who then informed him about the Himalayas.

How the Festival of Karam Became Popular

There were seven brothers of the Majhwar tribe who lived together. The six elder brothers used to go out to work, while the youngest used to stay at home to cook. He used to get his six sisters-in-law to cook and when it was done, he would take it to the fields to his brothers. This youngest brother also used to plant a branch of a Karam tree every day in the courtyard and dance before it with his sisters-in-law. This used to often delay the cooking. Now, one day, the elder brothers, coming home unexpectedly, found them dancing around the branch in the courtyard. They grew furious, tore up the tree in anger, and threw it in the river. Seeing this, the younger brother was enraged and left the house in a huff. Now, everything started to go wrong. Misfortune befell his brothers, and their family house collapsed. They lost all their wealth and were reduced to a condition of penury. The youngest brother too was suffering. His life was miserable. He could not find happiness anywhere he went, and also did not find a suitable job. Finally, one day, he spotted the Karam-deota floating in the river. He started to swim towards it to collect it, however, the deota forbid him, saying that he was a sinner. The youngest brother then propitiated the God by worshipping him. Finally, a satisfied God instructed him to go home. Upon arriving home, he discovered that all the previous problematic issues within his house had been resolved. The once dilapidated family home had been restored. The brothers were no longer in a condition of penury. On seeing and hearing everything from the brothers and sisters-in-law, the youngest brother informed that all the misfortune was because they had insulted Karam-deota. Ever since, the deity is worshipped by the people.

According to another similar story, once, there was a merchant, but he was very vain. One day, he returned from a long and a very successful trip abroad. His ship was laden with wealth and precious stones. He also wanted his family to immediately celebrate his return and perform a religious worship on his ship, both because he had earned immense wealth and due to his successful return. It was however the Karam puja day and as he approached his home, he saw his family celebrating the puja. The women were dancing around the Karam branch, and the men were beating drums. His wife, daughters, and sons were all busy celebrating the Karam puja. The merchant started to call everyone to draw their attention, but no one paid any attention. The merchant grew very angry. He went right into the middle of the puja, uprooted the Karam branches, and threw them away into the water. The deity was furious at this. No sooner had the merchant thrown away the Karam branches than his ship drowned into the depths of water, along with all the wealth in them. The merchant was devastated. Soon he went to seek advice from an astrologer to find out why his ship suddenly sank and how he could retrieve it. The astrologer told him that it was the curse of the Karam God which made the ship sink and the only way to get it back was to invoke the deity. The merchant again set out for another voyage, in search of the Karam deity. He found it in the middle of the sea. He then worshipped Karam Raja and the God then told him to perform the Karam ritual every year. The deity also instructed that his sons and daughters-in-law must fast for seven days and nights, and dance and sing during the Karam festival.

According to a third version, once there lived two brothers. Dharma was the elder brother and Karma was the younger one. Now, Dharma was very rich and Karma was very poor.

Once, there was no food or money for days together in the house of Karma and at the advice of his wife, he went to seek some financial help from Dharma. However, he was severely insulted by both Dharma and his wife. A very dejected and sad Karma was returning home, when he saw some women worshipping the Karam tree. The women understood his sad condition and advised him to worship the Karam deity for good fortune and prosperity. He followed the advice and soon, his bad days were over. Soon, others also started to follow him and worship Karam.

62

Why the Sun Is Hot, the Wind Dry, but the Moon Is Beautiful

This is a story from a long time ago, when there was no man on earth and the only living beings were the various parts of nature. At such a time, one day, the Sun, the Moon, and the Wind, went out to dine with their uncle and aunt, the Thunder and Lightning. At home, their mother remained alone, waiting for all the children to return. She was the most distant star you can see when you look up at the sky.

The mother kept waiting and waiting, while the children feasted merrily. Both the Sun and the Wind were extremely greedy and selfish. They enjoyed the feast and without ever thinking of taking some food to their mother, they started off for home. However, the Moon did not forget about her mother. In order for her mother to also enjoy the treat, the Moon set aside a small portion beneath one of her beautiful long fingernails, for every dish that was served at the large table.

At last, it was time to return home. When they arrived home, they saw that the mother was eagerly waiting. She was delighted to see all her children return home joyfully and asked, 'Did you all enjoy the feast?'

'Yes, mother. It was lovely. We enjoyed all the food that was served. We ate all of it. Uncle Thunder and Aunt Lightning were very happy to see us enjoying the food so much,' replied all the children of the distant star. The mother was indeed happy to hear this. Then hoping that they had brought something for her as well she asked, 'So, did any of you bring me back anything from the feast?'

The Sun, who was the eldest, replied in a rather surprised tone, 'I did not get anything for you. I went out to enjoy myself with my siblings, not to fetch dinner for my mother.' The Wind replied next, 'Me too, I did not get you anything either. You cannot expect me to get you anything just because I went out to eat.' The Moon spoke up now, 'No mother dear, I did not forget about you. Do get me a plate please.' And as the mother got a plate, the Moon shook out from her hands the choicest of food that she had collected from the feast.

The mother, the distant star, now spoke. She looked at the Sun and said, 'You went out to amuse yourself with your friends and feasted and enjoyed yourself. All the while, you never, ever thought about your mother even once. You shall be cursed. From now on, your rays will be forever hot and scorching. They will burn all that they touch. All of mankind will hate you and cover their heads when they appear in front of you.'

Thus, the sun remains hot to this day.

The Star then turned to the wind and said, 'As you too forgot about your mother because of your selfish nature, you too are doomed. You will always blow in the hot, dry weather, and shall parch and shrivel all living things. All of mankind will detest and avoid you from this very time.'

This is why the wind is hot and dry during the summer months.

Finally, she turned to the Moon and said, 'Dear daughter, since you remembered your mother and kept a share of the food, you will forever be cool, calm, and bright. No noxious glare will accompany your pristine rays and all of mankind will always call you blessed.'

And that is why the light of the moon is so cool and bright and liked by all to this day.

63

How Grains Were Distributed Throughout the World

At the very beginning of the world, there were no grains to eat. Men had only heard about grains being very precious and could only be found in the raised hood of the great cobra, which lived and ruled the netherworld. One day, their God Bhimsen, thought that it would be very helpful for man to have access to grains, so he decided that he would get it from the netherworld. Bhimsen sent a parrot to the underworld to get it. The bird flew down and found the cobra. Then, when the cobra was not looking, the parrot, very cautiously bit the cobra's hood and found a grain of kodon. The parrot immediately grabbed the grain within its beak and started to fly up and towards Bhimsen. Unfortunately, as it was flying over a thick bamboo jungle, the grain fell off from its beak. At that moment, a Basor was passing through that part of the jungle, as he was cutting and collecting bamboos to take home. He suddenly heard the sound of the grain crashing down on the ground. He bent down to pick up the grain, and just when he was about to touch it, he heard the grain saying, 'Don't take me now, but first go to your house and prepare a storage bin to keep me.' He went home and prepared the storage, and then returned to the jungle. He brought the grain and put it in the bin, and immediately, just like magic, the grain started to multiply several times, till the entire bin was completely full.

This news spread fast across the region and everyone came to see the storage bin. Now, everyone also wanted some grains.

The Basor agreed to give the grains, but with a condition. He said, 'Very well, I will give you my grains, but first you must eat at my house and Bhimsen must marry my daughter.'

Bhimsen heard this and understood that the Basor had cooked up a plan. He said aloud, 'Very well, I will come. Prepare the feast.' And soon, Bhimsen arrived. The Basor had already prepared the food and when the guests and Bhimsen arrived, he laid down plates made from leaves for all to eat. Everyone sat down to eat, the food was served, and right at that moment, Bhimsen clapped his hand and a severe storm of rains and wind swept away all the plates, along with the food on them. Bimsen finally said, 'Look, we have kept our word. Now you should too.' The Basor realized that he wanted to trick Bhimsen, but learnt his lesson instead. Thus, he agreed to follow Bhimsen's orders and gave sacks full of grains and bullocks for distributing to all mankind. Thus, with the blessings of Bhimsen, grains were dispersed across the land.

64

The Legend of the Beautiful Baiga Tattoos

The female of the Badi tribe, the Badnin, does the tattooing for the Baiga women (Baigin). There is a story about the creation of the Badi and Badnin.

Once, Lord Indra, the king of the Gods, was angry for some reason. Since he also controls thunder and rules over rainfall, he completely stopped the rains from descending upon earth. Soon, there was hue and cry across all the land, as it started to dry up and lay with a desolate parched look. All the crops in the field were drying up and the rivers were shrinking in size. There was no drinking water. All the animals and humans were suffering and many started to perish. Everyone could understand that a devastating and intense famine was imminent. This situation worried Lord Shiva and Goddess Parvati greatly. They called upon the deities, Naga Baiga and Naga Baigin, to persuade Indra to shower rain on earth. At that moment, Goddess Baigin thought that in order to appear before the king of God, she should be appropriately attired and wear suitable ornaments. Naga Baigin mentioned this to Shiva and Parvati. They understood and created the Badi and Badnin. The Badnin was given the task of decorating the body of the Baigin with tattoos. Since then, the women of the community have been decorating their entire body with wonderful and intricate tattoos.

65

How the Anatomy of Humans and Animals Came into Existence

At the very beginning of the creation of the world, all animals, including human beings, were very simple in construct. They did not have any proper digestive tract, neither did they have any vital organs, nor were there any bones. Thus, whatever they ate, passed through their bodies immediately and came out within seconds onto the ground, in the same state. It was as if the food was passing through a vacuous section.

Now, one day, Sankasur and his wife, Sirbhang, invited mankind to a feast, but they were not aware about the apathy of humans. To their surprise, they discovered that the poor people could not eat anything properly, and whatever delectable dishes were served, came out of their bodies immediately. This made both Sankasur and his wife Sirbhang ponder deeply. Sankasur wondered what they could do about this. At that time, Sirbhang had an idea. She said, 'Give me the cord around your waist.' When Sirbhang got the cord, she asked Sankasur to twist the large cord round and round. Then Sankasur was advised to stuff it inside a man's belly. Thus, was formed the main digestive tract. Once the main system was in place, Sankasur and Sirbhang set off to create all the other vital organs of the body. To make the liver, Sankasur took seven leaves of the karaya tree (*Sterculia urens*), to make kidneys, he got leaves of the takla tree (*Cassia tora*). With the flowers of the takla tree, he made teeth. Next was the turn to make the vital bone structure. With a stick, a hollow was made on the man's chest, and ribs were created, along with the backbone.

Once man was created, Sankasur and Sirbhang also corrected the animals in the same manner. Both men and animals looked complete now; all except the camel and the tortoise, who refused to cooperate like all the other animals, and their body structures remained half-finished. To this day, the tortoise has no teeth, and the camel's back is not straight.

Finally, after the creation was complete, Sirbhang took a bell and she was performing puja. Not being able to tolerate the ring of the bell, Sankasur suddenly took away the bell from Sirbhang's hands. In anger, Sirbhang made Sankasur open his mouth and she tied the bell inside his throat. Ever since we can see a bell inside our throats, which we refer to as the uvula, and this moves when we cough.

66

The Song about Lingo of the Maria and Muria Gonds

This is a song in reverence of Lingo, the founder of the Gotul. The original song was in Kongera of the Jhoria Muria Gonds. There are many versions of this myth and presented here is one of the popular ones.

Lingo was a boy of about twelve years. He was very brilliant, clever, kind, and gentle. Unfortunately, he did not have a favourable condition at home with the wives of his elder brother. One day, he left home as his elder brother sought to kill him, however, being a person with a pure heart, nothing could harm him, whether it be fire, iron, or any lethal weapon. Lingo kept fleeing and reached the banks of a river. There he built a house, where the walls were of fish scales, the beams of the roof were of snakes, and the top of the roof was covered with peacock feathers. There, within the beautiful house, Lingo started to lead a new life.

A gifted musician, Lingo could play eighteen musical instruments. His house was always an enchanting area of sublime essence, emanating from his wonderful music. Lingo's music was also magic. It attracted both boys and girls of the neighbouring villages, who flocked over to hear him at his wonderful house and often stayed back, listening to his music.

Lingo came to be revered as a God when he dissapeared. A shrine was made in his name in Semur Gaon in northern Bastar. The building or construction where Lingo's spirit is supposed to dwell is called the Gotul. Till date, almost every Maria and Muria village has its own Gotul.

67

Bhimasidi: The Lyrical Narrative of the Kondhs

The Bhimasidi is a famous lyrical epic of the Kondhs, sung by the Boguas.

According to the story of the epic, once, Bhima wanted to come down to earth by assuming a human form. Though his mother repeatedly warned him against getting associated with humans, as they are cunning and often crooked at heart, Bhima did not listen. Thus, he descended on earth by assuming the form of an emaciated, weak begger, whose body was full of blisters and wounds.

Roaming the surface of the earth, Bhima soon reached Beskapadar, a Kondh village. The name of the village chief was Urmadi Jani and he lived with his wife and two daughters—Konden Rani and Dumerani. The chief and his wife took pity on the poor beggar and offered him shelter. They gave him food and water, and provided him with a shelter as well. Though the chief and his wife were kind, their two daughters were not. They found Bhima's look repulsive, and considered him very ugly because of his wounds. One day, while the parents were not looking, they drove Bhima out of their house, and he started to wander around the streets of the village. In the meantime, the two sisters went for their bath in the village pond. Seeing the girls bathing, Bhima thought of teaching them a lesson. He invoked his father, Lord Pavan, the God of the winds, to blow away the clothes of the sisters into a jhapi (a round-shaped bamboo box in their house). Afterwards, Bhima also played other tricks with them and scared them by changing his form into various beasts and monsters, including a tiger and a bear. Finally, Bhima let the girls go and brought their clothes back. The sisters ran for their lives into their home and Bhima continued to wander across the streets, doing odd jobs and labours in various fields. Soon one day, he once again approached Urmadi Jani and requested him to keep him as his servant. He said that he wanted to repay the chief for the food and shelter which he had provided him when he had entered the village.

With his miraculous power, in no time, Bhima cleared and levelled the agricultural field. He cleaned all the weeds and bushes. The field was ready for cultivation within hours. After clearing the field, Bhima once again invoked his father, Lord Pavan to make the rains descend on the earth and make the soil suitable for ploughing. Overnight, the field was ready for cultivation, and the next morning, Urmadi Jani was overjoyed to witness the miracle. He praised Bhima for his work and requested him to stay in his abode. He secretly desired that Bhima would become his son-in-law. He also hoped that his girls would appreciate Bhima.

Soon, during his stay, Bhima performed many miraculous deeds. He discovered the intoxicating drink that can be made from the mahua tree (*Bassia latifolia*). He also discovered iron, gifted the blacksmith the bellow to create and mould iron, and taught how to tame wild buffaloes. Then one day, Bhima planted paddy, which did not yield and was drying up because of lack of rain. So, Bhima called the son of Urmadi Jani to set fire to the dry field. As the fire rose high into the sky, Bhima once again summoned rainfall and soon the fire was extinguished. From the ashes, Bhima discovered different kinds of paddy grains. Thus, Bhima gradually started to transform many aspects of the lives of the people. Then one day, the two sisters, Konden Rani and Dumerani discovered that Bhima was no longer the emaciated beggar whom they knew. Instead, he now looked handsome, tall, and powerful. Both the sisters came to know about the real identity of Bhima and they both wanted to marry him. The customs of the Kondh society permitted to marry both sisters. Thus, Bhima married both, lifted them up in his arms, and started off for his abode in the heavens. Unfortunately, the younger sister fell from his arms and turned into a fig tree (*Ficus carica*) on earth. Bhima told her that people will revere her and call her by her name, Dumerani, and worship her in Bhima's name. Thus, till date, people continue to worship Bhima under a fig tree.

68

How Humans Learnt the Appropriate Time for Harvesting

Once, Ponomosor saved the first human couple from the deadly fire which destroyed everything on the surface of the earth. He wanted them to resettle and start life anew on the surface, and he wanted them to start agriculture on earth. Thus, he advised them to cut down trees and burn them. In the clearing and on the ashes, Ponomosor advised the couple to plant pumpkin seeds. The tree soon grew and bore three fruits, out of which the first fruit grew slowly, while the second developed rapidly and ripened first. Ponomosor instructed the man and the woman to pick up the second fruit and sacrifice it in his name. When the couple cut open the vegetable, they found that the inside was filled with a variety of grains known as little millet (*Panicum miliare*). However, they did not know how to eat it and they powdered the grain and ate it raw. Till today, the Kharia offer a little powdered grain to Ponomosor during festivals.

The grain from the pumpkin lasted for a long time, by which time the third and last gourd had ripened. Ponomosor once again instructed the couple that it was time to cut down the vegetable and offer it to him. As instructed, the couple cut down the pumpkin and this time, they discovered the inside of the vegetable to be full of upland rice (*Oryza sativa L.*). Finally, the first pumpkin ripened and when the couple cut it open following the instructions from Ponomosor, they found the inside to be filled with lowland rice (*Oryza sativa L.*). Till today, when the crop is ripe enough and ready to be eaten, the Kharia reminisce the legend. Before harvesting the rice crop, they offer a cock to Ponomosor in remembrance of the legend of how Ponomosor taught them the ideal time for harvesting.

69

The Legend of Bhasmasura and the Gavri Dance of the Bhils

Once the Asura (demon) wanted to possess the ultimate power to control every living creature. He wanted to have the power to turn anyone to ashes simply by touching the head of the person. He knew that he had to pray to Lord Shiva to obtain such a boon, and thus, he sat in severe penance to seek the blessings of Shiva. Vrikasura sat in penance for six days and offered various parts of his body as aahuti (offering) to the sacrificial fire. On the seventh day, he decided to offer his head and just as he was about to chop his head off, Shiva appeared before him. Pleased with the dedication of the worship, Shiva asked Vrikasura, who was waiting for this moment, for a boon. He immediately asked for the powerful, destructive boon and Shiva had no choice, but to grant it to him. Hence, with the newfound power, Vrikasura came to be known as Bhasmasura (bhasma meaning ashes) and he decided to test the power immediately on Shiva himself. His plan was to reduce Shiva to ashes and then marry his consort Goddess Parvati. In fear, Parvati turned herself into a small bee and hid within the matted locks on Shiva's head and together, both fled from their abode. However, Bhasmasura had turned more ruthless with his new-found strength and he kept pursuing Shiva and Parvati. The chase continued till the end of the earth and this became a matter of great concern for all the Gods in heaven. Finally, to seek a solution, they approached Lord Vishnu, who immediately came to the rescue. He took the form of

Parvati and appeared before Bhasmasura. The Mohini Swaroop avatar (form) of Vishnu easily deceived Bhasmasura and he immediately proposed to the lady in front of him.

Though Vishnu (disguised as Parvati) agreed, he put forward one condition. He mentioned that Bhasmasura would have to dance like Shiva. Not really realizing that it was a trap. Bhasmasura readily agreed and started to dance. During the dance, Vishnu climbed onto Bhasmasura's shoulders and encouraged him to strike various poses. Suddenly, Vishnu proposed such a posture, where Bhasmasura needed to touch his own head. No sooner had he touched his head, than he turned into ashes immediately. Vishnu, the preserver, thus succeeded in destroying Bhasmasura. However, before dying, Bhasmasura asked for one last wish from both Vishnu and Shiva, that he should be remembered till eternity and he was granted the wish. Thus, to date, the story of Bhasmasura is repeated through the Gavri dance of the Bhils, which takes place across the Indian agricultural months of Bhadrapada and Ashwin (August–September and October).

The Asuras and the Beginning of Iron Smelting

According to a legend of the Asuras, they were traditionally referred to as Bir Asur, and they did not always smelt iron. This is the Asura legend about how they started their association with iron smelting.

A long time ago, King Bir Asur and his wife were travelling through a sal forest (*Shorea robusta*) in a palanquin, which was being carried by the Oraons. The palanquin bearers did not know the true identity of the king and queen. While passing through the sal forest, King Bir Asur exclaimed, 'How beautiful are the trees and how wonderful is this forest!' He thought a while and said aloud, 'These trees would produce very fine charcoal and can be very helpful.' Though the king said so, he did not have the idea of establishing an iron smelting site at that moment.

Seeing that the king and queen liked the forest, the palanquin bearers left them and went away to rest for a while. However, since the bearers did not return even after a long time, the couple started to search for a way to return home. Not being able to locate their way out of the forest, they decided to settle among the sal trees, which they admired so much.

Both the king and the queen had magical powers and they soon made a small hut and began to live upon the sal trees. The king used to travel deep into the forest every day, cut down sal trees, and burn them for charcoal. With the charcoal thus available, the king came upon the idea of smelting iron from the ore, which was also available there in plenty. The king was so engrossed every day with smelting iron, he would often forget to return home. He would stay away from his home for several days together. His wife started to get angry about this. She realized that the husband was also subsisting on the fruits of the sal trees and thus, she made the fruits bitter with her magical powers. This, finally, made her husband return home as he was hungry, and could not eat the bitter fruits. Till today, the fruits of the sal trees are bitter.

Thereafter, the king and his wife, lived in their hut and ate molten iron. They could get the charcoal from the sal trees and the king continued to pursue the occupation of iron smelting. He also conceived the idea of crafting various items from iron. Thus, he made the ploughshare, which he sold to the Oraons in exchange for rice and millets. Soon, when they had enough grains and pulses to eat, the royal couple realized that they can actually live on these, instead of the molten iron. Thus, they gave up the habit of eating molten iron and subsisted on rice, pulses, and millets instead. By this time, the king was old and was tired of smelting iron; he wanted to settle down with agriculture. In the beginning, the Oraons aided him in learning cultivation.

In order to learn the strategies of agriculture, the old man worked in the field of the Oraons for four days. He was helped by various groups of Oraons from time to time and they taught him everything about agriculture. The old man realized that agriculture was less tedious, and the old royal couple thus, continued with agriculture. In this way, gradually, the Asur gave up iron smelting and became agriculturists.

Southern Region

71

The Story of Kanyakumari

Once, the great demon Banasura was praying and meditating. Pleased with his austere devotion, Lord Brahma blessed Banasura, who then asked for a boon of immortality. However, Brahma told him that no being can be completely immortal. This made Banasura think for a while. Finally, he said that he wanted a boon of death only at the hands of a young virgin woman. This, Banasura thought, was impossible as a young woman would be too small, weak, and feeble to fight a mighty person as himself. Banasura's wish, in reality, had the hidden urge to take over the world and rule over everything. Such a wish, in itself, is a doom, as people harbouring such dreams misuse their power and create destruction all around. Little did Banasura imagine that misuse of great power, will ultimately meet its timely end.

Emboldened by the sanctification from the Gods and his new-found blessings of life, Banasura's strength increased further. He grew mightier than ever. His thousand arms had the strength of several thousand demons. Thus, becoming mad with his power, Banasura started to terrorize the heaven and earth. He left behind a trail of devastation wherever he ventured. All living creatures were afraid of him, including the Gods. Finally, one day, not being able to take the terror of Banasura anymore, the Gods went to Goddess Parashakti and pleaded to end the depravity and the terrors of Banasura. The Goddess listened in silence and understood that it was indeed a trying time, and if she did not intervene immediately, mankind would be annihilated. Thus, Goddess Parashakti, came down to earth in the form of a young girl and settled at the very southernmost tip of the land, so that she could keep a close eye on the entire nation. This southernmost tip came to be referred to as Kanyakumari, with the words 'kanya' meaning a young girl and 'kumari' meaning an unmarried girl. Gradually, the young girl grew into a beautiful woman and one day met Lord Shiva of nearby Suchindram. Goddess Parvati and Lord Shiva are destined by the heavens to be married across all their forms, incarnations, and rebirths, and thus, as a story of fate, Parashakti and Shiva fell in love. After a period of courtship, a wedding was planned. Both Parashakti and Shiva were extremely happy about the wedding and were eagerly waiting for the day. However, the gods became very worried. They knew that to kill Banasura, Parashakti had to be a virgin. They decided to stop the wedding at any cost. Finally, on the advice of the Gods, the heavenly sage Narada came down to earth and visited Kanyakumari and Suchindram.

Happy with the preparations of the marriage, Parashakti did not know what lay ahead. The region was all decorated. Everything was decked up and delicious food was being prepared, including many cauldrons of very brightly coloured rice. The aroma of the food and flowers mingled together to create an ethereal essence. The scheduled hour of the marriage was at midnight.

At the other side, at Suchindram, Lord Shiva rested a while and then prepared to leave for the marriage. The groom's marriage procession was just about to leave when sage Narada, taking the form of a rooster, started to crow, as if to announce the break of dawn. A startled Shiva looked up in horror and began to think that he had delayed the departure, and the auspicious hour of the marriage was over. Thus, Shiva and his marriage procession, returned to their place in Suchindram, and Shiva remained there. The temple of Lord Shiva is still to be found at Suchindram.

On the other hand, Parashakti waited and waited patiently for the groom and his procession but they never arrived. Then finally realizing that neither the groom nor his procession will be arriving for the wedding, in a fit of fury and anger, Parashakti upturned the cauldrons of coloured rice. This is believed to be still found, strewn across the beaches of the region where the sand is multicoloured. It is also believed that the nose ring of the Goddess glows and can be seen from afar. Very often, the glow from the ring can be seen from very far away in the ocean, and it has often been mistaken by sailors as the light from the lighthouse.

Thus, Parashakti remained a virgin and vowed never to marry. Over a fierce battle, she defeated and slayed the demon Banasura, and peace reigned on Earth. The Goddess stayed at the Kumari Amman temple on the beach with the coloured sand.

72

Saint Alphonsa: The First Woman Saint of Indian Origin

A nun in the Franciscan Clarist Congregation and an educator by profession, Alphonsa (christened Anna Muttathupadathu) from Kerala, was the first woman of Indian origin to be canonised as a saint by the Pope in 2008.

Born in 1910 in the village of Arpoorkara in the princely state of Travancore in British colonial India (which is now a part of the state Kerala), Alphonsa was also known as Alphonsamma. After leading a life of great service, she breadthed her last on 28 July 1946. Immediately, from the time after her death, hundreds of miraculous cures are claimed from her intervention, and many of them involved clubbed feet as she is said to have suffered from it herself. Two of these cases were submitted to the Congregation for the Causes of Saints as proof of her miraculous intervention. According to one such story, as narrated by Bishop Sebastian—once, when the Bishop was travelling in a small village in Wayanad, outside Manathavady, he saw a small boy, walking towards him. The boy trudged along with a walking stick with great difficulty on his calloused clubbed feet. The little boy approached the Bishop and the two got talking. The Bishop got to know that the little boy was ten years old and that his feet made him suffer greatly. The Bishop realized that the child was in great pain and he wanted to help him. He thus took out a bunch of holy pictures which he was carrying. He held out one of these that carried Alphonsa's picture and handed it to the boy and told him to pray to her. The child however replied that he could not pray to Alphonsa as he belonged to a different religion. The ten-year old also reasoned that he was born as differently abled, and there was no cure for him. The Bishop realized that the child was feeling helpless and prayed for his recovery nevertheless.

Several months passed by after that meeting and one day, a child and his father approached the Bishop at his home. Though, at first the Bishop could not recognize the little boy, after sometime, he remembered their meeting from several months ago. The father of the boy then mentioned that the boy had carried the photograph of Alphonsa with him and used to regularly pray to Sister Alphonsa. Very soon, after he began to pray, one of his foot got corrected. This surprised all the members of the family, and they all began to pray for the other foot, which too got corrected soon. The Bishop listened to the story and looked at the feet of the child. He could see that the child was standing without any difficulty. He could still see the calluses on the feet, which had formed on the skin from years of painful walking.

Thousands of people gather in the town of Bharananganam today, as they annually celebrate the feast of Saint Alphonsa from 19–28 July. Her tomb at St. Mary's Syro-Malabar Catholic Church in Bharananganam, has been designated as a pilgrimage site and several miracles have been reported by pious devotees.

73

The Story of Guruvayur Keshavan

The elephant Gajarajan Guruvayur Keshavan was donated to the Guruvayur temple of Kerala a century ago, on 4 January 1922, by the royal family of Nilambur. He served a long life as a temple elephant for over five decades.

According to lore, Keshavan was captured during the British colonial times in the Nilambur forest by the royalty of the region. Hunting was still not prohibited in colonial India and Keshavan was one of the twelve elephants who went to the royal courts. It is also said that the king was anxious about an impending attack of an armed rebellion which had spread throughout his region. He feared for his life and property, and sought the blessings of Lord Guruvayurappan. He promised that if the attack is warded off, he would donate one of his elephants to the temple. When the wish of the king did come true, he kept his word and he selected Keshavan, who was donated to the Guruvayur temple.

There are many legends associated with Keshavan. According to one such temple legend, Keshavan bent his front legs to allow only those who held the Lord's Thidambu to climb on his back. Everyone else had to climb over his hind legs. It is also believed that Keshavan held his head high and stood for hours while carrying the Thidambu. There is also another popular legend about Keshavan. Once, during the early 1930s, he was employed as a timber elephant and was sent to work in a forest along with his mahout. This forest was thirty kilometres away from the temple, and thus, everyone was astonished to see Keshavan return soon within the same day. It was more astonishing as his mahout was not there. It was indeed a marvel for all to wonder, how he travelled such a long distance without guidance, and everyone thought it was indeed the blessing of the Lord that Keshavan did not like being a timber elephant, even for a day, as he saw himself solely as part of the temple.

Keshavan has also won many prizes in the Guruvayur Aanayottam or Guruvayur elephant races. It is also said that he defeated Akhori Govindan, a famous elephant from outside of Guruvayur during the 1930s Aanayottam. In 1973, he was the first elephant to be honoured with the title of 'Gajarajan'.

Some Popular Legends of Mariamman

Long ago, there was a beautiful wife, Nagavalli of Saint Piruthu. She was known for her beauty and patience. The holy Trinity once decided to test her patience and paid a visit to her, disguised as three children. At that time, the Saint was not at home and Nagavalli soon got irritated with the tiring naughtiness of the children. She shouted at them and the Holy Trinity got very angry at her behaviour. They cursed her and condemned to lose her beauty and vanity. They told her that she will have scars all over her face, which resembles the scars created by smallpox.

When the Saint returned, he saw the ugly marks on her face and drove her away from the house. He also cursed that she will be reborn as a demon in her next life, and cause diseases to mankind which will make similar marks appear on the faces of all who got infected. The poor wife was completely crestfallen. However, later on, the Saint calmed down and told his wife that she will instead be reborn as a deity, and people will worship her to escape from the disease. The name 'Mari' in Tamil means the 'changed one' and thus she got the name, Mariamman.

The deity is also associated with the neem or margosa tree (*Azadirachta indica*), which is said to have curative powers. The neem leaf also often forms an integral part of the worship of Mariamman. Another legend speaks of the association of neem leaves with the deity. According to this story, dating to the Sanga period, once there lived a housewife, who got infected by small pox. As she was shunned by her family, she had to leave her house, and she went from door to door in the village, begging for food. As she walked, she held a bunch of neem leaves in her hand, fanning herself all the while to keep away the flies from settling on the sores on her body. She soon, recovered from small pox and people started to worship her for a speedy recovery from similar diseases like smallpox or chickenpox.

There is another legend which connects the deity to Goddess Kali, which states that Kali went down south where Bhairava followed her as Madhurai Veeran.

75

How Amnodr and Teikirshy Created Buffaloes

The Todas revere the Gods of the Mountains, and they believe that they reside on the Nilgiri peaks. They also associate them with their sacred buffaloes and dairies. There is a myth about the creation of the sacred buffaloes of the Todas, which is also associated with the creation of the very first Toda man and woman.

According to this myth, one day, Lord Amnodr (also often referred to as On) and his sister, Goddess Teikirshy, were visiting the plateau which lay at the top of the Kundah range in the Nilgiris. This plateau presently, stands as a ridge on the southwestern side of Mukurthi National Park, bordering Kerala. A very large ridge, it stands firmly across the Nilgiris. Upon reaching the region, Amnodr set up an iron bar, which stretched from one end of the plateau to the other. Then Amnodr stood at one end of the iron bar and brought out 1600 buffaloes from the earth. Along with the last of the buffaloes, hanging to its tail, came a man. This was the first Toda man, and thus were born the Toda buffaloes. Amnodr's herd were the ancestors of the Toda's sacred herds. Then Amnodr wanted to further expand the human population on earth. He took a rib from the right side of the man's body and created the first Toda woman.

On the other hand, Goddess Teikirshy, who stood at the other end of the iron bar, brought out 1800 buffaloes. These were the ancestors of the Toda's secular buffaloes.

Modern Todas believe that Goddess Teikirshy, rather than her brother created the Todas and their buffaloes.

76

Ayyanar of Chithakoor Village

It is said that once upon a time, he was the presiding deity of Singanam puri. This is very close to Chithakoor. It is believed that one day, while riding on his steed, Ayyanar reached Chithakoor and he liked the pleasant environment of the area, especially the water body. He thus decided to stay there. He visited the houses in the village, announcing that he liked the water body and wished to reside next to it. He also informed many of the wealthy people of the village to build him a hut near the water body. However, it was already past sunset and the people did not pay any heed to his calls, though the villagers understood that he looked like an important dignitary. Seeing the casual approach of the villagers, it is said that Ayyanar stated that in order to prove his divine presence, the villagers would see his warrior steed parked next to the water body in the jungle. Truly, next morning, as the villagers visited the water body, they saw an enormous statue of a horse next to the water body. The villagers realized their mistake and immediately took to building a hut from leaves and twigs for Ayyanar in that area.

It is believed that Ayyanar punishes any wrong doings in the village. Once, a stranger who was passing through the village, when the hut was being constructed, had taken away a stick from the construction. It is said that he lost his eyesight and only regained it when he promised to make amends, and replace the stolen stick with a thousand sticks. Till today, the deity is regarded with great reverence and consulted on many occasions to seek advice or help to solve disputes.

77

The Mighty Beerappa of the Kuruvas

Beerappa was the youngest son of Adireddi and Ademma and his real name was Elanagireddi. Ademma was a blessed mother as this youngest son was no ordinary one and was a 'varputra' or a blessed son. He had all the marks which showed his divine association, including a 'vaikuntha rekha' on his palm, a 'vinjamari' on his back, an 'amrita rekha' on his navel and the crown of a serpent on his head. As Elanagireddi grew up, he became a village head and looked after seven villages. However, his popularity was an eyesore for the families and wives of his seven brothers. Conspiring to put him into trouble and possible death, the seven brothers and their seven wives instructed him to go with his own bullocks to a place near Srisailam and cultivate hundred of acres of land. However, there was a termite mound under a tree in the area that Elanagireddi was sent to. There was also a belief that Lord Shiva had put a demoness on the tree. The brothers and their wives knew, that when Elanagireddi would cut the tree down, the demoness would devour him. However, unaware about this foul play, Elanagireddi proceeded to cut the tree down and raised his axe to give the first blow. Immediately and to his astonishment he saw many demons were rushing to attack him. These were the children of the demoness of the tree and Elanagireddi was not one to be scared easily. He fought bravely and fiercely, and killed all the children of the demoness. Devasted at the death of her children, the demoness went to complain to Lord Shiva, however, Shiva counselled her and said that Elanagireddi was a 'varputra' and all the land belonged to him. Shiva himself advised Elanagireddi to fell the tree and clear the land for cultivation. Elanagireddi obeyed and found a hundred acres of land for himself to cultivate upon.

One day soon after that, in Mount Kailash, Goddess Parvati asked lord Shiva for a sheep and he created a few. However, very soon, these sheep multiplied into many and were all over the mountains. Thus, Shiva sent these into 'nagaloka' or the netherworld and covered the mouth of the netherworld with a large slab of stone. Elanagireddi was ploughing in the adjoining region, and soon, his iron axe hit the large stone slab. He removed it to discover many sheep bleating inside. At this time, Shiva appeared before him and instructed him to rear the sheep and go to Kalyanapatnam. However, when Elanagireddi reached the city with his sheep, the King of Kalyanapatnam did not allow him or his sheep to enter the city. Everyone in the city used to worship Shiva and the King thus refused a nomad with sheep to settle in his city. Thus, Elanagireddi spent twelve long years on the outskirts of the city, roaming through the forests and leading a nomadic life. He got married twice in the meanwhile, and had seven sons. Elanagireddi, along with his family continued to live in the forest.

Seeing the plight of Elanagireddi for twelve long years, Shiva thought of teaching the King and the people of Kalyanapatnam a lesson. He thus refused the prayers being offered to his bull, Nandi. On the other hand, he instructed Elanagireddi to prepare a woollen blanket from the fleece of his choicest and best ram and take it as an offering to the people of the city, along with some meat. Though the people of Kalyanapatnam were shocked to see their prayers being refused, yet they did not accept the offerings of Elanagireddi. Seeing this, Shiva sent Revana Shiddeshwara to help Elanagireddi. As soon as Revana Shiddeshwara started his descent on earth, Elanagireddi along with his seven sons started to dance and rejoice and play drums—the 'birudulu'. Revana Shiddeshwara reached earth and sprinkled some 'haldi' or turmeric and 'kumkum' or vermillion on the strongest ram from the flock of Elanagireddi. It suddenly became excited and started to run amock among the people. It ran in every direction and killed many people. To save their lives, the people of the city, including the King , took shelter on a conical boulder or a 'sudigundu rai'. Finally, the people of Kalyanapatnam realized the divine and spiritual powers of Elanagireddi, and he started to be revered as a person sent by God. It is believed that the people of the city became followers of Elanagireddi thereafter. Shiva also conferred the title of Beeradeva on Elanagireddi as he was invoked through the playing of the musical instrument 'birudulu'. Later on, Beeradeva became Beerappa in popular parlance. The descendants of Beerappa are believed to be the present day Kuruvas as 'keru' in Kannada means wool.

The Kuruvas of southwestern Andhra Pradesh, also call themselves Elanati Kapus. The Kuruvas across the regions of Andhra and Karnataka are namely from two groups, 'unnikankanam Kuruvas' (those wearing woollen wrist bands), who are believed to be the descendants of the first wife of Elanagireddi, while the other group is 'pattikankanam Kuruvas' (those wearing cotton wristbands), who are considered to be the descendants of the second wife of Elanagireddi.

How Goddess Lakshmi Stayed Back in Hyderabad

The Qutub Shahi rule in the region of Hyderabad was a very prosperous one. It is often remarked that this was because of Goddess Lakshmi staying back in the region. According to this mythological story, Goddess Lakshmi was pleased with the generous King and founder of the city of Hyderabad, Muhammad Quli Qutub Shah, who was the sixth ruler of the Qutub Shahi dynasty. She thus, blessed the region and chose it as her abode. Any place which receives the blessings of Lakshmi, has always flourished and has been a prosperous one. It is also believed that the bad luck which accompanies the fall of a prosperous time or period is because Goddess Lakshmi leaves the region. Seeing that the region was doing well in terms of prosperity, the Goddess decided to leave and attend to lesser fortunate places, and bless them as well. The Goddess decided to leave one moonless or Amavasya (new moon) night. As she set off on her path at night, the city was asleep. Just as she approached the main gate, she was stopped by the guard, who was astounded at the sight of a bejewelled woman, walking alone at the dead of night, dressed in regal attire and also emanating a divine aura. This guard was of Abyssinian origin and was unaware about many local beliefs. He did not suspect that the lady in front of him could be Goddess Lakshmi but realized that she cannot be an ordinary person either. He felt a little uneasy while approaching her at first, but then he remembered his duties as a central gate guard. He then mustered enough courage to finally question her before opening the city gates. The Goddess was pleasantly surprised to see a mere mortal asking her identity and told him the truth. She also said that she had overstayed her time in the city and it was time she left to bless other regions. The guard stood listening silently. He was overwhelmed on hearing the Goddess speak. He felt like he was in a dream, and fear gripped him intensely when he heard the words of the Goddess. He could visualize the plight of the city without the blessings of Goddess Lakshmi. He kept on thinking of ways to make the Goddess stay back and started to plead with her, however she remained firm in her words. Finally, an idea struck the guard. He asked the Goddess to wait at the entrance gates till he returned after informing the king. The guard said that he was bound to lose his job if the words reached the royal courts that the Goddess had left the city, inspite of the gates being guarded at night. Lakshmi listened to the guard and thought for a brief while. She understood that it would be unfair for the guard if he lost his job because of her. Thus, the Goddess agreed that she would not leave the city, till the guard returned to his post next to the gate. The guard hurried to the royal court and informed Tana Shah. Though he was a benevolent monarch, he refused to believe the guard's story. After informing the king and on his way back, it is said that the disheartened guard took his own life. He was also frightened at the very thought of what would happen to the city's future if Goddess Lakshmi left the city. Thus, he never could return to his post at the main gates and Goddess Lakshmi, as promised, kept waiting for him to return. So, the Goddess stayed back in the city and Hyderabad continued to prosper for centuries. It is also believed that the strength of the blessings of Goddess Lakshmi also helped the city to recover inspite of the plunder by the Mughal army.

79

The Tradition of Women Priests at the Mannarasala Sree Nagaraja Temple

According to popular local legend, the Mannarasala temple came up in the place where sage Parshuram did penance to please Nagaraja, who agreed to eternally stay in the place and bless the land with his presence. There were mandara trees (*Erythrina variegate*) from which the place earned the name 'mandarasala' or the abode amidst the mandara trees. This name gradually transformed into Mannarasala. Over the years, the temple has been protected by members of the Mannarasala Illam and the eldest female member of the Mannarasala Illam becomes the chief priest. A popular story speaks of the initiation of the tradition of female priests.

Once, long ago, a massive fire broke out in the kavus (sacred groves) surrounding the temple. This devastating fire seriously injured many serpents in the kavus. At that time the residents of Mannarasala Illam were a Brahmin couple—Vasudevan and Sreedevi. Both being kind-hearted, they carefully nursed the serpents back to health. Nagaraja was touched by this show of devotion and dedication, and blessed the couple with a boon of twin boys, which were to be born soon. He also informed the couple that he would himself be reborn as one of them and would stay permanently in the area, showering prosperity on the lineage of the family, and also granting protection to all the devotees who would seek help. Thus, soon, Sreedevi gave birth to two boys. One of them was a human, while the other was a serpent—Nagaraja being reborn to bless mankind.

When the boys had grown up, one day Nagaraja advised his brother to marry to continue the lineage of the Illam. Thus, the marriage took place, and after blessing the couple, Nagaraja retired within a nilavara (a small cellar inside the house) to eternally stay aloof from the material world and devote his life to meditation. However, Sreedevi became extremely sad at the perpetual separation from her son and Nagaraja could not tolerate to see his mother's sadness. Thus, he allowed her to enter into the nilavara, once a year to conduct pujas for him. Ever since the main puja has been conducted by the ammas or the female chief priest of Mannarasala Illam. Even today, it is believed that Nagaraja meditates inside the nilavara and people refer to him as 'Appooppan' or grandfather.

Cochin Jews and Legend of Their Arrival in India

The Jews of Cochin have an interesting history. Much research has been conducted during the last several decades on the arrival of the Cochin Jews, considered to be the very first Jews to arrive in India. It is popularly believed that the Cochin Jews were known to have arrived in India in very ancient times and perhaps they came from Persia, after the destruction of the Second Temple.

Many of the legends concerning the Cochin Jews are connected to stories from the Bible, which speaks of the rule of King Solomon. According to the Bible, the rule of King Solomon was a prosperous one with a flourishing trade across the Red Sea, and the Indian Oceans. The 'First Book of Kings' describes the opulence of King Solomon and his and mentions the large number of items which originated from trade with India:

> And all king Shelomo's (Solomon's) drinking vessels were of gold, and all the vessels of the house of the forest of Lebanon were of pure gold; none were of silver; that was considered nothing in the days of Shelomo. For the king had at sea a ship of Tarshish with a ship of Hiram; once in three years the ship of Tarshish came, bringing gold, and silver, ivory, and apes, and peacocks. So king Shelomo exceeded all the kings of the era for riches and for wisdom.

A very similar description in the 'Chronicles' is also found about the trading interests of King Shelomo with India through today's Eilat. At the mouth of the Gulf of Aqaba, Eilat was one of the chief ports for the ancient sea trade with India, while another route was via Northeast Africa. According to one legend of the Cochin Jews, they arrived in India during the reign of King Solomon in the tenth century BCE and returned with ivory, monkeys, apes, and peacocks for his temple. There are also some Hebrew words for these objects, which seem to be direct translations from various Sanskrit and Tamil words, like the Hebrew for ivory is shenhabbim (elephant's tooth), which seems to be a direct translation of the Sanskrit word, ibhadanta.

There is yet another legend that mentions the arrival of the Cochin Jews to be around the first century CE at the Malabar Coast, following the destruction of Jerusalem by the Romans.

Many historians also speak of other legends that place the arrival of the Jews in Cochin to the time of the Assyrian exile in 722 BCE, the Babylonian exile in 586 BCE, or after the destruction of the Second Temple in 70 CE.

How Avvaiyar Met Lord Murugan

It is commonly believed that throughout the history of Tamil literature, there has been only one Avvaiyar. However, modern historians differ and mention that there have been at least three Avvaiyars at various periods of Tamil history. The earliest of them is believed to have been at the time of the Sangam period. Her poems, which are still famous, can be found in the 'Purananuru', 'Kurunthogai', and 'Natrinai'. There are many legends woven around this very famous poet. Once, Avvaiyar was travelling through a forest. It was hot and Avvaiyar was weary with hunger and thirst. She found some shade under a jamun tree and stood there wondering how to quench her thirst. Suddenly, she saw a young boy sitting on one of the tall and long branches of the tree, looking down and smiling at her. The sight of the boy sparked an idea in Avvaiyar's mind. She asked him, if he could be kind enough to gently shake the tree to assist in dislodging some fruits, so that Avvaiyar could quench her thirst, as well as her hunger. It was a simple request and Avvaiyar was not prepared for the question that came forth, instead of the fruits. The boy asked Avvaiyar, if she would like the fruits as 'sutta pazham' (cooked food) or 'sudaatha pazham' (uncooked food). Avvaiyar was amazed by this, and scoffed silently at the thought of cooked and uncooked fruits, thinking that the boy did not have any knowledge even about a fruit. However, she was tired and thought for a while, and finally asked the boy to throw down some 'sutta pazham', which she thought came closest to the boy's explanation of hot fruits. Hearing her reply, the boy started to shake the top branches of the tree vigorously and there was a shower of jamuns all around. As Avvaiyar picked up the nearest one, she blew on it lightly to remove the loose dust from the fruit, and to her amazement, the boy remarked, 'Grandma, are the fruits really so hot that you are blowing on them to cool them down?' Avvaiyar was amazed on hearing the boy's words. She thought that it was indeed intelligent of the boy to compare blowing on the fruits to cooling down hot food. Avvaiyar was humbled by the clever use of words, thinking that a mere cowherd can have such profound knowledge. She understood that the boy was no ordinary person and wanted to beg him to reveal his true identity. She looked up at the young boy, but saw that he had disappeared, and in his place sat Lord Murugan, smiling down at her. Stunned to find herself in front of divine company, Avvaiyar realized that the Lord came to meet her for a reason. Avvaiyar bowed down in obeisance and realized the infinite nature of knowledge, which Lord Murugan had imparted to her. Avvaiyar did pranam and sought the blessings of the Lord, and prayed to the Lord to aid her in her endless quest for knowledge. Avvaiyar understood that one should never become complacent enough to take pride in having acquired sufficient knowledge.

The Mythology of Kadayur Vellaiammal Koil

Lady Vellaiammal was born in a rich family of the Kongu Velalar community. While searching for a suitable groom for her, the parents one day saw Kangeyan, who had come to the village for Adhikarumapuram, to herd and look after the cattle belonging to the village. The parents of Vellaiammal noticed that Kangeyan was a very honest and hardworking individual and wanted to get their daughter married to him. The two families met, and the marriage alliance was happily confirmed between them. The parents of both the bride and the groom were happy at the proposed marriage. Soon, Vellaiammal and Kangeyan were married. As Kangeyan was still very poor, he asked for a piece of land for himself, on which he wanted to till and earn a living. The parents of Vellaiammal gifted a piece of land to Kangeyan. After marriage, Vellaiammal and Kangeyan continued to live near Vellaiammal's house and looked after the land which was gifted to Kangeyan. To everyone's delight, the land soon started to yield a bountiful harvest and the produce was more than sufficient to support the family and even keep a little in store. Life continued happily and within a few years, Vellaiammal and Kangeyan had three sons. The elderly grandparents were overjoyed and spent time with the grandchildren. However, this happiness was short-lived because soon, Vellaiammal's parents passed away one after the other. The death of the parents brought in more bad times. Vellaiammal's brothers, who did not want to give any part of the property to either Vellaiammal or her family, wanted to get rid of Kangeyan. They hatched a cruel plan and one day, they took Kangeyan to the forest and killed him. When they returned, the entire household was out looking for Kangeyan. Soon, the brothers spread the word around that Kageyan had actually deserted his family, his wife, and three sons and gone away. At that time, Vellaiammal was pregnant with her fourth child and was in a miserable state of mind. She could not believe that her dear husband would actually desert her or her sons in such an irresponsible manner. However, Vellaiammal's rough times had just begun. Soon, the brothers accused her of carrying the child of an unknown stranger, and thus drove her out of the house, along with her three sons.

A pregnant Vellaiammal, along with her three sons, kept wandering through the forests, looking for a suitable place to spend the night to shield her children and herself from the forest animals. Soon, the sardar of the place came riding down the same path, along with his sepoys. Vellaiammal tried to hide at first, but the Sardar's sepoys spotted her and her sons. Not trying to hide the truth, Vellaiammal narrated her sad story, and the Sardar believed it and sent for Vellaiammal's brothers. The brothers arrived and stood firm with their accusations that Vellaiammal was carrying a stranger's child. The Sardar insisted that he firmly believed that Vellaiammal was telling the truth. The brothers seemed to be in a fix and suddenly they thought of a plan. They decided to subject her to a few tests of virtue, intending to make them so challenging that she was sure to fail. Thus, firstly, the brothers insisted that Vellaiammal should bring water in an unbaked mud pot from the river and sprinkle it on the mud horse of Kadyeswarar temple and make that horse shiver. She should then sprinkle the water from the same unbaked mud pot on a dead piece of branch and make it sprout leaves and flowers. On hearing these demands of the brothers, the sardar became furious and wanted to immediately kill the brothers. However, Vellaiammal stopped him and thanked him for his belief in her and also said that she believed in her power and virtue and that she could easily complete the tasks. Just as she said, Vellaiammal completed both tasks. The mud horse started shivering with the sprinkled water and the dead branch suddenly started sprouting leaves and flowers. The whole village, along with the sardar and his sepoys did pranam to Vellaiammal and considered her to be a blessed one and a Goddess. The entire village performed obeisance before Vellaiammal, seeking her forgiveness, and the sepoys of the sardar drove the brothers and their families out of the village. Soon, Vellaiammal delivered a fourth son. The whole village rejoiced on seeing the bonny baby, and the elder brothers were extremely happy to see their new sibling. Vellaiammal lived for many years after that, and all the villagers sought her blessings for any auspicious occasion. When Vellaiammal passed away, the villagers installed a statue in the Kadaeswarar Temple. The descendants of her four sons consider her as the Goddess of their clan, and they look after the idol in the temple. The deity is particularly revered in relation to children, and all the descendants of the clan bring their children to the temple for their ear-piercing ceremony to this day. The story of Vellaiammal remains famous in the region and can be seen painted on the walls of the temple. Even today, people who face any household or domestic problems come to the temple of Vellaiammal to seek blessings or advice.

83

The Tradition of Offering Poovan Bananas at Korattymuthy

Korattymuthy is locally known as Hail Mary or Mother Mary of the Syro-Malabar Catholic Community at Koratty in Kerala. Also known as Our Lady with the Poovan Bananas (Poovankula Matha) the shrine is famous for its annual feast with the 'Poovankula', a special plantain, which is offered to the deity. A popular legend speaks of the beginning of this offering. Many years ago, a devotee of Korattymuthy was travelling to the shrine from Meloor, which is a hamlet around ten kilometres away from Koratty. He was bringing a bunch of a special variety of bananas, called the 'Poovan Pazham' to offer to the deity. When the devotee reached Muringoor, a rich landlord stopped him on the way. This landlord was supervising some work which was being done in his vast field. When he saw the devotee walking with the special bananas, he wanted to taste them. However, the devotee said that the whole bunch was for offering at the shrine. Unfortunately, the landlord did not like the refusal and forcibly plucked two bananas and ate them. No sooner had he eaten them, he started to develop severe stomach pain. The pain increased and doctors were called for, but no medicine could cure the man. Finally, it was advised that he should repent his misdeed and make reparations. The landlord immediately made arrangements and donated half of his land as an offering to Korattymuthy, and soon his stomach pain disappeared.

84

How Meer Ahamed Ibrahim (Periya Hazrat) Pursued His Education

The birth of Meer Ahamed Ibrahim (Periya Hazrat) is said to have been a miracle as he was born three years after his mother was blessed by Sultan Syed Ibrahim Shahid Badusha of Erwadi. An interesting legend mentions how he received his education. According to this, Meer Ahamed Ibrahim had left his home to attend to a madrassa, however, he was labelled by his teacher as a slow-learner. The teacher also admonished him and insisted that he leave the madrassa. A crestfallen Meer Ahamed Ibrahim was sad at the very thought of discontinuing his education and went to bed with a heavy heart, after praying to the Almighty Allah.

That night, Meer Ahamed Ibrahim had a dream. He dreamt that a large crowd of people was running and when he asked them, they replied that they were going to see Allah's Tajalli. He too joined the group of people, and they finally reached the top of a hill, where Allah's Tajalli was gliterring gloriously and everyone rejoiced. Then a voice told Meer Ahamed Ibrahim, that he was granted what he wished for.

Meer Ahamed Ibrahim woke up early the next morning and it was soon time for Fajr prayers. This time, Meer Ahamed Ibrahim's teacher asked him once again to leave the madrassa. The teacher further added that earlier he had asked him to leave as he considered him unfit to be taught, but that day, once again, he was requesting him to leave as he thought himself, a teacher, to be unqualified to teach him as he had been blessed by the Almighty. Thus, Meer Ahamed Ibrahim became educated with the greatest of knowledge. Soon, he returned home to his town in Madurai and started a madrassa to educate Muslims from all over Tamil Nadu. Many scholars of Islam in Tamil Nadu were his students and these scholars, in turn, started madrassas of their own.

Meer Ahamed Ibrahim was noted for his great expertise in the Islamic Fiqh laws. He was also appointed as the chief Kazi of Madurai and Kaziul Kuzaat by the then Nawab of Carnatic in India. He passed away in 1872, leaving four sons and a daughter.

Water Bodies: Bay, Ocean, Sea, and Others

85

How Lightning and Thunder Were Created

This is a myth concerning rainfall of the Duruwa community of Bastar region.

According to the story, once upon a time, long, long ago, when the world was still forming, there was water all around. This water was full of fishes. They were of various shapes, sizes, and colours, and everytime it rained, these fishes would come out to play, laugh, and enjoy. They would swim up and down, to and fro, and regale in the rhythm of the rain. In time, this play of the fishes became the lightning. During the same time, when everytime the fishes danced and it rained heavily, the dead souls who resided in the sky, who despised the loud laughter and play of the fishes, would gather together and pull a chariot across the sky, making an even louder noise than the fishes. This chariot was full of sharp metal objects which had no use in water, and so they resided in the sky. These were arrowheads, ploughshares, knives, sickles, and harrows. The dead would pull this chariot all over and across the vast horizon. Thus, the sound of the metal echoed throughout. This became the thunder. It is also believed that when gradually the earth was formed, sometimes, these metals fell down to the earth from the chariot, and thus, the earth started to get impregnated and began to bear rich fruit in the form of agriculture.

The Story from the Tendong-Faat Ritual Dance

This dance is performed as a worship for the Tendong hill of Sikkim. According to the legend represented through this dance, a long time ago, the mighty two rivers, Teesta and Rangeet were in full spate. The fury of the waters was so mighty that their level rose to a very great extent and all the surrounding hills were submerged. Men, women, children, plants, and animals were suffering because of the floods. At that point the Lepchas of Tendong hills started to pray to their God for a solution. Pleased with their ardent devotion and worship, God appeared in the form of a very large Kohomfo bird and began sprinkling chhang (a kind of millet beer) on the rivers. This had a miraculous effect. The moment the chhang drops fell on the rivers, the water started to recede rapidly. Soon, all the inundated areas were free of water once again. Plants started to grow back and men, women, children, and animals started to rebuild their homes, and once again carry on with their lives. It was then that the divine bird flew back to the heavens. The dance of the Tendong-faat is in remembrance of the Tendong hill, which is said to have given protection to the forefathers in their time of great calamity.

87

An Idu Mishmi Story: The Creation of River Brahmaputra

According to a myth of the Idu Mishmi community of Arunachal Pradesh (and Tibet), the Brahmaputra, referred to as Tallao, was the sister of Ringya, the Sun, and she lived in a great lake called Nimtubram. As the Sun lived in the sky, it could travel freely everywhere, but because the lake lived on land and was surrounded by very high mountains from all sides, she could never travel anywhere. Being trapped in one place, the water of the lake was stagnant and it never reached the plains to help mankind. Without a proper flow of water, it was very difficult to grow crops or sustain forests and jungles and this created a problem for man as well. There was a dire need for a channel of water to reach the place where man lived, but because Tallao was surrounded by so many mountains, it was not possible to manually make a channel. Thus, all around, everyone was facing problems because of the scarcity of water in the plains. Soon, a solution to the problems emerged. It so happened that a worm, named Taiyu, who lived very close to the banks of the Nimtubram Lake, dug a small hole and reached the water of the lake. It thus quenched its thirst. Water kept on trickling out of this hole in the bank of the lake. A cat, who was also thirsty, was passing by. He saw the water flowing out and wanted to have a drink. However, the trickling water was too muddy for the cat to drink. Thus, she made a bigger channel to the river and drank the fresh water from it. The cat then went off on its way. Upon witnessing the cat's remarkable intelligence, Tallao felt compelled to trail after it. Tallao followed the cat and as it wandered, it travelled and settled across many places which were parched because of lack of water. In this manner, a continuous stream was formed on the path that the river took as it followed the cat. Thus was formed the Brahmaputra. Unfortunately, the wanderings of the river soon came to an end as God Drakub made a wall in its path. The water of the river stopped flowing immediately and plants, animals, and humans began to die of thirst. This worried the deity Chainye, who went to Drakub and reminded him that mankind was suffering, and as it was he who had created the earth, he should also sustain it. However, Drakub did not want to remove the wall and sat firmly, keeping a watch on it. Chainye started to think of ways to make Drakub remove the wall. He realized, if he could be removed from his post of a sentry, the wall could be easily broken down in his absence. Chainye finally had an idea. He went and told Drakub that his wife was very sick and was dying, and that he should go and see her immediately. Drakub heard the news, but did not want to move from his post of vigilance. Next, Chainye told Drakub that his son was sick and dying, and once again, Drakub did not pay any heed. Finally, Chainye thought of another plan. He told Drakub that his mother was ill and dying in bed. This time Drakub got worried and wanted to go immediately and meet his mother. Thus, he left his place from the top of the wall and went home. When he saw that the wall was empty, Chainye broke the dam immediately, allowing Tallao to continue on its journey, till it reached down to the plains of Assam, and man and animals were revived.

The Story of the Pious Fish

This story is believed to have been narrated by Buddha while he was at Jetavanna, recounting the rains he caused to fall as a Bodhisattva in one of his previous births. In this particular incarnation, he took the form of a fish in a bright pond near Kosala and Sravasti. There was a severe drought and the Bodhisattva prayed to Pajjunna for the rains. It is also believed that the Bodhisattva's disciples at that time were the other fishes in the pond and Ananda was Pajjunna, the king of the Gods. This is a story from the 'Machha Jataka'.

Once upon a time, there was a beautiful pond near Kosala and Sravasti. This pond was full of wonderful aquatic plants. The water was clear and clean and one could see till the very depths of the pond. The waterbed had myriad creepers and flowers of various colours, which rendered a very ethereal look, and there were many plants growing around the banks which made the top of the pond look vivid, bright, and full of life all the year round. There were birds and bees all around the banks of the pond, fishes of different colours and sizes, and tortoises, swans, and ducks swam merrily all around. It was such a pretty sight that often passers-by would stop to marvel at the beauty of the impressive water body. In that pond, there lived a very large fish. He was no ordinary fish as he was very virtuous, pious, and was also a herbivore. He was known all across the pond as a fish who always followed the right path, took the right decision, and guided one and all in times of distress. This righteous fish was regarded with high esteem by all the fishes and other aquatic animals of the pond. If ever there was a problem, the animals would approach the large fish, and they knew that he would help to find a solution.

All around the year, life was beautiful in the pond and all the plants and animals lived harmoniously. However, difficult times soon arrived. It did not rain for a few days, which stretched on to weeks in the beginning, and this continued for many months. Finally, there was a severe drought everywhere. There was water scarcity all around. All the water bodies were drying up. All the plants were shrivelling and drying and all the animals were searching randomly for even the smallest waterhole to have a drink from. It was indeed a very grave time. Crops started to dry up and the agricultural fields lay bare and cracked from the lack of water. Men and animals started to fall sick and die from various diseases and starvation. The flora and the fauna of the little pond was also suffering. The water started to recede. There were patches of mud seen here and there. Many fishes and tortoises started to die, and was buried between the sticky mud. The wonderful creepers and the bright flowers, all drooped down and faded away. They lay dead across the mud patches of the pond, just next to the dead aquatic animals. The vultures found the dead fishes and tortoises and they started to encircle the pond on a regular basis in search of their food. The large fish was also suffering, but he was more concerned about his fellow aquatic beings dying all around him, including the beautiful plants. His heart was full of compassion. He could not bear to see the devastation around him anymore. He thought to himself, I must save my brethren from complete termination. I must pray to Pajjunna for rain. And thus, he took a bold step. He decided to swim up to the top of the pond to a muddy patch and waded somehow through the mud, dragging himself all along the way. It was getting difficult to breathe, and he could see the crows sitting on the bare branches of the trees, and the vultures flying high above waiting for their next prey. He knew that he could be hunted upon anytime, but he stood firm in his decision. He took a deep breath and kept dragging himself through the mud till he could clearly see the sky above. He looked up at the sky through his ruby red eyes and expressed a solemn statement of Sacchakriya—about perfect goodness with regards to his own virtue and good deeds. And he prayed to Pajjunna, the king of the Gods, 'My heart is sad and heavy to see all the people around me perish. My God Pajjunna, I am praying to you and yet there is no rainfall. How is it that I have always been a devoted and righteous person, and have been praying to you, yet there is no rain? It is customary to prey on another's meat for my kind and yet, I have never harmed another mortal and have survived only on grains of rice as alms given by kind people. This is the truth and I call upon you to send rains and succour my kinsfolk.' And he thus prayed, seeking rainfall to save his brethren from the woe.

The Bodhisattva's prayers reached heaven. The king of Gods Pajjuna answered his prayers and sent rains across the regions of Kosala and Sravasti. The whole day it kept raining and gradually, over the next few days and weeks, the rain brought back everything to life. The ponds and the ditches filled up, trees started to sprout green buds and leaves, and the aquatic plants and animals were relieved, to once again breathe normally, and find the joy to be at home and in water. Gradually the pond regained its lost lustre, and there was new life once again in the water of the pond. The righteous fish saved the flora and the fauna of not only the little pond, but everything else all around.

The Legend of Poubi Lai of Manipur

The Loktak lake of Manipur is a tourist attraction. It is home to a wide range of creatures and is also marked as an Important Bird Area (IBA). The lake is also known as the world's only 'floating lake'. Within the verdant landscape of the Loktak Lake echoes the famous legend of the aquatic dragon, Poubi Lai.

According to the story, Poubi Lai was a giant aquatic serpent, resembling a python and a large dragon. It used to live under the Loktak Lake and disliked human activities which disturbed the serenity of the waters. One day, Poubi Lai's siesta was rudely disturbed by the cacophonous activities of the fishermen of Moirang. Being suddenly thus awakened, it became angry and proceeded to destroy a significant portion of the habitation around the lake. Yet, its anger was not placated. Thus, it decided to destroy the whole of Moirang kingdom. It approached the king of Ancient Moirang and put forward a proposal. It demanded that the king should place one 'shangbai' (basket) of rice and one human in front of Poubi Lai everyday for him to consume.

Such a dreadful proposal filled the king with sorrow, but the people of the village had no option but to abide by it. Thus, every household began to take turns to provide rice and an individual to Poubi Lai. Then one day, it was the turn of a young man, who was quick in his wits. He realized that Poubi Lai has to be defeated somehow to make the people live in peace, and he needed to approach a powerful person for this. Thus, he went to the Kabui Salang Maiba—also known as Kabui Tomba. The Maiba was a priest or a shaman of the Kabui tribe in the Salangthel hill range of the Loktak Lake. Hearing the story from the young man, the Maiba decided to help the people in distress. Through his magical powers, he took a Tou plant, which is a local aquatic plant (according to another version of the legend, he took hold of a Khok Waa). He then proceeded to transform this plant into a powerful 'long' (the name of a nine-pointed javelin) and with this, the Maiba slayed the Poubi Lai after a fierce battle. Finally, peace returned to the kingdom and serenity prevailed once again on Loktak Lake.

Machher Biye from the Patua Songs of Bengal

This is a very old story from the Bengal region, which was formulated and has been kept alive through the performative art of the patachitra folk artists of the region. The artists are also called patuas or chitrakars (artists). As the tradition of the patachitra art goes, this story is painted across a long paper scroll and is described across many panels. The patua displays the scroll, points to specific panels and narrates the story.

This old story symbolically reflects one of the sad trajectories of life—the harassment of the weak at the hands of the powerful.

Oh Rangeela, let's go, we have to attend the marriage of the Dariya fish,
The Rohu fish says that I will carry the palanquin oh Rangeela;
Let's go Rangeela to the marriage of the Dariya fish,
The Catla fish says that I too will carry the palanquin oh Rangeela;
Let's go Rangeela to the marriage of the Dariya fish,
The Punti fish says I will go as part of the groom's procession, oh Rangeela;
Let's go Rangeela to the marriage of the Dariya fish,
Chanda fish says I will be the pasha (elaborate earring, covering the entire ear) of your ears, oh Rangeela;
Let's go Rangeela to the marriage of the Dariya fish,
The Bhutey fish says I will be the nolok (elaborate nose ring) of your nose, oh Rangeela;

Let's go Rangeela to the marriage of the Dariya fish,

Pankal fish says I will be the anklet of your feet, oh Rangeela;

Let's go Rangeela to the marriage of the Dariya fish,

The Prawn says, I will carry the pitcher of sweets for your marriage, oh Rangeela;

Let's go Rangeela to the marriage of the Dariya fish,

The Turtle says, I will carry your suitcases and trunks, oh Rangeela;

Let's go Rangeela to the marriage of the Dariya fish,

The Crab says, I will carry your basket of fruits, oh Rangeela;

Let's go Rangeela to the marriage of the Dariya fish,

The Shaipinal fish says, I will go to eat at your wedding feast, oh Rangeela;

Let's go Rangeela to the marriage of the Dariya fish,

The Hilsha fish says, I will play the madol drums at your wedding, oh Rangeela;

Let's go Rangeela to the marriage of the Dariya fish,

The Koi fish says, I too will play the madol drums at your wedding, oh Rangeela;

Let's go Rangeela to the marriage of the Dariya fish,

The Singhi fish says, I will sing at your wedding, oh Rangeela,

Let's go Rangeela to the marriage of the Dariya fish,

The Tangra fish says, I too will sing at your wedding, oh Rangeela;

All the fishes said, we will all attend your wedding feast, oh Rangeela,

Now, the Boal fish, was not invited to the wedding.

All considered him as a large demon. He was a big bully, who used to harass and devour small fishes.

The Boal fish saw the wedding procession moving along with the groom and the palanquin and suddenly disrupted

> the joyous occasion by jumping into the middle of the gathering and scaring everyone. He roared a thunderous laughter, as he continued with his destruction and killed many of the fishes. He finally hollered, 'Miserable fishes, how dare you not invite me to the wedding. I will eat you all.'

Thus, the maccher biye (marriage of the fish) met an unhappy ending.

91

The Origin of the Pushkaram River Festival

Once upon a time, there lived a pious Brahmin pundit by the name Tundila. After a severe penance, he was granted a wish by Lord Shiva—that he would be able to live in water and have the power to purify all the holy rivers for the betterment of mankind. So, Tundila stayed with Shiva, who took the form of water, one of his eight incarnations. Tundila came to be known as Pushkara, the one who caters to the needs of the whole world and the one who nourishes the world. Now, Brahma required water for creation. He prayed to Shiva to permit Pushkara to reside in his water carrier or kamandalu, and Pushkara remained within the kamandalu of Brahma. However, soon, sage Brihaspati or Jupiter, the preceptor of the Gods, wished to have Pushkara, because water was essential for the world and Pushkara's power to purify was unique. Pushkara was initially reluctant to leave Brahma's kamandalu, but finally agreed, on the condition that Brahma too would accompany him. Brahma found a way for this. He mentioned that Pushkara would stay with Brihaspati for twelve days when the latter was entering a specific zodiac sign, and also twelve days when Brihaspati was leaving that particular zodian sign. On all the other days of the period in between, Pushkara would stay with Brihaspati for only a length of two muhurtams or auspicious time in the afternoons. Brahma, accompanied by all the other Gods, would go to a holy river ruling the moon sign, in which Brihaspati was staying for the stipulated period. In this manner, it was decided by Brahma that Pushkara would stay with both Brahma and Brihaspati together. Thus, after every twelve years,

Pushkarams take place across twelve rivers and is celebrated for twelve days. People visit different holy rivers for a bath. The twelve major rivers of India which are part of this festival are Ganga, Yamuna, Narmada, Saraswati, Godavari, Krishna, Kaveri, Bhima, Tapati, Tungabhadra, Sindhu, and Pranhita. The Pushkaram festival is celebrated in each river according to the zodiac sign of that river. 2023 saw the celebration of the Ganga Pushkaram.

92

How the River Ganga Came Down to Earth

Once, there was a war between the Devas and the Asuras, in which the Devas were winning. Now, the Asuras hid under the sea and the Devas were unable to find them. They requested the great sage, Agastya, for help and he drank up the entire ocean. The Devas could easily defeat the Asuras who were hiding. They then asked Agastya to restore the waters of the ocean. However, the sage replied that he had already digested the water and could not restore it. The Devas and the others grew concerned about the dry ocean bed, but Lord Vishnu assured them that the ocean would soon be filled up. Many years later, in the kingdom of Ayodhya, the King Sagara was unhappy, as he had no heir to his throne. On propitiating the great sage Bhrigu, Sagara was granted a boon by which Kesini, one of his two wives gave birth to a son and the other, Sumati, gave birth to a gourd. The rind of the gourd burst open and produced sixty thousand sons.

When his children grew up, Sagara felt powerful enough to perform the Aswamedha sacrifice and dethrone the king of the Gods—Indra. Accordingly, and as per the rules of the sacrifice, he made preparations and let loose the horse to wander and graze at will across the pastures, near and far. Now, Indra, came to know the intentions of Sagara and assumed the form of an asura and drove away the horse to the nether regions. There, he made the horse browse near the place where the mighty sage Kapila was sitting in meditation.

In the meanwhile, a panic-stricken and anxious officiating priest of the Aswamedha sacrifice ran to inform King Sagara about the disappearance of the horse. This was a bad omen as it also meant that the sacrifice would remain unfinished. An enraged Sagara instructed all his sixty thousand sons to dig their way to the netherworld and regain the horse. As instructed, the sons of Sagara began to dig through the earth. As each son was digging, there were sixty thousand leagues being dug into the earth. From the severe discomfort, mother earth herself started to complain of the deeds of Sagara's sons to Lord Brahma. Brahma pacified mother earth saying that the sixty thousand sons were soon to meet their nemesis and all the problems will end. On the other hand, the sixty thousand sons of Sagara could not locate the horse, so they returned to their father empty-handed.

Sagara was even more furious than before. He told his sons to bring back the horse at any cost and not to step into Ayodhya without it. The sons now frantically started to search and dig in all directions. Their digging made them venture right through the earth and they reached the mighty elephants, who stood supporting the earth on their backs. However, the horse was nowhere to be seen. The sons kept digging, and finally, one day, they saw the horse grazing near the hermitage of sage Kapila. Now, the sons thought that the sage had stolen the horse and rushed towards him with the intention of causing harm. Though he was meditating, Kapila understood what was coming and it enraged him as the sons disturbed his meditation rudely. Kapila opened his eyes in anger and looked at the sons rushing towards him. Immediately they burnt into ashes. Not a single son survived to carry the news of the horse to king Sagara. Having died an unnatural and sudden death, the souls of all the sons wandered aimlessly, without attaining salvation (to be released from the emotional attachments of the material mortal world).

In Ayodhya, as Sagara sat waiting for his sons and there was no news, he sent his grandson, Anshuman, who was the son of Sagara's firstborn son. This firstborn son had taken to ascetism upon the birth of Anshuman. As instructed by his grandfather, Anshuman set off to search for his uncles. After searching far and wide, Anshuman finally reached sage Kapila's hermitage and saw the horse grazing nearby. He bowed down in reverence and after doing pranam, asked Kapila if he knew where his uncles were. Kapila was satisfied by Anshuman's humility and told Anshuman what had happened to the sons of Sagara. He also added that all the souls of the sons would attain salvation only if the holy waters of the celestial river Ganga touched their ashes. Anshuman did pranam and rode away with the horse to Ayodhya. He informed his grandfather, Sagara, about everything, and then completed the Ashwamedha sacrifice.

Now, Sagara began preparing to bring down the river Ganga from the heavens to the earth. Sagara ruled for thirty thousand years and during this time, as much as he wanted, he could never manage to bring down Ganga from heaven to the netherworld and to the ashes of his sons. Sagara passed away, bequeathing the task as a legacy to his grandson, Anshuman, but neither did Anshuman or his son, Dilip, succeed in completing the task. Finally, Dilip's son and Anshuman's grandson, Bhagirath was handed over the legacy.

Bhagirath was a very spiritual person. He performed severe austerities and propitiated the great Brahma, who agreed to order Ganga to descend to the earth. However, Brahma knew that the earth could not sustain the sudden and powerful descend of the torrential waters of the river. So, he instructed Bhagirath to propitiate Shiva and request him to receive the Goddess in his locks. Bhagirath accordingly underwent a further course of penances, at the end of which Shiva was propitiated and he consented to sustain the shock of Ganga's fall. Brahma then commanded Ganga to descend to the earth. The Goddess was not very pleased at the prospect of an earthly course and decided that she will completely flood the earth and take Shiva along with her to the netherworld. Thus, Ganga came down in terrible torrents, fuming and foaming, uprooting trees, drowning houses, tearing hillocks, causing landslides, and triggering mayhem in her course. However, she found an obstacle at Kailash as she had underestimated the power of Shiva, who caught her in his head and tied her up in his locks. The Goddess was unable to extricate herself from the maze of his hair and wandered aimlessly in his head. After much struggle, Ganga's fury calmed down a little, and her strength dissipated. Bhagirath, once again performed severe austerities to propitiate Shiva and persuade him to release Ganga from the locks on his head. Shiva was appeased and he released Ganga. She fell on earth, dividing herself into several branches, which gave birth to the sacred streams of India. One branch of the Goddess, followed Bhagirath, who rode swift and fast as the wind, guiding Ganga to the ashes of his ancestors. However, in the course of her flow, Ganga happened to flood the sacrificial grounds of sage Jahnu and the mighty sage drank up the whole river. Now, Bhagirath had to propitiate the sage. All the Gods too prayed to Jahnu to release Ganga. Calming himself down with the prayers, Jahnu allowed Ganga to flow out of his ear. After this, the course of Ganga was smooth and uneventful. Bhagirath led her to the sea and thence to the netherworlds, where the ashes of his ancestors lay. At the touch of the sacred waters of the Ganga, all the souls of Sagara's sons were released and they attained salvation.

As Goddess Ganga was brought down to earth from heaven with the severe austerities performed by Bhagirath, she is also often referred to as Bhagirathi, the daughter of Bhagirath. Ganga is recognized as Jahnvi, due to her reincarnation through sage Jahnu. The name of Bhagirath came to be associated with perseverance and persistence and any severe effort for a work that can only be achieved through hardwork. These kind of diligent efforts came to be referred to Bhagirath-prayatnam (labours of Bhagirath).

The Sad Legend of Jai of Chilika Lake

Kalijai hills in Chilka Lake is surrounded by very deep waters. The water also appears dark in colour to the layman's eyes because of its depth. The temple of the deity Kalijai stands on the hill. When one gets closer to the temple, it is almost an instant reminder of the popular legend of the land and also the famous poem which takes after it and was written by well-known Odia poet, Godabarish Mishra.
So goes the poem:

Sail carefully. Oh! Boatman.
Sail carefully
The girl fears the water,
People in the fort are waiting
The girl goes to her bridal home....

And thus, the poem brings to life a myth about a local deity and a legend from the past.

As the popular story goes, Jai was a young girl, probably in her late teens, who was travelling by boat to her husband's house for the first time after marriage. She was being accompanied by her father and other people. The in-law's house was in the Parikud Island of the Chilika Lake. As the travel drew on, Jai sat thinking about her life—about her father's house, about her friends, her mother, and many of the known faces—all of which she would not be seeing anymore. Her eyes welled up, and she choked with grief. Suddenly, her trance broke with the rocking of the boat. In the middle of the deep waters of the lake, the boat was swaying furiously. There was a sudden storm brewing, which started to cover the sky with thick dark clouds, the harbinger of the thunderstorm followed by torrential rains. Sitting in the rocking boat, Jai started to feel scared. She felt her distant memories fading in her mind as fear started to grip her. Jai's father began to caution the boatman. They were thinking of the water of the Salia River, but here, they were facing the turbulence of the sea, the Bay of Bengal, as the storm drew nearer.

Slowly the boat reached even deeper waters. The boatmen were struggling, but they were experts in the area and they thought that they could manage the situation. The people in the boat trusted them and so did Jai and her father. By now, the thick clouds were just overhead the little boat. They stretched far into the horizon and over the Bhaleri hills in the distance. Swiftly and in no time, they had covered the top of Jatia hills too and the clouds started floating all across the lake now. The deep waters of the lake reflected itself in the dark clouds above. With the clouds came gusts of very strong winds, creating high waves and froth on top of the splashing water. The waters of the lake, swirling around the boat, moved with purposeless yet determined vigour, evoking the fierce winds that created them. The ripples of the waves started to increase and the large waves picked up momentum to lash against the sides of the boat. The boatmen, though experts, knew their boundaries and the fact that they were no match in the face of the mighty fury of nature. Their efforts proved too feeble in the face of the mighty wind and the waves. The boat was picked up by the large waves and tossed around several times. It was bouncing up and sinking down the very next instant. The people inside the boat started to scream for safety. Suddenly, there was a loud noise, a tremendous force hit the little boat, and it came to a sudden stop. Before anybody could comprehend they found that they were lying on the banks of the lake. For the frightened people, it was the merciful moment that they were praying for. The boat had violently crashed against a massive rock on the island and broken down into pieces. All the people were thrown off the boat. They lay hurt and aching around the massive rock, and the moment they gathered their senses, they started to scamper for their lives and look for shelter. The broken pieces of the boat lay strewn across the banks of the lake and the jagged rocks, getting drenched in the strong rains, while the treacherous waves lashed against them. Finally, the storm abated. A very bright sun began to emerge gradually from behind the dark clouds, while the winds eased into a gentle murmur, occasionally falling completely still, as if to warn of the recent destruction. All the people who had taken shelter at various places, started to come out in search of each other. All the people were present, including Jai's father, but unfortunately, he could not locate Jai anywhere. Everyone, including the boatmen searched the banks all around, but Jai was nowhere to be found. The father was shocked beyond grief. The people and the boatmen soon returned in another boat but with heavy hearts.

Jai had vanished from the mortal world and to this day, it is believed that Jai still looks after all the boats which travel through the area. It is said that her voice, carrying through the hills, seems to be crying from a distance. No boat has ever capsized in the deep waters of the Kalahari hills as it is believed that the soul of Jai calms down the strong winds. Thus, the boatmen and the locals started to worship Jai as the Goddess Kalijai of the region. She is also considered as an avatar of Kali.

Kamaley Kamini and the Story of Dhanapati and Srimanta

Once upon a time, a merchant by the name, Dhanapati, was preparing for his travels to the island of Sinhala (the present Sri Lanka). To seek blessings for her husband's mercantile venture, Dhanapati's second wife, Khullana, made arrangements to worship Goddess Chandi. Khullana put in a ghot (earthen pot) for the puja and called Dhanapati to be a part of the ritual. However, Dhanapati was a devout worshipper of Shiva and refused to worship anybody else. He went and kicked aside the ghot which his wife had put in and this insolent act made the Goddess furious with rage. Khullana was pregnant at that time, but knew for sure that her husband's travel was doomed as the Goddess would not spare him. She bid adieu to Dhanapati with a heavy heart and prayed to Goddess Chandi for a safe journey and a safe return.

Dhanapati set sail for Sinhala with six large fleets. The journey began on a simple note but soon changed as all the six fleets were submerged due to a terrible storm. Dhanapati knew that Chandi had created the hurdle, but he remained steadfast in his determination not to plead in front of the Goddess. Though all six fleets were submerged, yet Chandi made sure that Dhanapati survived, keeping in mind the devotion of his wife Khullana. Dhanapati was saved by holding onto a floating log. As he floated along the mighty waters of the Bay of Bengal, near Kalidaha in Bengal, he had the fortune to witness the Kamaley Kamini avatar (form) of the Goddess

Chandi. Dhanapati was blessed and yet did not know how to assimilate this sighting to get back his fortune. So, when he finally did manage to find his way to Sinhala, he narrated his experience to the king of Sinhala. The king knew that sighting the Kamaley Kamini avatar is a good portent and wanted to witness it himself. He told Dhanapati that if he would be able to show the same to the king, then he would be awarded with half the kingdom, but if he failed, then he would be imprisoned for life. Dhanapati agreed, but was unable to show the Kamaley Kamini avatar to the king of Sinhala, as Chandi made sure that they will not be able to see anything even when they reached the exact area in the sea where Dhanapati had seen Kamaley Kamini. The king grew angry and imprisoned Dhanapati. As he sat serving time in prison, Goddess Chandi appeared in his dreams to instruct him to start worshipping her. However, a staunch Shaivaite, Dhanapati once again disagreed, as before. Chandi too, refrained from getting him out of his troubles, but waited for a more favourable time in the future. The good time did eventually come, but not before many, many years had gone by.

As Dhanapati was serving time in the Sinhala prison, his wife had given birth to a bonny baby boy. He was named Srimanta, and with time, he grew up to be a healthy and strong young child. He started his school in a local pathshala (traditional school), and under the guidance of his teachers, he soon became an excellent student. One day in the pathshala, the teacher asked him about his father's name and his whereabouts. Now, this is something that Srimanta never knew anything about. He went home and enquired about it from his mother. Khullana was reluctant to talk about the sad episode from the past, but finally narrated everything on Srimanta's incessant requests.

For Srimanta, the whole story of his father came as a shock. Though nobody knew that Dhanapati was still alive in the Sinhala prison, they all knew that Dhanapati set sail for Sinhala and never returned. Srimanta was also told the same by his mother. Thus, Srimanta decided one day that he must set sail for Sinhala too, for he was determined that his father was alive and that he could bring him back. Khullana realized that it was futile to stop Srimanta as he had already made up his mind to travel. Thus, though reluctantly, Khullana bid adieu to her son as Srimanta set sail with seven large fleets towards Sinhala. Before leaving, Khullana reminded her son to pray to Goddess Chandi in the face of grave danger where his life would be at stake, making him understand that the Goddess will protect him and also bring him home safely. Khullana wanted Srimanta to trust the Goddess and keep her in his heart always.

A diligent son, Srimanta, prayed to the Goddess and the journey towards Sinhala was not hampered with any sudden storms like Dhanapati's expedition had encountered. All the seven fleets kept moving steadily towards Sinhala across the Bay of Bengal. A spiritual son, Srimanta, also stopped by Neelachal or Puridham to pay homage to Lord Jagannath. After that Srimanta's ship passed by the cities of Kaladhautapura and Chandrasidhadweep and kept travelling for hundreds of yojanas (an ancient unit of distance, varying between about four and ten miles, depending upon the locality) before docking at Setubandha. There, Srimanta enquired from the locals about the distance to Sinhala and finally, once again, set sail. Very soon however, Srimanta realized that his ships were lost at sea and they were surrounded by a mysterious mist and very dark waters all around. It was at that moment suddenly, Srimanta saw the Kamaley Kamini avatar of the Goddess. It was more glorious and vivid than ever. The entire image gradually appeared out of the mist and over the waters. Srimanta saw a beautiful grove like a small island full of lotus blooms, buzzing with bumblebees and teeming with water birds. There were also various fragrant creepers of different flowers, including malati (jasmine or *Aganosma heynei*) and juthi (juhi or *Jasminum auriculatum*) flowers. All over the grove, the birds were flitting around and chirping melodiously, and in the middle of the grove, there was a very large, fully blossomed lotus. On top of the lotus sat a very beautiful lady, whose beauty was incomparable, for it was divine and horrifying at the same time. The lady sat, holding a struggling elephant in her left hand, and in the very next instant, she put the entire elephant in her mouth, which she had opened up large and wide. She devoured the entire elephant in one gulp. Within moments the lady also regurgitated or vomited up the same elephant, opening her mouth wide again. The elephant was once again back, struggling in her left hand. This event kept happening repeatedly, yet the lady did not look grotesque. She was devouring and regurgitating with the grace of a swan. Her large mouth, which opened up widely to devour the elephant, produced pearly white teeth which struck out like lightning. At the same time, she was also humming raagas and raaginis, and at times she would suddenly stand up and dance, raising her hands in the air. Suddenly many attendants and confidantes of the lady would surround her and dance with her. These were various deities, including the vidyadharis, daakinis, haakinis, and yoginis. The lady was bejewelled and to Srimanta, her beauty could only be compared to all the deities that he could think of, including, Saraswati, Sachi, Rambha, Arundhati, Satyabhama, or Lakshmi. The lady was sitting atop the lotus with as much elan as a swan. On her feet were tinkling anklets and her toenails shone brightly as ten moons. Her face was calm and radiated a glow like a full moon of autumn, and the sindoor bindi (vermillion bindi) on her forehead was as bright as the morning sun. The entire fragrance of the grove floated over the mist and the waters, and reached Srimanta, who was overwhelmed to witness this entire scene. Srimanta was dumbfounded. There were so many questions in his head: How can this entire grove exist within the sea with such exquisite creatures? Who can this lady be? How can anyone devour and regurgitate an entire elephant? Srimanta came to realize that what he saw was not a mere sight and it was indeed a blessing for him. Srimanta understood that he had witnessed the Kamaley Kamini avatar of the Goddess. Srimanta knelt in reverence and kept sailing. Soon, he realized that he could manage to find his way. It was not long before he reached Sinhala.

Upon reaching Sinhala, Srimanta approached the king and narrated the incident of sighting the Kamaley Kamini avatar at sea. The king, once again instructed Srimanta to show him the same. Just like his father Dhanapati, Srimanta was also unable to show the Kamaley Kamini avatar to the king. This time, the king instructed to behead Srimanta. Now, Srimanta remembered the wise words of his mother Khullana and he started to pray to Goddess Chandi. The deity appeared to help Srimanta in the guise of an old Brahmin woman and saved him from death. The entire army of the king of Sinhala was defeated and the king suddenly realized that he was dealing with divine forces. It was then that the king heard the story of Srimanta being Dhanapati's son and how he came all the way from Bengal to rescue his father. The king was full of remorse and repented. He wanted to show his gratitude towards both Dhanapati and Srimanta and sought their forgiveness. Finally, he arranged for the marriage of his daughter, Shushila with Srimanta.

Soon after that, Dhanapati set sail for Bengal, along with his son, Srimanta and daughter-in-law, Shushila. Upon their safe return, everybody became aware of the blessings of Goddess Chandi and since then, they started to worship her.

95

Biliku: The Deity of Storms and Thunder

According to the Akajeru legend of North Andaman, all causes of heavy rainfall and lightning are because of the deity Biliku, who lives in the sky. If she is angry, she sends intense storms and heavy rains on the people of the earth. Biliku also often throws her pearl shells in the storm and these strike as lightning. Once, mad with rage, Biliku had sent so much of rain, thunder, and lightning that it destroyed everything on earth. Nothing remained and it was all bare and empty. There were no plants and no animals. Then, one day, Biliku dropped a seed of the gurjun tree (*Dipterocarpus turbinatus*) from the sky. From this one seed, various kinds of trees started to grow on earth and life found a new meaning. Soon, the earth was covered with forests once again.

There is also another Akajeru legend about Biliku, when she used to live with man's ancestors on earth at Arkol. According to this story, one day, the Akajeru people caught some turtles and brought them to the camp. Biliku was sitting there. People asked her if she was interested in eating some of the meat. Biliku refused. So all the people put the turtles on top of the roof of the hut and went away. When the people left, Biliku ate all the turtles greedily and went off to sleep. When the people returned, they saw that the turtles were gone. They realized that Biliku had eaten them. They immediately left the camp and went away to Tebi-ciro, leaving a sleeping Biliku behind. Few days later, some people were passing by Biliku's place in a canoe. They knew that Biliku was deserted in this place as she had secretly eaten everything and left nothing for anybody.

These people were going turtle hunting. The minute Biliku realized where they were going, she called out to them and asked them to take her along. However, they did not agree as they said she had secretly eaten the turtles of the other group of people earlier. Biliku grew very angry at the answer. She had some round stones and pearl shells with her. She started to throw them at the people. The first shell did not hit them and it bounced back at Biliku and fell at her feet. Likewise, the second shell which Biliku threw also failed to hit the canoe or the people, and it bounced back at Biliku's feet. Finally, the third shell struck the canoe. It killed all the people in the canoe. This canoe and all of its occupants turned into reefs of rocks, which is believed to be still there.

After this, the other group of people, living at Tebi-ciro, called across to Biliku, saying, 'Come over to us. You can stay here.' Biliku replied, 'Very well, I will soon be there with you,' and so saying, Biliku climbed on the stone which she had created by killing the people of the canoe. This rock started to float on the sea, so Biliku stood on the rock and started to glide over water. Suddenly, when Biliku had only reached halfway across, her rock became heavy and both the rock and Biliku sank to the bottom of the sea. They became two big rocks, which can still be seen on the west coast of the North Andamans. It is believed that the shells and stones which Biliku was throwing were lightning and thunder respectively. Severe rainfall, accompanied by gusts of wind and thunder is a common phenomenon in the Andamans.

The Akakede Tsunami Myth from North Andaman

An Akakede myth from the North Andaman speaks about the catastrophe which befell on the ancestors of man when the water level rose so much that everything went under water.

Once, long ago, in the place called Cilpet, people used to collect a lot of honey. In the same place there used to live the local bird—Kopo-tera-wat. Thus, the Kopo-tera-wat bird became very angry, and in the evening, when the cicadae were singing, he deliberately started to make a lot of noise to disturb the singing of the cicadae. Goddess Biliku considered the cicadae to be her children, so she became very angry as the song of the cicadae was disturbed. In her fury, she sent heavy storm, rain, and thunder. The water level rose and the surrounding land started to get inundated. Very soon, all the small trees were submerged and only the top of a gurjun tree could be seen above the water. As a last resort, all the people took refuge in the branches of this tree. Mima Mite (Lady Dove) had managed to somehow rescue some fire and kept it alight under a cooking pot. The waters at length subsided, but the people did not know how to get down from the top of the tree. Mima Carami-lebek (a type of local bird) used to live on top of very high trees and she was also there sharing the space with man. She made a long piece of rope and with the help of this, she lowered all the people.

Madhukar Nouko Puja and the Story of Chand Saudagar

The 'nouko puja' or boat puja connects to an important storyline from the famous 'Manasa Mangal Kavya' of eastern India, dating to the time of the medieval period of the erstwhile region of Bengal (which includes present day Assam and also the country of Bangladesh). Held annually in open spaces with water bodies, the festival marks the gurmi or gurma or ojhas (spiritual healers), as well as the devotees gathering to pray and offer the ritual music and dance.

The story of the celebration of the very first 'nouko puja' is mentioned in the literary work of medieval Bengal, written by poet Ketakadas Khemananda. According to this story, Chand Saudagar was a very rich and famous merchant residing in Champak Nagar, near present day Chhayagaon in Assam. A well-known and devout Shaivaite, Chand only believed in the worship of Shiva. His dedication as a worshipper and his ardent devotion was well-known even in far-off places. Even Shiva himself knew and admired his devotion. Now, it so happened that Shiva had created a daughter who grew up in Nagalok and her name was Manasa. She grew up as the queen of snakes and knowing herself to be the daughter of Shiva, she wanted to receive equal respect just like Shiva. She also desired to be worshipped by all mankind on earth. Though Shiva knew that this was impossible, but knowing Manasa to be adamant, finally found a way. There was only one way to popularize her puja amongst mankind, and that was to request Chand Saudagar to conduct her puja. This would inspire others to conduct similar ceremonies. It was believed that if the common people saw Chand, as a strict worshipper of Shiva, worshipping a Goddess of snakes, they will also follow his path. Thus, Shiva thought that this will surely make Manasa famous on earth. However, the work seemed more difficult than it was assumed, as Chand refused to conduct the puja. Manasa subjected him to many ordeals which forced Chand to change his mind. In her fits of anger, Manasa started to trouble Chand and push him into various adverse situations. It began by drowning his fourteen ships at sea and killing all his seven sons. Very soon, after Chand experienced such misfortune, his youngest son, Lakkhinder also lost his life on the very first night of his marriage to Behula. Chand had taken all precautions to guard Lakkhinder's room for the night, however, Manasa's scheming mind found a way to kill the young man. Though the Goddess managed to even kill the last of Chand's successors, yet her struggles were far from over. Lakkhinder's widow, the young Behula, refused to give up on her dead husband. She floated down a river on a raft and reached heaven with her husband's dead body. She then prayed and appeased all the deities in heaven by performing a touching dance in front of all, including Shiva. Thus, finally Manasa was forced to grant her the blessing of life to Lakkhinder. She also brought back to life all the other seven sons of Chand, as well as all his fourteen ships which she had destroyed. However, all these blessings came with a staunch promise by Behula that she would make Chand conduct Manasa's puja on earth. Behula did manage to make Chand conduct the puja, though it was done with Chand's left hand, instead of the customary right hand. Nevertheless, Manasa was happy with Chand conducting the puja, and ever since, Manasa's puja became known across lands near and far.

The festival of 'nouko puja' celebrates the ending sequence of the mythological story from 'Manasa Mangal Kavya', where Manasa returns the fourteen ships of Chand Saudagar. According to the story, these fourteen ships were carried by four hundred snakes on their backs to the residence of Chand, who was overjoyed, and welcomed them to his home by conducting a puja with aromatics, lights, and the blowing of conch shells. Different musical instruments were played and dances were performed to celebrate Manasa's benevolence. Thus, at present, the festival includes building a grand float that resembles a boat, after Lakkinder's boat by the name Madhukar. The worship also celebrates all deities who were present in heaven, in front of whom Behula performed. It is believed that once Chand welcomed and worshipped all the fourteen ships at his home, people got to know and associate the worship of Manasa with fortune and wealth.

The Legend of Prince Vijaya

Long ago, in the capital of Banga, there lived a king who got married to the princess of Kalinga. The royal couple was soon blessed with a beautiful baby girl, Supadevi. At her birth, as was the tradition, a soothsayer was consulted, who mentioned that though the girl will grow up to be very beautiful, she will one day marry the king of beasts. Both the queen and king were heartbroken on hearing this. Supadevi, too, grew up with a heavy heart as she was aware from childhood about the prophecy and the very fact that her parents always remained sad because of her. One day, she decided to leave home and explore her life. She was ready to accept whatever came her way. Thus, unrecognized, Supadevi joined a caravan travelling towards the city of Magadha from Banga. Unfortunately, on the way, a ferocious lion attacked the caravan near Lala country (which is identified with Raar region or western parts of Bengal). Everyone ran in all directions to escape from the lion, however, Supadevi remembered her prophecy and started to follow the lion back to the forest. Though the lion was amazed at this at first, he understood that the girl stood fearless in front of him, and it was not long before they fell in love and started to live in the lion's cave. Soon, the girl gave birth to twins, a girl and a boy. The boy was named Sinhabahu, meaning lion-armed and the girl was named Sinhasivali. Growing up, Sinhabahu understood that his mother was different from his father, and one day, when Sinhabahu was sixteen years of age, he escaped with his mother and sister from the cave in which they stayed. They reached the city of Banga and Supadevi was remarried soon. On the other hand, the king of Banga had announced a hefty sum as a prize money for anyone who could kill the ferocious lion in the forest. Sinhabahu killed his own father and brought the lion's head as an offering to the king.

The grandfather of Sinhabahu and Supadevi's father, the king of Banga, rejoiced seeing the lion slain. Thus, soon after that, when the king of Banga passed away, the ministers and courtiers declared Sinhabahu as the new king. However he handed over the rule to his stepfather, Supadevi's husband and he retired to the region of his birth—the Lala region. There, he married his sister, Sinhasivali, as was mostly the custom in those days, and established a new kingdom with many villages. This was the kingdom of Sinhapura. A very prosperous rule ensued and Sinhabahu, together with his wife Sinhasivali, bore twin sons sixteen times. Thus, Sinhabahu had thirty-two sons. The eldest was named Vijaya and the second son was Sumitta. A very just and principled king, the subjects admired Sinhabahu as the ruler, and it was a prosperous rule. Soon, Sinhabahu consecrated Vijaya as the prince agent. Vijaya was destined to be a ruler soon, however, this went against the wishes of the subjects of the kingdom as Prince Vijaya had already earned a bad reputation for his many misbehaviours and conducts across the kingdom. In all of these, he was also accompanied by a band of friends, who were equally despised by the people of the kingdom. Thus, all the subjects of the kingdom went and complained to the king about Vijaya's misdeeds. The king warned him thrice and yet Vijaya refused to listen, and finally, he banished Vijaya along with his friends and families across the Bay of Bengal. While the men, along with Vijaya were sent on a separate ship, the women were sent on a second ship and the children were deported on a third one.

The ships sailed along the waters, and each one is said to have reached the shores of a different island across the Indian Ocean and the Arabian Sea, giving rise to the very first settlements on each island. The island where the ship of the children reached was the Naggadweep and the island where the women landed was the Mahiladweep. This Mahiladweep is believed to represent the present Maldives, and thus began the rule of queens in the history of Maldives. On the other hand, the ship carrying Vijaya and his male friends, landed first on the island of Supparaka, on the western coast of India, on the Arabian Sea. Finding the region unfriendly, they returned to their ship and kept sailing farther, and finally reached the island of Sinhala near the confluence of the Bay of Bengal, The Indian Ocean and the Arabian Sea. This was Sri Lanka.

The sixth chapter of The Mahavamsa ends with a mention of the legend of the arrival of Prince Vijaya to Lanka. The following chapters describe the meeting of Prince Vijaya with a Yakkhim, named Kuveni on the island, and the two children who were born from this marriage—a son named Jeevahatta and a daughter named Disala. Local legends also speak of these children to be the ancestors of the present-day indigenous community—the Veddas of Sri Lanka.

The following chapters of The Mahavamsa also speaks of how Kuveni's happiness was short-lived as Prince Vijaya soon married a princess from the Pandyan kingdom of southern India. Vijaya maintained a very cordial relationship with the kingdom of his in-laws and he ruled for thirty-eight years in Sinhala, but did not have any heir to the throne. Finally, towards the end of his rule, he wrote to his twin sibling, Sumitta in Singhapur, to come and take over the throne. However, Sumitta refused the offer as he too had advanced in age by then, and thus, made his son, Panduvasudev reach Singhal. Panduvasudev reached the shores of Lanka and was crowned the king and it is said that his dynasty ruled for the next six centuries.

99

The Minyong Myth about the Creation of the World

According to the Minyong myth, in the beginning, there was nothing but rocks and water. However, the rocks were not normal hard rocks as they had life in them. They were soft and supple and moved about. From these rocks, a female rock, Eling-Litung Tune was born. She grew up and gave birth to another female rock Peddong-Nane, who helped in creating the world from the great mass of water where the rocks lived.

When Peddong-Nane grew up, she married another male rock named, Eling-Limuk-Muktum and the first child was born. This was the very first fish, which went to live in a stream in the mountain. Next, Peddong-Nane gave birth to a big frog, and then a little frog, and then to the land frog. After that she gave birth to the insect Kungung-Pangam, which lives in water and finally, she gave birth to another fish, which went swimming in the sea—to accompany her child, the big fish.

After having completed her work on earth about the creation of life, Peddong-Nane left her home on earth and went to the sky to start another life to help in the process of creation from there. This was a second life, which began in the sky village named Engo-Takar. In the sky, she got married to Karba-Bojong and had many children—Ninur-Botte, Lomang-Botte, Doini-Nibu, and Darro-Rabbo. Finally, after growing old, Peddong-Nane breathed her last. One day after that, Doini-Nibu and Darro-Rabbo prepared rice beer in memory of their mother. When the millet was ready, they poured water over it.

A great cloud arose out of it and from this cloud was born Polung-Sabbo, the mithun.

A meeting was soon held to stabilize the creation of the Earth further, as there was still water all around. The big question was how to dry the water and make the earth appear? While everyone was deliberating, the deity Pulong Sabbo suddenly said, 'I can do it. I know how,' and saying so, he dug a great pit with his horns and all the water from everywhere rushed into it. Dry land started to appear all around. Thus, water was stored only in the seas and oceans, and the dry land was left for life to flourish. Soon, there were plants, animals, and humans across the earth and the rocks became stable. They became hard and stopped moving, thus creating hills, valleys, and mountains.

Anahita: The Bestower of Life

According to the Zoroastrian creation text, Bundahishn, the great cosmic ocean originated at the top of the Hara Berezaiti Mountain—'High Hara', which is at the centre of Airyanem Vaejah—the first of the lands created by Ahura Mazda. The sky revolved around this high mountain. This cosmic ocean was Anahita herself. The warm and clear water of this cosmic ocean flowed through a hundred thousand golden channels towards Mount Hugar, the 'Lofty', which is one of the daughter peaks of Hara Berezaiti. On the summit of Mount Hugar is Lake Urvis; the water of the cosmic ocean entered this lake and became purified. The water then exited through another golden channel of the mountain and divided into two parts at such great height that it was equal to the height of a thousand men. As the stream diverged into two, one was fresh water and the other was salt water. The fresh water drizzled as moisture upon the whole earth. This dispelled dryness of the air, and all the creatures of Mazda acquired health from it. From this was created humidity of the air and rainfall. The other saltwater stream ran down to the mythical sea created by Ahura Mazda, called the Vourukasha. The earth is said to rest upon this Vourukasha. Anahita flowed through the Vourukasha and purified all the seas and oceans of the world.

So, the waters of the cosmic ocean flowed down from the icy slopes of the high mountains, encircled the earth, and from the freshwater and saltwater bodies thus created, emerged all the animals and plants, including the aquatic ones. Thus, the world was created from the cosmic ocean—Anahita.

This veneration of water was an honour bestowed on the Goddess. She is not only regarded as the source of water, but water itself, and is referred to as being pure, swift in motion, and powerful. Her name represents the concept of moistness as well as strength. She is beautiful, is a strong maiden, and wears beaver skins. In Yt. 5.98, the divinity Aredvi Sura Anahita is described as one: '... round whom stood the Mazda worshippers with baresman in their hands'; which is the seat offered to a divinity to partake of the sacrifice being offered.

Anahita is described as royally attired and is said to wear a gold embroidered robe, a golden crown, necklace and earrings, golden breast ornament, and gold-laced ankle boots. She is visualized as riding a chariot drawn by four horses, named wind, rain, clouds, and sleet. In the Aban Yasht, the river divinity is described thus: 'the great spring Ardvi Sura Anahita is the life-increasing, the herd-increasing, and the fold-increasing who makes prosperity for all countries.' She is described as 'wide flowing and healing', 'efficacious against the daevas', which are supernatural entities with disagreeable characteristics, 'devoted to Ahura's lore'. She is associated with fertility and wisdom. Thus, she is said to purify the seed of men, the wombs of women, encourage the flow of milk for all newborns, make land fertile, and help both man and beast to survive. Being associated with wisdom, she is also the divinity to whom priests and pupils are believed to pray for insight and knowledge.

Jhulelal and the Unifying Spirit of Water

This is a famous legend that goes back to the time of a tyrant in the tenth century by the name, Mirkshah, who ruled Thatta. Once five representatives of the local Sindhi Hindu community were put under severe pressure by this despot Mirkshah for religious conversion, and they were given forty days to return and speak about their final decisions. In severe fear, the community members started to pray and summon Lord Varuna. All the members of the community fasted and prayed and sang songs for forty days in praise of Varuna. They did not cut their hair and wore no new clothes. Finally, at the end of the fortieth day, Varuna was pleased. He appeared before the Sindhis and told them that he would help them. He would be reborn as a mortal, as a son to Mata Devki, who lived in Ratanchand Lohano's house in Nasarpur. Following the legend, this day is revered till the present as a thanksgiving day, which comes after forty days of fasting.

Time passed slowly and after three months, everyone heard that Mata Devki would deliver a baby. Soon enough, one rainy day, amid torrential rain, Mata Devki gave birth to a bonny baby boy. As people poured in to see the newborn, they were astonished to see that the baby opened his mouth to show a vision of the Sindhu River flowing, with an old man sitting cross-legged on a pala fish. This was indeed a miracle, and everyone realized that their misery would soon be put to rest, and that God had truly answered their prayers.

The baby boy was named Udaichand. He was also lovingly referred to as Uderolal, while residents of Nasarpur called him

Amarlal. Like his birth, the boy was always surrounded by miracles. His cradle, where he lay, would keep swaying to and fro on its own, to calm him and put him to sleep. Thus, the boy got the famous name—'Jhulelal'.

However, misfortune soon struck as Mata Devki passed away. Ratanchand remarried soon. Meanwhile, as it was already many months since the time of Mirkshah's threat, the five representatives were once again summoned to speak about their final answer. By now, all the community members were confident about the arrival of their saviour. Thus, they requested for some more time. Mirkshah had already heard about the birth of a miracle baby, but was amused to even think that he would be harmed in any manner by a simple baby. So, he allowed the five representatives some more time, but also put to work his minister, Ahirio, as a spy, to supply him with important news from Nasarpur.

Ahirio was cautious from the very beginning. He had heard that the baby was no ordinary child and he did not want to take any chances. Thus, he dipped a rose in a bowl of liquid poison and took it to the child. However, he was bedazzled at meeting the child. When he offered the poisonous rose a miracle took place. The child took the rose, threw it at his feet, and blew a puff of breath into the flower. Immediately the child transformed into an old man with a flowing white beard, then gradually, the image changed into that of a young sixteen-year-old boy and soon, it transformed into Uderolal, with a blazing sword in his hand and a troop of warriors trailing him.

Ahirio knew that he had seen the Sindhu Lord, and immediately returned to Mirkshah and narrated the incident. However, the latter remained steadfast and did not believe the story. That night, Ahirio once again dreamt of the vision of the boy transforming into an old man, then a young boy, and then Uderolal. When the following day Mirkshah heard about the vision, he asked Ahirio to counter the threat, but the latter only told him to be cautious and not take any drastic step.

In the meantime, Uderolal was growing up and he had received the Guru Mantra. He was hardworking and extremely intelligent and helped his stepmother to make ends meet. From his very childhood, he was extremely empathetic. When his stepmother would give him baked beans to sell in the market, he would go instead to the banks of the Sindhu River. There, he threw half of the beans into the water and distributed the remaining half among the needy. After that, he would spend the rest of the day speaking of spiritual matters with the people who would pass by on the banks of the river. In the evening, when it was time for him to return home, he would dip a container in the water of the river and withdraw it. This would be miraculously filled with fine quality rice. This he would take home and hand over to his stepmother to feed the family. One day, Uderolal's father, Ratanchand watched this miracle and realized that he was a spiritually gifted boy, and no ordinary person. He would soon rescue them from the despotic ruler of the land.

On the other hand, Mirkshah asked his minister Ahirio to arrange a meeting with Uderolal. He realized that no work would be done by forcing the people to act against their will. By now Ahirio was a devotee of Daryashah, another name of Uderolal, the king of rivers. Ahirio went to the bank of the Sindhu River and prayed to the water God to come to his rescue, and an elderly man with white beard appeared on a pala fish. Ahirio realized that Khwaja Khizr and Uderolal were the same. He also watched in amazement when Uderolal jumped onto a horse and galloped away to meet Mirkshah, with a blazing sword in the other hand.

Uderolal explained to Mirkshah that all creations were made by God and each one referred to him by different names. However, Mirkshah did not feel like listening to a youngster and ordered to have Uderolal arrested. At the very moment when the soldiers advanced towards Uderolal, great waves of water rose from nowhere and a disastrous fire broke out in the palace. They feared they would get drowned in the mighty waves and while escaping, the routes were gutted with fire. Once again, Uderolal pleaded with Mirkshah not to be a tyrant and harass people on the basis of religion. By now, Mirkshah had realized how foolish he had been and that Uderolal was no ordinary warrior; in reality, he was a God for all religions. The moment Mirkshah sought forgiveness, the waters receded, the fire disappeared, and all the courtiers who were trapped and hurt in the water and the fire appeared to be fine once again, as if nothing had happened. Mirkshah was further convinced about the powers of Uderolal and understood never to differentiate people on the basis of religion.

Uderolal asked his Hindu followers to build a temple to commemorate the day of Mirkshah's transformation. He also suggested that a fire be kept alight every day within the temple, and water be made available for the 'holy sip'. Uderolal appointed his cousin as the first head of the religious sect, which believed in the spiritual strength of water. He also gave him seven symbolic things, which are important to the followers who were called Daryahi.

His work was complete, and soon Uderolal left the mortal home for his heavenly abode. However, soon he was heard again when his followers from various faiths were debating on whether to build a 'qaba' or a 'samadhi' in his memory. His voice boomed across the rains and thunder, which instructed to build a shrine which would be acceptable to all religious communities. Thus, the architecture would have the face of a dargah as well as that of a temple.

Since then the Sindhi community has been worshipping Jhulelal and also have the most famous greeting, 'Jhulelal-Bera hi paar' (Jhulelal—obstacles have been crossed) and it shows the unifying spirit of water.

102

The Amrit Sarovar

This story is according to a tradition recorded in *Panth Prakash* by Giani Gian Singh. According to the legend, Duni Chand was a very rich landlord and also a famous revenue collector of the sixteenth century in the Patti district. He had five daughters and a very prosperous household. Nevertheless, his major obstacle took the shape of excessive vanity. He believed himself to be superior to all, even to the Almighty. However, his youngest daughter, Rajani, was quite unlike her father. She was modest, kind, and empathetic towards fellow beings. Thus, she often faced rebukes from her father for what he considered as wasting her time. One day it so happened that Duni Chand got offended at one of Rajani's remarks as the latter mentioned that God alone was superior and blessed everyone with bounty, which cannot be compared to any mortal, including her father. These words seemed to sting Duni Chand and it hurt his pride. 'How can my own daughter even think about something like this? I am above all. I have money and I have power. I will show her soon, what a mighty man I am,' thought Duni Chand and he decided to teach his daughter a lesson. Finally, he made up his mind and got Rajani married to Vikram Datt, a very poor person from Patti, who was suffering from leprosy.

After the marriage Rajani left the household with her husband and remained devoted to him inspite of his infectious condition. The couple led a life of abject penury. Rajani used to make ends meet and provide food for her ailing husband, and herself, by begging from door to door for alms, and looking for free food at langars. Since her husband was unable to walk, she used to carry him in a basket, and they would rest sometimes under the shades of large trees. One day, while visiting a specific site where Guru Ram Das (1534–81) was working towards establishing a new area for settlement, Rajani discovered the langar which the Guru looked after. She saw a pond nearby. Its crystal clear water shone under the sky and close by on the banks of the pond stood a large beri or jujube tree (*Ziziphus mauritiana*). Rajani found the shade of the tree very cooling, and placed her husband near the tree to rest as she went to fetch some food from the langar of Guru Ram Das. Little did she know that a wonderful surprise awaited her upon her return.

While sitting under the tree, Vikram had a vision. He saw a crow having a dip in the pond and emerging from it with pristine white feathers. This inspired Vikram. Slowly and steadily, he started to drag himself towards the pond, and when he reached, he slowly lowered himself into the cool waters and bathed in it. This was a miracle bath. Immediately, Vikram could see that his leprosy has been cured. Soon, when Rajani returned with the food, she could hardly believe her eyes. Vikram sat under the tree, completely cured from his dreaded disease. The couple were overjoyed and went to narrate this wonderful miracle to Guru Ram Das. He decided to make the pond into a lined tank with proper arrangements and called the tank 'amritsar' or the pool of nectar. In due course, this name was also applied to the settlement around it, and thus the name of the city—Amritsar. The pool got the name Amrit Sarovar and lies within the Golden Temple premises. The beri tree, near the pond under which Vikram's illness was cured, came to be known as 'Dukh Bhanjani Beri', or the eradicator of woes.

The Earliest Settlements of Lakshadweep

There is a famous legend from Lakshadweep, which speaks about a possible discovery of the various islands of the region and their earliest settlements as a result of a shipwreck. The story traces its origin to the time when the region was under King Cheraman Perumal of Kerala. The story is also recorded in R. H. Ellis's *A Short Account of the Laccadive Islands and Minicoy* (1924). According to the legend, Perumal, one day, disappeared from his kingdom. No one could locate him anywhere, and finally, it was assumed that he had travelled to Mecca along with some new friends who were Arab merchants. Now, the absence of the King is a serious problem, and thus many search parties were organised. They started off on boats from the capital of Perumal, Cranganore, the present day Kodungallor, in various directions across the Arabian Sea and the Indian Ocean. In those days, Cranganore was an important harbour city, which also connected the town of Kochi to Mecca. Vessels of various shapes and sizes took to the water across the region, but they were unable to locate the King, or any trace of his ship. As days passed and the vessels continued their search, it is believed that one day, one of the boats of the Raja of Cannanore was caught in a fierce storm. The boat was stranded on the island, now known as Bangaram. It was a completely new territory for the people from the stranded boat, and they began exploring the region. Wandering in the area, the search party reached Agatti. They could proceed no further because of the rough weather. Gradually, after a few days, the weather became slightly conducive and the stranded party returned to the mainland of the Indian subcontinent. On their way back, they discovered many other islands. It is also said that soon, another group of sailors discovered the island of Amini and started living there. Gradually small settlements started to grow in various islands and the first ones to be inhabited were Amini, Kavaratti, Andrott, and Kalpeni. It is also believed that subsequently, people from these places started to migrate to other islands like Agatti, Kiltan, Chetlat, and Kadmat, and thus settlements started to spread across the region.

104

Sage Gautama and River Godavari

Once, there was a very severe drought in and around the region of the Brahmagiri Mountain. People, plants, and animals were suffering alike and dying of starvation. There was no rainfall, the wells, ponds, and riverbeds were dry. The agricultural lands lay bare and parched. All around there was only pain and death, and this continued for a hundred years. The great sage Gautama, living in the Brahmagiri mountain, was pained to see the dire situation all around. He decided to pray to the Gods to find a solution. Thus, he started a deep tapasya (meditation) on the Brahmagiri Mountain. He started to pray to Lord Varuna, the God of rains and water. Gautam continued his tapasya and finally, after six months, Varuna appeared before him. Varuna blessed him and made him ask for a boon. Gautama described the sadness and desolation all around, and asked for the boon of an immediate rainfall. However, Varuna mentioned that the drought was a part of the cycle of natural phenomenon and it is an equal part of life and death. This has been decided by the Gods. Death will follow new life, and one has to patiently wait. Gautama patiently listened and realized the truth behind what Varuna had just told him, but in his mind, he was still searching for a solution for mankind, and he finally found an answer. He asked for the blessings of a continuous flow of an everlasting divine water, which will also yield permanent results. Varuna agreed and instructed Gautama to dig a ditch. After Gautama finished digging, Varuna filled it up with divine water, saying, 'Let there be a perennial supply of water in this sacred ditch. This ditch will be famous henceforth in your name and everything offered to this water will be considered as a holy offering.'

Thus, the people in and around the Brahmagiri Mountain started to experience life once more. Crops started to grow; trees and plants started to sprout new leaves, fruits, and flowers. Starving children and the elderly, who were suffering the most, started to gradually regain their health. There were smiles once more on the faces of everyone.

At this point, when life was just getting back to its regular rhythm, Gautama started to face a problem with the very water of the ditch which he had helped to dig. It so happened that one day, Gautama had sent his sishyas (disciples) to get water. However, they were rudely stopped by the wives of other sages, who wanted to fill up their pitchers first. The disciples returned and narrated their experience to Ahalya, the wife of Gautama. Ahalya thought that there will be no problem at all if they go before the arrival of anybody else. So, this time, Ahalya herself set off to fetch water. She reached the ditch early. No one was there. She filled up her water pitcher and started off for home. However, news reached the other sages and they realized that Ahalya had tricked everyone. They became furious and wanted to teach Gautama a lesson. They decided to pray to Ganesha for this. Thus, when Ganesha appeared, all the sages asked him to create a situation where Gautama will be forced to leave the hermitage. Ganesha found this to be alarming and advised all the sages not to hurt someone who had only done good for all. The sages kept insisting and Ganesha was also bound to grant a blessing to the devotees who had prayed to him. Thus, finally, Ganesha relented, as he had no option. He took the form of a weak and feeble cow and started to graze in the field in front of Gautama's house. Gautama saw that the cow was grazing on his crops and wanted to shoo her away. He took some blades of grass and threw them at the cow to make her go away, instead, the cow suddenly fell down on the ground. When Gautama went to have a closer look, he realized that the cow had died. Gautama was horrified for he simply could not understand how a few blades of thin grass could kill any animal. However, Gautama knew the consequences of what had just happened in front of him. He knew that he had committed the biggest crime of killing a cow, which is against his religion, and which demanded immediate penance. Thus, Gautama, along with Ahalya, left the hermitage and started to circumnavigate all around the Brahmagiri mountain range in an act of penance, speaking to everyone they met and telling them about the sin that he had committed. To add to his penance, at every stop, he created a Shiva Lingam and started to pray to Lord Shiva to seek his forgiveness. Gautama felt this was the only way his sin could be atoned and he continued this for a very long time. Then one day, Lord Shiva appeared in front of Gautama and the latter asked him to accept his penance and release him of his sin. Lord Shiva however laughed and said that Gautama is one of the greatest sages and he has never committed any sin. Gautama was surprised at the answer. Lord Shiva now explained everything and instead of being angry, Gautama started to think of purifying all of mankind. Thus, he asked Shiva to bring river Ganga to the region to purify the mind, body, and soul of everyone. Shiva blessed Gautama, who started praying to the river Ganga. Shiva too began to communicate with Ganga and instructed her, 'O Goddess, in the Kali Yuga, the son of Vivasvat will be the twenty-eighth Manu. Till then, you will remain in this region.' Ganga heard the prayers of both Shiva and Gautama but said that she would only agree to be there if Shiva also stays with her. Thus, Shiva manifested himself through the Jyotirlinga at the site of Tryambakeshwar, meaning the three-eyed Lord. Till today, the temple of Tryambakeshwar is an important site and is one of the twelve jyotirlingas in the nation.

Thus, Ganga remained in the region and she was initially

referred to as Gautami and later renamed as Godavari.

All the men started to purify their body and soul by taking a dip in the water of Godavari. But she was reluctant to allow the sages who had been so cruel to Gautama, to have a bath in her water. However, Ganga finally agreed on Gautama's insistence, but mentioned that it would be limited to a small area. Gautama agreed and he dug a ditch for her to emerge from. Whoever had a bath in the ditch, would be purified. This ditch still remains as the famous Kushavartha Tirtha at the Tryambakeshwar temple.

The Arrival of the Parsis to the Subcontinent

The first chapter of *Qissa-i-Sanjan* begins with the Zoroastrians leaving Greater Khorasan, after the fall of the Sassanid Empire by mid-seventh century CE. The travellers first reached a port city near Bushire, in present day Iran. The life there was full of hardships as they battled continuously for their community against the locals. Through tough times, fifteen long years went by, and one day, the sage Dastur advised them to move towards Hindustan to seek a better life for all. He said, 'The period during which we were permitted by fate to eat and drink in this land has come to an end. It will be well if we leave this country. We must go out of this region forthwith, otherwise we shall all fall into a snare, and prudence will then be useless and our business spoilt. It will be better therefore for us to fly from these fiends to Hindustan, and run away towards Hind for fear of life for religion's sake.'

Thus, a ship was made ready for the sea. It hoisted sail with the men, women, and children and rowed towards Hind. The ship anchored immediately when it sighted land and this was the Island of Diu. This is part of the present Union Territory of Dadra and Nagar Haveli and Daman and Diu in western India. Diu is situated on an island in the Gulf of Khambhat (Cambay) on the Arabian Sea, off the southern tip of the Kathiawar Peninsula in southwestern part of the state of Gujarat.

The travellers took up home and stayed there for nineteen years, and towards the end, once again their wise sage Dastur said, 'O my enlightened friends, hence also must we move to another spot which will be our second home.' All the members of the community were delighted to seek an equally better place and they set sail once again towards Gujarat.

However, soon after setting sail, the vessel was caught in a raging storm at sea, which completely took all the members aboard by surprise. The large ship rocked from side to side, and frequently started to spin in such a manner as if it was stuck within a whirlpool. Water was splashing all around and it was almost on the verge of being capsized. All the members feared the worst and started praying to the Almighty:

> O Thou Wise One, come to our aid on this occasion and for once deliver us from this distress. Thou, All Conquering Warharan, befriend us and lead us to victory on overcoming this adversity. We shall not care for the tempest and give no place to fear in our hearts. Hearken then to the complaints of the helpless, and show Thou the way to us who are lost in this waste of waters. If we escape from this dreadful storm, if disaster does not confront us, and if we reach the realm of Hind with cheerful hearts and merry thoughts, we shall kindle a great fire to Warharan. Deliver us then from this strait and keep us sound and strong. We are resigned to everything that comes from the Lord, for save Him, we possess no other friend.

The Almighty came to the rescue. The storm soon subsided and the Fire of the Glorious Warharan saw them to safety as a soft wind started to blow, completely wiping off the stormy weather. All the travellers prayed, and just as the captain started to steer the ship, it reached the coast of Sanjan.

In that region lived a virtuous king, named Jadi Rana. The travellers approached the king and requested asylum. The wise Dastur said, 'O Raja of Rajas, give us a place in this city. We are strangers who have arrived in thy town and place of residence seeking protection....' The king welcomed them, but was suddenly struck with fear at the thought of accepting complete strangers into his kingdom. Thus, he questioned the Dastur about their religion and also about their beliefs. He further put up four clauses for granting asylum and said, 'O thou devout Dastur, tell us, first of all what are your customs? Let me first see what your beliefs are and we will then arrange for your residence here. Secondly, if we give you shelter, you must abandon the language of your country, and adopt the speech of the realm of Hind. Thirdly, as to the dress of your women, they should wear garments like those of our women. Fourthly, you must put off all your arms and simitars and cease to wear them anywhere. Fifthly, when your children are wedded, the marriage should take place in the evening. If you first give a solemn promise to observe all this, you will be given places and abodes in my city.'

The Dastur heard all of these from the Raja and agreed. He replied, 'O sagacious king, hearken now to what I say of our creed. Do not be heavy hearted on our account, for never shall any evil deed proceed from us in this land. We shall be the friends of all Hindustan. Know then for certain that we are the worshippers of Yazdan, One God, and have fled only for our religion's sake. We have abandoned all we possessed and borne many hardships on the road. Houses and mansions and goods and chattels, we have all forsaken, O auspicious prince. We strangers are of the seed of Jamshed, and revere the Sun and the Moon. Three other things also out of Creation we hold in honour, *viz.* the Cow, Fire, and Water. Thus, we adore the Fire, Water, Cows, and the Sun and the Moon likewise. It is the Lord who has created all those things that are on earth, and we pray to them because he himself has preferred them. Our kushti (sacred girdle) is made of seventy-two threads and we repeat when we tie it on, solemn professions of Faith....' Likewise, the Dastur also explained about the women, who were strictly aloof from everything, and also explained about their other customs, rites and rituals, marriages, and arms and weapons. Having listened carefully to the Dastur, the Raja realized that the strangers were peace-loving people and were genuinely seeking asylum and a safe place to reside. He thus agreed to grant them an area to live.

Soon, the people set off in search of an ideal place to settle down. Finally, after surveying the land, a spacious plain was chosen, where the soil was excellent. It was here that the travellers started to build their home. The Dastur gave it the name of Sanjan and soon, it was flourishing as much as their original home far away. The place came to be known as Sanjan from that day onwards.

After settling down, the Dastur, accompanied by many, visited the court of the Raja and sought permission to build a Fire Temple. They said, 'O Prince, you have given us a dwelling spot in this land. We now wish to install in the Indian clime, the Fire of Bahram (Warharan).' They also highlighted several crucial aspects which must be observed in order to consecrate the temple. The Dastur said, they needed to clear at least three farsangs (an ancient Iranian or Persian unit of measurement for how far a man can walk in a day, stone to stone) of land, so that the ceremonies, connected with the sanctification, may be duly performed. He also added that in order to consecrate the temple the presence of individuals from other faiths should be avoided, and there should not be any kind of noise around the temple which will interrupt the ceremonies. The Raja agreed and very soon all arrangements to build a temple were made. All the members of the community provided as much help as they could. The Raja also sent offerings of many kinds. Many of the travellers had bought tools with them from their homeland, and they used these to build the temple following their own spiritual beliefs and customs. Finally, the temple was complete and the aged Dasturs thus installed the Iranshah, beaming with light, in conformity with their own rites and rituals. Then, all the lay people and the Dasturs celebrated the new temple in the new land.

The sacred Fire is subsequently referred to in the story as the 'Fire of Warharan'. The first chapter ends by describing many of the descendants of the original settlers who moved and dispersed in various directions.

106

The Lonar Lake and the Myth of Lonasura

There is the mention of Lonar Lake of Buldhana district of Maharashtra in Skanda Puran and Padma Puran as well as in Ain-i-Akbari. There is a mythological story about this lake which speaks of a demon named Lavanasura, also known as Lonasura. According to the story, he was a very fierce demon and was going around destroying everything that he could lay his hands on. He even struck fear in the minds of the mighty Gods, who were completely traumatized, and they started to appeal to Lord Vishnu to seek help and bring an end to Lavanasura. The petrified men on earth also started to pray to Vishnu. Finally, listening to the pleas of so many people from heaven and earth, Vishnu decided to confront Lavanasura and teach him a lesson. He assumed the form of a handsome youth, Daityasudan, and enquired about the whereabouts of Lavanasura from his sisters. This hiding place was amid rocks and between mountains. Thus, Daityasudan located the place, removed the covering of the cave, and destroyed the demon. It is believed that the present Lonar Lake was the den and hiding place of Lavanasura, and the crater was created in the place where Lord Vishnu pushed Lavanasura into the netherworld after his death. When Daityasudan killed Lavanasura after a fierce battle, his blood and the salt from his body is said to have been mixed with the water. Thus, it is also believed that the water of the lake turned murky and also saline. Even today, the water remains high in alkalinity and salinity with a pH of 10–10.5.

According to another famous story from the Ramayana, Lavanasura was killed by Rama's youngest brother, Shatrughna.

107

The Story of the Creation of the World

The Jadu patachitra of the Santhals depict a story of the creation of the world and this is their very own mythology. According to this story, once, long ago, there was nothing—no plants or animals on earth, but there was only water everywhere. At that time, Thakur Jiu made various aquatic creatures including the crabs, crocodiles, prawns, fish, worms, and turtles. Then the creator thought of making humans, so he created two humans with the mud from the water and infused life into them. However, soon, the mighty Sun horse came down from the sky above and trampled upon these figures of mud. The mud figures were broken and everything else was destroyed in the process. Thakur Jiu was sad to see everything destroyed, and started to think of another way to create life and also to sustain it. He thus, created two birds, a gander and a goose from the dirt of his chest. He named these as 'has' and 'hasil'. He then gave life to the birds. They flew around happily and finally came down and settled down on his hands. Soon, Thakur Jiu noticed that the Sun horse came down once again, but this time to drink water, and as he drank, foam dripped from his mouth and fell on the water. On seeing the floating foam on the river, Thakur Jiu thought of beginning the journey of life with the two birds which he had in his hand. At first, though they refused to fly and settle on the foam, they finally agreed, and the birds sat on the foam like a boat, which rocked gently on the water. Now, Thakur Jiu wanted to create land around the boat so that mankind can be created. He thus ordered the crocodile, prawn, and crab to bring earth from under the water, but none of them could get the mud for Thakur Jiu. Finally, the worm approached Thakur Jiu and said that he can get the job done, but he needed a flat and dry surface to drop the mud. Thakur Jiu ordered the turtle to lend his back. Thus, as the turtle spread all his four legs towards the four quarters, the worm dived down deep into the waters, ate some mud, and came back to the surface. He then excreted it and the mud fell on the back of the turtle. The worm continued this for sometime and collected enough mud on the back of the turtle. Then Thakur Jiu asked the worm to stop and he set forth to create earth, land, hills, and the mountains. Thakur Jiu levelled the earth with a crusher, however, some of the lumps of earth remained so and got stuck within the mud. These elevated areas became the hills and the mountains and the levelled regions became the flat land. Finally, on the foam on which the two birds were floating around the newly created earth, Thakur Jiu planted some seeds and the grass began to grow. The two birds, has and hasil, the goose and the gander laid two eggs on the grass. These eggs soon hatched and from this, the first man, Pilchu Harem and the first woman, Pilchu Budhi were born. The bird parents fed them with juice squeezed from food on to cotton wool, and they grew up in a place called Hihiri Pipiri. Thus, Hihiri Pipiri is the legendry land in Santhal mythology from which the original people had come.

108

How the Khecheopalri Lake Was Formed

The waters of the Lake Khecheopalri in Sikkim is considered sacrosanct and it is believed that it has curative powers. There are many mythological stories associated with the origin of the lake, which is also considered a 'wish fulfilling lake'.

According to one of the stories about the origin of the lake, a long time ago, the region where the present lake stands, used to be a grazing ground, but had wild growth of nettle all over. The barks of the nettle have traditionally been used by the locals for various purposes. One day, a couple belonging to the Lepcha community was peeling off the bark of the nettle for their household need, when they were suddenly surprised to see a pair of conch shells fall from the sky onto the ground. This unexpected appearance of the conch shells was followed by a severe shaking of the ground and suddenly spring water burst forth from below. This water gradually filled up the area, and thus the lake was formed. The sacred Nesol text of Buddhist rituals, mentions that the lake is the abode of Tshomen Gyalmo or Chief Protective Nymph of the Dharma as blessed by Goddess Tara.

Among the other mythological stories associated with the lake, one says that the Guru Padmasambhava preached to sixty-four yoginis here. Another belief suggests the lake to be the footprint of Goddess Tara Jetsun Dolma, and she is also said to reside there. The lake is also said to represent Goddess Chho Pema. The footprints of Macha Zemu Rinpoche is said to be found on a stone beside the stupa near the lake. The lake is also worshipped by Hindus as it is believed that Lord Shiva once meditated in the Dupukney cave above the lake. Thus, Shiva is worshipped on Nag Panchami in the region.

Acknowledgements

This book has journeyed through difficult phases since its inception. Gratitude is owed to the unwavering support and steadfast encouragement of my family, whose invaluable assistance ensured the fruition of this project. Mini, Cindy, Gargi, Ma—this is all because of you.

I'm grateful to my editor at Aleph, Aienla Ozukum for initiating this literary voyage that has been enriching and enlightening.

Finally, this work is an ode to the world of storytelling, which spans diverse landscapes, cultures, languages, and experiences. I thank my dear readers, and hope this vibrant array of captivating narratives will shape your perception and connect you to our shared humanity.

Notes to the Stories

NORTHERN REGION

1. THE HARE-SHAPED MARK ON THE SURFACE OF THE MOON: This is a story from 'Sasa Jataka'. Animals and plants are variously represented in 'The Jataka' stories and they form vital parts of each one of them. All the Jataka stories, are also intrinsically related to nature, and this story is an important example of the same. The Jataka stories follow the belief that the Buddha did not attain enlightenment in one life. He became perfectly enlightened as a result of good deeds done in numerous earlier births across many centuries. In the rebirths, after he became conscious of his mission, he is spoken of as a Bodhisattva (Buddha elect) and the story of Bodhisattva's births are narrated in the Jataka tales.

2. HOW THE PARIJAT TREE CAME DOWN TO EARTH FROM THE HEAVENS: The tree is famously known as Parijaat, Parijat, or Night-flowering jasmine (*Nyctanthes arbor-tristis*). It is found across South and parts of Southeast Asia. The tree often grows to more than ten metres in height and its flowers are fragrant. These fragrant flowers are often used in festivals, rituals, and puja across South Asia. There is also a sacred tree in the village of Kintoor, near Barabanki, Uttar Pradesh, about which there are several mythological stories. These stories associate the tree as a Kalpavriksha (wish fulfilling tree) and it has appeared in the Bhagavata Purana, the Mahabharata, and the Vishnu Purana.

The fragrant flower of the Parijat tree is the official flower of the state of West Bengal in India, and of the Kanchanaburi Province in Thailand. The flower is variously referred to in different languages across South Asia, including India, like Harshringaar in Bihar's Mithila-anchal, Madhesh, Parijat, Shiuli or Shefali in Bengali, Xewelee in Assamese, Parijatha in Kannada, Parijatam in Telugu, Pavizhamalli in Malyalam, Pavazhamalli in Tamil, Paardak in Konkani, and Prajakta in Marathi. Outside India, it is known as Sepalika in Sinhala, in Sri Lanka, and Seikphaloo in Burmese in Myanmar.

3. HOW HARITI BECAME A PROTECTOR OF CHILDREN AND ALSO A PART OF SCULPTURE: The story of Hariti occurs in detail in 'Vinaya Pitaka' of the Sarvastivada School, the 'Mahavastu', and the 'Samyukta Ratna Sutra' of the Chinese 'Sutta Pitaka'. The Chinese pilgrims, Hiuen Tsang (arrived in India in 632 CE) and I-tsing (arrived in India in 673 CE), also mentioned in their writings that they saw many examples of monasteries with the presence of Hariti in both India and Nepal. Hiuen Tsang also mentions Peshawar, where a stupa was built in honour of Hariti by Emperor Ashoka, and people offered sacrifices to seek her blessings to obtain offsprings.

4. LEGEND OF SURDAS'S COMPOSITIONS ABOUT LORD KRISHNA: Surdas (1483-1563) was an important Bhakti poet, a follower of the Vallabha school of Vedanta. He lived and died in Braj. He is known for his 'Sursagar' (Ocean of the poems of Sursagar), which is a collection of poems, based on the stories of the childhood of Krishna found in the Bhagavata Purana.

5. THE STORY OF ADITI, THE DIVINE MOTHER OF ALL: In the Rig Veda, Aditi is mentioned more than 250 times, where all the verses praise her. She is believed to support the sky, sustain all existence, and nourish the earth. She is the personification of the infinite cosmos, the Goddess of motherhood, unconsciousness, the past, the future, and also of fertility. In the Rigveda, Aditi is a very important figure and she is often asked to guard the one who petitions her (Mandala 1.106.7; Mandala 8.18.6) or to provide him or her with wealth, safety, and abundance (Mandala 10.100;1.94.15). A mother to all beings, she is also associated with space and speech. In later texts, she is also often mentioned as a divine cow. The number of the sons of Aditi are also often linked to the twelve solar months of the year.

6. TO STAND UNITED LIKE TREES IN A FOREST: This is a story of Rukkhadhamma Jataka (from Book 1: Ekanipata, No. 74).

7. AMIR KHUSRO'S UNBOUND DEVOTION FOR HIS PIR: Hazrat Amir Khusro (1253–1325 CE) was born as Abul Hasan Yaminuddin in Patiali, in Uttar Pradesh. His father was Amir Saifuddin Mahmud. Khusru was a poet and a historian, and is considered to be one of India's greatest Persian-language poets. He enjoyed the patronage of many Sultans of Delhi. He was a dedicated follower of the saint of Delhi, Muhammad Nizamuddin Awliya of the Chisti Dervish order. His respect and devotion for his Pir is also reflected in the fact that, after his death, he was also buried next to the saint's tomb.

8. THE LEGEND OF SHAMBHALA: The concept of Shambhala plays an important role in Tibetan religious teachings, and has particular relevance in Tibetan mythology about the future. The Vishnu Purana also states that Shambhala is the designated birth place of the Kalki avatar (form) of Vishnu. According to this scripture, it is believed that through Kalki, in the imminent future, a new age known as Satya Yuga will be ushered in. It is described as a celestial place, where only Gods reign, and is also well-guarded by holy spirits.

In all the legends, the mention of the dark and evil forces is metaphorical and is believed to represent the basic decline in standards of living, thinking, and behaviour of mankind, as such ideologies like egoism, self-centeredness, and selfishness spread far and wide and pervade all life on earth. It is believed, that at such a time, when these evil forces will gain control, there will be a gradual deterioration of values and principles of honesty, truthfulness, piety, and empathy. Thus, the battle between the Dark Forces and Shambhala can be perceived through various layers of perspectives.

It is also important to understand that though the Kalachakra prophecies war, this goes against the basic tenet of non-violence of Buddhism. Thus, many interpret the war to be a representation of winning over the negative parts of oneself through positive energies, thinking, and principles. These two types of symbolic meanings about nature and all living creatures are passed down orally from teacher to student. The fourteenth Dalai Lama also noted during a speech at Bodh Gaya in 1985, at the Kalachakra initiation, that Shambhala is no ordinary physical place, but a pure land, and one needs merit to go there through their karmic connections.

9. THE DREAMS OF QUEEN TRISHALA: All the dreams of Queen Trishala reflect an ecclesiastical connection between spiritual liberation and the rhythm and energies of nature. The guided path of salvation is charted out by virtues, which imbibe all their forces from nature. Thus, the spiritual path and awakening is always blessed with the gentle touches of nature.

10. SOME TALES FROM THE JANAMSAKHIS: Guru Nanak Devji (1469–1539 CE) was born in a village called Talwandi, nearly forty kilometres away from Lahore in present day Pakistan. In his early twenties, he moved to Sultanpur on the main road between Lahore and Delhi, and worked as a clerk in the Lodi administration. When he was about thirty, he had a remarkable spiritual experience and a direct encounter with God, which changed the course of his life forever. The stories of Janamsakhis are narrated by the Sikh community about the childhood days of Guru Nanak Devji and his engagement with various social issues. They also highlight his honesty, truthfulness, and devotion.

Guru Nanak Devji travelled to many places. Early Sikh sources also speak of his travels to the Middle East. He preached his messages in the form of beautiful hymns, called 'shabads'—the words as a guide from darkness into light. He was accompanied by his friend and musician, Mardana. Guru Nanak Dev Ji sang of the oneness of God and the equality among people. The anecdotes shared among his disciples provide insight into the profound teachings he imparted. The Janamsakhis are legendary biographies of Guru Nanak Dev Ji. The story of the giant fish speaks about faith in God, and about doing hard work, while sharing everything with fellow beings. This story has been depicted in art, namely the Paheri (Guler) and the Murshidabad schools of art, and both dating back to between 1755–1770. An unpainted image is preserved at the Government Museum and Art Gallery in Chandigarh, India, and a painted version is at the Asian Art Museum, San Francisco, USA.

11. THE STORIES OF SAINT LAL DED: Lal Ded was born in the early 1300s in Kashmir into a Hindu family and she was married into a Brahmin family of Pampor. It is believed that her life at her in-laws was very rough and she would spend most of her time in meditation, which would bring solace to her troubled mind.

In life I sought neither wealth nor power,
Nor ran after the pleasures of sense.
Moderate in food and drink, I lived a controlled life,
And loved my God.*

Her 'vakhs' remain famous till date. There are many lores in oral traditions about Lal Ded and her miracles.

12. PHULAICH—FLOWER FESTIVAL OF HIMACHAL PRADESH: During the course of the festival, many deities are worshipped, including Mahasu, Kali, Usha, Chandrika, amongst others. During the festivities, drums are occasionally played, and bugles are blown. These are commemorative parts of the festival, celebrating the remarkable feat of the ten men who ascended the hill and collected the flowers, as per the legend. According to tradition, one man from each family proceeds to go up the hill to collect the flowers. They spend the night up on the hill, collect the flowers and come down the next morning. Often tourists and vacationers throng the place during the festival and also participate in various events.

13. THE STORY OF THE CHARKULA DANCE: Only womenfolk perform this dance with 108 oil lamps on their head. The burning lamps are organized, in a tiered, circular, wooden, pyramid-like structure. This is generally a solo dance and when one woman completes her performance, the Charkula is passed on to the next solo dancer. Since the lamps are heavy, the dancers are trained well before the performance and also placed on a special diet to carry the weight of the lamps on their heads.

The Charkula dancers dance to the beat of a huge drum with one face, called the bamb. The dance is also accompanied by other instruments like chimta and jhanj, all of which provide rhythm to the dancer. The faces of the dancers remain covered with a veil and only the lamps are prominently visible. The performances are set to the tunes hailing Lord Krishna.

The legend and the performance both pay obeisance to the mighty forces

---

*Lal Ded- 5th verse- from- Kaul, Jayalal 2018 Lal Ded. Sahitya Akademi: New Delhi. Parimoo, B. N. 2013 The Ascent of Self. Motilal Banarsidass: New Delhi.

of nature, which are overwhelming on one hand and yet subtle, mild, and tender. They remind us of the life-giving forces of nature. In front of both these forces of representation, humans can only bow down in reverence.

14. HARIYALI DEVI OF UTTARAKHAND: The Indian epic, The Mahabharata mentions the story of the birth of Lord Krishna. There are various local interpretations of many parts of this story and this is one of them. The deity is also worshipped as Bala Devi and Vaishno Devi.

The Hariyali Devi temple is surrounded by the Himalayan Mountains and forests, and it is situated at a height of 1,400 metres. The Devi also harbours Van Devi or Forest Spirits and the felling of trees is prohibited. Only the branches of trees which have fallen off, are allowed to be taken away. This also helps to protect the biodiversity of the area.

NORTHEASTERN REGION

15. THE ORIGIN OF THE DAOPHANG AMONG THE DIMASA: The story presented here has an interesting touch. Not only does it speak about a close association of the community with nature, but also their ethos of handloom weaving. The story highlights the significant role of the matriarch as a decision-maker and also the matrilineal nature of a family. As a prominent figure, she exhibits the capacity not only to choose a fitting home for her children, but also to identify a suitable place for herself for her own retirement in later years. This is an important lesson from the myth of the Dimasas, and it is a role which also reflects a close association with nature.

The Dimasa community is one of the oldest indigenous communities of the northeast and can be mostly seen in Assam. They belong to an Indo-Mongoloid group of people. The word Dimasa is formed from the confluence of three words from the Dimasa dialect—'di' meaning water, 'ma' meaning big or great and 'sa' meaning son. Thus, it forms the literal meaning of being the son or descendants of a big river. This also relates to the fact that the Dimasas consider themselves to be the descendants of the Brahmaputra River.

Weaving is an integral part of the community. Traditionally all women were taught to weave. However, in recent times, many men can also be seen to be a part of the profession. The daophang is a traditional loom, and presently there are three types of daophang in use. Every household has a daophang in their front or backyards or in a separate room, which is referred to as the 'daophangkho' or the room for the loom. There are numerous enchanting folk songs traditionally sung by women, accompanying the art of weaving.

16. THE LEGEND OF KEIBU KEIOIBA FROM MANIPUR: Keibu Keioiba is a mythical creature in Meitei mythology of Manipur. He is described as having the head of a tiger and the body of a human.

The appearance of a mythical creature, which embodies humans and tigers is a common appearance across mythologies and folktales of many other states of Northeast India, including Nagaland, Meghalaya, Assam, among others. Often referred to as the stories of the 'tiger people', they express the belief that the human consciousness can merge with that of a tiger. The tiger man or the woman is thus, the liminal human-animal being, who belongs to the community, but moves across alternate realities. However, often these are expressed negatively, like in the story presented here.

This exact story is also part of popular folklore of erstwhile Bengal region (including the present country of Bangladesh). It features among the compiled collection of folktales, published in 1911 in the book titled—*Tuntunir Boi* (The stories of the tailor bird) by noted author, publisher, poet and illustrator—Upendrakishore Ray Chowdhury. He is the father of poet, author, and illustrator Sukumar Ray and grandfather of auteur, author, illustrator and Bharat Ratna, Satyajit Ray.

17. HOW THE MIZO FESTIVAL OF PAWL KUT ORIGINATED: The festival of Pawl Kut is held after the paddy harvest in January. Thus, the Mizo name for the month of January is 'Pawl kut thla' or the month of Pawl Kut. Children and women, especially, take great pleasure in participating in the festival. New clothes are worn and good food is served. Children usually have 'chhawnghnawt', in which they feed each other meat, eggs and rice. The Mizos have three annual festivals called 'Kut'. All of these mark the three different stages of the agricultural processes of their lives. These three festivals are 'Chapchar Kut', 'Mim Kut', and 'Pawl Kut'.

The Mizo are an ethnic group and are native to the state of Mizoram but are also found in other neighbouring states of Northeastern India. The name also includes many related ethnic groups or clans inside the Mizo group.

18. THE LUSHAI STORIES OF THE CREATION OF THE WORLD: This is a story of the Lushai tribe of Tripura. This is another tribe under the Kuki-chin group of tribes and they were traditionally found mainly in Kanchanpur sub-division of North Tripura. They practice jhum cultivation and thus, agriculture forms an important part of their lives, which is evident from the story mentioned here.

19. THE ORIGIN OF SOME ETHNIC COMMUNITIES OF MANIPUR: A close analysis of myths and legends of various communities often speak of their travels, migrations, and settlements as well as resettlements in the past. These often provide vital information to support historical documents. These stories also speak of all the communities having a close bond with nature and diligent efforts to find a peaceful place to reside in.

The Anal are some of the oldest settlers of present-day Manipur and the community can be found both in India and Myanmar. The Anal is also one of the '66 Naga Tribes' of the Naga ancestral homeland. They speak their own language—Anal.

The Thadous are also found in India and Myanmar. The Thadou language belongs to the Kuki-Chin subgroup of the Tibeto-Burman language. It is widely spoken across Manipur and is the second largest language after Meiteilon (the Meitei language).

The Chiru is a small tribe of Manipur with their own set of customs and beliefs.

The Lamkang is a Naga tribe of Manipur. They also reside in Myanmar. They share close cultural and language similarities with the Anal community.

The Purum are an Old Kuki tribe of the Manipur Hills. Apart from India, they are also in Mayanmar. They speak Purum, which is a Tibeto-Burman language.

The Koireng of Manipur are referred to by the Thadou/Kuki as Kolhen. Originally they were called 'Kolren', meaning men of the east and their oral traditions speak of their travels from far away lands in the east.

20. HOW TEZPUR GOT ITS NAME: Tezpur is an important city on the northern banks of River Brahmaputra in Assam. The story of Usha and Aniruddha is from the Srimad Bhagavatam. A popular story, it has found expression in many places in popular culture as well, including paintings, novels, dance dramas, and films. The story is, once again, a reminder of the many creation stories which narrate the pattern of renewal of life after a cataclysmic episode; life, peace, and harmony are once again restored among mankind.

21. THE STORY OF RIJU DUNE: The Gallong segment of the Adi tribal community is mostly seen in the West Siang district of Arunachal Pradesh. It is performed towards the later part of autumn, from November to December. Both men and women participate in the dance. The leader of the dance is called the Min. All the dancers repeat the lyrics of the Min and swing their hands while moving forward and backward to the rhythm of the song.

22. THE LEGEND OF THE ORIGIN OF THE GREAT HORNBILL: These are Sumi Naga stories about the origin of the colourful hornbill. It is also an integral part of most of the tribes of Nagaland. The hornbill is held with great esteem among the Nagas, which is also evident in the famous Hornbill Festival of Nagaland. The usage of the hornbill feather in the traditional attire signifies prestige and honour. In India, nine species of hornbills are found, and Nagaland is home to five of them, including Oriental Pied hornbill, Rufous-necked hornbill, Wreathed hornbill, Brown hornbill, and Great hornbill. Unfortunately, at present, the Great hornbill is also said to be endangered.

23. THE LEGEND OF U THLEN: Reptiles frequently hold prominent roles in the mythologies of various cultures worldwide, featuring both favourable and unfavourable depictions.

24. HOW ECLIPSES BEGAN: The Bugun tribe of Arunachal Pradesh was formerly known as Khowa, and they are mostly seen in the Singchung subdivision of West Kameng district of Arunachal Pradesh. They are one of the earliest recognized scheduled tribes of India. According to their legend, they are the descendants of a single forefather, named Achinphumphulua.

25. WHY HOUSES ARE BUILT ON STILTS IN MIZORAM: Mizoram, often also called as the 'Land of the Blue Mountains', has evergreen ranges, exotic flora, and dense bamboo jungles. There are many sparkling waterfalls and rivers, and also the Phawngpui, which is also called The Blue Mountain, which has the highest peak in the Mizo hills in Mizoram. It has an elevation of 2,157 metres. It is in the southeastern region of Mizoram, near the Myanmar border.

26. HOW HUMANS LEARNT TO UNDERSTAND THE NATURE OF ANIMALS: Sangpangtu is a symbolic celebration of the Ao Naga festival—Moatsu. This is celebrated in the first week of May every year, and various rituals are performed during this period. Moatsu is a harvest festival, which is observed after the sowing is done. It is celebrated as a period of recreation after the stressful days from the work in the fields, sowing seeds, cleaning up the tsubu (well), and also repairing of houses. The Moatsu festival is observed through many songs and dances.

27. THE SAD LEGEND OF NOHKALIKAI FALLS: According to many, the howling and eerie sound of the wind and the water might have given birth to the sad story of the Nohkalikai Falls. Meghalaya is also referred to as the 'abode of the clouds'. Nohkalikai Falls is a famous tourist destination. It is the highest plunge waterfall of India, standing at 340 metres (1,115 feet) and is surrounded by verdant and exotic natural beauty. It is located near Cherrapunji, one of the wettest places on earth.

28. THE LEGENDS OF UNAKOTI: Unakoti is 178 kilometres from Agartala, the capital city of Tripura in the Unakoti district. The site has a thirty feet head of Shiva, known as Unakotiswara Kal Bhairava, along with the sculptures of the Goddesses Ganga and Durga and many other deities, including Hanuman and Ganesha. The place has many festivals and an annual mela (fair) known as 'Ashokastami Mela', held in the month of April, which is visited by thousands of pilgrims.

EASTERN REGION

29. THE NABAGUNJARA FROM SARALA DAS'S MAHABHARATA: In Sarala Das's Mahabharata, the Nabagunjara is considered a variant of the 'virat-rupa' of Vishnu, who, by assuming the form, merges his own divinity into the animals in a manner of tribute to the animal world, and thus to the environment.

Sarala Das was a very famous poet and his other famous works of literature include Vilanka Ramayana, Chandi Purana, and Laxmi Narayana Vachanika. The Nabagunjara is often mentioned as the unique and original display of Das's genius and creativity. This version of the Mahabharata is also often referred to as the 'Sarala Mahabharata'.

The Nabagunjara occupies an important part in various traditional artworks and architecture of Odisha and is a common motif in the patachitra style of traditional artwork of Odisha. The Nabagunjara-Arjuna scene is sculpted at the northern side of the temple of Jagannath in the Puri district of Odisha. The Nila Chakra disc, on top of the Jagannath temple also has eight Nabagunjaras carved on the outer circumference, with all of the Nabagunjaras facing the flagpost. The Nabagunjara is also displayed on Ganjifa playing cards of Puri district and Ath-rangi Sara in Ganjam district. This particular set of cards is referred to as the Nabagunjara set. Within the set of cards, the one marked as the king, shows the Nabagunjara, while the card marked for the minister has Arjuna.

30. A MUNDA SONG OF BIRTH AND DEATH: This is translated from Munderi. The song speaks about various aspects of our lives and leaves an important lesson for all, as it highlights equality between men and women, and their equal need to preserve the balance of prosperity amidst nature and our lives. The poem also highlights the aspect of the bride price, which is a traditional custom and thus, having a girl in the house is seen to be more significant.

The Munda tribe is traditionally from parts of Jharkhand, West Bengal, Assam, Tripura, Madhya Pradesh, and Odisha. The headman of the village is also known as Horohon or Mura. The Munderi language is spoken in large parts of India and there is also an encyclopedia of the language—*Encyclopaedia Mundarica* (16 Volumes) by Reverend John Baptist Hoffman (1857–1928) and other Jesuit scholars.

31. HOW THE KOJAGARI LAKSHMI PUJA CAME TO BE POPULAR: Lakshmi is considered as the deity of prosperity, good health, wealth, and bounty. Lakshmi is worshipped all over the country and in specific parts of eastern India; she is worshipped on full-moon days of each month and also on each Thursday of the week. An annual puja also takes place on the full-moon day of the Indian agricultural month of Ashwina (September–October). This full-moon is also referred to as 'Kojagori Purnima' (purnima meaning a full-moon) and the puja is referred to as 'Kojagori Lakshmi Puja'. In the eastern parts of India, there is a mythological story attributed to the puja which takes place each month.

The present story is specifically associated with Kojagori Lakshmi puja of Ashwina. This specific puja is mostly performed within households, and the story highlights the people within a house seeking blessings for a prosperous life and overall well-being. This is reflected through the presence of judicious thinking, wise decisions, benevolent efforts, and wise spending, among others. Often these are believed to be blessings of the Goddess of prosperity—Lakshmi.

32. THE ORIGIN OF THE KARENS OF THE ANDAMANS: This is a story of the Karens from the Andaman Islands and this story of origin is still preserved within the Karen community till today. The original story is in the Karen or Karenic languages, which is often considered to be affiliated to the Sino-Tibetan languages, though many critics also opine otherwise. According to the Karens, their name derives from the Burmese words for 'shyness' and 'politeness'. Research about the earliest history of the origin, travels and migration of the Karens still continues. In the Andamans, the miniscule Karens can be traditionally found in Middle and North Andamans. This story indicates a possible travel from their original homeland in the north, which is also often stated to be in Central Asia. It also suggests a possible association with China and their settlements in Burma, followed by the Andaman Islands, and finally a friendly acceptance within the inhabitants of the Andamans.

Historically, the Karens trace their beginning to the Andaman Islands nearly a century ago, around 1925. There is a legend associated with the arrival of the first Karens to the island. Responding to an advertisement of a British scheme—a year's ration free for settlers in the islands, who are willing to work in the massive timber trade, the first Karens arrived in the islands from Myanmar.

The Karens have great regard for nature and consider keeping it pristine and clean. Over the decades, the isolation and reticence of the Karens have helped them to preserve their culture, despite the turbulent times in history.

33. LIMBU MYTH ABOUT RITUAL OFFERING OF NEWLY HARVESTED FOOD GRAINS: The mundhum, based on oral literature of the Limbu language, gives an important insight into the basic understanding of nature and society in the Kirat community, including thoughts about the universe, birth, and death. This story also follows the pattern of thanking God for a harvest season and seeking blessings for an upcoming prosperous harvest.

34. CREATION MYTHS OF BIRDS, BEASTS, AND FISHES OF THE ANDAMAN: It is understood that the introduction and the practice of fire in an organized manner, provided through non-natural sources, began during the colonial times across the Andaman Islands. This was especially true for the few zones that witnessed construction of various public spaces by the British administration during the colonial times. Outside these areas, however, the significance of fire had existed for centuries together and was considered as an important and also sacrosanct part of nature. Thus, the stories reflect its various associations, including being an aid in helping to create life across the region.

35. HOW BONBIBI HAS BEEN PROTECTING THE SUNDARBANS: Bonbibi, Dakkhin Rai, and Gazi are generally placed together. It is also believed by the devotees that it shows how people from various creeds and castes coexist and come together to a common agreement while dealing with the forest. According to popular belief, Bonbibi, the woman of the forest was chosen by Almighty Allah. She protects people who work in the Sundarbans against the wrath of Dakkhin Rai, who is considered a greedy man-eater and a demon, who is half a Brahmin sage and half a tiger. The people of the region identify themselves with Dukhey and are convinced that Bonbibi protects all who believe in her. It is also believed that when one enters the forest, one should not be greedy and only take what is needed to sustain oneself. This is a belief in folklore, but it also reflects an important part of forest protection.

There are various rural theatres which often narrate this story of Bonbibi and Dakkhin Rai. The story can also be found in present day folklore books or graphic novels. There is a very famous poem, composed in 1686 called 'Ray-Mangal', composed by Krishnaram Das. There is also a booklet, *The Bonbibi Johuranamah*, written by Abdur Rahim towards the end of the 1800s, which narrates the story of Bonbibi. Interestingly enough, though this was written in Bengali, yet it is formatted from back to front, to emulate the Arabic script.

36. A HALBI STORY OF THE MOON, STARS, AND THE SUN: Similar stories of explanations of natural occurrences form significant parts of myths from around the world. This is a traditional story of the Halbi language. This story was originally written in Devanagari by Chingaru Ram Baghel. The Halbi language is an Eastern Indo-Aryan language with influences of both Odia and Marathi. The script is also of Odia and Devanagari. It is spoken across the central part of India.

37. THE LEGEND OF TAI PAK KUNG OR TONG ATCHEW: The main Chinese temple is a low-roofed structure, painted bright red and covered in Chinese calligraphy. Behind the temple, stands a small temple of Dakkhin Ray, the deity of the Sundarbans, and across the road is a temple of Bonbibi from the Sundarbans. Today, the tomb of Atchew is a pilgrimage for many Chinese, who have previously migrated out of Kolkata to far-off lands like the USA or Canada. They often visit the tomb of Tai Pak Kung. This is mainly seen around the time of the Chinese New Year. As a symbolic gesture, they burn paper money and incense sticks and offer food and wine in front of the sanctum. During the time of the Chinese New Year, for a few weeks annually, the small town of Achipur comes alive with the visiting pilgrims. They pay homage to their ancestor and seek blessings for a prosperous year ahead, and the general well-being of man and nature. There is also another idol of Atchew in the Sea Voi- Yune Leong Futh Church in Black Burn Lane, in Kolkata.

38. WHY THE SKY WAS PUSHED BACK FROM THE EARTH: An interesting aspect is highlighted through the story about keeping the household and its surroundings clean. The act of cleaning a house during festivals or rituals is seen across the world. Though such activities are often associated with propitiating the deities, however, they also have an important message of generally keeping the surroundings clean and maintaining health and hygiene where one resides.

39. HOW THE TWELVE MONTHS OF THE LEPCHA CALENDAR CAME INTO BEING: This is a creation story of the Lepchas, especially heard in the Darjeeling and Sikkim areas. There are however, many variants of this story. The mention of the changing forms is a reflection of each month of the year closely embodying various aspects of the environment. It is also an act of paying reverence to the manifold aspects of the natural world. Such instances of the months of a year, being associated with the representations of various animals is also seen in many other calendars of the world, like the Chinese calendar.

40. THE STORY OF THE ORIGIN OF BHADU SONGS: There are historical records that mention Nilmani Singha Deo as the king of Kashipur of Raghunathganj subdivision of Purulia. His wife's name has been variously mentioned as both Anupkumari and Kalavati. Bhadrabati is often stated to be their own daughter and researchers point out that she was born in 1841. She lived for 17 years and in 1858, a day before her marriage, she seemed to have lost her life in some tragic accident. Thereafter, a grieving king started the month-long mourning with songs, which gave rise to the concept of Bhadu brata songs and a final puja to be held on the sankranti. Though the historical records of the royal family mention Nilmani Singha Deo and his wife Anupkumari/Kalavati, there is no mention of Bhadrabati. Often researchers mention this as a possible deliberate attempt to remove the name of the princess, who seems to have tarnished the reputation of the family. Such omissions are common across pages of history of the world. On the other hand, it is also often stated by researchers that the story of Bhadu got entwined within an already existing set of harvesting rites of the region, making it part of local lore, which eulogises the local King Nilmani Singha Deo, his deeds and his family members. In the absence of further historical records, it is difficult to explain the existence of Princess Bhadrabati and her life and death, but the oral traditions do testify that the story still remains an integral part of local mythology. It has remained famous through decades and has been mentioned across several rural theatres and musical performances. The remains of the historical palace of Nilmani Singha Deo still stand as a testimony to the Bhadu songs—an important aspect of local life.

The festival is celebrated with Bhadu brata songs in the Indian agricultural month of Bhadrapada (August–September), followed by a puja on Sankranti. It is observed across various districts of West Bengal, including Purulia, Burdwan,

Bankura, Birbhum, and West Mednipur. Bhadu festival is also celebrated in some parts of the adjoining states including Bihar and Jharkhand. Famous academic Prof Ashutosh Bhattacharya had comprehensively mentioned them in his works many decades ago. Bhadu festival coincides with the time of harvesting and it is also considered as the worship of Lakshmi or the Goddess of prosperity during the harvesting season. It is also suggested that one who performs the month-long Bhadu brata songs, will be blessed by the various avatars of Goddess Lakshmi like, Yasholakshmi, Bhagyalakshmi, and Kulalakshmi. Thus, Bhadu is also considered the deity of the harvesting season, which is observed in celebration of the new harvest in the month of Bhadrapada.

41. THE STORY OF TAPOI: The story of Tapoi is a famous legend from Odisha, closely connected to water and its prosperous blessings. The legend is recited in the Khudurukuni osha. Celebrated mainly in the coastal region of Odisha in the month of Bhadrapada (August–September), it is also related to the festival of Boita Bandana or Bali Yatra, which is observed in the region during the time of Kartik Purnima in November (the full moon of November). Thus, the celebration is very closely linked to water and is in remembrance of their prosperous trading activities in the past. They traded with various regions of South and Southeast Asia, including Sri Lanka, Java, Sumatra, Vietnam, among others, using biotas (boats). As the merchants would sail far, their family members would pray for their safe travel and return, which is also emphasised through the story of Tapoi, which particularly mentions her brothers who travel to Bali for trade. The very essence of the story is the safe return of the merchants, the prosperity which followed therein and the ending of oppressive and stressful times.

The rites and rituals of the festival involve the worship of Goddess Mangala, which differs slightly from urban to rural regions. In the rural regions, the Goddess is worshipped at the dhinkishala (where rice is pounded). Within urban areas, where it is difficult to find a water body, the rituals take place within the home, but with familiar arrangements. The Goddess is offered khuda bhaja (broken rice), ukhuda (flattened paddy sweetened with molasses), chuda (flattened rice), kanti kakudi (cucumber), lia (fried paddy), misri (rock sugar crystals), and various types of fruits. Since the main offering is khuda, the name 'Khudurukuni'is derived from it. Girls fast and pray every Sunday, including narrating the story of Tapoi. The fourth and last Sunday witnesses the final pompous celebration.

42. THE MAHABHARATA AND THE MANY CONNECTIONS WITH PURNIA:

The city of Purnia is the administrative headquarters of the district of Purnia in Bihar. Apart from its mention in the Mahabharata, the region's history can also be traced back to the very ancient times. The Mithila kingdom or the Kingdom of the Videhas became a major political and cultural centre of ancient India (along with Kuru and Panchala) during the late Vedic period (1100-500 BCE). The kings of the Videha kingdom were called Janakas. This Videha kingdom was later on incorporated within the Vajji confederacy, which had its capital in the city of Vaishali, which is also in Mithila.

One and a half thousand years later and during the Mughal rule, Purnia was an outlying military province and its revenue was mostly spent on protecting its borders against tribes from the north and east. In 1757, after Calcutta was captured by the East India Company, Purnia's local governor raised a rebellion against Siraj-ud-Daullah and in 1765, the district came under British possession, along with the rest of Bengal. On 14 February 1770, the district of Purnia was formed by the East India Company.

WESTERN REGION

43. HOW CORN WAS CREATED FOR HUMANS: The corn is respected and valued by the Warlis, who are agriculturalists, and the presiding deity of corn is Kanseri Mata. Though the method of story narration may have changed over the years, this story of Mother Corn or Kanseri Mata had a system and time of narration in the past. Traditionally, the story of corn would be narrated at night during the harvesting season on a threshing floor. Any man, who knew the full story used to narrate it to the accompaniment of 'ghangali' (a two-stringed instrument). Traditionally, this narration was considered a sacrosanct act, almost like worshipping the corn deity, and thus the man on whose threshing floor the narration used to be held, would wave a lamp at the narrator, apply red vermillion on the forehead of the narrator and place a coconut in front of him. After the narration was finished, the coconut would be broken and distributed to all in an act of distribution of prasad after a puja is complete. This also goes to portray the significance of the narrator and the listener in the sociocultural ethos of the Warlis.

Interestingly enough, the story also reflects class and caste differences, with the marginalized being maltreated by the upper castes, though the supply chain is closely connected to all the people of the society. It was only after the calamity which befell mankind after Kanseri Mata's departure, that an apology, from necessity, was created to seek her forgiveness, which also sought her inclusion.

The method of distribution of agriculture, food, or the mention of the food chain also follows closely the format of narration of the Kahankar and Ahankar. It is believed that it is important to be open-hearted and distribute and share one's assets, and float on top like the Kahankar, rather than just accumulate and remain stagnant like the Ahankar.

44. BHAGAT DHANNAJI: The story significantly weaves nature and life with spiritualism. The Shaligram Shila itself is an important part of nature as they are a variety of stones, and most typically a particular variety of fossils of ammonite shells from the Devonian-Cretaceous period of 400 to 66 million years ago. These are generally collected from the riverbed or banks of the Kali Gandaki River, which is a tributary of the Gandaki River in Nepal. It represents Lord Vishnu. The mention of Lord Krishna blessing the harvest, further associates the story with the procreative abilities of earth and the sustenance of life. Dhanna Bhagat is also known as Dhanna Jaat or Dhanna Bairagi or just Sant Dhanna and was a mystic poet and a Vaishnav devotee, whose three hymns are present in the holy Adi Granth. Dhanna Bhagat Ji is said to have served the needy and the holy men with dedication and devotion since his very childhood, and when he grew up, he went to Kashi and got initiated into Vaishnavism by the Vaishnav saint Swami Ramananda. In the village of Duan Kalan, there is a Gurudwara of Sant Dhanna Bhagat. There are many depictions of the story of Bhagat Dhanna in the scroll paintings of the Garoda community of Gujarat. They normally depict legends and also paint horoscopes for newborn babies. The picture scrolls are known as tipanu in Gujarati, meaning 'recording' or 'remark'.

45. THE STORY OF JAMSHED AND JAMSHED-I-NAOROZ: The Naoroz celebrations across India, Afghanistan, Azerbaijan, Islamic Republic of Iran, Iraq, Kazakhstan, Kyrgystan, Pakistan, Tajikistan, Turkey, Turkmenistan, and Uzbekistan were declared as an Intangible Cultural Heritage of Humanity by UNESCO in 2009. Naoroz or Nowroz, meaning a 'new day' is an ancestral festivity, marking the first day of spring and the renewal of nature. It involves various rituals, festivities, ceremonies, and cultural events, along with special meals with loved ones. New clothes are worn, visits are made to the homes of family and friends, and gifts, especially for children, are exchanged. In India, it is celebrated by the Zoroastrians on the spring or Vernal Equinox on 21 March each year.

Though Naoroz is celebrated worldwide in March, it arrived 200 days later in India and it is celebrated in the months of July–August with the Parsis in India following the Shahenshahi calendar, which does not account for the leap year. As a mark of celebrating spring and a new harvest season, Naoroz celebrates life and a new beginning with the sun. The warmth of the sun spreads to infuse new life among one and all, including plants and animals. Thus a new year begins on a holy note to thank the Almighty and also seek blessings for a prosperous year ahead. The story speaks of the creation of the world according to Zoroastrian beliefs and one can understand the significance of the sun in the story, in relation to creation and protection of the world. It is also important to mention that the concept of Naoroz is an integral and important thought and it binds all people of the community together. Thus, the Parsis in India celebrate the Naoroz in March, according to the Iranian calendar, followed by the second celebration according to the Shahenshahi calendar between July and August.

46. THE ABHANGS OF SAINT TUKARAM AND HOW THEY BECAME FAMOUS: A well-known poet from Maharashtra, Tukaram is best known for his devotional poetry called *Abhanga* and community-oriented worship with spiritual songs known as kirtans. It is unknown, though, how many poems Tukaram composed, but the first book which contained his poetry was published with 4607 poems. This book was published in 1873 from Indu Prakash Press, funded by the colonial government in Bombay (now Mumbai). This has also seen many reprints over the years. There have been numerous manuscripts of his poems, but none of them could be attributed to the handwriting of Tukaram. Some poems could be found only in few manuscripts, while they are absent from others, and the poems vary between manuscripts. Tukaram is also considered a significant figure in the history of Marathi literature. There was a nearly complete translation of Tukaram in English, titled, *The Collected Tukaram*, by J. Nelson Fraser and K.B. Marathe, published in Madras by the Christian Literature Society (1909–1915). A more recent translation of Tukaram's works has been done by Dilip Chitre, titled, *Says Tuka* (1991).

There are various beliefs which speak of the beginning of the tradition of the annual pilgrimage of the warkaris to Pandharpur. Though it is said to have been in existence for more than eight hundred years, the annual visit during the Ashad and Kartik months is said to have been initiated by Vitthalpant, the father of Warkari Sant Dnyaneshwar in the thirteenth century. This tradition was continued by Sant Tukaram in the seventeenth century on Ashadi Ekadashi. Later on in 1685, the youngest son of Tukaram, Narayan Maharaj, is said to have begun the tradition of carrying the padukas of both the Saints to Pandharpur. This tradition of the twin processions continued for a couple of centuries, till towards the beginning of the first quarter of the nineteenth century and thereafter it changed. This was under the initiative of one of the descendants of Tukaram, a devotee of Sant Dnyaneshwar—Haibatravbaba Arphalkar, a courtier of Scindias, the Maratha rulers of Gwalior. He is credited with having organized, the pilgrims into what is seen at present, including making it a single and united procession, carrying the paduka in a palkhi (palanquin), having horses in the procession, and organising the warkaris into Dindis or specific groups. Today, apart from these two, around forty other palkhis take part in the pilgrimage. Nearly 250 groups or Dindis join the prilgrimage and the procession from various places. The warkaris cover more than 200 kilometres during the month of Ashad on foot from Dehu and Alandi to the famous Lord Vitthal temple in Pandharpur.

47. THE STORY OF GUGGA PIR: Gugga is also famously referred to as Goga, Jahar Veer Gogga, Gugga Pir, Gugga Jaharpir, Gugga Chohan, Gugga Rana, Gugga Bir, and Raja Mandlik. He is worshipped variously across northern India, including, Rajasthan, Himachal Pradesh, Haryana, Uttarakhand, Punjab region, Uttar Pradesh, Jammu, and Gujarat. In all these regions, he is a warrior hero of the region and also venerated as a saint and a snake God. Thus, the association of nature is an important aspect. He has been especially popular in Rajasthan, and since the seventeenth century, has also been worshipped in the western Himalayas, possibly because of migration from Rajasthan.

His shrine in Tikkar, in Kangra, in Himachal Pradesh, has eleven idols and an umbrella made from Tor leaves (Casuarina). People come here to seek cure from various diseases, especially those suffering from snakebites. During the festival, various stories of Gugga Pir are sung by the people from Bajati community to the accompaniment of various instruments like 'damru', 'dhol', 'thali', 'chimta', 'ghunghroo', and 'chhena'. It is also believed that Goga was born in 900 CE to Queen Bachhal, daughter of the Rajput ruler Kanwarpala, and King Jewar in Dadrewa of Chauhan clan in Churu district of Rajasthan. The region that they ruled stretched from Hisar in Haryana to Sutlej in Punjab.

48. WHY THE CITY OF PUNVARANOGAD LAY DESOLATE: There is another version, probably dating to the eighth century. According to this version, in order to fight against the oppressive King Punvar, the Sanghars, the villagers, sought help from the cavalry from Western Asia. Seventy-two horsemen came and camped on the high hill near Punvanarogad. They seized the fort and killed the king. Then, the Sanghars named the hill, Kakadgad, in honour of the leader of the warriors, Kakad, and called the warriors Yakshas, after the fair-skinned demigods of that name. The Sanghars also made seventy-two horsemen images and put them on a railed platform in Punvaranogad with their faces towards the south. They also started a fair, dedicated to Jakhs, or the 'Jakh Botera no Melo' or 'Mota Jakh no Melo', held on the second Monday of Bhadrapad, (September–October), every year on the foothills of Kakadbhit.

The symbolism of horses is a vital part of the story, which is also an important part of nature. Votive offerings of horse effigies, variously made from cloth, stone or burnt clay, are documented in different villages across India. In many cases, the symbolism of the horse is a mark of gratitude with reference to conception, birth, or cure of a child. This is also associated with the procreating powers of nature. Horses are also an important part of the historical past that speaks of visits of foreigners from outside, and also a pattern of a thriving trade. In the collective folk memory, the religious symbol of the horses remained embedded and thrived through folk traditions, even long after the foreigners had left, or the actual events or historical incidents had taken place. In 1830, a large number of Indo-Sassanian coins buried in a copper vessel were excavated, in Punvaranogad. There are also traces of ruins of a large boundary wall, within which are the broken remains of two palaces, a mint, and a temple of Mahadev—all made from stone.

49. HOW THE TOWN OF JEJURI BECAME KHANDOBACHI JEJURI: The various versions of the myths surrounding Khandoba continues to reflect

the gradual transformation of a folk deity into the mainstream and classical pantheon, and thus the association with Shiva, Parvati, and Ganga. He has also been referred to as Khandehrao and is also a very famous and most popular family deity; or Kuladaivat in Maharashtra and North Karnataka regions; the patron deity of few, who were traditionally considered warrior, farming castes, Dhangar community and also Brahmin castes; also many others who were traditionally considered hunter-gatherer tribes and native to the hills and forests of the region. Much is known about the mythological stories of Khandoba from oral traditions and folk songs, and also from the text—Malhari Mahatmya. All of these speak of the victory of Khandoba over the demons Mani-Malla and about his marriages. There are over six hundred temples of Khandoba across the Deccan that variously include the regions of Nasik in the north of Maharashtra to Davangere towards southern Karnataka, the Konkan Maharashtra in the west to the western Andhra Pradesh in the east. A six-day festival is also celebrated at Jejuri to mark the victory of Khandoba over the demons Mani and Malla. This festival takes place from the first to the sixth lunar day of the bright fortnight of the month of Marghashirsha (December–January). It is believed that on the sixth day, which is the Champasasthi, Khandoba slayed the demons.

50. THE LEGEND OF HOW THE SIDDI RULERS OF JANJIRA TOOK OVER THE FORT: The Siddis are said to have been from Abyssinia and brought over at one point as slaves. The Siddi rulers of Janjira initially held the title of 'Wazir', but after 1803 the title of 'Nawab' was officially recognized by the British Raj. They were entitled to an eleven-gun salute by the British authorities after the 1903 Coronation Durbar.

51. THE WADDAR COMMUNITY AND THEIR TRADITIONAL WORK: This old tale from long ago is almost lost from the pages of most modern publications. Though the association of the community with digging tanks, wells, and dams is a traditional concept, yet the story highlights some important aspects, including abject poverty and several hardships through seclusion and marginalisaion. They are also a geo-historically dislocated pan-Indian peripatetic community, found in many parts of India, including Andhra Pradesh, Telengana, Karnataka, and Maharashtra. The community is also seen in other parts of South Asia, including Pakistan, Nepal, and Sri Lanka (Ethnologue Report, 2009).

52. KARNI MATA: THE PROTECTOR OF COWS AND KRISHNA SAARA MRIGA: As the legend suggests, the association of Karni Mata with animals makes her an important deity who protects cattle. She is considered a warrior sage of the Charan community and is also revered as an incarnation of the warrior Goddess Hinglaj. She is also the official deity of the royal families of Bikaner and Jodhpur and at the request of the rajas of these families, she even laid the foundation stones of both Bikaner and Mehrangarh forts. Her

famous temple is at Deshnok, near Bikaner.

53. THE STORY OF TANA AND RIRI: The story highlights an important aspect of Indian classical music, its association and relation with nature. A raag from Indian classical music follows an array of melodic structures with musical motifs. Each raag also provides the musician with a musical framework within which to improvise. The improvisation by the musicians and singers involve creating notes, sequences and repertoire which will include only the notes allowed by the raag and will also maintain the rules allowed by that specific raag. Each raag is also supposed to be sung in particular times of the day as well as seasons; each one is supposed to have immense influence on the psyche, mind, and emotions of the singers and listeners. The story also connects spiritualism and environment by speaking of Tana and Riri's performances, which were only fit to be performed in front of a deity and this, in turn, were connected to the life-giving forces of nature through water and rainfall. Today, Tana and Riri's story is also reflected in a sacrosanct temple in the region, and there is also an annual Tana Riri music festival held every year.

54. THE STORY OF THE SEVEN SISTERS AND ONE BROTHER OF GOA: The various festivals and processions of these deities are spread across several months. It is established that the deities of seven sisters and one brother is also a part of popular worship from all over India, from the northern Ganges valley to southern regions of Tamil Nadu and Karnataka. These deities are also worshipped to cure diverse ailments, and they are known by various names in different regions. They are also often associated with the Sapta Matrika of the Puranic tradition, but this is also often refuted by many researchers. It is believed that these deities are much older and had their origin in the very early beliefs of man concerning earth, water, the life-giving forces of nature, and the protection of life on earth against diseases and death. Thus, the seven sisters and one brother are often said to resemble various aspects of Mother Nature. It is also interesting to note the close association of the story of the seven sisters and one brother to our everyday lives. The tale resonates with present day family stories, a brother who does wrong, a sister who corrects him, an anger which creates a rift, siblings still staying together, and sisters helping each other in times of need.

55. THE STORY OF WAGHOBA: This is a story from Kartod in Maharashtra. Waghoba refers to big cats, including tigers and leopards. The worship, which is extensively seen among the Warlis, reflects a degree of reverence between man-nature relationships and that of the concept of coexistence that comes within shared regions. The worship of the Waghoba also helps to understand a need for conservation and focus on ecological dimensions. The Waghoba is also worshipped by the Koli and the Thakkar communities.

In 2021, an extensive study, titled 'Sharing Spaces and Entanglements with Big Cats: The Warli and their Waghoba in Maharashtra, India' was published in the Frontiers in Conservation Science which studied 150 sites of Waghoba worship across Maharashtra. The Kartod village is the biggest temple of Waghoba.

56. SAO JOAO FESTIVAL OF GOA: The Nativity of John the Baptist is one of the oldest festivals of the Christian Church.

The feast of Sao Joao in Goa is held at such a time, when the monsoon has just commenced, and thus amid the fresh greenery, all the water bodies are filled up, including rivers, ponds, and wells. The celebration of St John's birth in Goa is believed to coincide with this life-giving aspect of nature during the monsoons. Jumping into the well is believed to be symbolic of both, signifying the baby jumping in the womb and also the baptism in the river Jordan. The men, wearing kopels (flower crown) during the festival, is also believed to connect to St John's natural attire.

CENTRAL REGION

57. HOW BADA DEV CREATED THE WORLD: This is a very popular Gond myth about the creation of the world, and it has also been depicted often in their artwork in a static form, where Bada Dev is mostly represented at the centre and often appears to personify water. Surrounding this are depicted other life forms which are part of the story, including the crab, earthworm, and the spider, among others. In these paintings, there is mostly the portrayal of the Saja tree (*Terminalia tormentosa*). According to the Gond belief, Bada Dev resides in the Saja trees, which are quite abundantly found across Madhya Pradesh.

The Gond art traditionally, portrays ritualistic idols, motifs, depictions of the natural world, and the harmony between all creations, including plants, animals, and humans. These are painted in an elaborate pattern of lines and dots.

58. HOW THE SANTALS LEARNT MUSIC AND DANCING FROM THE GODS: Music and dance is an important part of the Santal festivals and worships. They form such an integral part of their sociocultural and religious ethos that this story elaborates upon a divine origin of music and dancing, which accords a very significant space to performing arts. Through their music and dance, they not only express their emotions, but also reach out reverentially to all elements of nature, including the sacrosanct spaces of the Gods. Quite prevalent across, mainstream media culture, the Santal rhythm is also often depicted in modern media across cinema and music.

59. KOYA PUNEM OF THE GONDS AND THE LEGEND OF PAHANDI PARI KUPAR LINGO: The legend is especially seen among the Pari Kshetra of Nagpur, Wardha, Bhandara, Seoni, and Balaghat districts. The horoscope

of snake in Gondi language is called Kupar. The basic concept behind the ideology of Pahandi Pari Kupar Lingo emphasizes the importance of collective unity among individuals, advocating for an organized, 'phratrial' community life. His philosophy stated that peaceful people should not be hurt or harmed and harmful beings must not be protected. Although Punem's philosophy is not documented in any written script, it is prevalent in the conduct and lifestyle of the 'Gonds'. Kali Kankali shrine and the Kachargarh pilgrimage, over the years, have become an important part of the lives of the Gonds. The Kali Kankali myth survives through various folk songs in the Gondi language and worship. Verrier Elwin also mentioned about this in his *Myths of Middle India* (1949), in which he spoke about three mythology stories about her, including, 'The Tamarind', 'Rajnegi Pradhan', and 'Dewar'. Kali Kankali is also mentioned in Christoph von Fürer-Haimendorf's legends of Adilabad in *The Raj Gonds of Adilabad* (1948).

60. WHY THE VINDHYAN RANGE IS LOWER THAN THE HIMALAYAS: The Vindhya Mountain has been an important landmark across history as it is also often regarded as the traditional geographical boundary between northern and southern parts of India. Both the Indian epics, the Ramayana and the Mahabharata mention the Vindhya Mountains and it also appears prominently in many other mythological stories. The Vindhyas have been noted in many of these ancient texts for its dense vegetation and the many tribes who used to live in and around the region.

Geographically, the Vindhya Mountain is a broken range of hills, forming the southern escarpment of the central upland of India, The Vindhya Mountain extends from Gujarat till near Varanasi in Uttar Pradesh. The Vindhya is also important geologically as the 'Vindhyan Supergroup' is one of the largest and thickest sedimentary successions in the world. The earliest known multicellular fossils of eukaryotes, a filamentous algae, which dates back to 1.6–1.7 billion years ago, has also been discovered from the Vindhyan basin.

The Himalayas is a fold mountain, which is still growing. It is one of the youngest mountain ranges of the planet and consists mostly of uplifted sedimentary and metamorphic rocks. The Himalayas is also a mountain range which separates the plains of the Indian subcontinent from the Tibetan plateau. This range has some of the world's highest peaks, including the Mount Everest at 8,848.86 metres, the highest peak in the world. The Himalayas touches across five countries, including India, Bhutan, Nepal, China, and Pakistan. The northern Himalaya is the northern boundary of the state of Himachal Pradesh and is also the international border with China and Tibet. The southern foothills have the state of Uttar Pradesh. The region is rich in fossils, lakes, and glaciers and is the point of inception of several perennial rivers, as well as their tributaries and distributaries, which drains across the entire region, including all the countries which the Himalayas surrounds.

61. HOW THE FESTIVAL OF KARAM BECAME POPULAR: This is an agricultural festival, which according to Durga Bhagwat is celebrated by the Baiga, Majhwar, Sahis, Savar, and Gond in Madhya Pradesh, and few adjoining regions. Bhagwat cites this story as mentioned in *The Gazeteer of the United Provinces, Mirzapur*, pp.103–104 (Bhagwat pp. 65–66). The second version of the story mentioned here is from the Pauri Bhuiya of Odisha, which was recorded by S. C. Roy (Bhagwat, pp. 66–68). The third version of the story, is in E. Dalton's *Descriptive Ethnology of Bengal*, pp. 259–60 (Durga Bhagwat. pp. 67–68). The singing and dancing of the festival are both communal as well as household ones. The music and dance celebrate the harvest and compliments the growth of a good season of crops. Across decades, the interpretation of the music and dance have changed. As Bhagwat mentions it has ceased to be looked upon as a festival dance and is seen more as a traditional social dance. The stories here allude to the celebration as associated with prosperity, and a good agricultural season.

62. WHY THE SUN IS HOT, THE WIND DRY, BUT THE MOON IS BEAUTIFUL: This is a very old story from the Deccan region. Since the sun, moon, stars, wind, thunder, lighting, etc. are vital parts of the nature surrounding us, they are often the protagonists of similar myths and legends, which explain the characteristics of these vital aspects of nature.

63. HOW GRAINS WERE DISTRIBUTED THROUGHOUT THE WORLD: Interestingly enough the story reflects a spiritual connection between divinity, the labour behind agriculture, and the precious harvest which is reaped thereafter. The results of a harvest are seen as a gift of the Gods as of nature.

The Bhaina community lives on the fertile plains of Raigarh and Bilaspur districts of Madhya Pradesh. They work as farmers and labourers.

64. THE LEGEND OF THE BEAUTIFUL BAIGA TATTOOS: Different tribes have their specific and unique tattooing patterns. They also believe that the tattoos are also the only ornaments which will go with them to the afterlife when they die. The tattoo patterns usually draw inspiration from nature, where various parts of the nature around us are symbolically represented. This includes fire, crops, grains, peacocks, pair of hens, chariot, flowers, trees, eyes, etc. The Baigas also believe that the pain the Baigin (woman) endures during tattooing, prepares her for the pain of childbirth.

65. HOW THE ANATOMY OF HUMANS AND ANIMALS CAME INTO EXISTENCE: This is a Kahar story from Bilaspur. The bell inside the throat is the uvula, a fleshy extension at the back of the soft palate, which hangs above the throat and can be seen when the mouth is opened wide. Interestingly enough, the plants mentioned within the story remain significant within the community for their various medicinal qualities.

66. THE SONG ABOUT LINGO OF THE MARIA AND MURIA GONDS: The Hill Maria and the Muria Gond tribes were originally from the Abujhmar mountains in Bastar in Southeast India. Within the song, there are extensive descriptions of Lingo's beautiful house.

Over the years, a lot of research has been conducted on the Gotul of the Murias, and especially famous is the work of Verrier Elwin, *The Muria and their Ghotul* (1947). The Gotul is like a religious dormitory, where boys and girls between the age groups of eight to eighteen, interact, sing, dance, and sleep. At the entrance hangs a dhol (drum), which represents Lingo. The rules of a Gotul differs from village to village; while at some places only the men and boys are allowed to sleep, at other places, both girls and boys are allowed.

67. BHIMASIDI: THE LYRICAL NARRATIVE OF THE KONDHS: The story of Bhimasidi is famous as the mythical epic of the Kondhs, which is sung by the Boguas, who are a distinct offshoot of the Kondhs. The epic song represents a tale performed in the narrative poetry form. The song is particularly sung by the priests and Gurumai, assisted by a musical string instrument. The Bhimasidi has basically two parts—the first section mentions the birth of the hero and the second section mentions his heroic deeds.

68. HOW HUMANS LEARNT THE APPROPRIATE TIME FOR HARVESTING: The Kharia is an Austroasiatic tribal ethnic group from east-central India. Originally, they spoke the Kharia language, which belonged to the Austroasiatic languages. There are three divisions among them—the Hill Kharia, Delki Kharia and Dudh Kharia. Ponomosor, also referred to as Bhagwan is the supreme power of the Kharia, and is revered by every member of the community. He is also worshipped to protect the village from all evils and during any crisis situation. The Kharia regard the sun and its rays as the symbol of Ponomosor.

69. THE LEGEND OF BHASMASURA AND THE GAVRI DANCE OF THE BHILS: Also considered as Gavri nachh or Rai Dance, it is a dance drama, combining mime and dialogue. There are four types of characters in Gavri—Gods, humans, demons, and animals. In the symbolic character of Bhasmasur, the central character, Rai-Bhuria wears an extraordinarily artistic mask and is also the central figure of Gavri. The scenes enacted are called Khel, Bhav, or Sang. The narrator is called as Kutkadiya.

This story has been performed by the Bhils for centuries. The dance highlights the legend and also various stories associated with Lord Shiva. Any courtyard or crossroad in the village is chosen as the performance area. Two or three Bhil villages combined together, organise the play. Interestingly enough, the villagers organise Gavri in the villages where their daughters or sisters are married to. All the members, who participate in the dance, consider it to be a sacrosanct act. Sometimes, the number of characters increases to a hundred or more. The dance drama continues for over a month and begins on the day after Rakshabandhan (this festival is usually in the month of August).

70. THE ASURAS AND THE BEGINNING OF IRON SMELTING: The Asurs are a very small minority community. They are an Austroasiatic ethnic group and traditionally used to live in Jharkhand across the regions of Gumla, Lohardaga, Palamau, Latehar districts, and also some areas of the neighbouring states. Traditionally, they were iron smelters, though many moved to agriculture later on. Iron made by the community is very famous and is said to have anti-rust property, and the processes are much safer, cheaper, and eco-friendly. However, with time, this important tradition as well as occupation of the Asurs have dwindled. Even as early as the early 1960s, Verrier Elwin mentions that the iron smelting work of the Asurs had almost entirely disappeared from Neterhat. He also points out that one of the reasons for the non-availability of charcoal for the process was due to the official restrictions on tree cutting. He also mentioned that if this could be properly organized, and helped, the Asurs could continue with their traditional craft. However, in present times, this activity seems to be further dwindling, according to very recent reports from dailies and weeklies. In the last few years the Asurs are sometimes invited for workshops to demonstrate their iron-smelting skills, which is also part of the effort to inspire the continuity of their tradition.

The Asurs also believe Mahishashura, the Asura king from popular Indian mythology, to be their ancestor. According to the story, Goddess Durga slayed Mahishashur, who was a ruthless king, after a very fierce battle, and this is celebrated during the Durga puja in the months of Chaitra (March–April) and Ashwin (September–October). However, since the Asurs believe Mahishashur to be their ancestor, they mourn during the period of Durga puja as they see it as an unjust act of killing. Mahishashur is also revered by other tribes as well.

SOUTHERN REGION

71. THE STORY OF KANYAKUMARI: The temples of Lord Shiva and Goddess Parashakti are at Suchindram and Kanyakumari respectively. According to scientific explanations, the coloured sand of the beach is because of the presence of many minerals including zircon, monazite, garnet, and rutile. The southernmost region of Kanyakumari is also considered sacrosanct as it is the meeting place of three very significant water bodies—the Indian Ocean, the Arabian Sea and the Bay of Bengal. Being the confluence of the three, it is also called the 'Triveni'. Bathing in the waters of the Triveni is considered sacrosanct.

Kanyakumari is also famous for the Vivekananda Rock Memorial, built in 1970 to commemorate the visit of Swami Vivekananda to the area in 1892, where he attained spiritual enlightenment while meditating. It is said that he swam two hundred metres to the rock.

72. SAINT ALPHONSA: THE FIRST WOMAN SAINT OF INDIAN ORIGIN: On 12 October 2008 (Sunday), Pope Benedict XVI announced the canonisation of Sister Alphonsa during a ceremony at Saint Peter's Square. The world, along with many Indians present in Rome for the ceremony, rejoiced at this momentous occasion. In the homily, Pope Benedict XVI, recalled Alphonsa's life as one of 'extreme physical and spiritual suffering.'

To mark the event, a chapel was constructed at St. Mary's Forane Church in Bharananganam, where the Franciscan Clarist Sister was laid to rest. In 2009, the Reserve Bank of India issued a 5 Rupee Commemorative Coin to celebrate the birth centenary of Saint Alphonsa.

73. THE STORY OF GURUVAYUR KESHAVAN: Gajarajan Keshavan stood over 3.2 metres or 10.5 feet in height, making him the tallest elephant in Kerala at that time and is still considered to be one of the tallest among all temple elephants of the region. With increase in his popularity, the Devaswom board honoured him with the title of Gajarajan or the king of elephants in 1973. He passed away on Guruvayur Ekadasi, on 2 December 1976. His death anniversary is still mourned in Guruvayur and his statue is garlanded by fellow temple elephants.

Temple elephants continue to be an important part of the sociocultural and religious ethos of Kerala, and there are many stories and legends associated with many of these animals. They are often decked in full regalia and they take part in festivals, like the temple festival of Thrissur Pooram. These festivals are also tourist attractions, and people from near and far often travel to see the large mammoths all decked up. Though these temple elephants are domesticated, there are also many debates about reports of maltreatment of these large animals at various levels, which suggest that these animals must not be domesticated but should be allowed to live in their natural environment.

74. SOME POPULAR LEGENDS OF MARIAMMAN: Mariamman has been and continues to be worshipped variously across Tamil Nadu and some parts of Karnataka and Kerala. She is also considered as the village deity across many villages. There are multiple myths which are famous in relation to several of the temples in each of these places. She is also considered to be the deity from whom blessings for a good rainfall is sought as the word 'Mari' according to the Tamil of Sangha Period means 'rain', and the word 'Amma' means mother. So, for a very long time, the deity has been worshipped to seek blessings for better rains to sustain the agricultural economy.

Thus, concerning prosperity and general well-being, Mariamman is also associated with wishing health, which also includes prayers to ward off diseases, a practice which continues till present. Even as recent as the pandemic of the 2019 coronavirus there were reports about the deity being worshipped across various places. These include a temple of 'Corona Devi' within the premises of Kamatchipuram Adhinam at Kamatchipuram, near Irugur on the outskirts of the city, and a makeshift temple set up by a priest at Kerala's Kadakkal in Kollam district, among others. These recent reports also bring to mind the worship of Mariamman a century ago, during a plague in Coimbatore at the famous Plague Mariamman Temple. Still existing, this temple is located near the parking lot in between Big Bazaar and Raja Streets, and is estimated to be a little over hundred and fifty years old. The popularity of the deity goes to the time when the region saw the plague epidemic in 1936. Coimbatore saw the outbreak of the plague in 1903 first and several times thereafter, including in 1909 and 1917. Thousands of people died in Coimbatore. Several efforts of civic authorities followed which also saw the initiation of inoculation, maintaining cleanliness and generally extending helping hands to all in need. Even today, the city remembers the various public and private initiatives in the domain of civic infrastructure and environment.

Often, Mariamman is also considered as part of the seven sister deities. The names of these sisters vary from place to place, however, mostly they are referred to as Poleramma, Ankamma, Muthyalamma, Dilli Polasi, Bangaramma, Mathamma and Renuka or Yellamma or Mariamman. There are several stories associated with the Seven Sister deities in each place. They are also often considered as resembling the Sapta Matrikas, who are famous in different parts of India. However, many critics opine otherwise.

The story of Mariamman reveals many aspects of the inclusion of a folk deity within mainstream beliefs. Often mythologies, legends and folktales also reflect many discriminatory beliefs and practices. The stories of the deity associated with a housewife meeting with ill-fated circumstances through family or social pressures are all unfortunate reflections of the same. Such tales of woe, concerning women are many, and they variously include incidences to indicate a woman 'falling from grace', being inflicted by a curse, having an infectious disease, and as a result of all these beliefs, she is either thrown out of her house or made an outcaste of the village.

75. HOW AMNODR AND TEIKIRSHY CREATED BUFFALOES: The Toda religion considers their buffaloes sacrosanct. Thus, cattle herding and dairy work forms an important and revered part of their community. Holy dairies are built to store buffalo milk. The Toda dairies and their herds have various degrees of sanctity, with each level having its own ritual practices.

Traditionally, the Todas are pastoralists, living in the Nilgiri Mountains of South India. Though many have moved out in recent times to adjoining regions in search of jobs, they used to conventionally live in settlements called 'munds' across the Nilgiris. Primarily each 'mund' had around 4–10 homes, one or two temples and a buffalo pen near their abode.

The buffaloes of the Todas occupy a special place and are referred to as Toda Buffalo, a breed of the Asiatic Water Buffalo. Among the Indian breeds of buffaloes, the Toda Buffalo is a unique breed, genetically isolated and only confined to the Nilgiris. Unfortunately, in recent times, there has been a marked decrease in the Toda Buffaloes, and local conservationists have been steadily working to revive the population. According to the Central Institute for Research on Buffaloes, the existence of this buffalo can be traced back from the earliest reference of Finicio in 1603, who wrote about the Toda tribe, their buffaloes, and the milk and butter they get from them.

76. AYYANAR OF CHITHAKOOR VILLAGE: The very essence of the story speaks of the close relation of the village deity with the general well-being of the people and protection of the environment. Ayyanar is the main guardian deity of the villages of Tamil Nadu, and surrounding him are seen many colourful and terracotta steeds. Located mostly outside villages, the temples are generally open to the sky. In many temples, he is also present with his consorts, Poorna and Pushkala.

Chithakoor is a small village in the Pudukkottai district of Tamil Nadu. The Ayyanar here has a whip in one hand and has Pooranam and Pushkalam, who are his consorts next to him. It is also believed that one day Ayyanar appeared in the dream of a villager, instructing him to construct a tiled temple for him. Thus, the hut was replaced by the temple. Ten days before his festival, Ayyanar is taken to his original village, Singanampuri.

77. THE MIGHTY BEERAPPA OF THE KURUVAS: The story of Beerappa has long been studied by anthropologists. It provides an understanding of the early history of the pastoral communities of Deccan, and their beliefs, practices and livelihoods. Considered traditionally to be the God of shepherds, the Kuruvas of southwestern Andhra and Kuruvas of Karnataka, Beerappa is depicted as the chief devotee of Mallikarjuna. The myth stated here highlights the emergence of Beerappa from the status of a human to that of a divine being.

78. HOW GODDESS LAKSHMI STAYED BACK IN HYDERABAD: Such stories of Goddess Lakshmi are often part of popular lore in many regions across India, with the Goddess personifying the very essence of prosperity and general well-being. This particular lore explains an important and prosperous period of history. The Qutub Shahi dynasty ruled the Golconda Sultanate in northern Deccan Plateau (Telangana) from 1512–1687 CE. Muhammad Quli Qutub Shah (1565–1612 CE), founded the city of Hyderabad on the southern bank of the Musi River and also built the architectural centrepiece of Hyderabad, the Charminar. He was the sixth ruler of the dynasty and his reign is considered to be one of the most important and prosperous times of the Qutub Shahi dynasty. Quli Qutub Shah's successor, Abul Hasan Qutub Shah, also known as Tana Shah (1672–1686 CE) was the eighth and last ruler of the Qutub Shahi dynasty. He was an inclusive ruler and the ministers in his court came from different religious backgrounds. Mughal emperor Aurangzeb attacked the region and arrested Tana Shah in 1687. Tana Shah later died in prison in 1699. The region however flourished once again and soon attained its lost glory, which continued for centuries later. The monarchs always had a prosperous region under them. Even the last Nizam or monarch of Hyderabad, Nawab Mir Osman Ali Khan, is ranked as one of the wealthiest individuals of all time. At the time of the independence of India in 1947, the Princely State of Hyderabad was the largest princely state in British colonial India, and Nawab Mir Osman Ali Khan was the Nizam of Hyderabad from 1911–1948, when the Princely State of Hyderabad joined the new nation and the constitution of India. Nawab Mir Osman Ali Khan of Hyderabad, at the time of the independence of India was also listed as one of the wealthiest persons in the world. He was also a visionary and contributed considerably for the development of Hyderabad. He helped to introduce many public spaces and institutions, including electricity, university, airport, high court, railways, and roads, among others.

79. THE TRADITION OF WOMEN PRIESTS AT THE MANNARASALA SREE NAGARAJA TEMPLE: The Mannarasala Sree Nagaraja temple is located at Harippad in Southeast district of Alappuzha in Kerala. It has many lush green sarppakavus (serpent groves), which are the home to many species of plants and reptiles. These plants are also considered important for medicinal purposes. The kavus (sacred groves) as well as the temples are also host to many serpent idols. The female chief priest is succeeded by the second eldest female member of the family. The high priest is referred to as 'Amma' or mother. The appointment of women as the priestess follows a particular pattern. When a woman is appointed as the next Amma, she has to take the vow of celibacy and adopt an ascetic way of life.

80. COCHIN JEWS AND LEGEND OF THEIR ARRIVAL IN INDIA: The arrival of the first of the Jews to India is channelled through the blessed waterways in history, which has supported a very prosperous trade for a long time, until their arrival in the subcontinent later on. Thus, the Bible mentions the first of the Jews in relation to India and their involvement through trading activities through merchants and ships. The Book of Esther, dating to the second century BCE, cites decrees enacted by Ahasuerus, relating to the dispersal of the Jews throughout the provinces of his empire, from Hodu to Kush, where Hodu was India in Hebrew and Kush was Ethiopia. The Talmudic and Midrashic literature also speaks of perfumes, spices, plants, animals, textiles, gems and crockery which were either from India or bore names of Indian origin. On the basis of various legends, historians often ascertain a period of the early Middle Ages as the arrival of the Jews in Cochin. Preserved within India is also evidence of some of the earliest documentations of the Jewish settlements. These are on two copper plates, which are now preserved within Cochin's Pardeshi Synagogue. Engraved in local language, they reference Bhaskara Ravi Verma, a fourth century ruler of the Malabar, granting privileges to Joseph Rabban. The inscription also states that the King granted the Jews the village of Anjuvannam 'so long as the world and

moon exist.' Anjuvannam meant five castes, since the Jews were believed to be the 'lords of the five castes of artisans'. The Jews are believed to have continued in Anjuvannam for a thousand years till the extinction of the line of Rabban and dissension arising between two brothers of a noble family for the chieftainship of the principality.

Much later, the twelfth century Christian and Muslim travellers also mentioned about the Jewish settlements around Cochin, with the main community in Cranganore, north of Cochin. Even later, in 1686, the Jewish Dutch traveller, Moses de Pavia noted the presence of 'Malabaree Jews' in Cochin, who had their very own synagogues. Many of the Cochin Jews migrated to Israel between1953–54 with only about a hundred Jews staying back in India. At present there are only very few Cochin Jews remaining in the region.

81. HOW AVVAIYAR MET LORD MURUGAN: The Pazhamudirchoali Murugan Temple, which is one of the six shrines of Murugan in the Arupadai Veedu Temples in Tamil Nadu, is believed to be the area where Avvaiyar met Lord Murugan. The worship of Murugan is associated with the general well-being of the people. It is believed that his worship brings copious rainfall, provides bountiful harvests and blesses people with intelligence and fame. Similar blessings of Murugan echo through the present story, as the little boy came to feed the intelligent but hungry Avvaiyar. The conversation which is supposed to have transpired between Murugan and Avvaiyar forms an important philosophical piece, which is still considered relevant.

82. THE MYTHOLOGY OF KADAYUR VELLAIAMMAL KOIL: Being a local deity, it is intrinsically connected to the natural and sociocultural ethos of the area. The very association of the elements of forest, water, mud and animals, woven within the story of Vellaiammal, also reflect the close nature of the village deity, which is considered sacrosanct for the protection, as well as the well-being of the village. It is also interesting to note the trajectories of the life of Vellaiammal, who had to undergo the hardships as a single mother, and the difficulties and adversities which she had to undergo in order to be accepted as part of the society. The storyline thus, also draws attention to similar adverse situations which many women, as well as widows and single mothers have to undergo under the ruthless folds of the patriarchal society. Kadayur is six kilometres away from Kangeyan on the Kangeyan–Coimbatore Road. Many celebrities of the region also consider Vellaiammal as their family deity.

83. THE TRADITION OF OFFERING POOVAN BANANAS AT KORATTYMUTHY: The shrine is also known as the 'Lourdes of Kerala'. A very busy travel destination for many believers, it is in the Archdiocese of Ernakulam, Angamaly. The date of the establishment of the church is 8 September 1381, which is also mentioned in the official website of the church.

It also mentions the popularity of the church during the period when Sakthan Thampuran (1775–1790) reigned over the erstwhile Cochin Province. The church is especially known for the Lady's Feast with the Poovan bananas, which is celebrated in the month of October on the Saturday and Sunday, following the tenth of October. The Poovan kula or the Poovan banana is the main offering here. The festival has many customs and one of the important aspects is 'Thulabharam' with 'Poovan kula', a ritual involving devotees offering their body weight worth of plantain. The offering also associates the deity with an important agricultural product of the region and thereby also connects the deity with the harvest cycle of the area.

84. HOW MEER AHAMED IBRAHIM (PERIYA HAZRAT) PURSUED HIS EDUCATION: Periya in Tamil means elder or big. The Madurai Maqbara refers to the Dargahs of three Sufi saints, Mir Ahmad Ibrahim, Mir Amjad Ibrahim and Abdus Salaam Ibrahim, situated in the Kazimar Big Mosque in Madurai in Tamil Nadu.

WATER BODIES—BAY, OCEAN, SEA, AND OTHERS

85. HOW LIGHTNING AND THUNDER WERE CREATED: The Duruwa tribe traditionally belonged to Chhattisgarh and Odisha regions. This is an interesting story which not only reflects upon the close association of rainfall and agriculture, but also metaphorically speaks of the gradual use of metal in agriculture, which also aided in the domestication of plants and animals in history.

86. THE STORY FROM THE TENDONG-FAAT RITUAL DANCE: The Tendong-faat is a ritual dance of the Lepcha community of Sikkim. The dance follows the Buddhist lunar calendar, and it is performed on the fifteenth day of the seventh month of this lunar calendar (corresponding to August–September). The focus of the dance is the worship of the Tendong hill and it is inspired by many local legends.

87. AN IDU MISHMI STORY- THE CREATION OF RIVER BRAHMAPUTRA: The Idu Mishmi is a language of the sub tribe by the same name of the Mishmi group, who lives in various districts of the state of Arunachal Pradesh, including Dibang Valley, Lower Dibang Valley, Lohit, East Siang and Upper Siang, and also in Zayu County of Tibet. The Brahmaputra River originates in the Manosarovar Lake and flows through Tibet, then enters India through Arunachal Pradesh, flows through Assam, goes into Bangladesh (where it is known as Jamuna), and finally flows southwards into the Bay of Bengal. The mention of the lake in the story is the place of the origin of the river and the wall is the many dams, which are built across the Brahmaputra River.

There are also many beliefs about the origin of the Brahmaputra. It is also considered to be a male river and the son of Brahma and Amogha, who was the wife of sage Shantanu. The sage placed the child in between high mountains like the Kailash, Gandhamadana, Jarudi and Sambwartakka and he grew into the great lake, Brahmakund. There is also a story which says that sage Parshuram came to have a holy dip in the water of the Brahmakund and he axed the side of the mountain, releasing the water of the lake and making the river flow. Parshuram was seeking atonement for the sin of killing his mother with an axe, at the orders of his father. But so great was the sin that the axe refused to come off from his hand. In order to release the axe, Parshuram went on a pilgrimage and reached the Brahmakund. After a dip in the holy waters, the axe came off from his hands.

The Brahmaputra River has other myths about its origin in other religions as well. According to a belief in Buddhism, the Chang Thang Plateau was a great lake and one day a compassionate Bodhisattva felt that the water from the lake should reach mankind below. This river, which was created was the Yarlung Tsangpo with Tsangpo meaning 'Great River'. The Bodhisattva proceeded to create an outlet through the Himalayan mountain ranges for the flow of Yarlung Tsangpo to flow down and reach the plains. The river thus flowed through gorges, jungles, forests, and across Tibet. The region through which the river flows is considered holy. There are many myths about magical places residing amid this holy land, including beyuls lying deep in the Himalayas where ageing is slowed down and all animals and plants have magical powers, and also the mysterious land of Shangri-La, considered to be the doorway to paradise on earth.

88. THE STORY OF THE PIOUS FISH: The story is from *Machha-Jataka* (No. 75), Cf. Cariya-pitaka (P.T.S. edition) page 99. The concept of 'Sachhakriya' can be explained as a declaration of truth regarding one's own virtue and is believed to have miraculous strength of creating a wonder which can benefit one and all. In this story, the righteous fish makes the declaration and is blessed by rain.

89. THE LEGEND OF POUBI LAI OF MANIPUR: The legend of Poubi Lai is considered an important part of the beliefs of the Meitei people of Manipur and there are many lores which surround the myth of this giant aquatic serpent. The story has also been variously represented in popular culture across the last few decades. The twenty-one feet long wooden sculpture, created by Karam Dineshwar in 2002 deserves special mention. This was exhibited at the Manipur State Museum in 2002. Later on, it was also exhibited at the National Museum, New Delhi, Indian Museum, Kolkata and in 2010, it was exhibited at the Quai Branly Museum, Paris. The carvings belong to the permanent collection of the Indira Gandhi Rashtriya Manav Sangrahalaya (IGRMS), Bhopal, and it was declared an 'Object of National Importance' and registered under 'AA' category of the museum collections. The story of

Poubi Lai is also performed as a dance drama.

Referred to as the lifeline of Manipur, the Loktak Lake is the largest freshwater lake near Moirang in the central plains of Manipur. It is known in Meitei as Loktak Paat and provides habitat to biota and livelihoods to people. It is the house of many 'phumdis', which are floating islands and are heterogenous masses of vegetation, soil and organic matter at various stages of their decomposition. Among the floating islands, the Keibul Lamjao National Park is the only floating National Park in the world. In 1990, the lake was included under Ramsar Convention as a 'Wetland of International Importance'. However, during recent times, increasing activities due to human interventions have witnessed a disturbance in the eco system of the lake and its surrounding regions. The legend of Poubi Lai also represents this continuous tussle between man and the environment, and adds a degree of reverence to the ferocity of nature if it is disturbed beyond control through human activities.

90. MACHHER BIYE FROM THE PATUA SONGS OF BENGAL: The patachitra folk artists of this particular story are from the Naya village of West Mednipur district of Bengal. The common subject of all the patachitras generally vary from local mythological stories to the various episodes of the Ramayana and the Mahabharata. Across the last few decades, these artists are also seen to depict various recent topics with a social message, including deforestation and afforestation, child education, female child education, vaccination, oral polio vaccination, health and hygiene, coronavirus pandemic, economic crisis, health crisis, and migrant problems, among others. Traditionally, the chitrakars also used to use natural dyes from nature as the colour of their scrolls, including juices from flowers, barks, leaves, turmeric, lamp soot, etc. However, in modern times, in order to sustain their paintings for longer periods of time or to travel for exhibitions, the chitrakars use synthetic colours from the market.

The chitrakars are also often employed by government organisations to act as a traditional medium to deliver performances about various socially relevant messages to the masses. These attempts have received many accolades, and the reach and acceptance of the messages of the chitrakars have always helped to highlight the effectivity of traditional media. The chitrakars are thus, artists, who are storytellers, painters, singers, lyricists, and performers—all rolled into one.

91. THE ORIGIN OF THE PUSHKARAM RIVER FESTIVAL: The story, above all, highlights the significance of recognising the importance of water as a life-giving source for all on earth. There are many such water legends which often speak of this extremely important gift. It is also a reminder to all, to conserve and preserve this life-giving source and hopefully, create a better life for all.

The Pushkaram festival is associated with the astrological sign of the planet Jupiter. This story is, according to a legend in astrology, treatise, the Jataka Parijata (1426 CE). It is believed that each river is associated with a particular zodiac sign, and the river for each year's festival is based on the zodiac sign where the planet Jupiter or Brihaspati will be at that time. The Pushkaram festival is also considered as part of medieval astrological lore, and the names of twelve rivers vary depending on the regional traditions. Thus in Maharashtra, the Bhima River is associated with the Scorpion sign, and in Tamilnadu too the Tamraparni is associated with the Scorpion sign. Theoretically, the festival continues as long as Jupiter remains in the corresponding zodiac sign.

Bathing festivals are considered a pious act and the Pushkaram, celebrated after every twelve years at each of the twelve rivers in India, witnesses many devotees taking active part in doing snana (bath), dana (charity), japa (chanting), archana (worship) and dhyana (meditation). The associated temple towns also witness a festive atmosphere as millions of pilgrims gather around for the celebrations. The Pushkaram for each river lasts for the whole year, but the first twelve days of Jupiter's entry into a rashi or a zodiac house, and the last twelve days when the planet exits from the rashi, are considered to be particularly auspicious days. A dip in the waters, on any one of these twenty-four days, is believed to erase all sins. It is also considered an auspicious time to conduct shraddha or last rites for deceased relatives, and to offer libation to the Gods (tarpan).

92. HOW THE RIVER GANGA CAME DOWN TO EARTH: The Ganga River originates in the Himalaya Mountain at Gomukh, the terminus of the Gangotri glacier. The ice melts from the Gangotri glacier to form the Bhagirathi, which flows down to be joined by the Alakananda River, officially forming the Ganga River. The geography of the river is prominently divided across upper, middle and lower reaches, till it empties into the Bay of Bengal. Across its course, the river forms prominent landforms, including rapids, cataracts and waterfalls in its upper and middle stages, meanders and creates oxbow lakes in its middle and lower stages, and delta at its mouth, where it joins the Bay of Bengal. The Ganga and its adjoining watershed also support one of the most fertile and densely populated regions on the planet, and its intricate web of waterways has also been photographed from space by the crew of the Space Shuttle Columbia on mission STS-87. This photograph is available over the internet for free viewing.

Considered as a sacred river, there are many mythological stories associated with the Ganga, and it is also considered to be the path to attain salvation after death. The story of its travel down to earth, which is reproduced here, is a very famous one from the Mahabharata. The story also speaks about the force of the river, eroding mountains, creating rapids and waterfalls, or creating floods in the low-lying regions, until finally, the river meets the

Bay of Bengal. There are many other texts as well as the Ramayana, which also speaks of the creation of Ganga, which is referred to as the daughter of Himavan and Menavati. Brahma had created Himavan, who later became the King of the Himalayas. Menavati, who got married to Himavan, was the daughter of Meru. Ganga was their firstborn, and after some years, another daughter, Parvati, was born, who was an incarnation of the Mother Goddess Shakti. When Ganga grew up, the Devas took her to heaven and she took the form of a river and flowed there.

In the 'Bhagavata Purana', there is another story which speaks of the creation of Ganga and her descent to earth. Lord Vishnu, in his Vamana avatar (form) had appeared in the sacrificial arena of the Asura king Mahabali to measure the universe, and had extended his left foot to the end of the universe. As his left foot expanded, the nail of his big toe pierced a hole on the ground and pure water of the Causal Ocean (which is the origin of material creation and a space where Lord Vishnu lies, and also creates the material world) entered this universe as the Ganga River. Now, as the waters washed the lotus feet of Lord Vishnu, which were covered with reddish saffron, they assumed a gentle pink colour. As Ganga touched the feet of the Lord, it came to be referred to as Bhagavat-padi or Vishnu-padi- meaning that it emanates from the lotus feet of Bhagvan. The waters of Ganga is said to have then settled down in Brahmalok or the abode of Brahma, before descending down to earth, at the request of Bhagiratha.

93. THE SAD LEGEND OF JAI OF CHILIKA LAKE: This myth is after the legend of the region, which inspired the poem, 'Kalijai re Sandhya' by noted Odia poet Pandit Godabarish Mishra (1886–1956). Odisha's coastline is often prone to very strong storms and cyclones. The poem is an important reminder of the cyclonic weather, lest one gets caught in mid-water. A beautiful, heart-rending and famous piece, the poem has also been sung by many. However, many critics often question the reality behind any actual incident which may have taken place. In the book, *The History of Parikud*, published in 1930 and written by Dr Radha Charan Panda, it is mentioned that the temple of Kalijai was built in 1717 by Shri Jagannath Mansingh, who was the king of Bankad, which is presently known as Banapur.

94. KAMALEY KAMINI AND THE STORY OF DHANAPATI AND SRIMANTA: This story is from the 'Chandi Mangal Kavya' from erstwhile Bengal region (including the present country of Bangladesh). This forms an important part of Bengali literature of medieval times. The texts eulogizes Goddess Chandi or Abhaya, who were primarily folk deities, but subsequently is identified with mainstream deity Chandi. There are two stories of the text, which probably survived as oral traditions before they were finally penned down from the sixteenth century onwards. The mythology produced here is part of the second section or the 'Banik Khanda' (Merchant Section), which looks into the narrative about the merchant Dhanapati and his two wives, Khullana and Lahana and their lives. The story of Kamaley Kamini speaks primarily of the constructive and destructive powers of nature, woven into the character of a woman, through whom these features are represented. Such a depiction in itself speaks of the sublime, yet vicious balance of nature—an understanding of which is considered to bring peaceful existence.

There are many poets who composed the 'Chandi Mangal Kavya', including Dvija Madhab or Madhabananda, also known as Madab Acharya in 1579 and also Kabikankan Mukundaram, dating to 1544. The earliest text of the *Chandi Mangal*, which has been recovered is by Manik Datta, from Malda, dating to 1785. *The Mangal Kavyas*, including *Chandi Mangal*, helps to understand a lot about the contemporary society, culture, religion and politics of the medieval times of Bengal.

As the story of 'Chandi Mangal Kavya' is famous, many sections of the main story have been reproduced in various lore, stories and architecture during the previous centuries, including folkart, like the patachitra folk paintings of Bengal. The story has also often been depicted across temple architecture. The terracotta panel in the Navaratna temple in Dey para (locality) in Bishnupur district (Joypur region) in West Bengal, depicts the story of Srimanta sighting Kamaley Kamini at sea.

95. BILIKU—THE DEITY OF STORMS AND THUNDER: The region of Andaman is prone to heavy rains, thunder, lightning and floods and these, being preserved in the memory of the locals are reflected variously in their myths. Biliku is believed to be the Goddess of the northeast monsoon, as well as lighting, thunder and all erratic floods. Tarai is the God of southwest wind and monsoon. Interestingly the myths weave natural phenomenon within their storylines.

Akajeru is an independent and nearly extinct Great Andamanese language. It was one of the four dialects once spoken in North Andaman. The other three remaining dialects of this language are the varieties of the remaining traditional groups of the island—Akachari, Akabo and Akakhora. Radcliffe-Brown had reported in 1922 and 1933 about the four tribes of North Andaman—Akachari, Akakora, Akabo and Akajeru.

When the British established a Permanent Settlement and a Penal Colony in 1858 in Port Blair on South Andaman, the Akajeru inhabited the southern portion of North Andaman and the northern extremity of the Middle Andaman. It is estimated the total number of people of all four native groups were only 1,500 in 1858. During the early part of the nineteenth century, their estimated number was around 3,500, which steadily declined because of imported diseases, including pneumonia, syphilis, measles and influenza, to which the inhabitants had no immunity. Finally, by the end of the nineteeth century the situation was very serious as the Greater Andamanese were facing complete extinction. In the 1951 census, a total of only twenty-three Greater

Andamanese and ten Sentinelese were reported, including Akajeru, Akakora and Akachari. It is reported that the numbers have grown slightly and by 2013, Greater Andamanese were reported to be slightly more than fifty in number.

96. THE AKAKEDE TSUNAMI MYTH FROM NORTH ANDAMAN: The Akakede group of languages from North Andamans is an extinct group of languages which has been officially reported to have disappeared between 1930 and 1950. However, it is interesting to note that though the language has ceased to exist, this story remains famous from the region. A close study of lighting, rain and thunder from the Andamans also suggests significant environmental occurrences, which is typical for its geographical location. These stories also aid various ethnographic studies of the region.

97. MADHUKAR NOUKO PUJA AND THE STORY OF CHAND SAUDAGAR: Held sometime between January and February, the 'nouko puja' begins on the day of Saraswati Puja or Vasant Panchami or Sri Panchami and is held across few places in lower Assam Brahmaputra Valley and extensively across Barak Valley. The festival and the storyline reflect respect for the riverine ecology of the region. It also connects to the essence of both environment and nature on one hand, and trade on the other, thus connecting an ethos of prosperity that a flourishing environment and biodiversity begets. Thus, the larger storyline of 'Manasa Mangal Kavya' also reflects the basic essence of nature and the significance of conservation and preservation. The storyline also represents man's continuous battles of survival against the forces of nature.

The storyline of 'Manasa Mangal Kavya', which the festival follows, is the famous poetry from erstwhile Bengal region (including the present country of Bangladesh), which is also said to have originated as part of oral traditions and was written down later, during the medieval time in Bengal. This poetry is known through various names and there are different versions which have been written by many authors. It is also referred to as 'Manasa Purana' or 'Manasa Bijaya'. According to Sukumar Sen, there are fifteen versions of the text, while D. C. Sen has mentioned fifty-eight authors. Interestingly and also as mentioned by Edward C. Dimock Jr in his 'The Goddess of Snakes in Medieval Bengali Literature', all of these varied versions have the basic story of Chand Saudagar, Manasa, Behula, and Lakkhindar as the centre point, but each one carries its own unique style of presentation, including slight variations in style, language, and details within the story.

98. THE LEGEND OF PRINCE VIJAYA: This is a story from the Mahavamsa-the Theravada Buddhist chronicle from Sri Lanka, which mentions the beginning of the history of Sri Lanka with the arrival of Prince Vijaya and the establishment of a ruling dynasty thereafter. This legend from Sri Lanka is also a well-known one and has been variously reflected across many works from Bengal. One such famous work is a Bengali poem of eight paragraphs by Satyendranath Datta (1882–1922), titled 'Amra' (Us). This includes a simple

reference to the legend in its second paragraph as it mentions the two lines: 'Our son Bijoy Singha won over Lanka, Has left behind marks of his bravery on its soil'. Thus, there are many other famous poets and authors, who have also composed verses with reference to this legend, including Dwijendralal Roy (1863–1913). Even the famous Bengali poet Michael Madhusudan Dutta (1824–1873) had also gathered and compiled notes in English to write an epic poem about the legend of Bijoy Singha, however, it could not be completed because of his untimely death. Thus, the legend of Prince Vijay (variously referred to in Bengali as Bijoy Singha) is famous across South Asia; however, many critics often question the historical truth within the story and often just speak about it as being part of local myth and legend.

The Veddas mentioned in the legend is also spelled as Veddahs. They have been accorded indigenous status at present in Sri Lanka and have sub-communities like Coast Veddahs, Anuradhapura Veddahs, and Bintenne Veddahs.

99. THE MINYONG MYTH ABOUT THE CREATION OF THE WORLD: The Minyong are a sub-group of the Adi people of the state of Arunachal Pradesh, and this is a Minyong myth about the creation of the world from a vast body of water. Various myths often describe the creation of the universe from water bodies. In this particular story, it is interesting to note the mention of the creation of rocks and water, the quintessential features of the surface of the earth, which has been part of creation for thousands of years.

100. ANAHITA—THE BESTOWER OF LIFE: According to the Bundahishn, the Zoroastrian Book of Genesis, water is the second good creation of Ahura Mazda. Avan is the Divinity or Energy of Ahura Mazda, presiding over all waters. The name 'Avan' is derived from the word 'Aap' or 'Aapo.' It is the divine and cosmic force which sustains the entire cosmos. In the Avesta, this divinity is called Ardvisura Anahita—the Pure and the Immaculate. In the Zoroastrian calendar, the tenth day of the month is dedicated to the waters. Zoroastrians offer thanks by observing the Maidioshahem Gahambar. This is a mid-summer Gahambar or seasonal feast, celebrated in the month of Tir from Roj Khorshed to Daepmeher. In India, Parsis observe the Avan nu Parab or Parab of Ava according to the Shehenshahi calendar. This is the day of worship, which is the Avan roj nu Parab in the month of Avan Mah (i.e. the tenth day of the eight month of the Zoroastrian calendar) and this is a day of special reverence for offering worship to the great nourisher and purifier of the world. This day is celebrated as the birthday of the waters. For Avan roj nu Parab, prayers are recited before any natural and pure body of water including the well, river, and the sea, along with flowers and natural rock. Sugar and oil lamps are lit before dusk near the wells.

101. JHULELAL AND THE UNIFYING SPIRIT OF WATER: In the Rig Veda, there are many verses in praise of the Sindhu. Though many historians speak of the word 'Sindhu' as a sea, it is popularly believed to signify the river Indus. Thus, the word speaks about the Sindhu River, which also blesses with fertile soil, agriculture and life. In the Vishnu Purana, the Dasarna River in Sindh has been identified as the Sindhu River. The Sindh River is also often believed to be identical with the Kali Sindh River.

The legend speaks of not only the spiritual aspects of water, but also about water being the source of life, energy and existence. Interestingly, the mention of the pala fish also shows an aspect of strength and bravery as it is a fish, found locally and is often consumed, but it swims against the current, which is an act of courage, reflected in the legend.

102. THE AMRIT SAROVAR: The story is about the sacredness of water and its vital blessings for life, which is akin to rebirth or washing off all sins and looking forward to a new beginning. The Amrit Sarovar is still considered a sacred place in the Golden Temple premises and a holy dip is thought to be very sacred for spiritual cleansing. The beri tree mentioned in the story is among the three historical trees in the Golden Temple complex. It is believed to have been here since the time of Guru Ram Das, who is said to have founded the holy pond or sarovar, and the city of Amritsar. The other two beri trees inside the complex are the 'Ber Baba Budha Sahib' and 'Lachi Ber'. *Panth Prakash* was written by Giani Gian Singh, who completed the book in 1867 and it was published in 1880. Giani Gian Singh was the first to write about the history of the Sikhs from the birth of Guru Nanak Dev to the last decade of the nineteenth century. He wrote the book in Brij, explaining the life of ten Sikh Gurus and the various sacrifices made by Sikhs, Dal Khalsa, Sikh Misals and Sikh Sects. He has also mentioned that the main background and influence of his book is the books of Ratan Singh, Bute Shah, and many other stories narrated by elderly people in those times.

103. THE EARLIEST SETTLEMENTS OF LAKSHADWEEP: Though this is a very famous legend, yet it remains unsubstantiated. What the legend however highlights is the close association of the islands with the nearby mainland. Thus, it is not improbable that migration may have taken place and settlements may have occurred in various waves. Some of these settlements may have even taken place just a century ago. Evidence of these recent settlements is provided in R. H. Ellis's *A Short Account of the Laccadive Islands and Minicoy* (1924), where Ellis mentions Bentley's reference from 1795, speaking of the islands of Agathi and Kiltan as having only a limited hundred people, while Kadamat was still uninhabited.

Archeological and historical records about the earliest settlements of Lakshadweep speak of a similar relation to the mainland, which in recent years have been studied through mitochondrial DNA analyses of individuals from the islands. According to recent studies from 2019 by Mustak, M. S., Rai, N., Naveen, M.R. et al., there is a strong founder effect for both paternal and maternal lineages and a close genetic link of Lakshadweep islanders with the Maldives, Sri Lanka, and India. Most of the Lakshadweep islands share the haplogroups specific to South Asia and West Eurasia, except Minicoy, which shares haplogroups of East Eurasia. Thus, the majority of human ancestry in Lakshadweep is mainly from South Asia, with minor influences from East and West Eurasia.

104. SAGE GAUTAMA AND RIVER GODAVARI: This story is from the Kotirudra Samhita of the Shiva Purana. Brahmagiri is a mountain range in the Western Ghats, and is located in Nashik district of Maharashtra. The Tryambakeshwar temple is located near it. The origin of the Godavari River is considered to be near Tryambak. The river Godavari flows eastwards and meets the Bay of Bengal, after crossing several states of India, including Maharashtra, Telengana, and Andhra Pradesh and covering 1,465 kilometres. It drains 312,812 square kilometres and has many tributaries which flow through the entire region. The river Godavari also has many folklores associated with it and this river helps many economic activities around the region.

105. THE ARRIVAL OF THE PARSIS TO THE SUBCONTINENT: Some accounts state that about 18,000 Parsis came in waves of seven. Five of these groups landed in Diu, one at Variav, near Surat, and one at Cambay in Gujarat. The Sanjan Stambh or the Sanjan Memorial Column was constructed in the year 1920, to commemorate the arrival of the Parsis at Sanjan. This column mentions the date of arrival as 936 CE. Sanjan Day is celebrated in November, which is attended by many Parsis from the area as well as many other places.

In the absence of the history of the early years of the Zoroastrian settlers, the Parsis of India, this narrative, Qissa-i-Sanjan which is in the form of a poem, holds significant importance in shedding light on the early years of the settlers in the Indian subcontinent. The original poem was written in 432 verse couplets in 1599 CE by a Parsi priest, Bahman Kaikobad, whose name is signed in the conclusion and is assumed as the date of authorship. This is also several centuries after the described events have taken place. His story is based on the lore of priests and speaks of the history of the Zoroastrian community from the days of Zoroaster to the late fifteenth century. This work was translated into French in 1771 by Abraham Anquetil-Duperron and by the beginning of twentieth century, the poem was widely known. The account variously describes how the settlers fought foreign invaders, their failure in the same, and their flight. The narrative closes with a chapter on the conveyance of the 'Fire of Warharan' to Navsari.

Though the Parsis revere and variously worship all five elements of nature, fire holds an important part in their spiritual belief. They consider it to be the purest element. Fire is associated with light, warmth, energy, and the cause for creating life. Thus, every rite, ritual, and ceremony involves the presence of sacred fire.

106. THE LONAR LAKE AND THE MYTH OF LONASURA: The story is an interesting example, which reflects a gradual inclusion and adoption of many natural phenomenon around us within the folds of oral traditions, including myths and legends. Geographically, the lake is located in Buldhana district of Maharashtra. There are several temples surrounding the Lonar Lake and most of them lie in ruins, except the temple of Daityasudan at the centre of Lonar town. This is dedicated to Lord Vishnu. This temple is dated to the Chalukya dynasty (ruled over central and southern India between the sixth and twelfth centuries) and is a good example of the Hemadpanthi style of architecture. In about 1600 CE, Abul Fazal wrote in his Ain-i-Akbari about the lake, 'These mountains produce all the requisites for making glass and soap. And here are saltpetre works which yield a considerable revenue to the State, from the duties collected. On these mountains is a spring of salt water, but the water from the centre and the edges is perfectly fresh.'

The Lonar Lake has undergone extensive study by various experts, including geologists, archaeologists, ecologists, naturalists, historians and astronomers. Numerous academics and scientists from institutions across India such as The Physical Research Laboratory, The University of Sagar, Central University and Geological Survey of India—all under the Government of India—have contributed to this research. Additionally, international organisations, including the Smithsonian Institution, USA and the United States Geological Survey have also been involved in the study of the Lonar Lake. Situated within the Deccan Plateau, it is a massive plain of volcanic rock, created by eruption, around 65 million years ago, and it is understood that the Lonar Crater was created as a result of a meteorite impact. The water of the lake is both saline and alkaline. In November 2020, the lake was declared as a protected Ramsar site. Biological nitrogen fixation was discovered in the lake in 2007. There have been extensive studies conducted on the rocks of the lake. In 2019, a study conducted by IIT Bombay revealed the minerals in the lake soil to be very similar to the minerals found in the moon rock brought back during the Apollo Programme. Previously, the crater's age was estimated to be around 52,000 + -6,000 years, but much newer studies have suggested an age of 576,000 = 47,000 years. The lake's ecosystem is also under threat. It is often a cause of concern due to the drying up of the percolation dam nearby. The closure of streams which flow into the lake, as well as various other factors like illegal constructions around it, sewage dumping in the waters of the lake, the lake being used for bathing and washing purposes, illegal deforestation, and excavations, among others, are also subjects of apprehension. These causes are a real threat to the region, and hopefully, some constructive planning in the future can help to rejuvenate the lake.

The lake can be viewed while travelling over the region in an aeroplane, and is often even announced by a generous pilot to the travellers to look down to have an aerial glimpse. The aerial view is splendid and is probably the reason why another mythology story was inspired in its honour. It is popularly believed that when Lord Rama was travelling back to Ayodhya with Sita, after killing the demon King Ravana, he is said to have looked down at the lake. Being mesmerized by the spectacle, he is also said to have pointed out the same to his wife and both were fascinated by the great aerial view from the sky.

107. THE STORY OF THE CREATION OF THE WORLD: This story is after the Santhal patachitra from Purulia district of West Bengal, which is also part of the Chhotanagpur pleateau region. This story narrates the landscape surrounding the region, which is hilly and undulating with monadnocks. The story also speaks about the significance of various elements from nature in the lives of the people, including the goose, the gander, and the grass. From the grass, especially sabia grass and bamboo, various items like baskets are made. The patua folk artists are quite famous for their artwork. There are many patuas who reside across the region of Majramura village in Kashipore block, which has the largest cluster. There are also patua families in Raghunathpur, Burrabazar, and Bharatpur. All patuas carry the last name of Chitrakar, meaning an artist. The patachitra or the folk paintings which the patuas create are scroll paintings, which are 8–12 inches in width and vary in length, depending on the length of the story. The colours of these Jadu patachitra are very simple and generally monochromatic with various shades of grey, brown and white, depicting all the characters in the story. The story in the scroll painting is depicted on small panels, and each panel is marked by a decorative border. Apart from Jadu patachitra, they also paint other episodes from various mythologies, including Madanmohan Leela, Krishna Leela, Raas Leela, among others, which also show the influence of mainstream religion and culture on folk beliefs.

108. HOW THE KHECHEOPALRI LAKE WAS FORMED: The Khecheopalri Lake, is locally referred to as Sho Dzo Sho, meaning, 'Oh Lady, sit here'. It is located near the Khecheopalri village in the west of Gangtok in Sikkim district, and is considered sacrosanct to both Hindus and Buddhists. The lake forms part of the Buddhist religious pilgrimage circuit, involving Yuksom, the Dubdi monastery in Yuksom, Pemayangtse monastery, the Rabdentse ruins, the Sanga Choeling monastery and the Tashiding monastery. It is intriguing to observe how birds diligently clear away even the tiniest leaves that fall onto the lake. This makes the lake stay clear and clean always. This lake is also an integral part of the sacred valley of Demazong, meaning the 'valley of rice', and this valley is considered to hold hidden treasures which have been blessed by Guru Padmasambhava.

Topographically, the lake was formed due to the original scooping action of a glacier. The water is collected in the depression, caused by the glacier. Thus, the lake was the original region of ancient precipitous glaciers and forms the southern bank of the Lethang Valley. The vegetation surrounding the lake includes broadleaved mixed temperate forest, and the vegetation within the lake comprises of Macrophytes, Phytoplankton, and Zooplankton.

Bibliography

'Achipur-Places of Interest in South Bengal', *Kolkata Tours*. http://www.kolkatatours.in/south-bengal.php?target=Places-of-Interest-In-South-Bengal&place=Achipur

'Aditi': Hindu deity', *Encyclopedia Britannica*. https://www.britannica.com/topic/Aditi

'Amrit Sarovar', *The Sikh Encyclopaedia*. https://www.thesikhencyclopedia.com/biographical/famous-women/rajani-bibi/

'Anahita', *Encyclopedia.com*. https://www.encyclopedia.com/social-sciences/encyclopedias-almanacs-transcripts-and-maps/anahita

'Anahita', In *Wikipedia*. https://en.wikipedia.org/wiki/Anahita

'Anal in India', *Joshua Project*. https://joshuaproject.net/people_groups/16211/IN

A. R. Brown, *The Andaman Islanders*, 2nd ed., Cambridge: Cambridge University Press, 1933.

A. R. Brown, *The Andaman Islanders*, Cambridge: Cambridge University Press, 1922.

Aathira Perinchery, 'Worshipping Waghoba: Faith Meets Conservation in Maharashtra Where Humans and Leopards Share Space', In *Mongabay*, 4 October 2021. https://india.mongabay.com/2021/10/worshipping-waghoba-faith-meets-conservation-in-maharashtra-where-humans-and-leopards-share-space/

Alfred Radcliffe Brown, *Puluga of Andaman*, UK: Cambridge Universiy Press, 1933, pp. 196–197. https://www.sacred-texts.com/asia/tai/taitp.htm

Amir Khusro and Indian Riddle Tradition Author(s): Ved Prakash Vatuk Source: *The Journal of American Folklore*, Apr. - Jun., 1969, Vol. 82, No. 324 (Apr. - Jun., 1969), pp. 142-154

Amir Khusro Author(s): Kunwar Narain Source: *Indian Literature*, May/June 2018, Vol. 62, No. 3 (305) (May/June 2018), pp. 65-66 Published by: Sahitya Akademi.

Ananya Bhattacharya, 'Santhal Pata of Majramura' in *Tribal Culture of India*, Delhi: The Indian Trust for Rural Heritage and Development, 2019, pp. 71–72.

Aniket Mahapatra, 'Bouddho-oitijjher Aloke Bener Meye- ekti uponnash' (Looking at the novel Bener Meye through the perspectives of Buddhism). In *Nalanda Journal*, 2020–2022, p. 81.

Annu Jalais, 'Bonbibi: Bridging Worlds', *Indian Folklife*, Serial No. 28, January 2008, pp. 6–8.

Anuradha Goyal, 'Shirgaon Lairai Devi and the Seven Sisters of Goa', *Inditales*, 6 May 2021. https://www.inditales.com/lairai-devi-seven-sisters-of-goa/

April Holloway, 'Mysteries of the Kingdom of Shambhala', *Ancient Origins*, 5 April 2014. https://www.ancient-origins.net/ancient-places-asia/mysteries-kingdom-shambhala-001529

Arnapurna Rath, 'Ecological Consciousness and the Tale of the Nabagunjara from Folk Odisha', In *Fundamatics*, 10 January 2020. https://fundamatics.net/ecological-consciousness-and-the-tale-of-the-nabagunjara-from-folk-odisha/

Ashok Biswal, *The Kaliani Wind and Other Jungle Stories*, New Delhi: Pustak Mahal, 1 January 2012.

Ashok Ganguly, 'Bengal's Town Where Bhadu Gaan Originated', *Get Bengal*, 8 November 2017. https://www.getbengal.com/details/bengal-s-town-where-bhadu-gaan-originated

Ashok Mathur, 'Gavri- The Incredible Play of Bhils' In *Royal Harbinger*, 5 September 2019. https://www.royalharbinger.com/udaipur_News_9390.html

Asia Society, 'Legends of the Indus', New York:19 May 2008. https://asiasociety.org/arts/visual-arts/legends-indus

Avantika Halflongbar, 'Weaving in indigenous Dimasa community of Assam: Social entrepreneurs can revive the age-old traditional knowledge by using social media and e-marketing platforms', In *Heinrich Boll Stiftung*, 19 December 2019. https://in.boell.org/en/weaving-indigenous-dimasa-community-assam

B. N. Parimoo, *The Ascent of Self: A Reinterpretation of the Mystical Poetry of Lalla-ded*, New Delhi: Motilal Banarsidass, 2013, pp. 206.

B.N. Parimoo, The Ascent of Self. Kotru, Lal Ded Her Life and Sayings.

B. Ramadevi, 'The Saint of the Masses', *The Hindu*, 3 March 2014. https://www.thehindu.com/features/friday-review/history-and-culture/the-saint-of-the-masses/article5746486.ece

Banglanatak, 'Desert Music: Soul of Western Rajasthan'. https://artsandculture.google.com/story/desert-music-soul-of-western-rajasthan-banglanatak/twUBeELO1jFemw?hl=en

Beheroze Shroff, 'Indians of African Descent: History and Contemporary Experience,' *Souls*, 10:4, 9 December 2008, 315-326.

Bilal Habib, 'Beautiful Lal Trag Park in Ruins in Pampore' In *Kashmir Reader*, 14 August 2020. https://kashmirreader.com/2020/08/14/beautiful-lal-trag-park-in-ruins-in-pampore/

Book Excerpt, 'Five poems by Lal Ded, the Kashmiri mystic who merged erotic and spiritual longing in her poetry', *Scroll.in*, 6 February 2018. https://scroll.in/article/867201/five-poems-by-lal-ded-the-kashmiri-mystic-who-merged-erotic-and-spiritual-longing-in-her-poetry

Book Excerpt, 'Five poems by Lal Ded, the Kashmiri mystic who merged erotic and spiritual longing in her poetry', *Scroll.in*, 6 February 2018. https://scroll.in/article/867201/five-poems-by-lal-ded-the-kashmiri-mystic-who-merged-erotic-and-spiritual-longing-in-her-poetry

British Library, 'The Migration of the Zoroastrians from Iran to India: Qiṣṣah-'i Sanjan'. https://www.bl.uk/collection-items/qissah-i-sanjan

'Charkula Dance', In Madhya Pradesh GK, 27 October 2015. http://www.madhyapradeshgk.in/2015/10/charkula-dance.html

C. B. Varma, 'The Illustrated Jataka & Other Stories of The Buddha'. https://ignca.gov.in/online-digital-resources/jataka-stories/012-the-mighty-fish/

C.A. Soppitt, A Short Account of the Kuki-Lushai Tribes on the North-east Frontier, Assam: Assam Secretariat Press, 1887.

Catherine Gilon, 'Conserving the Toda Buffalo Before it is too late', *Mongabay*, 26 May 2020. https://india.mongabay.com/2020/05/conserving-the-toda-buffalo-before-it-is-too-late/

Cecil Henry, Bompas, *Folklore of the Santal Parganas*, London: David Nutt, 1909, p. 26.

Chapchar Kut, Festivals of Mizoram. https://www.tribaltoursinindia.com/festivals-of-mizoram/

Chiranjeevi Kumar, 'Lalleshwari: The Light of Wisdom in Valley' In Blogpost of the writer, 8 November 2019. https://www.jammukashmirnow.com/Encyc/2019/11/8/LALLESHWAR-The-light-of-wisdom-in-valley.amp.html

Clara Lewis, 'Ethnogaphic Study of Warli Tribe Documents 150 Waghoba Shrines', *The Times of India*, 27 June 2021. https://timesofindia.indiatimes.com/city/mumbai/mumbai-ethnographic-study-of-warli-tribe-documents-150-waghoba-shrines/articleshow/83881741.cms

Corinne G. Dempsey 'Lessons in Miracles from Kerala, South India: Stories of Three "Christian Saints.' *History of Religions*, 39:2, 1999, 150–176.

Cyrus H. Gordon, 'Legendary Wisdom of Solomon', *Britannica.com*. https://www.britannica.com/biography/Solomon/Legendary-wisdom

'Dreams of Mother Trishala', *Jainworld.com*. https://jainworld.com/education/jain-education-material/jain-stories/dreams-of-mother-trishala/

Darshi Vasavada, 'The Untold Story of Tana- Riri', Blog post, 1 December 2018. https://darshivasavada.wordpress.com/2018/12/01/the-untold-story-of-tana-riri/

Debraj Mitra, 'How a Trader Became a Deity', *The Telegraph*, 1 November 2018. https://www.telegraphindia.com/west-bengal/how-a-trader-became-a-deity/cid/1408157

Deepanjan Ghosh, 'Achipur and India's first Chinese Settler', *Live History India*. https://artsandculture.google.com/exhibit/achipur-india%E2%80%99s-first-chinese-settler-live-history-india/7QLCgSL39EveLw?hl=en

Devika. B, 'Myths and Legends of Famous Serpent Temples in Kerala', In *Overview*, 20 August 2020. https://www.sahapedia.org/myths-and-legends-major-serpent-temples-kerala

Dharmendra Kanwar, 'Gavri- The Dance of the Bhils', In *Tribal Culture of India*, New Delhi: Indian Trust for Rural Heritage and Development, 2019, pp. 5–6.

Dhee, 'The Warli and Their Waghoba', In *Current Conservation*, 23 May 2022. https://www.currentconservation.org/the-warli-and-their-waghoba/

Diana Eck, *A Sacred Geography*, New York: Harmony Books, 2012.

Digambar Ghodke, 'Language and Culture of the Waddar Community in Maharashtra', In *Shiksan Prasarak Sanstha's Sangamner Nagarpalika Arts*, 2016, pp. 69–70. https://www.researchgate.net/publication/311922163

Dilip Chitre, *Says Tuka: Selected Poems of Tukaram,* Mumbai: Poetrywala Paperwall Media and Publishing Pvt Ltd, 1991, pp. 121, 128, 130, 131, 145, 153, 155.

Durga Bhagvat, 'Folktales of Central India', In *Asian Folklore Studies*, Vol. 31, No. 2, 1972, pp. 1–89. https://doi.org/10.2307/1177489. https://www.jstor.org/stable/1177489

Durga Bhagwat, *Indian Anthropologist*, 36:1 & 2, 2006, pp. 23–44, p. 27.

E. H. Man, *On the Aboriginal Inhabitants of the Andaman Islands*, London: The Royal Anthropological Institute of Great Britain and Ireland, 1932.

Edward Cowell, (ed.), The Jātaka or Stories of the Buddha's Former Births, Cambridge: Cambridge University Press, 1895, pp. 34–37. https://jatakastories.div.ed.ac.uk/stories-in-text/jatakatthavannana-316/

Edward C. Dimmock, 'The Goddess of Snakes in Medieval Bengali Literature', In *History of Religions*, Vl 1, No. 2, USA: University of Chicago Press, 1962, pp. 307–321. https://www.jstor.org/stable/1062059

Edward Horace Man, *The Andaman Islanders: On the Aboriginal Inhabitants of the Andaman Islands, Report of Researches into the Language of the South Andaman Island,* UK: White Lotus Press, 1885, pp. 202–203, 212–213.

Elwin, *Myths of the North-East Frontier of India*, p. 41.

Elwin, *Myths of the Northeast Frontier of India*, p.18.

Elwin, *Specimens of the Oral Literature of Middle India*, p. 319.

Elwin, *Specimens of the Oral Literature of Middle India*, p. 71.

Elwin, *Specimens of the Oral Literature of Middle India,* p.163.

Elwin, *Specimens of the Oral Literature of Middle India,* pp. 217–218.

EMN, 'Hornbill, the Naga Cultural Totem Spanning Generations', In *Eastern Mirror*, 30 November 2019. https://easternmirrornagaland.com/hornbill-the-naga-cultural-totem-spanning-generations/

Esther David, *Bene Appetit: The Cuisine of Indian Jews*, Gurugram: Harper Collins India, 2021, p. 57.

'Folktales of India- Tales from Nagaland- the legend of Hornbill'. www.wearetrip.in.https://www.youtube.com/watch?v=kNfbZ8raS4s

Faizal Khan, 'This filmmaker takes on the issue of gender bias in Parsi community through her art', *Financial Express*, 11 August 2019. https://www.financialexpress.com/lifestyle/this-filmmaker-takes-on-the-issue-of-gender-bias-in-parsi-community-through-her-art/1672287/

Folklore Foundation, 'Lokaratna' Vol. IX, ISSN No.2347-6427, 2016, pp. 69–70.

Frances M. Woods, 'Moon and Sun Story', 1972. https://www.sil.org/resources/archives/87791

'Gavri- The Incredible Merumatyam of Rajasthan', In *Various Colours of Rajasthan*, 13 June 2018. https://www.rajasthanstudy.co.in/2018/06/gavri-incredible-merumatyam-of-rajasthan.html

'Guru Nanak and the Monster Fish'. *Heritage Lab*. https://www.theheritagelab.in/guru-nanak-and-the-monster-fish/

G. N. Devy, 'Tribal Verse', New Delhi: *NCERT*, 2021–22, p.168.

Gaia Tree, 'Tattoo Art of the Baiga Tribe', In *Gia Tree Gallery of Indigenous Art*, 7 October 2015. https://www.gondtribalart.com/tattoo-art-of-the-baiga-tribe/

Gazetteer, 1880, pp. 234–236. https://www.google.co.in/books/edition/_/dLUBAAAAYAAJ?hl=en&gbpv=1&pg=PA210

George van Driem, *Languages of the Himalayas: An Ethnolinguistic Handbook of the Greater Himalayan Region, Containing an Introduction to the Symbiotic Theory of Language*, Leiden: Brill, 1 January 2001. This book states: 'The Aka-Kol tribe of Middle Andaman became extinct by 1921. The Oko-Juwoi of Middle Andaman and the Aka-Bea of South Andaman and Rutland Island were extinct by 1931. The Akar-Bale of Ritchie's Archipelago, the Akakede of Middle Andaman and the A-Pucikwar of South Andaman Island soon followed. By 1951, the census counted a total of only 23 Greater Andamanese and 10 Sentinelese. That means that just ten men, twelve women and one child remained of the Aka-Kora, Aka-Cari and Aka-Jeru tribes of Greater Andaman and only ten natives of North Sentinel Island ...'. Probably, for these forms and constructions there is 'very little difference (...) between the four tribes of the North (Aka-Čari, Aka-Kora, Aka-Bo and Aka-Jeru)', as Radcliffe-Brown explains.

GetBengal, 'Bijoy Singha – the Prince of Bengal who Went on to Rule Sri Lanka!, 11 June 2020. https://www.getbengal.com/details/bijoy-singha-the-prince-of-bengal-who-went-on-to-rule-sri-lanka

Government of Assam, 'Sonitpur District Profile'. https://sonitpur.assam.gov.in/portlet-sub-innerpage/legend

Gurmehar Kaur, 'Sikh Dharma', *Guru Nanak Storyteller*. https://www.sikhdharma.org/video-gurdwara-bair-sahib-at-4-am-guru-nanak-550-celebrations

Harbans Singh and Dharam Singh, *Concise Encyclopaedia of Sikhism*, Patiala: Punjab University Publication Bureau, 2013, p. 542. https://archive.org/stream/Concise EncylopediaOfSikhism/ConciseEncylopediaOfSikhism_djvu.txt

Harbhajan Singh, Giani Gian Singh Krit Sri Guru Panth Parkash Vich pesh dharmik itihasik chetna da sahitshastri Pripekh, Unpublished PhD Thesis submitted to Punjab University, 2020, Sodhganga. http://hdl.handle.net/10603/301717

Hariyali Devi, Jasoli. https://www.pilgrimaide.com/temples/haryali-devi-jasol

Henry Whitehead, *The Village Gods of South India*, London: Oxford University Press, 1921. https://archive.org/stream/VillageGodsOfSouthIndia/Village-Gods-Of-South-India_djvu.txt

'India's First Women Saint.' *Reuters.com.* October 11, 2008.

IANS, 'Asur Tribe from Jharkhand to Showcase Iron Smelting Skills this Durga Puja', *The Indian Express*, 12 October 2016. https://indianexpress.com/article/lifestyle/art-and-culture/asur-tribe-from-jharkhand-to-showcase-iron-smelting-skills-this-durga-puja-3070949/

Indira Gandhi Rashtriya Manav Sangrahalaya, 'The myth of Gugga Pir', *Indian Culture*. https://indianculture.gov.in/images/gugga-pir-kangra-himachal-pradesh

Ipsita Chakravarty, 'The legend of Tong Atchew- the First ancestor of the Chinese in India', In *Scroll.in.* 28 January 2017. https://scroll.in/magazine/826383/the-legend-of-tong-atchew-who-was-the-first-ancestor-of-the-chinese-in-india

Ishan Kukreti, 'Himalaya's Magical Grove', *Down to Earth*, 15 January 2018. https://www.downtoearth.org.in/news/forests/himalaya-s-magical-grove-59410

J.Sampath. 'Welcome to Madurai : Maqbara in madurai, Madurai Maqbara, Maqbara Photos, Maqbara history'. madurai.jbss.in.

Jason Soares, 'Earth Cult and Tale of the Seven Sisters', *The Times of India*, 25 July 2018. https://timesofindia.indiatimes.com/city/goa/earth-cult-tale-of-the-seven-sisters/articleshow/65135387.cms

Jean Camille, 'Myths and Legends', *American India Foundation*, 29 January 2013. https://aif.org/myths-and-legends/-

Jesse Buck, 'The Sugar in the Milk and the Augmented Historian', A thesis submitted for the degree of Doctor of Philosophy at The Australian National University © Copyright by Jesse Canaan Roe Buck 2018. https://openresearch-repository.anu.edu.au/bitstream/1885/197150/1/Buck-thesis-2020.pdf

Jews of Cochin. *Encyclopedia.com* https://www.encyclopedia.com/humanities/encyclopedias-almanacs-transcripts-and-maps/jews-cochin

Jhulelal, 'Rivers in Mythology'. http://117.252.14.242/rbis/Mythology.htm-

Jiwan Pani, *Celebration of Life: Indian Folk Dance*, New Delhi: Ministry of Information and Broadcasting, 2000, pp. 76–78.

Jiwan Pani, *Celebration of Life: Indian Folk Dance*, pp. 87.

John Shakespear, *The Lushei Kuki Clans*, London: Macmillan and Co., Limited, 1912, pp. 41–42.

Joshua J. Mark, 'Anahita', *World History Encyclopedia*, 4 February 2020. https://www.worldhistory.org/Anahita/

'Khecheopalri Lake', In *Wikipedia*. https://en.wikipedia.org/wiki/Khecheopalri_Lake

K Krishnamurthy, *Mythical Animals in Indian Art*, New Delhi: Abhinav Publications, 1985.

K. J. Save, 'The Warlis', *Archaeological Survey of India*, Bombay: Padma Publications Ltd. 1945, pp. 173–179.

K.K. Leuva, *The Asur- A Study of Primitive Iron-Smelters*, New Delhi: Bharatiya Adimjati Sevak Sangh, 1963, pp. 141–143.

Kannan Somasundaram, 'Tana and Riri: The Gujarat Geniuses Tansen Turned to', *The Times of India*, 23 November 2010. http://timesofindia.indiatimes.com/articleshow/6977859.cms?utm_source=contentofinterest&utm_medium=text&utm_campaign=cppst

Karen Organisation of Minnesota, 'Karen History: Migration to Burma'. https://www.mnkaren.org/history-culture/karen-history/

Kausalya Santhanam, 'From the Shadows', In *The Hindu*- Metroplus, 15 February 2011. https://www.thehindu.com/features/metroplus/From-the-shadows/article15445328.ece

Keibu Keioiba, *Wikipedia.* https://simple.m.wikipedia.org/wiki/keibu_keioiba

Keibu Keioiba. https://en.everybodywiki.com/Keibu_Keioiba

Koratty Feast, Kerala.com. http://www.kerala.com/pages/koratty-feast

Koratty Muthy Church History, Official webpage of the church. https://korattymuthy.org/koratty-muthy-church-history/

Koratty Muthy's Feast, *Just Kerala.com*, 2017. https://www.justkerala.in/culture/festivals-of-kerala/koratty-muthys-feast

Kynpham Sing Nongkynrih, 'U Thlen: The Man-eating Serpent', *India International Centre Quarterly*. Vol. 32, No. 2/3, 2005, pp. 33–38.

'Legend of Nohkalikai' In *Wikipedia*. https://en.wikipedia.org/wiki/Nohkalikai_Falls

'Lonar Crater Lake and Vishnu as Daityasudan in Skanda & Padma Purana', In *Fact*, 4 March 2015. https://www.booksfact.com/mysteries/lonar-crater-lake-and-vishnu-as-daityasudan-in-skanda-padma-purana.html

'Lord Krishna lifts Govardhan Parvat', In *Vedas and Puranas*. https://vedapuran.wordpress.com/short-stories/krishna-stories-bal-kannd/lord-krishna-lifts-govardhan-parvat/

Lakshmi Sharath, 'Kanyakumari Guide: Beaches, Temples & Tri-Coloured Sands', *Natgeo Traveller*, 14 November 2016. https://natgeotraveller.in/kanyakumari-guide-tricoloured-sands-and-a-goddess-who-got-stood-up-at-her-wedding/

Lokesh Ghai, 'From Earth Grew Rice, from Rice Grew the Warli Art', *Garland Magazine*, 29 May 2019. https://garlandmag.com/article/warli/

Lonar Lake, In *Wikipedia*. https://en.wikipedia.org/wiki/Lonar_Lake

'Madurai Maqbara, Tamil Nadu, INDIA | Ajmer Sharif Dargah – fathia Sharif – Esaal e Swaab – Sufi Prayer for Deceased – World Sufi Shrines'. Archived from the original on 24 April 2018. Retrieved 24 April 2018.

'Mother Godavari should flow with all its glory', *Hans India*, 13 March 2015. https://www.thehansindia.com/posts/index/News-Analysis/2015-03-13/Mother-Godavari-should-flow-with-all-its-glory/137144

'Mount Meru: Mythology', In *Britannica.com*. https://www.britannica.com/topic/Mount-Meru-mythology.

'Mount Meru', In *Wikipedia*. https://en.wikipedia.org/wiki/Mount_Meru

'Myths and Legends: How Birds and Fishes were Created- Chapter IV'. https://www.sacred-texts.com/asia/tai/tai04.htm- pp-207-208

M Frere, *Old Deccan Days or Hindoo Fairy Legends Current in Southern India*, Philadelphia: Lippincott's Press, 1870, pp. 194–195.

M. L. K Murthy, 'The Emergence of Folk Gods in the Religion of Kuruvas and Gollas of Andhra Pradesh', *S.M.Katre Felicitation* Volume, 51/52, (1991–92), pp. 563–572. https://www.jstor.org/stable/42930441

M. Madhavankutty, 'Elephants in Rituals and Festivals of Kerala', In *Sahapedia*, 24 September 2019. https://www.sahapedia.org/elephants-rituals-and-festivals

M. R. Narayan Swamy, 'Connecting the South Asia dots through common cultural heritage', *South Asia Monitor*, 25 February 2022. https://www.southasiamonitor.org/books/connecting-south-asia-dots-through-common-cultural-heritage

M.D. Muthukumaraswamy, 'Finding ecological citizenship inside the archives of pain: Famine Folklore', In *Indian Folklife* (editorial), Volume 1, Issue 3, October 2000, pp. 3–4.

Maccha-Jātaka, Fausboll, ed., pp. 329; Maccha-Jātaka, Chalmers, trans. https://obo.genaud.net/dhamma-vinaya/pts/kd/jat/jat.1/jat.1.075.chlm.pts.htm.

Madhusudan A. Dhaky, *The Vyala Figures on the Medieval Temples of India*, Varanasi: Prithivi Prakashan, 1965.

Maharashtra Government Gazetteers Department. https://gazetteers.maharashtra.gov.in/cultural.maharashtra.gov.in/english/gazetteer/KOLABA/places_Janjira%20Fort.html

Mahendra K. Mishra, 'A Hero of the Mahabharata in Folklore of Central India', *Folklore Foundation*. https://folklorefoundation.org/a-hero-of-the-mahabharata-in-folklore-of-central-india/

Mahendra K. Mishra, 'Oral Epics in Kalahandi' p. 97. www.folklore.ee/folklore. doi:10.7592/FEJF2004.26.mishra

Malini Nair, 'How Kerala Mistreats its Star Elephants in the Name of Piety', *The Times of India*, 14 June 2020. https://timesofindia.indiatimes.com/blogs/toi-edit-page/how-kerala-mistreats-its-star-elephants-in-the-name-of-piety/

Mamgain M.D, Himachal Pradesh District Gazetteers Kinnaur Vol 3, Ambala: 1971 pp. 120–122. https://archive.org/stream/dli.csl.3010/3010_djvu.txt

Mannarasala Shree Nagaraja Temple, Mannarasala.org. https://mannarasala.org/

Margaret Lyngdoh, 'Tiger Transformation Among the Khasis of Northeastern India: Belief Worlds And Shifting Realities', In *Anthropos*, Bd. 111, H. 2, 2016, pp. 649–658.

Migrator, 'The Chhinlung Rock and the Legendary Rain: Mizoram', *The North East Today*: 20 November 2016. https://thenortheasttoday.com/travel/

northeasts-seven-sisters-legends-myths/cid2547049.htm

Migrator, 'The Legend Behind Nohkalikai Falls: Meghalaya', In *The North East Today*, 20 November 2016. https://thenortheasttoday.com/travel/northeasts-seven-sisters-legends-myths/cid2547049.htm

Ministry of Culture, 'Sanjari: Folk Music of Nagaland by Onetoshi Jamir' India, 20 July 2018. https://indianculture.gov.in/video/sanjari-folk-music-nagaland-onetoshi-jamir-sanjaarai-naagaalaainda-kae-laoka-gaita

Ministry of River Jalshakti, Godavari River Management Board, Govt of India. https://grmb.gov.in/

Miranda Shaw, *Buddhist Goddesses of India*, New Jersey: Princeton University Press, 2015.

Mohammed S. Mustak, et al., 'The Peopling of Lakshadweep Archipelago', *ResearchGate*, May 2019. https://doi.org/10.1038/s41598-019-43384-3, https://www.nature.com/articles/s41598-019-43384-3

Mohit M. Rao, 'A little Myanmar in the Andamans', 24 September 2018. https://www.thehindu.com/society/a-little-myanmar-in-the-andamans/article24894384.ece -

Nalini Ramachandran, 'Jumbo Tales: A Tribute to Guruvayur Kesavan- The Celebrated Chief Elephant of the Temple', *Swarajyamag*, 14 January 2022. https://swarajyamag.com/books/jumbo-tales-a-tribute-to-guruvayur-kesavan-the-celebrated-chief-elephant-of-the-temple

Nandita Bhardwaj, Tirna Ray, Smita Mishra Chaturvedi, *Storytellers @ Work*, New Delhi: Katha Publications, 2004, p.193.

National Geographic Resource Library (online), 'Ganges River Basin'. https://www.nationalgeographic.org/encyclopedia/ganges-river-basin/

Nawa Raj, Subba, 'An Overview of the Association between the Myths and Proof of Lepmuhang Mundhum and Matsya Puran', *ResearchGate*, 1 November 2019. https://www.researchgate.net/publication/337869915_An_Overview_of_the_Association_Between_the_Myths_and_Proof_of_Lepmuhang_Mundhum_and_Matsya_Puran

Neeraj D, 'Kinnaur's Phulaich Fair- Festival of Flowers (Ukhyang)' In *Mysterious Himachal: Land of Faith and God*, 2 January 2017. https://mysterioushimachal.wordpress.com/2017/01/02/kinnaurs-phulaich-fair-festival-of-flowersukhyang/

Nila Kanth Kotru, *Lal Ded Her Life and Sayings*, Srinagar: Utpal Publications, 1989.

Nilanjana Bhattacharjee, 'Situating the Cult of Manasa and Nouka Puja within the MangalKavya Tradition', October 2021, In *Sahapedia*.

Noshir H. Dadrawala, 'Avan Ardvisura Anahita – The Divine Purifier', *Parsi Times*, 24 March 2017. https://parsi-times.com/2017/03/avan-ardvisura-anahita-divine-purifier/

Noshir H. Dadrawala, 'Qissa-e-Sanjan: The Tale of Sanjan', *Parsi Times*, 12 November 2016. https://parsi-times.com/2016/11/qissa-e-sanjan-tale-sanjan/

Noshir H. Dadrawala, 'Questions Answered- Part-1'. http://parsizoroastrianism.com/Tenets/qstns33a.html

NT Desk, 'An Ancient Tale of Siblings', *Navhind Times*, 5 May 2019. https://www.navhindtimes.in/2019/05/05/magazines/buzz/an-ancient-tale-of-siblings/

Odisha Tour, 'Kalijai temple and Island, Chilika Lake, Khorda'. https://odishatour.in/kalijai-temple-chilika-khordha/

Onaiza Drabu, 'Queens, poets, academics, mystics: A calendar celebrates 12 inspirational women of Kashmir', In *Scroll.in.* 5 January 2019. https://scroll.in/article/908064/queens-poets-academics-mystics-a-calendar-celebrates-12-inspirational-women-from-kashmir.

Ornella D'Souza, 'Seven Sisters of Goa', DNA, 31 December 2018. https://www.dnaindia.com/just-before-monday/report-seven-sisters-of-goa-2701878

P. R. Ramachander, Kadayur Vellaimmal Koil, In *Village Gods blogspot.com*, 9 March2014. http://villagegods.blogspot.com/2014/03/kadayur-vellaimmal-koil.html-

P. Thomas, *Epics, Myths and Legends of India-A Comprehensive Survey of the Sacred Lore of the Hindus, Buddhists and Jains*, Bombay: D. B. Taraporevala Sons and Co. Pvt. Ltd., 1961, pp. 152–53.

P.C. Roychoudhury- Bihar district gazetteer- 1968.

Palash Vaswani, 'Mythological Trail of Manav Sangrahalaya', Blog post. https://www.dsource.in/resource/mythological-trail-manav-sangrahalaya/trail/9103

Pallavi Mishra, 'Khudurukuni Osha: A cultural tale of Odisha', *Utkal Today*. 8 June 2020. https://www.utkaltoday.com/khudurukuni-osha/

Pankaja Srinivasan, 'How Coimbatore Dealt with Epidemics in the Past', In *The Hindu*, 28 March 2020. https://www.thehindu.com/society/history-and-culture/coimbatores-chronicler-rajesh-govindarajulu-on-past-epidemics-in-the-city/article31191454.ece

Patron Saints Index- Saint Alphonsa of India.

Paul Thomas, *Epics, Myths and Legends of India- A Comprehensive Survey of the Sacred Lore of the Hindus, Buddhists and Jains,* Bombay: D.B. Taraporevala Sons and Co. Pvt. Ltd, 1961, pp. 178–179.

Pavani Mbagahawattha, 'Kuveni, the Queen of Lanka', *South Asian Today*, 20 May 2020. https://www.southasiantoday.com.au/article-75-kuveni-the-queen-of-lanka-details.aspx

Pr Kungsong Wanbe, 'Koren's (Koireng) Affinity with Tribes Inside and Outside India', In *E-Pao*. http://epao.net/epSubPageExtractor.asp?src=manipur.Ethnic_Races_Manipur.Koren_Koireng_affinity_with_tribes_inside_and_outside_India_By_Kungsong_Wanbe

Pradip Bhattacharya, 'Innovations in the Oriya Mahabharata', In *Boloji.com*, 15 May 2016. https://www.boloji.com/articles/49137/innovations-in-the-oriya-mahabharata

Purnia divisional commissioner office front view- Bihar government- Official website- www.purneadivision.bih.nic.in

R. H. Ellis, *A Short Account of the Laccadive Islands and Minicoy*, Madras: Asian Educational Services, 1992, p. 15. 1924https://archive.org/stream/LaccadiveIslandsAndMinicoy/Laccadive%20Islands%20and%20Minicoy_djvu.txt

Radha Sarkar, Hariti, Buddhist Deity, IGNCA (Indira Gandhi National Centre for the Arts). https://ignca.gov.in/PDF_data/Hariti_Buddhist_deity.pdf

Raja Thatha, 'Alphabetical Index of Village Gods of Tamil Nadu', Blog post, 19 June 2018. http://villagegods.blogspot.com/2018/06/alphabetical-index-of-village-gods-of.html

Raja Thatha, 'Chithakoor Ayyanar (Sevuga Perumal)', Blog post, 22 February 2010. http://villagegods.blogspot.com/2010/02/

Rajesh Govindarajulu, 'The Plague Chronicles', The Hindu, 31 October 2014. https://www.thehindu.com/features/metroplus/society/The-plague-chronicles/article11091036.ece

Ramya Nair, Dhee, Omkar Patil, Nikit Surve, Anish Andheria , John Linnell, and Vidya Athreya, 'Sharing Spaces and Entanglements With Big Cats: The Warli and Their Waghoba in Maharashtra, India', In *Frontiers in Conservation Science*, 23 June 2021. https://doi.org/10.3389/fcosc.2021.683356 https://www.frontiersin.org/articles/10.3389/fcosc.2021.683356/full

Raoul Zamponi and Bernard Comrie, *A Grammar of Akajeru: Fragments of a Traditional North Andamanese Dialect,* London: UCL Press, 11 November 2021. https://www.jstor.org/stable/j.ctv1nnwhkb.6

Raphael Meyer, 'Jews of India- The Cochin Jews', *The South-Asian.com*, March 2001. http://www.the-south-asian.com/march2001/jews_%20of_india_cochin_jews1.htm

Remigius de Souza, 'Universal Holistic Definition of Environment in Five Words'. Blog Post, 10 November 2011. https://remidesouza.blogspot.com/2011/11/

Ria Gupta, 'Unakoti, Tripura: The Story behind the Lost Hill of Faces', In *Conde Nast Traveller*. 1 February 2022. https://www.cntraveller.in/story/unakoti-tripura-the-story-behind-the-lost-hill-of-faces-monuments-of-india/

Ritika Pandey, 'A magical visit to the Lonar Crater with Stargazing Mumbai'. https://stargazingmumbai.in/a-magical-visit-to-the-lonar-crater/

Robert Chalmers, Edward B. Cowell (ed.) 'Rukkhadhamma Jataka' No. 74. Vol. 1- *Ekanipata*, 1895. https://obo.genaud.net/dhamma-vinaya/pts/kd/jat/jat.1/jat.1.074.chlm.pts.htm

'Samudra Manthan: The legend behind eclipses', *Amar Chitra Katha*, India: Amar Chitra Katha, 26 September 2020. https://www.amarchitrakatha.com/mythologies/the-legend-behind-eclipses/

'Sao Joao Festival in Goa', In *Wikipedia*. https://en.wikipedia.org/wiki/S%C3%A3o_Jo%C3%A3o_Festival_in_Goa

Sajjad Shahid, 'Myths and Legends of Hyderabad', *The Times of India*, 21

October 2012. https://timesofindia.indiatimes.com/city/hyderabad/myths-and-legends-of-hyderabad/articleshow/16895962.cms?from=mdr

SANDRP, 'Northeast Wetlands Review 2017: Remove Ithai Barrage on Loktak Lake', *South Asia Network on Dams, Rivers and People*, 31 January 2018. https://sandrp.in/2018/01/31/north-east-wetlands-review-2017-remove-ithai-barrage-on-loktak-lake/

SANDRP, 'Ramsar Wetlands Crisis 2020: North East India', *South Asia Network on Dams, Rivers and People*, 1 March 2020. https://sandrp.in/2020/03/01/ramsar-wetlands-crisis-north-east-india/

Sanjay Sharma, 'Fulaich- The Festival of Flowers in Kinnaur', In *Hub Pages*, 21 July 2019. https://discover.hubpages.com/travel/Fulaich-The-Festival-of-Flowers-in-Kinnur.

Sarah Stewart (ed.), *The Everlasting Flame: Zoroastrianism in History and Imagination*, London: SOAS University of London, 18 December 2013, p. 34. http://minorityaffairs.gov.in/sites/default/files/The_Everlasting_Flame-Zoroastrianism_in_History_and_Imagination.pdf

Sarmaya Trust, 'Bada Dev', In *Sarmaya.in*. https://sarmaya.in/objects/indigenous-tribal-art/bada-dev/

Satyabrata Das, 'Sarala Mahabharat: Tales of Subversion (Part-II)', In *Orissa Review*, November 2007, p. 52.

Shahpurshah Hormasji Hodivala, 'Kisseh-e-Sanjan', translated from Studies in Parsi History Bombay, 1920, pp. 94–117. http://www.avesta.org/other/qsanjan.htm

Shernaz Cama, 'Jamshedi-Nvroze', Parzor Foundation. https://artsandculture.google.com/exhibit/jamshedi-navroze/gQVK2nwe

Shramrao Koreti, 'Religion of the "Gond" Tribes of Middle India', In *South Asia Culture, History & Heritage,* 2015, pp. 87–90.

Shri Nallathangal Temple of Vatrayiruppu. https://temple.dinamalar.com/en/new_en.php?id=771

Shrikala Warrier, *Kamandalu: The Seven Sacred Rivers of Hinduism*, London: Mayur University, 2014.

Shruti Chakraborty, 'Bring forth the rains! Indian folklore and tribal practices to invoke rainfall', New Delhi: *The Indian Express*, 5 July 2018.

Six Poems from Surdas Author(s): Surdas Source: Mahfil, 1963, Vol. 1, No. 2 (1963), pp. 24-26 Published by: Asian Studies Center, Michigan State University.

Soma Ghosh, 'Navagunjar: Interesting Depictions in Indian Art', Blogpost, 5 December 2021. https://deccanviews.wordpress.com/author/wordlist123/

Srushti, 'Shocking Story of the Breathtaking Nohkalikai Falls', In *Native Planet*, 3 April 2018. https://www.nativeplanet.com/travel-guide/shocking-story-of-the-breathtaking-nohkalikai-falls-003646.html

St. Mary's Forane Church, Koratty, Official webpage of the church. http://www.korattymuthy.com/

Staff Reporter, 'Folk deity Gugga Dev', *Free Press Journal*, 1 October 2021. https://www.freepressjournal.in/bhopal/madhya-pradesh-folk-deity-gugga-dev-at-indira-gandhi-rashtriya-manav-sangrahalaya

Subba Rao, 'When Vindhya Grew Tall', In *Katha Kids*, 14 October 2016. https://kathakids.com/mythology-for-children/when-vindhya-grew-tall/

Sukumar Sen, Bangala Sahityer Itihas, Vol.I, (Bengali), Kolkata: Ananda Publishers, 1991. (Reprint 2007), p. 423.

Surjit Singh, '"Dukh Bhanjani Beri" at Golden Temple laden with fruits after over a decade', *Hindustan Times*, 29 May 2018. https://www.hindustantimes.com/punjab/dukh-bhanjani-beri-at-golden-temple-laden-with-fruits-after-over-a-decade/story-8avD2agNqM0jORorzldErK.html

'Tana- Riri the Legendary Sisters for Indian Classic Singers of Vadnagar'. https://sites.google.com/site/nagarnkgktg/hestory-of-nagar/nagar-tana-riri

'Tendong-faat', *Gauri Jog's- Indian Dance School*. https://www.gaurijog.com/indian-dance-education/indian-folk-dances/folk-dances-from-sikkim/tendong-faat/

'The Abode of the Virgin Goddess-The Call of the South: Part Three: Kanyakumari', 2 April 2009. https://kaminidandapani.typepad.com/my_weblog/2009/04/the-abode-of-the-virgin-goddess.html

'The Boy Who Became a Hornbill- Zeme Folktale'. In *Naga Journal*, 21 March 2020. https://nagajournal.com/the-boy-who-became-a-hornbill/.

'The Chiru Tribe of Manipur', 20 April 2020. https://www.ne.cab/tribe/chiru-tribe/

'The Crowning Glory that is the Kopel of Flower Crown at Sao Joao', In *Its Goa*, 23 June 2018. https://itsgoa.com/crowning-glory-kopel-sao-joao/

'The Lamkang Tribe'. https://www.ne.cab/tribe/the-lamkang-tribe/

'The Lonar Crater: The Mesmerizing Union of Religion and Science', In *Stargazing*. https://stargazingmumbai.in/the-lonar-crater/

'The Purum'. https://www.encyclopedia.com/humanities/encyclopedias-almanacs-transcripts-and-maps/purum

'The Ratnas of Samudra Manthan', *Amar Chitra Katha*, India: Amar Chitra Katha 14 May 2021. https://www.amarchitrakatha.com/mythologies/the-ratnas-of-samudra-manthan/_

'Tibeto-Burman languages', *Britannica*. https://www.britannica.com/topic/Tibeto-Burman-languages

'Toda People', *New World Encyclopedia*. https://www.newworldencyclopedia.org/entry/Toda_people

'Todas', In *Encyclopedia.com*. https://www.encyclopedia.com/humanities/encyclopedias-almanacs-transcripts-and-maps/todas

'Tukaram Throwing His Abangas in river', *Bhagavatam-katha*. http://www.bhagavatam-katha.com/tukaram-trowing-his-abangas-in-river/

T. W. Rhys Davids, *Buddhist Birth Stories: or, Jataka Tales, Volume 1*, London: Trübner & Co, 1880. (The oldest collection of folk-lore extant: Being The

Jatakatthavannana- first time written in the original Pali by V. Fausboll and translated by T.W. Rhys.) https://www.gutenberg.org/files/51880/51880-h/51880-h.htm

Talilula Longchar, *She Who Walks With Feet Facing Backwards and Laughs in the Wilderness- Ao Naga Narratives of Aonglemla,* New Delhi: Zubaan Books, 2019, p. 35.

Tamilnadu Tourism, 'Nallathangal Temple, Vathirairuppu (Watrap), Virudhunagar', Blogsite, 4 January 2017. https://tamilnadu-favtourism.blogspot.com/2017/01/nallathangal-temple-vathirairuppu.html?m=1

Tana and Riri. *Wikipedia*. https://en.wikipedia.org/wiki/Tana_and_Riri

Tanvi Mittal, 'The Karen of Andaman Islands: Labor Migration, Indian Citizenship and Development of a Unique Cultural Identity', *ResearchGate*, April 2015, pp. 19–20.

Tapaskumar Bandopadhyay, 'Bhadu gaaner utsa sandhane', (Bengali- In Search of the Origin of Bhadu Songs), *Anandabazar Patrika*, 19 February 2018. https://www.anandabazar.com/west-bengal/bhadu-festival-is-one-of-the-most-ancient-festivals-in-bengal-1.758665

The Joshua Project 2022 Bhaina. The Joshua Project began in 1995 as part of the AD 2000 and Beyong Movement. From 2001 through 2005, Joshua Project was at different times informally connected with Caleb Project, ICTA and World Help. Since 2006, this has been a work of the ministry of Frontier Ventures. https://joshuaproject.net/people_groups/16401/IN

The Mizos, 'Aonglemlatsu- 5 Nasty Mythical Creatures from Northeast India', 11 October 2021. https://www.themizos.com/2021/10/5-nasty-mythical-creatures-from.html

The Pluralism Project, 'Guru Nanak', Harvard University. https://pluralism.org/guru-nanak

P.Thomas *Epics, Myths and Legends of India*, Bombay: D.B Taraporevala Sons & Co, 1961, p. 135.

TLN Team, 'Know the History & Significance of Parsi New Year', In *The Live Nagpur*. 16 August 2021. https://thelivenagpur.com/2021/08/16/know-the-history-significance-of-parsi-new-year/

UCLA, Social Sciences 'Tukaram'. https://southasia.ucla.edu/religions/gurus-saints/tukaram/

Unakoti District Tripura Government, 'Unakoti Heritage Site'. https://unakoti.nic.in/tourist-place/unakoti-heritage-site/

Usha Nilsson, *Makers of Indian Literature- Surdas*. Sahitya Akademi. New Delhi. 1969

Verrier Elwin, (reprint) *When the World was Young*, New Delhi: National Book Trust, 1995, pp. 12–13, (Original 1961, pp. 74–75).

Verrier Elwin, *Myths of the North-east Frontier of India*, New Delhi: Gyan Publishing, 2017, pp. 82–83.

Verrier Elwin, *Specimens of the Oral Literature of Middle India: Myths of*

Middle India, Madras: Oxford University Press, 1949, p. 328.

Viggo Fausbøll (ed.) *The Jātaka Together With its Commentary Being Tales of the Anterior Births of Gotama Buddha,* London: Trübner and Co, 1875, pp. 51–56.

Walter Kaufmann, 'The Songs of the Hill Maria, Jhoria Muria and Bastar Muria Gond Tribes', In *Ethnomusicology*. Vol. 4, No. 3, September 1960, pp. 115–128 (cited here, pp. 1–2). https://doi.org/10.2307/924499

Wendy Doniger, *On Hinduism*, New Delhi: Aleph Book Company, 2013.

Wilber Theodore, Elmore, 'Dravidian Gods in Modern Hinduism- A Study of the Local and Village Deities of Southern India', University of Nebraska, Vol XV, No.1, 15:5, 1915.

Wilhelm Geiger, *The Mahavamsa or The Great Chronicle of Ceylon*, UK: Oxford University Press, 1912. https://archive.org/stream/mahavamsagreatch00geigrich/mahavamsagreatch00geigrich_djvu.txt

William J. Wilkins, 'Aditi and the Adityas', *Hindu Mythology, Vedic and Purānic,* Calcutta: Thacker, Spink & Co, 1900, p. 17.

Xing Zhang, and Tansen Sen, *The Chinese in South Asia*, New York, London: Routledge, 2013, pp.205–26.

Yazdi, 'Sagan Ni Machhi', *Zoroastrians.net*, 9 September 2015. https://zoroastrians.net/2015/09/09/sagan-ni-machhi/

Zarafshan Shiraz, 'Parsi New Year 2021: Date, History, Significance, Celebration of Navroz in India', *Hindustan Times*, 16 August 2021. https://www.hindustantimes.com/lifestyle/festivals/parsi-new-year-2021-date-history-significance-celebration-of-navroz-in-india-101629089758147.html